Carol Marinelli recently filled in a form asking for her job title. Thrilled to be able to put down her answer, she put 'writer'. Then it asked what Carol did for relaxation, and she put down the truth—'writing'. The third question asked for her hobbies. Well, not wanting to look obsessed, she crossed her fingers and answered 'swimming'— but, given that the chlorine in the pool does terrible things to her highlights, I'm sure you can guess the real answer!

Canadian **Dani Collins** knew in high school that she wanted to write romance for a living. Twenty-five years later, after marrying her high school sweetheart, having two kids with him, working at several generic office jobs and submitting countless manuscripts, she got The Call. Her first Mills & Boon novel won the Reviewers' Choice Award for Best First in Series from *RT Book Reviews*. She now works in her own office, writing romance.

Also by Carol Marinelli

Heirs to the Romano Empire miniseries

His Innocent for One Spanish Night
Midnight Surrender to the Spaniard
Virgin's Stolen Nights with the Boss

Wed into a Billionaire's World miniseries

Bride Under Contract

Also by Dani Collins

Marrying the Enemy
Husband for the Holidays

Bound by a Surrogate Baby miniseries

The Baby His Secretary Carries
The Secret of Their Billion-Dollar Baby

Diamonds of the Rich and Famous collection

Her Billion-Dollar Bump

Discover more at millsandboon.co.uk.

IF THE CROWN FITS…

CAROL MARINELLI

DANI COLLINS

MILLS & BOON

First published in Great Britain 2024
by Mills & Boon, an imprint of HarperCollins*Publishers* Ltd,
1 London Bridge Street, London, SE1 9GF

www.harpercollins.co.uk

HarperCollins*Publishers*, Macken House, 39/40 Mayor Street Upper, Dublin 1, D01 C9W8, Ireland

If the Crown Fits… © 2024 Harlequin Enterprises ULC

She Will Be Queen © 2024 Carol Marinelli

His Highness's Hidden Heir © 2024 Dani Collins

ISBN: 978-0-263-32032-9

11/24

This book contains FSC™ certified paper
and other controlled sources to ensure responsible forest management.

For more information visit www.harpercollins.co.uk/green.

Printed and Bound in the UK using 100% Renewable Electricity
at CPI Group (UK) Ltd, Croydon, CR0 4YY

SHE WILL BE QUEEN

CAROL MARINELLI

MILLS & BOON

PROLOGUE

'SLOW DOWN, SAHIR...'

Sahir turned. He'd been a little relieved that the ancient steps carved in the bedrock were so narrow that there could be no conversation, and Mother was some considerable distance behind.

Queen Anousheh of Janana was unsuitably dressed for a rugged walk.

The wind was blowing her black hair into her eyes and her elegant robe was clearly a hindrance. Naturally, his delightfully eccentric mother was in full make-up. Even her footwear was jewelled.

It didn't usually slow her down, though.

Sahir retraced his steps and offered his hand for the steepest incline. 'Why are you wearing palace slippers?'

'They are my walking shoes.' She smiled.

Sahir had not been looking forward to this. It wasn't just that at thirteen he felt a little old for the annual picnic his mother insisted upon. It was more the fact that when they eventually got to the top there was an awkward conversation to be had.

Sahir, much like his younger brother and sister, had grown up vaguely aware that their mother had a *confidant*—whatever that meant.

As heir to the Janana throne, Sahir spent his summers being tutored in protocol and Janana's intricate laws—and a few years ago he had discovered that their mother had a lover!

Sahir had kept that knowledge to himself, but this particular summer their mother's disinhibition had meant his younger siblings had worked things out for themselves.

Something *had* to be said.

'It has to be you,' Ibrahim had said, always happy to avoid a task and volunteering Sahir. 'You're going to be King one day.'

'Mama's going to leave Papa!' Jasmine had sobbed dramatically. 'Oh, poor Papa.'

'She is not going to leave him.' Sahir was firm with his sister. Even if he was cross with Mother, he felt defensive towards her. 'As Queen, she's done nothing wrong—the law states that she can take a confidant—and anyway, Father might have—'

He'd halted abruptly, deciding not to reveal that the King was allowed a *haẓiyya*, or second wife. Not only would Sahir prefer not to deal with more drama from Jasmine, he could not begin to fathom his austere father invoking such a rule.

'Papa should be kinder.' Ibrahim had been indignant. 'He's miserable and always cross…'

'He has a lot on his mind,' Sahir had reminded him sharply. 'These are troubled times. The King has to focus on peace for our land—not dramas within the palace walls.'

Growing up, they'd all heard their mother taunting the King whenever she felt she was being ignored—telling him that she would take it up with her confidant…saying that at least *he* listened to her, at least *he* noticed what she wore…

It had all come to a head this summer.

Ibrahim had seen her one night, all dressed up in lipstick and jewels, and their mother had urgently warned him not to tell.

And Jasmine, after a bad dream, had tried to get to her mother's bedroom. But the entrance to the *syn* wing had been locked…

'There were no maidens and she took for ever to answer,' Jasmine had sobbed to Sahir. 'Then she wouldn't let me in… just sent me back to bed…'

More worryingly for Sahir, he had seen the sour expression on Aadil's face when a lavish delivery had arrived for the Queen.

Aadil was Sahir's protection officer, but Aadil's father was the King's senior advisor, and if this reached the King's ears there would be trouble.

Sahir knew every rule, and he knew that while a confidant was allowed, all parties *must* be discreet.

Increasingly, Queen Anousheh of Janana was not.

'Oh, Sahir…' Mother was breathless as she reached the top.

'Give me a moment.' She caught her breath as Sahir spread out the rug and blankets he had brought up earlier. 'It looks wonderful.' She smiled. 'Look at all the treats you have brought. It is good for you to learn to do this without servants...'

'I make my own bed at school,' he said, opening the hamper he had carried up the cliff steps and pouring her some iced tea. 'Here.'

'Thank you.' She drank it thirstily. 'What I am saying is that it is good to know these special places.'

Sahir resisted rolling his eyes. Last year they had climbed dusty palace stairwells, the year before they had explored caves... 'The places you take me to are practically inaccessible.'

'Exactly.' Mother smiled. 'So you can do things without others always knowing. You might want a little privacy one day...'

Mother was a fine one to talk about privacy, Sahir thought as they sat drinking iced tea and eating the delicacies Sahir had sourced while they made small talk. Or rather, while Mother attempted to squeeze conversation from her thirteen-year-old son, talking about his life in London and his school subjects, trying to find out about his friends.

'It's a shame Carter didn't come this year.'

'He's spending the summer in Borneo with his grandfather.'

'Poor Carter. To lose all his family like that...' She gave a pensive sigh. 'Does he speak of them?'

'No.' Sahir shook his head. 'He never has.'

Years ago, his friend Carter's mother and baby brother had been killed in a crocodile attack—his father had perished attempting to save them. Sahir only knew what had been said at school or in the press. His friend had never discussed it. Not even once.

'Sometimes it's as if he's forgotten them.'

'He hasn't,' Mother said with certainty. 'Be there for him, Sahir. Always invite him to join us for holidays and celebrations. Speak their names...'

'I've tried.'

'You'll know when the time is right.'

The desert was like an orange fire behind the palace, and

the ocean was pounding on the rocks below. Sahir looked to the city skyline beyond.

Janana was a land of contrasts…beautiful and fierce, delicate and wild, mighty yet conversely fragile.

Sahir knew his history, and even if his father was distant and remote he was fiercely proud of him. King Babek of Janana had fought long and hard to have a thriving capital and CBD, with state-of-the-art hospitals, hotels and designer shops, even though the elders and council had been strongly opposed.

For his mother, Queen Anousheh, it was the ancient city and the desert that were her passion.

They both gazed towards the palace, taking in the magnificence of the ancient citadel. From this vantage point the *setarah*—star structure—was evident, but not so the hidden passages and stairs that led to the unroofed centre tower—outwardly bland, glorious within—with its view of the night sky the jewel.

The palace, though a sight to behold, bore the scars of history. Centuries ago an earthquake had devastated Janana, razing buildings, wiping out villages. The fracture had stretched to the palace, where an entire wing had been reduced to rubble, killing the then Queen as well as many palace staff.

Shortly after the earthquake the King had taken his own life, throwing the beleaguered country into further chaos and turmoil. In consequence the lineage had changed, and so had some of the marital laws. New legislation had been put in place to ensure such a tragedy could never befall the country again. Any future king or queen must have but one passion—the Kingdom of Janana.

Love was for commoners, not their rulers.

'It is such an eyesore,' Mother said, following Sahir's gaze to the destroyed wing.

'It serves as a reminder,' Sahir responded, repeating his teachings. 'A ruler's heart can belong only to his country.'

'Well, once your father brokers peace I am going to fight to have the wing rebuilt and the palace returned to its former glory.'

Mother always had grand plans.

'Sahir,' she ventured, perhaps attempting a gentler approach with her very self-contained son. 'I know that love is forbidden for a monarch, but I do believe that a heart is for sharing.'

'Yes,' he agreed. 'A king's heart is divided equally amongst his subjects.'

'I want you to listen to me.' Mother put down her refreshments to speak. 'Just because you are going to be King, that doesn't mean you have to agree with everything the elders—'

'I don't always agree,' Sahir interrupted.

This topic was one he wrestled with himself. He knew his mother must be lonely, even if she smiled and laughed. And yet he could understand the demands placed upon his father.

'I am learning, and not yet King,' he said. 'Until that time I shall abide by all the teachings.' He turned to face her. 'You do!' At thirteen he had not quite mastered being as aloof as his father. 'Especially the ones that suit you.'

'Pardon?' She blinked.

It had to be said, and it fell to him. 'Your discretion is lacking.'

'Sahir…?' Her head was cocked to the side, her hazel eyes curious. Perhaps she was unsure about the warning being given. 'What are you saying?'

Sahir held her gaze and refused to blush. Nor did he allow a glimpse of his agony at having this conversation. His voice was deep, that of a man, and he held on to his trust that it would remain steady now.

'There is no place in the palace for an imprudent confidant.'

To his surprise, she laughed. 'Oh, Sahir.' She laughed so much she wiped tears from her eyes. 'You can be so staid at times—just like your father.'

'He is King!'

'Yes…yes.' She took a breath, pressed her lips together and composed her face. 'You are right.'

'Mother, please…' Now his voice croaked…now fear surfaced. Sahir had done his best to reassure Jasmine, but he too was scared of what might happen. 'Be more careful.'

'Sahir…' She held his chin. 'You were right to speak to me.

It will be addressed. Now, let's enjoy the rest of our picnic. To-morrow you fly to London, and soon you'll be back at school.'

Sahir nodded, but then frowned. 'Mother?' There was a trickle of blood coming from her nostril. 'You're bleeding.'

'It's the climb,' she said, reaching for a napkin. 'Is there any ice in the hamper?'

'Of course.' He felt dreadful, even if it was quickly sorted. 'I should not have said anything.'

'Sahir,' she reassured him. 'I'm fine.' She put her arm around his tense shoulders, as if she knew how much this conversation had killed him. 'I know it took courage to discuss this with me.'

'You'll be more careful?'

She nodded. 'Everything shall be fine.'

Three weeks later he was summoned from class and told his mother was gravely ill.

Mid-flight home, Sahir was informed that Queen Anousheh was dead.

CHAPTER ONE

'MY DECISION HAS been made.'

Crown Prince Sahir of Janana's deep voice caused a few shoulders to stiffen before his team rapidly stood up to bow. His appearance at the double doors to the dining room was a little unexpected—after all, he was supposed to be upstairs, preparing to attend a wedding.

His Belgravia home was elegant—a white stucco building with a balcony that ran from the lounge to the principal bedroom. To the rear, the gated garden offered secure elevator access to the main residence, and it was large enough to contain flats for staff.

Ultimately, though, when he was in London, it was Sahir's home.

It didn't feel that way this late morning.

His dining room, often used to host small receptions or private dinners, was serving this morning as a meeting room. The silver candelabras had been removed and the gleaming oak covered with a leather protector.

On Sahir's way down from his rooms he had passed palace staff carrying his formal attire for tomorrow up to his dressing room.

Given Sahir's main residence was the palace, he was more than used to staff coming and going there—but in London he had his own staff, as well as a hand-picked team that accompanied him.

The arrival here of the palace entourage felt like an intrusion.

Not only were they several hours early, but Aadil—now the King's chief advisor—had joined them.

Aadil had been a thorn in Sahir's side since childhood. There was a lot of history between the two men—decades worth—

and in all that time there were few pleasant memories Sahir could summon.

It had been Aadil who had coldly informed him of the Queen's death.

'Your Highness,' Sahir was greeted now, as he crossed the room and took a seat at the head of the table.

Even caught unawares, with his raven hair wet and his face unshaven, still there was no question that Sahir was the absolute authority as he signalled for them all to be seated before addressing the subject being debated.

'Only minimal security is required today. What else?' He turned to Pria, his private secretary.

'Some minor revisions for tomorrow,' she said, handing him an updated plan. 'It's a tight schedule. We need to leave here ten minutes earlier.'

'I see.'

Sahir flicked through it, his dark eyes missing nothing, noting that other updates had been added beneath the names of certain guests now attending tomorrow's function. Little prompts to aid conversation.

The King and Queen of a neighbouring kingdom had recently become grandparents again—good to know…he would offer congratulations.

Then he saw an added suggestion. Say *Alf mabrook!*

A thousand congratulations.

While a common saying, it seemed a little excessive—especially for the less than effusive Sahir.

He read on.

A sultan's brother-in-law had passed away—he would offer his condolences on behalf of Janana.

But there was another prompt… Say *Atueatif maeak*—I take my sympathy to you.

Just a little more personal—personable, even?

And yet Sahir was neither.

'Sir, should the opportunity present itself…'

Aadil started droning on about some other European royals who would be there tomorrow.

'There was an exquisite gift sent for your birthday—a bejewelled gold amphora,' he went on. 'Perhaps a light reference...?' He turned to Pria. 'Do we have a photo?'

'No need.' Sahir raised his hand to halt Pria from searching through her tablet. 'It will be just a brief greeting.' He looked across the table to Aadil. 'You will have people thinking I'm on something...'

His protection officer Maaz smothered a smile, and even Pria pinched her lips, trying not to giggle. Away from the palace Sahir was a touch lighter, with small flashes of his spirited and wilful mother a little more on display.

'Sir...?' Aadil frowned.

'I thought a member of the Janana royal family must always be composed—not running around shaking hands, gushing...'

'It's a fine line, sir.'

'Not for me.' Sahir was not making light of things now— he could be as rigid and severe as his father. More so, even.

The sudden death of his mother had devastated Sahir, and had served as a rapid lesson in the merits of an icy demeanour and shielding his emotions.

There was a solid black line around his heart.

Impenetrable to all.

Unlike his father, he did not consult aides on his every move, nor meet endlessly with Hakaam, the 'teller' who read the skies.

Sahir relied upon himself.

If he needed wisdom or guidance then he went alone to the desert—sat with the land rather than searching for answers in long since burnt-out stars.

'Gentle conversation, sir...' Aadil persisted.

'I am not gentle,' Sahir reminded him. 'However, I am a gentleman, and I shall greet all parties respectfully.'

They went through the rest of the plans for tomorrow. He would leave his residence at ten and join the motorcade forty-eight minutes later. He would be back by six p.m., and his flight for Janana would leave at eleven.

'Thank you.'

He went to stand, but Aadil would not leave things there, the question of security clearly still on his mind.

'Your Highness, I must emphasise the high-profile nature of these visitors.'

Sahir felt his jaw grit as Aadil spoke on.

'It would be remiss of us not to increase security.'

'The ceremony today is a private affair,' Sahir responded calmly. 'As for the reception—it's little more than dinner. It's a closed venue, with a select group of guests.'

Carter Bennett, his long-time friend, had in recent weeks married a virtual stranger. The happy couple were now hosting an intimate celebration of the event in London.

However, the post-wedding reception was so low-key that had Sahir not already been in London on royal business he'd have struggled to justify attending. His heavy schedule had for once worked in his favour, though, and he'd agreed to act as Carter's best man. His duties were light. They included attending the cake-cutting at the bride's mother's nursing home, followed by dinner at a nearby restaurant.

The event was so informal he'd been told not even to prepare a speech.

Sahir did not want his presence there to be an issue, and told Aadil the same now. 'Carter has his own security arrangements. Even so, he selected the venue with my requirements in mind.' He turned to Maaz who, along with another officer called Layla, was on his protection team today. 'You're happy with things?' he asked.

It was Layla who nodded. 'The guests have all been vetted. Carter knows not to share your title. The restaurant has been swept and is being watched now, and I'll relieve them as soon as the bridal party arrives. Maaz is about to head to the nursing home.'

'Excellent,' Sahir said. 'As I have already stated—minimal security for today.'

His dark eyes held a strong warning as they met Aadil's, almost daring him to challenge.

'Sir...' Aadil wisely acquiesced.

Sahir dismissed his team...for now.

Most of them were looking forward to an unexpected day off, but a select few remained—and of course Aadil lingered.

Apparently there was one final matter to deal with before Sahir dressed.

Faisal, his major-domo, placed a wedding congratulations card in front of him. Sahir went to take up the jewelled pen he used for royal matters, but then hesitated—after all this was personal.

So little was personal in Sahir's life and so, even though it perhaps mattered not, he requested his preferred ballpoint pen—a twenty-first birthday gift from Carter.

'What is the bride's name?' Sahir asked, pen poised.

'Grace,' Faisal said. 'Although you could just put *To the newlyweds...*'

'Thank you.'

He loathed writing cards, and usually only his signature was required, but given it was Carter...

He wrote some fluff about wishing them every happiness for the future, then scrawled his name, pleased, for once, to leave out his title as Faisal briefed him about the wedding gift that had been selected.

'A two-branch silver and rose gold candelabra from the Setarah collection. The bobèches depict—'

'Thank you,' Sahir interrupted.

He knew the collection. Several pieces were here in London, and while he might have quipped that he hoped the groom would get to keep it in the divorce, the thought wasn't shared.

He made small talk only and never discussed personal matters.

With anyone.

Usually, he loathed giving his heritage away, but Carter, a skilled architect, was working with him on plans for the palace restoration, and would appreciate the treasure more than most.

With the card and gift sorted, he headed to the principal suite.

It was rather like dressing for a full English wedding, Sahir thought as he stood in his dressing room and Faisal handed him his attire.

'Pity,' Sahir commented quietly.

'Sayyid...?' Faisal queried.

'It's a shame that it's just a quiet dinner and a few photos. I actually like a good English wedding.'

'You have been to many,' Faisal agreed.

Faisal helped him into the jacket of his morning suit and arranged the boutonniere on his lapel. An unusual choice, Sahir thought, glancing down at the lilac flower with peacock detail on some petals. To his mind it was rather too large…a touch inelegant, even…

But apparently it was a water hyacinth, and had been flown in from Borneo for the occasion. The bride had insisted, Carter had told him.

Of course she had.

The newly rich were very good when it came to making demands!

Once he was dressed and ready to collect the groom, Layla took Sahir through the final details.

'I'll follow behind. Both Maaz and I shall be outside the nursing home and later the restaurant. If the press arrives, or there are any security issues…'

'There won't be.'

Sahir was confident, but he understood his staff had to be sure and listened as Layla told him the updated security code for the private garden and the exit route at the restaurant.

Sahir memorised it easily, repeating it back as he pocketed the key he would use should the code fail.

His phone buzzed, and he saw that it was Carter calling. 'I'm just on my way,' he told him.

'Change of plan,' Carter informed him. 'We'll meet at the nursing home. Grace wants me to have some time with her mother prior to cutting the cake, to ensure she's calm.'

'Sure.'

'And, Sahir… I know you think this is all about my grandfather's will—'

'Carter,' he cut in, 'it doesn't matter what I think.'

'Look, I know you're not a fan of marriage…'

'Nor were you.'

'Things change, Sahir. People change.'

Sahir had no desire to change, though, and no desire for a cold marriage. And he certainly did not want love. He'd already managed to stall things—there was a private agreement in place with his father that the matter of his marriage would be addressed only when he turned forty.

Although now he was thirty-five, it seemed a little too close.

'You got to choose your bride,' Sahir said to his friend. 'And I am sure you made a wise choice.'

'I have,' Carter said. 'Hey, at least you get to choose your second...'

'True.' Sahir let the small joke pass, even if it irked. His friend knew a little of Janana's royal ways, and he would never understand them. 'Carter, you know I shall always wish you well.'

'I do—but could you also extend that courtesy to Grace?'

'Of course.' Sahir wasn't lying—he hoped that both parties got whatever it was they needed from this union. To him a marriage was as transactional as that. 'I wish you both well.'

'Good.'

'And speeches?' Sahir checked. 'Are you sure you don't want—?'

'It's an informal dinner,' Carter interrupted swiftly. 'No need for speeches.'

'As you wish.'

'I'll meet you at the nursing home. Text me when you arrive.'

'Certainly.'

'Thanks,' Carter added, 'for managing to be here today.'

'Of course,' Sahir said.

'It means a lot.'

Sahir frowned as the call ended. Carter sounded as if this marriage actually *meant* something to him.

But his cynical nature soon returned, and a black smile was on his face as he collected the card and gift Faisal had left out.

Of course this had nothing to do with love.

Driving out of the underground garage in his sleek silver car, he found that he was relieved for some time alone—a rarity for Sahir.

London was looking stunning—and yet he drove away from

the gorgeous centre to the outer suburbs, occasionally glanc-ing in the rear-view mirror to see Layla driving the car behind. Maaz, as arranged, was already parked opposite the nursing home.

Sahir pulled into the car park outside a very plain-looking building indeed. Layla followed him, parking a suitable dis-tance away.

He glanced around for Carter, and was about to text that he was there when a taxi pulled up and a pair of black stilettoes peeked out, followed by a lot of purple silk.

Glancing in the rear-view mirror, he saw Layla idly lean-ing against her vehicle, though he knew she was watching carefully… It irritated Sahir. Why was everyone considered a threat? They would have already vetted the guests—discreet checks would have been made, the guest list gone through with a fine-tooth comb.

He was soon given a swift update by phone, and he glanced at Layla's text.

Bridesmaid. Violet Lewis.

Sahir was sorely tempted to fire back that he'd rather worked that out—he doubted there were many calls for silk ball gowns on a Saturday afternoon around these parts. But, yes, the stun-ning dress was apt, given her name! The shade was violet, he corrected, not purple.

He thought it a vivid choice when he saw the woman's co-louring. Her skin was very pale, especially given it was early September and the end of summer. Her blonde hair was worn up, though there were tendrils blowing in the breeze. She had a purse on her wrist, and from that she took out her phone to pay the driver. She looked happy and carefree, completely un-aware that she was being watched by his protection officers. She even laughed at something the driver said.

Sahir watched idly as she retrieved a carefully wrapped sil-ver box with an awful lot of curled ribbons, and then laughed again. He found himself tempted to open the window a touch, mildly curious not so much about what was being said, more to discover the sound of her laughter.

She waved to the driver and then, with that same hand, lifted the hem of her gown and walked in her high heels across the rather dour car park. Her pale shoulders were exposed by the gown, and she moved with flair. She could be walking the red carpet and being photographed, rather than arriving unseen and avoiding potholes.

Sahir remained in his car, in no mood to make small talk with the bridesmaid, who was now peering through the glass door. Clearly the bride and groom weren't in sight, for she fired off a message on her phone.

But then, as the taxi drove away, her demeanour rapidly changed.

When most women might be checking their appearance in a hand mirror, or perhaps pacing a little, instead those straight shoulders slumped and she leant against the wall and closed her eyes.

Formerly bright and breezy, she now cut a solitary figure in her gorgeous gown. A sad figure, even, because she'd placed a hand on her stomach, as if calming herself, and was muttering like an actress rehearsing her lines, getting ready to step into her role...

Sahir was suddenly on high alert. Possibly his staff were right...perhaps Violet Lewis was in fact a threat...

Though not the usual kind.

Sahir found that he wanted to go over to her and engage in some of that hated small talk.

For he sensed that he was glimpsing the true Violet Lewis.

CHAPTER TWO

VIOLET WAS VERY good at giving herself pep talks.

Oblivious of the luxurious silver car and its driver, she was focussed on psyching herself up for the happy event.

You've got this, she told herself. *Just smile and get through today, for Grace's sake...*

It had been a very tricky week.

She should be used to them by now.

Once a social worker had described Violet's life as a rollercoaster ride.

Violet had begged to differ.

Oh, it was more than a rollercoaster. There were waltzers and ghost trains, halls of mirrors... It felt as if she'd been handed life entry to a theme park the moment she'd arrived on planet earth. A social worker had been present in the delivery room, waiting to whisk her away. Then her childhood had been a mixture of chaotic parents interspersed with foster homes.

She'd ached for peace.

For a home...

For a normal family...

Her one glimpse of that had been Grace and her mother, whom Violet had grown up calling Mrs Andrews. Both had been so very kind. There had been cake or a biscuit after school, sometimes help with her homework. At times Mrs Andrews would be putting on some washing and had offered to add her uniform, giving Violet a dressing gown to put on. Sometimes she'd trim her hair. Mrs Andrews had been the one to help with her first period, and had always had plenty to spare when it came to products.

'I bought far too many,' she'd say. Or, 'They were in the sale.'

Josephine Andrews had been more of a mother than her own.

At sixteen, Violet had torn up her theme park ticket.

With the help of a new and wonderful social worker, as well as encouragement from Grace and Mrs Andrews, she had been offered a full time job at the local library and had moved to semi-independent living. She'd had her own room, kitchen and bathroom, and had been responsible for all the bills. Without the chaos of her parents her little home had been tidy, and her bills, even if it had meant living on a lot of soup, had always been paid on time.

She'd soon become fully independent, moving into a flat of her own choice, and though her flatmates had changed over the years—Grace being the latest—she remained there to this day.

Her parents, though they had long since moved away, had left her quite a reputation to contend with.

Now, at twenty-five, Violet was pretty much unbreakable—or at least she appeared that way.

She was cheeky and fun…and everyone thought her a little 'out there'. Thanks to her quick wit and voracious nature, some considered her bold, and even a bit of a flirt.

In truth, it was all a façade. Violet had learnt long ago never to show weakness, let alone fear. Her upbringing meant she was suspicious of men, and had barely been kissed, but lately she was doing her level best to get over all that, and had even joined a dating site.

Her job at the library had always been her saving grace. She loved her work and her colleagues, considered the regular clients her friends, but last Monday her lack of schooling and formal qualifications had finally caught up with her. The powers that be had decided on a restructure, and an HR woman she had never even met had informed Violet she was being given two weeks' notice.

The library was her *place* in the world. As her family structure had changed, as flatmates had come and gone, her workplace had been her constant.

The news, though not entirely unexpected, had shattered her. Not that she'd shown it. But it had shaken her so much that just yesterday she had asked to use a precious week of annual leave before returning to serve out the final week of her notice.

Financially a poor choice, perhaps—after all, she'd soon have plenty of time on her hands.

Emotionally, it had been her only one.

Violet hid when she was hurt, and this had wounded her.

She hadn't told a soul—not even Grace, who was all floaty and insisting this marriage to *the* Carter Bennett had nothing to do with money.

Violet had long been worried that Grace was heading for a financial crisis as she cared for her mother.

She had tapped Carter's name into the library computer the very second she'd heard it, and blushed at the groom's reputation. Then she'd sighed when she'd read about his billion-dollar empire and his wrestling for his grandfather's estate—marriage was the key that would release it.

Oh, Grace…

Still, she thought as she breathed in the late-summer air, it wasn't Grace's choice of husband that was filling her with dread. It was the thought of the little ceremony ahead…

When Violet had been around eighteen, things with Mrs Andrews had changed.

It had started with the occasional offhand comment, which Violet had brushed off. Then a couple of rather spiteful things had been said, which Violet had tried to ignore. It had culminated in a dreadful confrontation, when Mrs Andrews had accused her of stealing a necklace—even threatening to call the police.

That had been awful enough, but it had been the doubt from Grace that had hurt the most and almost cost them their friendship.

But Grace had finally broken down and admitted that her mother had become suspicious and terrified of everyone, and then she had sadly been diagnosed with early onset dementia…

Mrs Andrews hadn't known what she was saying, and Violet accepted that, but her accusation had been so personal, so hurtful, so caustic… Especially from the woman whom she'd adored since she was a little girl.

And the doubt from Grace, no matter how brief, and the

glimpse of the knowledge that she might be dropped by her friend had devastated Violet, even if she'd never let it show.

Violet hadn't really seen Mrs Andrews since, but now she was about to.

Mrs Andrews barely recognised even her own daughter, but Grace wanted one happy photo…one shining picture on her wedding day…with those she and her husband were closest to.

Violet felt ill at the thought of it—terrified, not just for herself but of any confrontation that might ruin Grace's special day.

Perhaps she should suggest not going in?

It was something Violet was still pondering as the doors to the nursing home opened. It was the groom—Carter. Violet recognised him not just by the morning suit but by her little snoop on the internet, so she fixed on a dazzling smile and, pulling herself from the wall, greeted the man who was—from all she had read—a completely reprobate groom.

'You must be Carter…' Violet said—and didn't add *the man taking advantage of my friend*…

Instead, determined to get through this day, she smiled and shook his hand.

Only when Carter had appeared did Sahir get out of the car and approach.

'Sahir.' Carter shook his hand. 'Thank you for being here today.' He introduced the bridesmaid. 'This is Grace's close friend, Violet.'

'Violet.' Sahir nodded, and briefly met eyes that were a vivid blue, though they barely met his. Her interest was clearly fixed on the groom.

With the introductions made, Carter caught sight of the box Violet held. 'We said no gifts!'

'Oh, people always say that…' she dismissed, her voice trailing off as Carter turned and peered through the door of the nursing home.

Sahir watched as, with Carter's back turned, Violet Lewis's smile faded and her blue eyes narrowed in suspicious assessment.

Ah, so she wasn't sure about this union either!

'Here comes Grace,' Carter said, and Sahir watched as the single bridesmaid in this very small celebration turned her smile back on like a light.

'Grace,' Carter said, 'this is Sahir.'

Well, the bride wasn't quite the gold-digger he'd been expecting. She looked sweet and natural.

Sahir was not being cold in his expectations. Not only was he aware of the financial implications of this union, his status meant that at several weddings he'd attended Sahir had been placed in the awkward situation of dealing with a bride determined to flirt—and not with her groom.

Indeed! It was, at times, quite perilous being a prince.

'It's so lovely to meet you, Your… Sahir.' Grace's smile wavered, and he knew Carter would have warned her not to reveal his status. She was clearly unsure how to proceed. 'Carter told me you've worked on a lot of projects together.'

'Indeed…' Sahir nodded.

'We'll only be spending a few moments in there,' Grace explained. 'Mum seems good today, but she can get a little confused.'

'I understand.'

Grace turned her attention to Violet then. 'Oh, you look incredible! Your dress…' Her jubilation faded when she saw the parcel Violet held. 'We said no gifts.'

'You did,' Violet agreed, and Sahir blinked as she went on to elaborate. 'Honestly—it's really the most annoying thing to find on a wedding invitation. As if I wasn't going to buy you a present!'

'We meant it,' Grace said. 'There's nowhere to put it.'

Sahir saw she really was a bundle of nerves as she tried to hand Violet a spray of flowers.

'And you have to hold these…'

'Here,' Sahir offered, and relieved Violet of the box. 'I'll keep it in my car.'

He did so, placing her gift next to his. To his own surprise, curiosity got the better of him and he briefly peeked at the attached tag.

Violet's message was far more effusive than his!

Something about *soulmates…eternal happiness…*

Yet for all Violet's written hopes for them, as he returned to the small party the bridesmaid seemed reluctant to go in.

'Grace,' she said to her friend, 'why don't I just wait out here?'

'But I want you in the photos. The photographer's already inside.'

'I do tend to upset her, though.' Violet lifted her hand in a wavering gesture. 'Perhaps we can just have photos of us outside? Or at the restaurant later?'

'Violet, she won't even recognise you—she barely even knows who I am now.'

Sahir's curiosity was piqued—why wouldn't Violet want to be recognised?

'Ready?' Carter checked, and Grace took a breath and nodded.

It really was a rather odd function…

The couple walked ahead, and as he held the door open Violet stepped in, all smiles as the photographer clicked away.

'Gosh, I thought we'd have a moment to…' Violet muttered, more to herself than him, as they stood outside a lounge room where the small celebration was taking place.

As the bride and groom walked in to the oohs and ahs of the residents he looked away from the happy couple to the bridesmaid.

'Our turn now,' she said, and gave him a smile—no sign now of the nerves that he'd witnessed when she'd been alone outside.

Then he met her eyes…clear, sparkly and that gorgeous shade of blue.

No sign there either.

'Shall we?'

He offered his arm as they were summoned. Moving the bouquet to her other hand, she took it, and he briefly caught her wrist.

There was his sign.

In that second he felt her pulse tripping in panic, felt the ice of her skin. And beneath the perfumed air that surrounded her was the indescribable yet to a trained warrior unmissable scent of fear.

Sahir glanced over. There was nothing in her expression that gave it away. Her hand had positioned itself on his arm, her fingers were as light as a little bird's foot wrapped around a finger, and there was not even a slight tremble that he could detect on the bare arm next to his.

But for whatever reason, Sahir knew she was terrified.

'You'll be fine,' he offered.

'Of course.'

It was a very sedate affair.

There was a small cake on a silver stand, champagne and sherry had been served, and waiters were poised to serve afternoon tea to the residents.

The bride's mother seemed too young to be in the nursing home. She sat there in a high-backed chair, her hair the same deep brown as her daughter's and her skin smooth, with hardly a line.

'A wedding?' She looked at her daughter. 'Why didn't you tell me? I need to get ready.'

'You are ready,' Grace responded, clearly used to reassuring her. 'In a moment or two we're going to cut the cake.'

'Grace?' she checked. 'You're getting married?' She peered at Carter. 'To him?'

Carter, as if he hadn't been there before, politely shook her hand. 'Mrs Andrews.'

'Violet…' The mother of the bride smiled in delight when she saw her. 'You're here too?'

'Hello, Mrs Andrews.'

She let go of his arm and stepped forward to embrace the seated mother of the bride.

'Josephine,' she corrected. 'I keep telling you to call me that. I haven't been called Mrs Andrews since…'

Then she frowned, and there the pleasantries ended.

'You've got a nerve…' She started to rise from her seat. 'Thief!'

'Please, Mum…' Grace was frantically trying to calm her

mother down and throwing anxious, awkward looks towards her bridesmaid, who stood, frozen, as the tirade continued.

'Violet Lewis!' Mrs Andrews sneered. 'The apple doesn't fall far from the tree.'

Only then did Sahir realise that Violet was wearing a dusting of blusher—her face had turned so pale that the pink now seemed gouged into her cheeks. In fact, she looked like a porcelain doll, her eyeshadow, mascara and lipstick painted on to pale, pale features.

Yet still she pushed out a smile. 'I'll go. I'm upsetting you...' Her voice was bright, though a little too high.

Sahir heard the swish of her gown and the click of her heels as she moved quickly out of the room.

'Damn thief!' Mrs Andrews ranted. 'We all know it was you!'

'Mum...' Grace was pleading, but clearly torn, and when Carter stepped in to help, she ran after her friend. 'Violet...'

As he was best man, and very used to taking control, Sahir did his duty and tried to help Carter calm the mother of the bride—but to no avail.

'Who's he?' Mrs Andrews demanded, eyeing him with suspicion. 'What's he doing in my home?'

And Sahir knew it was best that he too leave.

Even though she'd been half expecting it, so many dreadful memories were flooding back, and Violet was deeply shaken as she walked briskly down the corridor.

'Violet, wait!' Grace was clearly distressed as she caught up with her. 'Mum doesn't mean it...'

'I know that. She's confused and doesn't know what she's saying...'

Grace looked as if she was on the verge of breaking down. 'I honestly thought things would be okay...'

'And they shall be,' Violet reassured her. 'So long as she doesn't get another glimpse of me. Go back in and enjoy things. I'll wait outside...' She gave her brightest smile. 'You can make it up to me with champagne later.' Violet squeezed Grace's hands. 'Forget it happened.'

Violet couldn't forget it, though.

She stepped outside and took a huge breath, determined not to cry. Her nails were digging into her palms as she tried to steady her breathing, and she felt a hot tear splash out.

'Damn,' she cursed, thankful that she was alone. Well, apart from a woman leaning on her car—but she was too busy looking at her phone to notice.

Even so, Violet moved to the side of the building.

It was possibly a throwback from her childhood, but Violet loathed the thought of anyone seeing her upset or knowing that she was feeling vulnerable.

Yet despite her efforts to contain them, the tears kept right on coming.

She scrabbled in her purse, even while knowing she hadn't brought a tissue. Violet was simply too used to picking herself up and carrying on rather than caving in to tears.

Just not today.

She sniffed and dabbed under her eyes, then saw the black ink of running mascara on her thumbs.

'Here…'

She started as she saw the best man was offering the pocket square from his morning suit. 'I'd ruin it,' she sniffed. 'You'd never get your deposit back.'

'Take it.'

'Please go.'

'I can't. It's my duty to ensure things go smoothly.'

'So, I'm part of your *duty*?'

'You are,' he said, relieving her of the bouquet.

Having placed it on the ground, he held out the square of silk again, but she didn't notice. Her eyes were closed and she was back to leaning against the wall and scolding herself. 'Stop it, Violet.'

Sahir had another suggestion. 'Breathe.'

She did as he said and inhaled deeply, and then she did it again, before speaking urgently. 'Grace mustn't see how upset I am.'

'I'm sure she doesn't expect smiles after all that.'

'I don't cry…' Violet attempted to explain the anomaly this was. 'I mean, I *never* cry.'

'Violet, you did suggest not going in.'

'I did.'

'Grace should have listened.'

'Yes, but…' It felt important to defend her friend and explain that her tears weren't all Grace's fault. 'It's not just her mother that's upset me…' She gulped. 'It's been a wretched week.'

She took out a mirror from her purse and tried to dab at her black tears, then gave in and asked for the silk square.

It just made things worse, spreading mascara like soot across her pale cheeks.

'Allow me…'

Sahir went back around to the front of the residence and discreetly waved at Layla to stay back.

It didn't feel like enough, though.

Usually he snapped his fingers, or passed problems on to someone else, and he knew Layla was poised to come over.

But he doubted Violet would appreciate an audience.

Taking out his phone, he fired off a quick text to tell Layla it was a private situation, and then stepped into the nursing home for some supplies to deal with a teary bridesmaid.

There wasn't much on hand!

He returned with only a bottle of water.

Violet was hunched over, holding herself, her body a ball of tension as she fought not to cry.

'Stand up,' he said, pouring water on the silk. 'And do as I say.'

'I don't want you to see me,' she admitted, but she did as she was told and unfurled herself.

'Too late,' he said, his voice matter-of-fact. 'Now, drop your shoulders.'

'Why?'

'Because we want you to appear happy and serene for Grace, and we have ten or fifteen minutes to achieve that.'

She sniffed.

'So, drop your shoulders and chin up.'

'Okay…' She forced protesting shoulders down, and when she elongated her neck he saw that it was flushed, as was her chest.

To Sahir's surprise he found he wanted to take her in his arms, to let her cry, but he chose to focus on the task he'd just outlined—to return her to order rather than let her fall further apart.

'I'm truly sorry about this,' she said, and shuddered as he very carefully dabbed her cheeks with the cool silk.

Gosh, her eyes seemed almost familiar, he thought, though he'd never met her before.

'Look up,' he instructed, dabbing gently at the little flecks of black mascara that clung to her fair lashes, and although she did as instructed, she voiced a question.

'How do you know how to do this?'

'I have a very emotional sister.'

Her full, trembling mouth smiled.

Almost.

Then, as he worked on wiping away the streaks on her cheeks, he listened as she tried to explain the anomaly that this was.

'I'm honestly the last person to cry. I mean that. Grace would be so upset if she saw me.'

'Don't think about it now, or you'll get upset again. Think…'

'Happy thoughts?' she scoffed.

'Neutral thoughts,' he corrected, but then he paused, for usually he was not one for admitting that he was anything other than completely together. Nor was he one for sharing the tactics he used when a surge of emotion threatened to hit him, and how he managed to remain impassive even in the most trying of times. 'It works. Just focus on something that you find neither happy nor sad.'

'Such as…?'

'It's different for everyone…something that doesn't excite you.'

'Filing the late returns,' she said. And even though he had no idea what that meant, at least she was talking. 'I don't hate it; I don't enjoy it. I just…' But then she took a shuddering breath and her tears were starting again. 'Oh, I'm going to miss...' She shook her head as if trying to clear it. 'What's your neutral?'

'I have many.'

'Share one.' Her voice sounded urgent. 'Please!'

Those stunning eyes moved to meet his, and while Sahir usually had a plethora of neutral thoughts he could rapidly summon, for a second or two he had none. Her eyes *were* familiar. They were the same deep intense blue of the lapis lazuli embedded in the walls of the observatory. The colour of a clear night sky, with flecks of gold and silver. But they were by far too enchanting to explore.

Instead of dabbing her cheeks, he moved his hand so it rested on the wall by the side of her head as he attempted to find something neutral.

'Cricket,' he said, and saw her nose wrinkle. 'At my school they were very serious about it.'

'Did you play?'

'I had no choice—I was very good at it. I have excellent hand-eye co-ordination. I was captain in my final year.'

'Yet you hate it?'

'No,' he reminded. 'Neutral.'

He knew she smiled—not because of her lips, but because he saw her tears dry and how her eyes shone with the escape he briefly gave her—so he gave her a little more.

'My birthday is in July—the middle of cricket season. I would get tickets to matches, a piece of cricket art, another bat...' He said it with all the lack of enthusiasm those gifts had mustered, and yet he smiled as he shared the memory.

His smile stole her breath—and also the newly found calm he had so recently brought. For how could she summon neutral thoughts as he smiled right into her eyes? How did she attempt neutral when she was suddenly aware of the proximity of his mouth and the fact that his hand rested on the wall behind her head?

He could never know how nervous this moment made her.

Or that she'd never enjoyed male company, even though she'd tried.

How could this man know that she didn't do eye contact when she was staring so readily and so deeply into his eyes?

He was exquisite—but how hadn't she seen it until now? Possibly she'd been far too busy trying to work out the playboy groom to pay attention to his suave, good-looking friend.

On the periphery of her vision she'd noticed the elegant man climbing from a silver car, and as they'd walked to the lounge she had been a little too aware of his exotic scent, but very deliberately she'd paid him little heed.

Another rich playboy, going along with the charade...

Now, though, she met eyes that were as black as night—or were they a very dark navy? She could just make out the iris. His hair wasn't just black, it was raven—a true blue-black, and a shade she'd never seen.

'Breathe,' he told her again, and she was grateful for the reminder—even though it wasn't the prior upset that had caused her body to malfunction again, it was the shock of such beauty close up.

Violet took in his stunning bone structure, his sculpted cheeks and straight nose, then moved her gaze down to lips that were so perfect they had to be the prototype...the one God and the angels had first designed. Every other mortal had got some variation, for these lips she was now staring at were perfection. A little large, but not anything other than deliciously so, and there was a neat pale line around the cupid's bow that made her breath hitch. And how did you get a razor into that cleft in his chin...?

She watched his lips as they spoke. 'Your cheeks are very pink,' he said.

'Yes...' Violet croaked, putting her hands up and feeling their heat as he removed his hand from the wall.

'Can you calm them? So Grace doesn't see you've been crying?'

'Yes, yes...' She went into her bag, pathetically pleased he'd blamed the sudden burning flush on her earlier boo-hoo.

She opened up her compact, but she was all fingers and thumbs. Without a word he took it, but first he offered again the use of the square of silk.

'Blow your nose.'

She did so noisily, frantically trying to think of something to say so that he didn't notice her sudden, almost violent attraction.

It was something she'd never encountered before, and she was flailing as he opened the compact and dabbed powder on her cheeks.

'What's your sister's name?' she asked.

'Jasmine,' he said, as he powdered the tip of her reddened nose. 'She used to cry all the time.'

'And now?'

Sahir said nothing in response.

'Now?'

'Now she's tougher—or perhaps she cries to her husband rather than me.'

He offered the bottle of water for her to gulp and it really helped. Not just with the tears, but to snap her back to her normal senses. Yes, he was being nice, but if he was a good friend of Carter's... Well, according to Violet's research, he must be an utter bastard too.

She must not lose sight of that!

'Why are you looking at me the same way you looked at the groom?'

'What way was that?'

His gorgeous eyes narrowed, imitating hers.

'Birds of a feather...?' Violet said.

'I don't understand.'

'Flock together,' she added, but then felt guilty. After all, the same had long been said about her. Yet she at least had broken the cycle and flown the coop.

'So, you are suspicious of this union?'

'It's not my place to say.'

Even if they both refused to say it outright, it would seem they were both in agreement—this marriage really was a farce.

Still, whether it was his emotional sister, or his hordes of previous women-friends, he knew about repair jobs with make-up, Violet decided as she peered into the mirror.

'Wow, even I'd hardly know. Thank you, Sahid.'

'Sahir,' he corrected.

'Oh, yes…' She took a breath. 'Sahir.' She nodded, as if locking it in as they emerged around the side of the care home. 'And thank you for not asking what that was all about.'

They parted ways as the doors opened and the couple emerged.

'Don't thank me yet,' Sahir murmured, his voice low and for her ears only.

And it might just as well have been dipped in chocolate and slathered in cream, because it was the closest thing to vocal seduction Violet had ever known.

'After all,' he added, 'the night is still young.'

CHAPTER THREE

IF SAHIR HADN'T seen Violet so distraught for himself, he would never have known. She was smiling and throwing confetti, seemingly without a care in the world, as the bride and groom climbed into a waiting vehicle.

'Get in, you two,' they urged.

'I am *not* getting in your wedding car,' Violet said—even if she could see it would house plenty and there was champagne waiting inside. Some traditions stood! 'I'll get a taxi.'

'Violet,' Grace insisted, 'I wouldn't put it past you to get the driver lost.' She looked to Sahir. 'Honestly, she has no sense of direction.'

'I got here, didn't I?' Violet said, taking out her phone to summon a taxi.

But it would seem the best man had things in hand, for he told her to put away her phone.

'I'll take care of your bridesmaid,' Sahir assured Grace.

He already had, Violet thought as she enthusiastically waved them off.

'Wave!' she prompted.

'I am not as good an actor as you,' he said, still convinced this marriage was a farce. 'And aside from that I don't wave...' Sahir paused, then refrained from telling her that his waving was reserved for work. 'Let's go.'

His car lit up as they approached, and then there was an awkward moment when she had to wait for him to open the door, as she had no idea how to do it herself.

'What happened to door handles?' she asked, sinking into soft leather and trying not to notice the more concentrated version of his scent as the doors closed on them and Sahir drove off. 'And don't you have a passenger mirror?'

It slid down at the push of a button and she rather wished she hadn't asked, as it was rather higher quality than her dusty compact. 'Yikes...'

'You look fine,' he told her. 'You recover quickly!'

'I do.' She topped up her lip-gloss, but then her hand went to her stomach.

'Are you going to cry again?' he asked.

'No, I'm just starving.'

'Do you want to stop for something to eat?'

Violet frowned at the odd offer. 'We're going for a sit-down dinner.'

He glanced at the time. 'There'll be champagne and hors d'oeuvres for the first hour or so.'

'I'll be fine.'

Sahir *felt* her sideways glance, and her shameless curiosity didn't bother him. Really, he was more than used to being stared at.

'Did you get them a gift?' she asked.

'Yes.'

'Even though it said not to on the invitation?'

'I didn't notice.'

He chose not to mention that his staff dealt with all that.

'So, what did you get them?'

He was grateful for Faisal's description of his gift, though he downgraded it a touch. 'A candlestick.'

'Oh, I wish I'd thought of that. I'm usually good at gifts, but I've never struggled so hard.'

Sahir stared ahead; she was good at talking too!

'I wish they'd done a gift registry.'

'They clearly didn't want anything.'

'Well, you got them something.'

'True.' He glanced over, saw her full lips and pointy nose, and thought she was like no one he had ever met. Gorgeous, chatty, teary, funny...

'So, what did you end up getting them?' he asked.

'Guess.'

'I'm not guessing.'

Violet waited for him to do just that, but to no avail. Clearly he didn't wave *or* guess.

'A vase.' She sighed. 'How boring is that? I spent double my usual wedding present budget—triple, actually, given Grace is such a good friend. But I just couldn't come up with anything more exciting.'

He made no comment.

'A tulip vase,' she elaborated. 'I was going to get a rose bowl, but I *do* like tulips. At least while they last...'

Even though he still offered no response, she happily carried on.

'I get them on a Saturday sometimes, after work. But they're generally all collapsed by Monday.'

On and on she chatted.

'Still, they make my Sundays happy.'

They sat for ages at some traffic lights. He could see Layla driving the car behind him, Maaz the one in front, and yet it felt like just the two of them.

Finally Grace paused.

'In Janana,' he said, 'where I am from, tulips were once considered more valuable than gold.'

'No!'

'True.'

'Wow! Well, I'll send Grace and Carter a bunch when they're back from their honeymoon, they'll be searching for a suitable vase, and...bingo!'

'Bingo?' He frowned as the lights changed to green and he pulled off.

'Ta-da!'

His frown remained as he concentrated both on her words and the road.

'They'll remember my gift!' she explained.

'Unless they already have a tulip vase.'

He turned and saw her slight pout. Usually pouts irritated him. Violet did them exceptionally well, though, and she even slumped for effect.

'I'm sure they don't,' he said kindly. Glancing at the time, he saw that it was approaching six. 'We're almost there.'

'I don't mind being late.'

'Well, I do.'

'I bet you're always on time.'

'Of course.' He nodded. 'You?'

'I try to be,' she said. 'But I'm always rushing, and sometimes…'

He glanced over. 'Sometimes?'

Violet didn't answer. She was sure a man as confident and measured as Sahir didn't curl up and hide from the world at times.

'Well,' he said into the silence, 'we're right on time.'

'Yay,' Violet said, but without enthusiasm. And then, still staring ahead, she admitted, 'I'm a bit nervous.'

Usually she'd never reveal such a thing. But, given her performance outside the nursing home, it seemed a little too late to play it cool.

'Why?'

She hesitated, not used to sharing her fears. 'I've never been to a French restaurant—at least not a posh one.'

'It's very relaxed there.'

'I'll hardly know anyone,' she said. 'Well, apart from Grace and a couple of her friends from school, who I never got on with. They're married now. I didn't get an invitation to their wedding.'

'At least you didn't have to come up with a gift for them, then.'

That made her giggle a bit. 'Oh, and her cousin Tanya will be there…even though she's barely been around since Mrs Andrews got ill. She's insisted on bringing her children.'

'I'm used to children at weddings.'

'Well-behaved ones?' she asked, and he nodded. 'Just you wait! Oh, and Tanya doesn't like me either.'

They were pulling up outside the restaurant. It was elegant beyond words; in fact the whole street was just like a postcard. She honestly didn't want to go in, but knew that she had to.

'Even the lampposts are posh.'

'Violet,' he said, and she turned at the calm delivery of her name. 'Why don't we stand close to the kitchen, get some hors d'oeuvres as soon as they come out, and then you can tell me why you are so unpopular?'

'Deal.'

The bride and groom were just getting out of their car under the instructions of their wedding photographer. Violet liked the way Sahir handed over his keys to the doorman and explained their gifts were in the car... He just took care of all the details.

'Our turn,' he said, and they moved in for photos.

She smiled brightly for the camera, seeing that Sahir didn't seem to do much of that either.

He was very...remote.

No.

Polite?

Yes, but that wasn't quite the word...

Formal!

'Let's go in.'

Again he offered his arm, and she liked his formality... how he made walking into somewhere that should be daunting rather easy.

'Allow me,' he said and relieved her of her bouquet.

He placed it on the table with other gifts—clearly most of the guests had disregarded the couple's wishes.

'Now they'll be stuck with a hundred kettles and toasters,' Violet said. 'Serves them right.'

Sahir, while he didn't really understand a world that had kettles and toasters, got the drift.

He liked *her* drift...her constant, ever-changing drift...

And that quietly surprised him.

Sahir was used to chic and sophisticated women. His dates were vetted and they all knew from the outset that their relationship was going nowhere. They were just happy for the elevation his status would bring them, the gifts and the baubles…

Of course Violet wasn't a date, and she endlessly surprised him.

Having escorted her to the back of the room where she was handed a glass of icy champagne, he noticed she shook her head as the trays of hors d'oeuvres started to come out.

'I thought you were starving?' he said.

'I am, but I want something sweet.'

'That's later…' he said, then frowned when the 'starving' Violet politely declined everything.

He had a word with the waiter, and soon she stood there with a plate of cakes and pastries all of her own.

'Thank you!' Violet smiled, biting into a tiny chocolate ice cream cone, smaller than her little finger, and made just for her. 'Gosh, that's better.'

'You have a sweet tooth?' he said.

'Sweet *teeth*,' she corrected, and then worried she'd misled him. 'Actually, you said it properly. I was making a little joke.'

'I know.'

And suddenly Violet wanted to know more about him. 'Have you and Carter been friends for a long time?'

'Since boarding school,' he said. 'Yes, a long time.'

'You work together now?'

'We have worked together on a couple of projects.'

Sahir didn't really know how to explain them without giving his status away, so he turned the conversation to her.

'What about you and…?' He had to think for a moment. 'Grace.'

'We've been best friends since infant school.'

He frowned.

'Since we were five or six years old. She moved here after her parents broke up.'

'Ah…'

'I guess we grew up together. I spent more time in her house than my own.'

* * *

Violet took a breath, thinking back to long-ago days and how lovely Mrs Andrews had always been. How it had felt more like home than her own.

'I shouldn't let it get to me, but I do wonder…'

'Go on…' said Sahir.

'No.' She smiled. 'Best forgotten.'

As Sahir caught up with a couple of people he clearly knew, one of the awful old schoolfriends made a beeline for Violet.

'Violet, it's been ages!' she declared. 'Where are you living now?' Her eyes widened when Violet told her she was still at the same flat. 'Still?'

'Yes.' Violet smiled.

'What about work?'

'The library,' Violet said, not really wanting to add that she'd just been let go.

She kept her smile on as she heard about Mrs Glass Ceiling's stunning career, and then her husband, who'd been a real bully at school, came over. She found out that he'd entered politics.

'He's been nominated to stand…'

'Fabulous,' Violet said, and then stood by as he droned on and on about politics and by-elections and then offered his fake, practised smile.

'So tell me about you, Violet…where are you working now?'

His wife answered for her. 'The library.'

'Still?' he checked. 'You had a Saturday job there when we were at school?'

'Yes,' Violet said, keeping her smile in place.

'So what do you do there now?' he persisted, clearly aghast when she told him she was doing much the same, as if he'd expected her to be running the place by now. 'Don't you get bored?'

'Never.'

She didn't know quite what to say next, but thankfully Sahir came over.

'Violet, we need to take our seats.'

Violet found she was seated at the end of the top table, next to Sahir.

'Phew!' Upset from the small exchange she forced a smile. 'I thought we'd have to be bookends.'

'Were those two your friends from school?'

She nodded.

'They upset you?'

'No,' she lied, but was actually touched he saw through her façade. 'A bit. I'm probably just being overly sensitive.' She gave a tight shrug. 'They were banging on about their wonderful careers.' She knew she wasn't making sense so just said it. 'And I've just lost my job.'

'Okay…'

'Even Grace doesn't know yet.'

'She's not going to find out from me.'

'I just need to get through tonight.'

'And you shall.'

He sounded so sure.

'Thank you,' she said.

'For…?'

'Your help today.'

She was grateful to him for looking out for her. Oh, she knew it was all duty, and that nobody wanted to see the bridesmaid falling apart. But it was just nice that he'd noticed the hellish time she was having.

'It'll be Cousin Tanya next…'

'Breathe?' he suggested again, only he said it very kindly. 'We'll talk about it later,' he offered. 'Only if you want to.'

'Thank you.'

'For now, you are going to smile.'

'Yes!'

And she did just that, taking a breath, so grateful to have him in on her secret—or rather secrets. Because he shared her suspicions about the bride and groom too—although admittedly they looked incredibly happy.

It was nice to be here with him. And he was delightful company—taking her through the French menu and managing not to make her feel stupid at the same time.

'I don't want the cold cuts,' she said as she pondered it closely. 'And I am not eating blue cheese. What's bouillabaisse?'

'Fish stew.'

'Oh…'

'You take your food seriously, Violet?'

'I don't think so—I'll eat anything.'

Actually, he wasn't very talkative, she thought, possibly a little aloof and stern, and yet he behaved decorously, his focus on both the people beside him as well as the proceedings—so much so that a woman who must be the wedding organiser came and had a word in his ear.

'Excuse me a moment,' Sahir said.

Violet watched him walk off, stand and speak with the organiser, and as he did Grace leaned over. 'How are things?'

'Wonderful.' Violet smiled. 'Are you enjoying yourself?'

'It's perfect—well, except for what happened earlier…'

'Stop!' Violet warned her. 'It's forgotten.'

Thanks to Sahir, Violet thought. She shuddered to think of the blotchy mess Grace might have come out to see had it not been for him.

'What's Sahir doing?'

'I've no idea.' Violet shrugged, and then as he made his way back to them saw that the wedding gifts were being moved.

'Everything okay?' Grace asked anxiously as he took his seat.

'Of course,' Sahir reassured the bride. 'I've suggested we move the gifts to make room for dancing.'

Content with that, Grace got back to her dream day, but Violet wasn't so easily fobbed off.

'What's happening?' she asked.

'Later,' he said.

She gave a contented smile as she took a sip of her newly poured wine, knowing somehow that he *would* tell her later, and that there were conversations to be had away from the top table.

Then she put down her drink.

'You don't like it?' he checked.

'It's fine.' Violet smiled—after all she was hardly a wine connoisseur.

Sahir must be, though, for he took a sip of his own glass, and realised it wasn't at all to her sweet taste.

And again he was being a gentleman, taking care of her in little ways, for he spoke to the waiter, and soon she was being poured a glass of far sweeter wine.

He noticed her likes.

And when he did speak it was *always* a treat.

'Left and to the rear, wearing floral...' Sahir said as the starter was served.

'What about her?'

'Is that the cousin who doesn't like you?'

'Correct.' Violet smiled. 'Tanya. How did you know? Because she has children with her?'

'Hardly *with* her,' Sahir said.

And she had to smile, because the kids were play-fighting on the small dance floor.

'She keeps looking at you,' he said. 'And I agree...she doesn't look very approving.'

'Hmmm...' Violet said. 'She never liked me—even as a little girl.'

He carried on eating as she explained.

'I think she expected Grace's full attention when she came to visit her.' Tanya really was casting her dirty looks, she saw. 'She probably thinks she should have been asked to be bridesmaid.' She turned her face to his ear. Not to whisper, just speaking in a low voice to one side. 'She thinks I really stole the necklace—the one Mrs Andrews was so upset about.'

'Ah!'

'I'm sure when she tells the story, she conveniently forgets that it was found. Still, as someone said, never let the truth get in the way of...'

She couldn't complete the quote, let alone remember who'd said it. His scent was divine, his ear was as perfect as an ear should be...and, oh, that jaw was so smooth, yet she could see the dark shadow beneath the skin.

Sahir was the most beautiful man she had ever seen, let alone spoken to.

He must have wondered why she'd paused, for he turned his face to her. She saw those dark liquorice eyes, and as their eyes met there was a light tension between them that had her abruptly turning from his gaze.

As the starters were concluded he told her that it wasn't just Grace's cousin looking over.

'There are a few men looking your way...although not with critical eyes.'

'Oh, please...'

'Seriously.' He nodded. 'If you promise you won't turn to look, I shall tell you who your admirers are.'

'Okay.' She needed no excuse to keep staring at him, but was delighted to have one. 'Who?'

'Have you noticed the tall gentleman with blond hair?'

'Really?' Violet gave a delighted smile. 'He's gorgeous!'

'Actually,' Sahir said, 'my description was incorrect—he isn't a gentleman! His wife is at home with their new baby—not that that will stop him.'

'How do you know?'

'He was at my school.'

'Oh...' She glanced down at that delectable mouth and guessed it had been working magic for a very long time. 'And you were an angel, I suppose?'

'Not at all,' he said, almost reluctantly leaning back as her plate was removed. Then they faced each other again. 'But I always made it clear that short term was all I wanted.'

Violet blinked quite slowly, absorbing his words, hearing the subtle warning.

'Your blond admirer makes promises he has no intention of keeping,' said Sahir.

She stared back, wondered what his reaction would be if she told him she was a virgin, and that really she'd barely kissed a guy.

But then she stopped wondering. Because that didn't matter right now. All that mattered was his look, and how she felt that if she were to lean forward now and meet his lips, her mouth would know exactly what to do.

The main courses arrived.

To her relief, rather than fish stew, a rich beef bourguignon was placed in front of her. She glanced down at his plate and saw that he'd been served the same dish—no need to offer to swap!

'I requested the beef for us both,' Sahir said.

'I wouldn't have minded…'

'Violet?' His eyes both smiled and called her a liar. 'You are the fussiest eater I've ever met.'

'I'm honestly not.'

Violet *should* have felt irritated, and yet she was delighted instead.

She'd asked for an extra napkin. And then another. Then given him a glimpse of her lack of cleavage and turned him on as she did so.

'I don't want to spill anything,' she'd explained, tucking herself in.

Sahir found himself ridiculously attracted to Grace's unconventional friend.

'When are the speeches?' she asked now.

'There aren't any.'

'Oh!'

She ate very methodically, he saw, avoiding all the vegetables.

'What about the dancing?'

She loaded her fork and pushed off a pea.

'Do you and I have to…?'

She popped silky mashed potato into her mouth.

'I doubt it,' he said. 'There's no formal order for proceedings—just dinner and a dance if people choose to.'

He watched her chew, even though there was surely no need to, and was arrogant enough to be certain she was disappointed that they didn't *have* to dance.

God, she was fun to tease—and that was something he so rarely did.

Still, he was oddly put out when, in a lull between the main course and dessert, with the plates all cleared and some couples dancing, she nudged him with a question.

'What about the silver-haired guy? I think he's looking at me.'

Sahir glanced around the room, then saw to whom she referred. 'No. Anyway, he's a bit old,' Sahir pointed out—even though he knew that he and Mr Silver-Hair had been in the same year at school!

'I don't mind that,' Violet said. 'There's something attractive about maturity. I'm sick of guys my age. So...' She met his eyes. 'Is he looking at me?'

'I already told you—no.'

'Really?' She frowned. 'My mistake... He must be making eyes at you.'

As the bride and groom headed to the tiny dance floor, Violet popped a mint in her mouth and proceeded to top up her lip-gloss—no discreet bathroom exit for her.

And now, with her lips so shiny and kissable, Sahir found he wanted a taste of that after-dinner mint more than he had ever wanted anything.

Or rather, he wanted that minty mouth on his...

She stood up and shook off her many napkins—an accidental dance of the seven veils—and he sat there, a little stunned by the impact of her company.

'I'm going to dance,' Violet declared.

He watched her head to the small dance floor...watched as a silver head turned and a blond man moved to stand. And, yes, there was a reason Sahir enjoyed a traditional English wedding...

'Hey,' he called.

As Sahir caught her wrist, a flutter, a thrill...something that felt like a warm breeze from an open door...brushed through her as he turned her around.

'For the sake of tradition, I believe the best man and bridesmaid dance together.'

Oh, they do, Violet thought, smiling because her plan had worked, and this gorgeous, delectable man was hers for the next few minutes.

It was nice to dance with someone so elegant, so beautiful and so magnificently scented.

'What a lucky bridesmaid I am,' she said, breathing him in.

She was bold, a bit cheeky, but it covered up so much shyness, so much hurt. But then she winced, wondering if she was being too much. And then he spoke in her ear.

'What a fortunate best man…'

She closed her eyes at his velvet words and fought not to lean on him, just absorbing the moment.

'Your dress is perfect.'

'I know!' She nodded as she leant on him anyway, but then she wanted to share what a find the dress had been and so she pulled her face up to his, and being so close up to those lips and eyes was a reward in itself. 'I only found out about the wedding on Monday.'

'I did too,' he concurred.

'The Saturday before, I was getting my hair cut and someone was bringing these dresses back.'

'I'm lost…?'

'My hairdresser rents out dresses.'

'Okay…'

'Well, I saw this one and I kept hearing it calling to me as I sat there. Anyway, I ignored it—because I had no reason to hire a ball gown—but then I found out about the wedding. Grace wanted me to go to some designer, but I told her I'd already seen the most perfect dress.'

'So you went back?'

'Yes, only they didn't want to hire it to me because it's booked out for a wedding next week—the bride's actually wearing it. I had to beg, and promise it will be returned by Monday, but for tonight it's all mine.'

'I want to see the back,' he said, and raised her hand.

She actually twirled, and it was fun.

So much so she did it again.

He glimpsed the straight spine, the pale, slender back, and he didn't need a second look to know that she was exquisite…and just breathless enough that, as the music slowed, she returned her head to his chest and leant on him a little more.

He was being incredibly respectful, she thought, even as he held her close. For it felt not quite close enough, and she felt like a mouse who wanted to burrow into him.

She experienced the odd temptation to move in just a fraction, for more of this bliss. And yet, it was a polite dance.

And then she felt the warmth of his palm on her waist, and his cheek next to hers, not quite touching, and she wanted to feel that smoothness in a way that felt new.

'There are so many moving parts to you, Violet...'

Sahir's low voice tickled her ear.

'What do you mean?'

'The missing necklace...the dreadful week...the tears... the smiles...'

Damn, the desserts were coming out. Their dance was over and they were soon back at the table—but now she was itching for more physical contact.

'I chose this for you,' Grace informed Violet, as the most perfect chocolate mousse was served, and Violet gave a smile of delight and sank in her spoon.

'Goodness!' Violet closed her eyes as she tasted it. 'That's incredible.'

Yet despite the deliciousness Violet didn't quite finish it, because the dancing had started up again and she was back in Sahir's arms, resting her head on his chest. She reminded herself that she was terrified to kiss—dreadful at it—and yet she had never, ever wanted to kiss someone so badly.

It was all part of a bigger problem. Her childhood had been confronting at times. The company her family had kept had ensured she put a chair to her door at night, and not every foster home had been perfect.

Violet had quickly worked out that showing fear made her vulnerable, and had adopted a chatty, breezy persona. Her teenage years had been even worse. Visiting her father in prison, she had experienced comments and looks from some of the men there. Instead of quivering, she'd spoken up and out, even when she was scared on the inside.

Now, at twenty-five, she wanted to trust…wanted what came so naturally to others to unfold for her.

Yet any hand closing around hers felt like a vice, and any mouth on her own caused a dreadful panic, even though she fought it, persisted, hoping that in the end it would fade.

Why, when she ached for affection, didn't she want to kiss anyone?

Or have sex?

She didn't even like touch…

Only, Violet amended, it would seem that suddenly she did. Sahir's touch.

The sense of unease she seemed to have lived with for ever had dimmed. In fact, it had dispersed completely—only noticeable by its absence. For in his arms, with the brush of his cheek against hers as he moved closer to speak, she imagined his lips finding hers…

Sahir's low voice didn't jolt her—it felt like a caress. At least until her dizzy mind deciphered his words.

'The music has stopped.'

Violet blinked, as if snapped from a trance. 'So it has…' She pulled back from his embrace, a little flustered as to where her mind had just been, for it felt as if they'd kissed. 'I was miles away.'

'And me.'

CHAPTER FOUR

'I BELIEVE THE cake is coming out.'

Sahir unravelled her reluctant arms and peeled her body from his.

'They've already had a cake,' Violet grumbled—but only because she'd far rather dance. 'And I don't really...' She halted, deciding not to mention that she didn't like fruit cake.

Perhaps she was a fussy eater after all, Violet pondered, retaking her seat at the top table. Only Sahir didn't join her. Instead he stood by the dance floor, speaking with the bride and groom.

'They lied,' Sahir said when he came back.

'About what?'

'There will be speeches after all.'

'Oh,' Violet said.

'Slightly irregular order, though,' he said. 'If the cake is to be cut now.'

'Irregular?' Violet frowned.

'Usually the cake is cut at the end.'

'Only if you're a stickler for protocol.'

'I am.'

She didn't envy Sahir having to make this particular speech. The bride's parents were both absent, the groom's family all dead.

She swallowed. 'Are you going to mention his family?'

Sahir didn't respond, and she wondered if he was pondering the same.

The cake was being cut, and as coffee was served, slices came round...

Fruit cake.

Violet chopped it up, to look as if she was eating it, nibbling on the white icing and hoping the speeches were short as she wanted so badly to dance again.

There was no father of the bride, so the groom spoke first, thanking his bride, the bridesmaid, and also the guests.

'Sorry to tear you away from an excellent cricket match…'

A few of the guests groaned, and then Carter glanced over to his best man.

'Sahir, I'm sure you weren't best pleased when I told you the wedding was today.'

Sahir spread his palms, as if admitting it had been a difficult choice he'd been forced to make to attend the wedding and not the match.

She was the only one here who knew his true feelings on cricket, Violet realised. And it *thrilled* her to share in a tiny secret. So much so that beneath the table she pressed her knee against his leg and he pressed back.

She wasn't flirting, and nor was he—it was just a moment shared, Violet thought as the groom moved his speech on.

'I've attended several weddings, where—as many of you have reminded me—I've repeatedly stated that you'll never be getting an invitation to mine.' His voice moved from light-hearted to reflective. 'But then I met Grace, and everything changed…'

'Please…' Violet muttered, but for Sahir's ears only.

'Violet,' Sahir warned. 'He's about to toast you.'

Whew! Just in time she pushed out a smile as everyone raised their glasses.

'To the bridesmaid!'

Then, with Carter's speech over, it was time for some slushy words from Grace. Violet felt anxious as she watched her friend give her heart to him in front of everyone. So much so that as the speech drew to a close she found she was twisting the white napkin in her hand.

'Carter,' Grace said to her husband, 'I'm so excited to take this journey with you.'

Violet could hear the adoration in Grace's voice and it worried her—because Grace seemed to be entering this marriage with a heart brimming with hope. Yes, Grace was strong—after all, she'd been through a lot with her mother—but life had taught Violet to be tough, to *expect* to be let down, and she was terrified that her friend was about to be.

But then she felt Sahir's hand come over her own, in a gentle prompt that she was letting her suspicions show, and she put down the napkin.

'You seem to think he's playing her,' Sahir whispered, making the hairs in her ears tickle. 'Have you considered it might be the other way around?'

'Not for a second.'

'Perhaps they are both happy with their choice?'

'I hope so.' Violet nodded. 'I really do. And if that is the case...' She met his eyes. 'Perhaps you ought to mention...' She swallowed, loath to give this suave man any advice.

As if he'd take it!

As Sahir stood and took the microphone a deep hush descended. The guests had been still and quiet for the bride and groom, but there was something about Sahir that had the waiters stopping, the bar staff too. He commanded the room.

'Good evening,' he stated, and looked to the intimate gathering. 'Most of you I already know, or we've been introduced tonight, but for those I haven't met I am Sahir, a long-time friend of the groom.'

He got the formalities out of the way—complimenting the bride, accepting the toast to the bridesmaid, and Violet duly raised her glass. She was curious to hear him speak. He told the guests how he and Carter had shared a dormitory at boarding school. How some summers Carter had joined his family in Janana.

He said nothing to embarrass the groom or his bride. It was rather formal and really a very polished speech. Still, Sahir's voice made her toes curl. It was heaven to have an excuse to look at him properly, even if she could only really see his back as he turned to address the bride and groom.

His suit was perfection. It skimmed his broad shoulders and contoured his torso and moved as he spoke. His hair too was immaculate, cut into the nape of his long neck...

Then she heard a slight shift to his tone.

'Before we came to the restaurant this evening I had the

pleasure of meeting Mrs Josephine Andrews—Grace's mother.' He looked directly at Grace. 'It was wonderful that she could share in this day.'

Violet watched as Grace pressed her lips together and nodded, clearly moved that her mother had been properly named and mentioned.

'And, Carter…'

Violet found she was holding her breath.

'I never met your parents, but from all I have heard about them Sophie and Gordon would have been thrilled to be here today.' He looked right at Carter. 'I am your oldest friend, and I'm proud to be your best man, although I wish—as you must— that this speech was being delivered by Hugo.'

Violet watched as Carter briefly looked down and reached for Grace's hand, before everyone raised a glass to the people missing tonight.

It was the first time Violet had truly considered that this love might be real.

Just as that thought formed, Sahir moved his speech to a close, ending it on an upbeat note. 'I believed Carter when he said he'd never marry.' There was laughter all round. 'It is good to prove him a liar…' He raised a glass. 'To Grace and Carter—we all wish you every happiness.'

As everyone took a sip of champagne Sahir sat down. Unlike every other mortal, he didn't ask her if that had been okay, or if he'd said too much.

Violet turned to him. 'I think I'm going to cry.'

'Not yet…' He turned and gave her a slightly bemused smile. 'It's your turn to speak.'

'No!' She shook her head. 'I don't do speeches.'

'Violet…' Grace whispered loudly, urging her to stand.

'I can't,' Violet protested. 'I've never…'

'You'll be wonderful.' Beneath the table, Sahir gave her thigh a tiny squeeze. 'It's all very low-key…just keep it short.'

Violet stood on shaky legs and wished she could be as effortless and polished as Sahir.

She had never given a speech—well, just once, for Mrs Hunt at the library, when she turned sixty.

And she'd stuffed that up.

Then she saw her beaming friend, thought of her gorgeous dress, and knew she was the most polished she was ever likely to be. As well as that, she could feel the little aftermath of that touch on her thigh and it was a nice distraction.

'This is all so unexpected,' she began. 'The wedding...giving a speech...'

Violet smiled brightly at the select invitees, and then looked at the glaze on Grace's eyes. Even if she wasn't certain about this marriage, perhaps being happy for a little while was enough...

'I was hoping Grace would bring me back a nice surprise from her trip to Borneo,' she told the audience. 'A toy orangutan, or even a tea set...' She heard laughter. 'And I did get a surprise—just not quite what I had in mind. I suspect she and Carter have been a little too busy to shop.' Violet smiled at her friend. 'So I'll have to wait for something gorgeous after the honeymoon.'

She picked up her glass and toasted the seemingly happy couple.

'To Grace and Carter—you owe me a present.'

She sat down to happy applause, and of course worried that she'd got it all wrong.

'Well done,' Sahir said.

But suddenly there was no time to discuss speeches, or anything. She saw Sahir glance down at his jacket and heard the buzz of his phone.

'I'm just heading out for a moment,' he told her.

'Sure.'

Sob!

She politely shook her head at Mr Blond when he approached, and said her feet were killing her, and then for a moment she sat alone.

She looked at Grace, her eyes closed as she danced with her husband, and then she looked at the groom and how tenderly he held his bride.

Was it love?

After all, who was she to judge when love was something she'd never really known?

Could it be that Grace and Carter were for real?

'You've got a nerve.'

Violet turned to see a derisive look from Tanya. She hadn't seen her since *'the incident'*.

'You might have managed to convince Grace,' she went on. 'But we all know you took advantage of Aunty Jo.'

'Tanya...' Violet took a breath, upset that Tanya still held such resentment. 'It's Grace's wedding—'

'And there you sit, as if butter wouldn't melt in your mouth.'

It dawned on Violet that Tanya's resentment was probably because neither she nor her children were at the top table. 'I honestly think—'

'There's nothing *honest* about you, Violet.'

She breathed in sharply, both at the accusation and also at the sudden sound of Sahir's voice.

'No need for introductions! You must be Tanya.' He was being utterly charming, and clearly hadn't a clue what had just been said. 'I've heard so much about you.'

'Oh!' Tanya positively glowed. 'Yes, I'm Grace's cousin.'

She turned on her charm for Sahir, and as they stood chatting Violet left them to it and took a seat back at the table. She felt silly all of a sudden, wondering if she'd misread the closeness they had shared. Was he simply suave and delicious with everyone?

The night was winding down, and she rummaged in her bag for her phone, to call a taxi.

Two accusations in one day were just too much, and Grace would barely notice if she was gone... She just wanted to slip away.

'Hey.' Sahir was beside her. 'Where are you going?'

'I think I've had enough.'

'We're supposed to wave them off.'

'You don't wave,' she reminded him, but then her shoulders slumped. Of course she had to stay to the end. 'I'll head off after the happy couple leave.'

'Do you need a break?'

Violet nodded. 'I might just nip to the ladies'.' Though knowing her luck another blast from her past would be in there. 'Or just sit somewhere else.'

'I have a key.' He showed it to her.

'To where?'

'There's a courtyard near the main kitchen.'

She frowned. 'Why would you have a key to that?'

'In case there's an issue.'

'Or in case you want to go for a snog?'

She made him laugh. She was direct, and funny, but also, he understood, suddenly wounded and sad.

'No, it's because…' God, he did not want to explain the complexities of his life—he wanted to escape them. But thankfully Violet came up with her own reason.

'Because you're the best man?'

'Yes!' He nodded, content with that explanation. 'I asked for the gifts to be locked up out there.' He told her a part of the truth. 'Cousin Tanya's children were trying to open them. Take it…go and have a little break. You've done incredibly well.'

'Honestly?'

'Here.' He handed her the key. 'Take your time.'

'I don't know…'

'Do you want me to come?' he offered, and before she could give any response, spoke on. 'For that talk?'

'What talk?'

'The one I said would have to wait.'

Violet thought for a moment. Yes, she had hoped to talk to him later. She'd been looking forward to it, in fact.

This time with Sahir had been wonderful—it was others who had soured the night. And so she nodded.

'I'd like that.'

'And me.' He glanced to the happy couple, who were draped around each other. 'I doubt they'll miss us.'

He took a bottle of champagne and she discreetly followed him, but it was all a bit of a maze.

Some events you didn't want to attend turned out to be the most surprising of pleasures, she thought, as she unlocked a door and found a courtyard lit with fairy lights. It was the size of a small bedroom, really, but it felt like a magic garden...

'Oh, my...' Violet breathed and handed him the key, sighing in relief as he locked them in the courtyard and the wedding inside faded. 'I can stop smiling now.'

'Yes,' Sahir said. 'It's just us.'

She just closed her eyes and stopped smiling, and it was possibly as nice as taking her heels off would be later.

'Tell me about this dreadful week,' he said.

'I don't want to bore you.'

'If you do, I shall put up a hand for you to stop.'

She giggled. He made it so easy to just be herself.

She took a seat on a small stone bench. 'Your speech was lovely.'

'Stop trying to change the subject. I want to hear about you. You said you lost your job?'

'I found out I was being let go about ten minutes after I found out about the wedding. Well, they've offered me a part time role at a library on the other side of London, but it's less money and it would mean moving.' She sighed despondently. 'Usually I'd discuss it with Grace, but...' She put her hand up, gestured to the laughter and music. 'I didn't want to bring the mood down.'

'Talk to me, if you like.'

Violet thought for a moment. It had been so hard not talking about it.

'I don't want to leave,' she stated. 'I've been there for more than ten years.'

'You look too young to have worked anywhere for ten years.'

'I started there when I was fourteen, just on a Saturday, then I did a couple of evenings a week, then worked full time when I was sixteen.'

She took his rather messed-up silk pocket square out of her purse and blew her nose.

He was thankfully silent, and he stood rather than sat, but

not in an overbearing way...more in a way that gave her space as she sat and pondered her life.

She looked around the pretty garden, its walls dulling the sounds of laughter. It was a relief to escape, and even better not to be hiding from the world alone.

'Do you want a drink?' he offered.

She nodded, and he popped the cork and handed her a glass of champagne.

'Cheers.'

'To what?' Violet asked, but she did clink his glass. 'I've got no job, no qualifications, and my flatmate has just gone and got married...'

'You mean Grace?'

Violet nodded. 'The flatmate I had before Grace used to cook fish for breakfast...the one before that had this awful boyfriend... There's quite a list.'

'Do you have to share your flat?' He winced. 'Sorry, that's thoughtless.'

'Believe me, it's the same question I'm asking myself. But, yes...' She took a sip of icy champagne. 'There aren't many jobs near me, though. Well, not that I've seen.'

'Could you take the part-time job for now? Move closer...?'

'I don't want to move.'

'Because you don't want to be away from your family?'

'No.' For the first time she gave a frustrated shake of her head. 'Nothing like that.'

Violet had been open with him—more open than with anyone—but she chose not to answer that one. She just gave him a shrug, brushed the question off.

'It's just been a bad week.' She rolled her eyes. 'Oh, and I had a dreadful date on Saturday, just to kick things off...'

'Haircut day?'

'That's the one.' She smiled, appreciative that he'd been listening. 'He seemed nice, but when we met he was all about himself—how he went to the gym, how he took care of his body... Do you know? I felt judged when I ordered dessert!'

'In my country you are judged if you *don't* eat dessert.'

* * *

Violet smiled for the first time since entering the garden, and for Sahir there was a surge of triumph at watching her lighten, seeing the return of her gorgeous smile.

He gave a shake of his head, as if to clear it. He'd been right when he'd said there were a lot of moving parts to Violet—a lot of life, a lot of personality, and dots he would rather like to join up.

'Had you been dating long?' he asked, disliking no-dessert guy immensely—or rather, the thoughts he conjured.

'No. Just chatting online.'

'Online?'

'Yes. He described himself as "laid-back and easy-going".'

'Doesn't that mean you'd have to do all the arranging and he'd have no problem with you getting the bill?' Her little laugh made him smile and he was curious. 'So, how would you describe yourself?'

'Laid-back, easy-going...'

'Violet!' He chided her for her fib, calling her out, and was gifted another smile.

'I don't really,' she admitted. 'My bio describes me as "outgoing and friendly", and I guess I am. I just...'

She was more than that, he thought, but she didn't know how to reveal her fears and wants or insecurities.

'I'd be dreadful online,' Sahir admitted, and watched her put her elbows on her knees and look up as he spoke. 'I'd have skipped straight past the "outgoing and friendly" Violet, and look at what I'd have missed...'

'That's nice of you to say.' She smiled again as she gazed up at him. 'It's hard out there—not that you'd know. I can't imagine you'd have to resort to going online.'

Sahir said nothing at first, just looked at her sitting there, a little pensive and doleful, yet still but a second away from a smile. That much he knew about Violet. A thought came then—one he'd never so much as briefly entertained before. He had wealth, stature and dates aplenty, but when it came to the future Violet Lewis had something he'd never know—choices.

She also had the prospect of love.

It wasn't something he wanted.

Sahir had grown up knowing he could never be too close to another person, and that it was forbidden to love your wife. After the death of his mother, he had better understood the reason for that law—for how did you run a country on the edge of war, as his had been then, while dealing with the loss of the love of your life?

Certainly he did not want a confidant or a second wife. One would be enough to deal with, let alone two!

Sahir had asked that the subject of his marriage not be discussed until he neared forty. The King was growing impatient, though. The elders too… He doubted it would be put off until then.

No, he would not be going online. His bride would be selected for him, with the welfare of both their countries in mind. It was the one area in his life where he had no say in the matter.

Sahir answered her at last. 'We all have our own mountain to climb.'

'We do,' she agreed. 'Thanks for being there for me today. You've made things a whole lot better.'

'So have you.'

'I mean it,' Violet said.

She sat up, taking in a breath.

Yes, Sahir thought, she'd faced a few demons today.

'Don't worry about Mrs…'

He paused. Usually he was brilliant at summoning names—half his life was spent doing just that, and talking with people he barely knew—and yet since Violet had stepped out of that taxi minor details were proving a little difficult to recall.

'Andrews?' she finished for him.

'Yes.'

'And thank you for saving me from my brilliantly successful, very happily married schoolfriends.'

'If it's any consolation, the two of them were having a big argument outside when I was on my phone,' Sahir told her. 'And as for people like Tanya…'

'I thought you two were getting on?'

'No, I was trying to divert her from being so awful to you.

My mother used to say that a snake waits in the shadows to strike.'

'Used to?'

He nodded, but said no more on the subject than that. 'I saw Tanya make a beeline for you the moment you were alone,' he told her.

'Is that why you came over?' she asked.

'Of course. I knew she was going to attack.'

'But you were so nice to her.'

'No. I was *polite* to Tanya. With you, I'm nice…' He offered his hand. 'One more dance?'

'Can't we stay out here a little longer?'

'I meant, let's dance here…'

It was a lovely slow dance, but he could feel her question coming—her need for more information.

'Your mother used to…?' she checked.

'She died when I was thirteen,' Sahir said. 'It was…' He took a breath. 'I was told it was sudden.'

'Told?'

'I'm not so sure. I wish I had acted sooner,' he admitted. 'Noticed things.'

Sahir had told her only a little, yet it was by far more than he had ever told anyone.

He looked down at her. 'Do you find that people talk to you, Violet?'

'All the time. Clients at work, people on buses… I'm the one they sit next to…'

'Taxi drivers?' he added.

'Oh, yes.' She smiled, and her eyes were misty, her next words soft. 'Not so much you, though.'

'You have no idea…' Sahir said.

He was beyond private—no one knew his thoughts—and he tried to pull back control, lighten the topic.

'Let's work on your online bio. How about "gorgeous"?' he started.

But the thought of helping her meet another man didn't lift his mood, so instead he gave up on conversation and lightly kissed her pale shoulder. Then he opened his mouth. As his tongue met her flesh she exhaled sharply, and he lifted his head as she jolted.

'Okay?' he checked, a little bemused by her reaction, and was pleased to find she was smiling.

'Don't stop,' she told him.

So he got back to the shoulder he'd made wet.

'I actually got a shiver down my spine,' she told him. 'I never really got what that meant before.'

'Good,' he said, and his lips moved along her collarbone to her neck, then up to her gorgeous mouth.

Violet stopped him, as if she had something she thought she really ought to say. 'If I'm honest, I think you'd skip past my bio.'

'How come?'

'Because I've never...*been* with anyone.'

'Sorry?'

'I've barely kissed, let alone slept with anyone.'

Sahir met her eyes. Yes, there were so many parts to Violet—but he had a rather urgent question.

'You didn't put that on your bio?'

'Of course not!'

'Because you'd get every—' He stopped himself.

'I do know!' she shrilled, all indignant.

And then he saw her pink cheeks, and she hid her head in his chest as they continued their dance.

'Dreadful, isn't it?' She sighed.

'Of course not,' he said.

'Then why are you holding me like it's a duty dance now?'

'I'm not,' he refuted, even though she'd made a very good point.

'If my date hadn't been so mean...'

'Can we stop talking about him?' Sahir snapped, appalled at the thought of Violet with him. With anyone. 'Were you going to sleep with him? Someone you'd just met online?'

'I wanted it out of the way.'

'It's not a chore! It can actually be...' He halted, perhaps for his sanity's sake. 'Well, you'll find out for yourself,' Sahir said, and then a little too hastily added, 'Someday.'

Only that little addition didn't help his sanity either. He didn't want to entertain even the thought of her with another man—certainly not while holding her in his arms.

Violet wanted to find out.

And not just someday.

Today—or rather tonight.

With Sahir.

She wasn't surprised at the sudden strain between them.

She was good at a little flirting, even if it was usually an act. Yet with Sahir it had been so natural.

'I had a pretty wild family,' she told him.

It was too much, and too hard to explain, but they were dancing more easily now, and he smelt so divine, and *gosh*, he was good to talk to—or was it that he simply didn't say that much?

She was brave enough to lift her head and look at him now. 'And in trying not to emulate them I think I went too far the other way. Became too cautious...'

'Go on...' he invited.

'Now, when a guy finds out I've never slept with anyone, they seem to assume I'm saving myself for a reason. That I want a husband.'

'You don't want to marry?'

'Absolutely I do.' Violet nodded. 'Not yet, though. I want a gorgeous life, with babies and...' She gave a contented sigh, thinking of everything she'd never had. 'But before all that I want to sort myself out. Maybe when I'm about thirty...'

'That's the age you'll be all sorted?' He smiled.

'I hope so.' She nodded. 'How old are you?'

'I just turned thirty-five, and believe me...'

Sahir paused, reminding himself that his future was more than sorted. It just didn't feel that way right now.

Thankfully she didn't notice his silence, just chatted on.

'For now, though, I just want to date...have some fun while I work things out. The trouble is, I don't think I've ever really wanted to...'

That pulled him out of his own head. 'Have sex?' he asked.

'Oh, it's far worse than that,' she admitted. 'I don't even really like kissing. I've never wanted to…never felt compelled…'

Violet chewed her lip, because she'd been utterly honest with Sahir so far.

However, as of now, she was lying.

'Never?' he checked, his hands hovering near her torso and warm on her waist.

'Maybe a little once…'

'Possibly tonight?'

'How did you know?' She laughed.

'I think we were kissing on the dance floor,' Sahir told her. 'Not physically, but… I don't know the word in English. *Takhatari*…in our minds…'

'Imagining?' she asked.

'Both imagining,' he said. 'At the same time.'

'Ooh, *takhatari* kisses. I like that.' Whatever it meant. 'And you're right—I was thinking about you, about kissing you, maybe…'

She watched his dark eyes looking up somewhere to the left, as if he was really thinking about things, and then they came back to her, and for the first time she saw their colour, the tint on the edge of his pupils as raven as his hair.

'You want to "get it out of the way"?' he accused, using her own words.

'No.' She shook her head. 'It doesn't feel like that with you.'

'Violet, I'm only here for tonight.' He was terse, back to holding her at a distance again. 'And as much as I'd like to kiss you, and maybe more…' He inhaled sharply. 'Given you've never done anything before, I think you deserve to be wined and dined and…'

'Stop being polite.' She stared back at him. 'If you don't fancy me, just say so. And if there's a Mrs Sahir at home, or—'

'Violet,' he cut in. 'I don't like that word.'

'What word?'

'"Fancy". It is…'

'What?'

'Teenage.'

'Okay, then.' She thought for a moment. 'I'll put it more maturely. If you're not attracted to me...'

'I'm intensely attracted to you,' he said, and he pulled her in, kissed her neck.

She closed her eyes as lust swept like a turning tide low inside her stomach.

'But I fly back home soon,' he went on. 'I don't do romance—and, believe me, I *am* a bad choice.'

'I think you're the perfect choice.'

'How so?'

She smiled. 'Because I'm twenty-five and I have never even come close to being so intensely attracted to anyone. And I don't care if I never see you again...' She looked into his eyes and ran a hand through his raven hair. 'Well, I care. But I think you'll be rather deliciously missed and very fondly remembered.'

'Violet,' he said. 'That's a really bad reason to sleep with someone.'

'Oh, so you only sleep with someone when you have excellent, well-thought-out reasons? Tell me, Sahir, what are they?'

'I can tell you why we shouldn't,' he volunteered. 'I don't bed virgins.'

'*"Bed"* virgins!' She laughed. 'Gosh, that's old-fashioned. Well, then, for tonight I shall remain un-kissed and un-bedded.'

She knew she'd hit every nerve, and it had him pulling her right in. She slipped her hands beneath his jacket.

'You are...' He stopped, as if trying to find a word to describe her. 'Irresistible.'

'So are you.' Violet nodded. 'And you have no idea how long I've waited to feel like this.'

'Like what?'

'Ready.'

She wasn't begging, she was tempting him. And her mouth was right by his, and she was completely free to be herself, to cajole and tease. Because he made it so...

His shirt was crisp beneath her palms and she thought of the skin beneath, and of tasting his breath while locked with his eyes. And whatever *takhatari* kisses were, they must be sharing them again, because she could feel her breath catching, feel him hardening against her stomach…

Violet vowed to herself that if he didn't kiss her this second, she would walk away.

Fortunately, there was no need to walk away.

Because he answered her demand, his lips lightly brushing her own.

The soft contact was so welcome it almost made her startle, because it was all that had been missing. He cosseted her lips, indulged them tenderly till they were attuned to his. And then he delivered more…still soft, but a deeper peek at further treasures as his tongue met the tip of hers.

For Violet, this was usually the moment she involuntarily rebelled—the moment when her body shrilled because it was too close to another. Were she with another man right about now she'd revolt—pull her head back in alarm, press her lips closed. Tonight, though, or rather with Sahir, it felt exactly right and, closing her eyes, she found there was only the soft thrill of bliss, followed by a new and fervent desire to reciprocate.

I'm kissing, Violet thought as their mouths meshed softly. And he allowed her tongue to toy with his until she had to taste him more deeply and he obliged.

His hand moved to the back of her head, exerting a gentle pressure as his mouth took command. And the crush of his lips, the slow revelling of his tongue, had the fire that had been kindling in Violet igniting, shooting flame in directions she'd never so much as sought before.

She was by far too eager as her hands came to his hips, tugging at his shirt, desperate to feel his skin, yearning for a deeper taste. To be guided straight to more bliss.

Sahir must have felt her need for escalation, and yet he refused to reciprocate, or cave to her demand. Instead she felt the sure placement of his hands on her cheeks as he moved his mouth back.

'We're being called.'

'No.'

Oh, but they were—she could hear Carter's voice.

'Where's Sahir?'

They stood, foreheads resting on each other, as Grace joined in with the search.

'I have to say goodbye to Violet.'

There was no avoiding the world.

'Go that way.'

Sahir pointed to an exit she hadn't even seen.

'It will take you out by the restroom. And tidy up,' he told her, while tucking his shirt in, then straightening his tie 'I'll say I had to make a phone call.' He gave a wry laugh. 'Actually, I do.'

And then what? she wanted to ask, unsure if this was it—if a kiss was the only wish she'd be granted.

But rather than ask, she wiped her lip-gloss from his cheek... oh, and the other one. Gosh, even his chin.

Yes, she'd better go and tidy up!

And now, after such a nice kiss, she was being shown the red card.

'I'll say goodbye here...' Sahir told her.

'Okay.'

'I have appointments tomorrow, and then I fly...'

'You already said.'

There was a knock on the door they'd entered through, and as she slipped out through the other exit he took out his phone and started talking in Arabic.

Carter called his name, opening the door the moment she'd slipped away.

Damn.

She stood in the tiny bathroom, frantically smoothing her hair and toning down her cheeks.

She wasn't stinging from rejection—she'd grown up with it, refused to react... She was just annoyed that Sahir was doing what he considered the right thing by her.

What he didn't get was that she'd been waiting a long time to feel so right, so sure, so...

Damn.

Why did she have to get a decent bastard?

* * *

'There you are!'

Grace was smiling as Violet duly came out of the restroom, her lip-gloss back on, her smile in place, trying to act normal—as if her legs knew how to walk and she hadn't just glimpsed paradise.

'We're heading off,' Grace told her. 'Carter's just rounding up Sahir.' She rolled her eyes. 'I know he doesn't like me...'

'You don't know that.'

'He thinks it's all about money...' She looked at Violet then. 'You think so too.'

'Not any more,' Violet admitted, and gave her friend a hug. 'I love you, Mrs Bennett...'

'I love you too,' Grace told her, then whispered, 'Don't tell a soul...you're going to be an aunty...'

Violet tried not to squeal. Because even if she wasn't technically going to be an aunty, they were closer than many sisters and it was just the most wonderful news. So brilliant that even deep kisses and sexy Sahir were momentarily forgotten as the news sank in.

'I'm so happy...' She hugged Grace tighter. 'Oh, my, God...'

She felt dizzy, and then suddenly guilty that she'd been so wrong about them both. And as the party headed out to the waiting car, and she saw the smiles on the newlyweds' faces and realised that she'd been trusted with a precious secret, a huge wave of emotion hit her—a delectable moment when everything felt right in the world.

Indeed, one kiss was all Sahir would be granting. What a kiss, though...

The afternoon and evening had raced by, and the wedding had been made both interesting and fun—and fun wasn't something Sahir either sought or was particularly used to.

And now it would seem it was over, because duty had tried to call—the reason he'd had to slip off earlier, even though his phone was effectively off, save for one particular line.

'Did you find out who was trying to get hold of me?' he asked Pria.

'It was an error,' Pria told him. 'They were checking procedures for tomorrow.'

Reassured, he headed out to the street and stood on the other side of the carpet from Violet, hands in his pockets, watching Carter and Grace get into the car. He glanced down the street and saw Maaz a couple of doors down, and Layla in her car.

Very deliberately, he was doing all he could not to look at Violet.

Once the newlyweds had gone, he'd head back to the restaurant, wish Violet goodnight and then he would head home.

He could still smell Violet's meadowy scent on his jacket, still feel the slight sheen of her gloss on his mouth—or was that more a case of wishful thinking?

He was in no mood for a virgin.

Okay, he was very much in the mood for a certain virgin—but he was trying to do the right thing here.

Grace threw the bouquet, and—phew! Violet didn't even leap to catch it, instead that blond bastard caught it.

'Flowers for your wife!' Violet called out, and Sahir smothered a smile as she put him in his place for eyeing her up earlier.

Violet Lewis should write on her bio that she was independent and tough—that she knew what she wanted for her first time and losers need not apply.

Oh, and she could also add gorgeous and mind-altering too.

And sexy as hell.

There was a vulnerability to her too, though...

Sahir stood as the car containing the happy couple was driven off and some things never changed—of course he did not wave.

One thing had changed, though...

As they walked back into the restaurant he watched Violet reach for her purse. Somehow knew she wasn't going to linger just to be turned down...

'Violet?'

'Please.' She put up her hand. 'I don't need the farewell speech—'

'Violet,' he interrupted. 'I don't want tonight to end either.'

He adored the way her eyes widened.

'But I do fly home tomorrow, and as I said...'

'Oh, gosh...' She waved tomorrow away. 'I know all that. And Grace and Carter must never, ever know...'

'Agreed.' He smiled. 'I just have to get rid of some people.'

'Were you all meant to be going off to a club?'

'Something like that,' Sahir said, not wanting to burst this incredible bubble they'd found by talking about his protection officers or revealing his title. 'Can you wait for me in the garden?'

'Yes.'

Discreetly he slipped her the key. 'I shan't be long.'

Her eyes told him she'd wait...

CHAPTER FIVE

VIOLET TURNED THE key and stepped into the courtyard. Her heart hadn't stopped hammering since their kiss. He was the first person she'd truly coveted—the first person she'd felt an actual need for.

As someone who'd practically brought herself up it was new and unfamiliar.

She'd felt looked after by him from that moment outside the nursing home.

More, she'd been completely herself.

She'd hidden her tears and upset from Grace, dragged out her happy smile for her old schoolfriends, and then, when Tanya had been such a cow...

Her children had run wild, Violet thought, looking at the table full of half-unwrapped gifts.

She was checking that her box didn't rattle when her eyes caught sight of the most beautiful silver candelabra. As she went to pick it up she briefly wondered if it been secured somehow, because it barely moved, but then she realised she hadn't been expecting it to be so heavy...

Gosh, it was beautiful—seriously so.

She stared at it closely. The parts that caught the wax were different colours—one silver, one a rosy gold.

She sat on the little bench, still holding the candelabra. She was excited for the night and the adventure ahead. Okay, and a teeny bit nervous, Violet admitted. And she felt suddenly shy as he came through the wooden door.

'Running off with the silver?' he teased.

'I think my arm would fall off if I tried to run off with this.'

She both blushed and smiled, but his words hadn't hurt or offended, and she hadn't jumped as if she was being accused, as she so often did. Violet was simply pleased to see him.

'I was just admiring it.' She frowned then, remembering he'd said he'd bought them a candle stick. 'Is this your gift?'

Sahir nodded. 'It is…' He paused. 'Carter and I are working on a project together in Janana.'

'So, this is from your country?'

'Yes.'

'Gosh.' She went to hand it to him, but paused again to take in its absolute beauty. It was so solid, and yet so intricate. 'This part is different,' she said. She couldn't stop staring. 'The wax catcher. Perhaps they ran out of silver and had to use brass?'

It was rose gold, and the bobèches—or wax catchers, as Violet described them—depicted a full moon with Mars in opposition to the sun.

To Sahir's surprise he wanted to share that with Violet—to sit on the bench and tell her about the Setarah collection, even to describe the palace, how it was shaped like a star.

She tried to hand it to him, but it was truly heavy, and she pulled a funny face as he took the weight.

'Beats my tulip vase,' she said as he replaced it on the table, and then she stood.

'Here.' He gave her his jacket and suggested that instead of walking out through the restaurant they leave by the rear exit.

'Are you famous?' she asked as they walked down a cobbled side street. 'It's all very cloak and dagger.'

'In some circles.' He nodded. 'I guess you could say that.'

They walked along another beautiful street and then came to a gate. She looked at the very smart house that backed onto a formal garden as he punched a code into the gate.

'You live here?' she checked as they walked through the garden and he entered another security code, and another…

'When we get in,' he said, 'if you just want a drink—'

'If you send me home after a drink I'll be *extremely* upset!'

She would—because for her whole life she'd been looked at as second rate. Sahir made her feel first rate.

Sahir would be her first.

Her eyes widened and then narrowed as she took in the size

of his residence, frowning when she saw the dining table. 'Are those the same candle—?'

'Do you really want a tour?' he asked.

'No.' She laughed as they stepped into the lounge and she pointed to a decanter. 'But I'll have a glass of that.'

'Not if you're staying,' he said. 'I want us both to remember this…every last moment.'

She thought she should feel shy, but it had faded, and there was not even a glimpse of it.

The light of the moon was streaming in through the French doors and she looked out at a glorious balcony.

'Oh, my goodness…' she said.

Under any other circumstance she would have been tempted to step out, for the view of London must be stunning from there…but as he came and stood behind her there was something rather more vital occupying her attention.

He removed his jacket from her and kissed her shoulder, as he had in the courtyard, and instead of opening the French doors she turned around.

'Are you nervous?' he asked.

She considered his question, then she turned clear blue eyes to him. 'No.' She shook her head. 'I'm…'

She swallowed, because this felt so right, so perfect, that something told her it could only ever have been him. It was as if last weekend's date and every dreadful date she'd walked away from before had been mere signposts that had turned her away and somehow led her to a place she felt she perfectly belonged.

'I feel happy.'

'So do I.'

He brought her back into his embrace, as if they were dancing again, though he pulled her closer than he previously had, and his cheek was next to hers. This time she allowed her skin to rest on his and breathed him in. She closed her eyes as his mouth moved as she had wanted it to on the dance floor. It created a warm path to her lips, and she parted them.

His kiss was different from the one in the courtyard. There, she had felt restraint…now it was warm and slow. She wasn't fighting the feelings he evoked, just letting them ripple through her. Feeling the silk of his hair beneath her fingers and how her breasts ached as her arms reached behind him...how his hands on her hips guiding her in made her feel warm and aching down below.

So much so that she moaned into his mouth and briefly pulled back. 'Turns out I do like kissing.'

He smiled and got back to her mouth, and just for a moment he lost concentration. For it had dawned on him that he hadn't particularly been a fan of kissing either...

Or of feeling happy.

Until this night...

They stood staring at each other, mouths almost together, exchanging the sensual air. He touched the top of her arm and stroked it.

His touch made her hungry...it made her weak, it made her bold. She did something she never had before. She kissed his neck...ran her mouth over the scratchy throat that had been so smooth just hours ago. It made her desperate to see it dark and shadowed and rough in the morning.

'Careful,' he warned.

'I don't want to be careful,' she whispered, breathing into his sexy ear.

He adored every word, every moment, every taste of her skin and the feel of her awakening to him. He loved feeling her desire building and, yes, he wanted to be her first.

There were not enough hours in the night to do all that he wanted, but he wanted more of that laughter, more of everything...

There would be no sleeping tonight.

He wanted her shoes on his floor. He wanted her earrings by his bed, her perfume on his pillow and traces of her everywhere.

Taking her hand, he led her to the principal bedroom.

The covers were turned back, the side lamps on, and he re-moved her earrings very carefully.

'They're not expensive,' she said, because he was treating them with such care, placing them neatly by the bed.

And he wasn't shy either, because he went to the bedside table and saw her swallow as he took out some condoms and then lifted the lid on a small container.

'What's that?' she asked.

'Oil.'

'For me or you?'

'Both.'

She dipped in her fingers and the fragrance was like every season condensed on her fingers, so subtle.

'I don't think I need it,' she whispered, and he was aware of her own arousal. 'And as for them…' She pointed at the con-doms. 'I'm on the pill. Or do you always use them?'

'Absolutely.'

There could be no chance of an unplanned pregnancy. He always wore a condom, to protect both himself and his partner.

Only this was something he had never encountered before.

A woman who wanted just him and just this.

So was it a kick of rebellion as he replaced the condoms in the drawer?

Or trust?

No, for he trusted no one.

And yet, here they stood, and he wanted every moment of this night, every inch of her naked skin.

He pulled her to him and found the little side zip of her dress.

'Violet…' he whispered—for, as she'd said the dress had been calling her, she had been calling to him all night.

It was pure silk, and it fell as such, and he loved her pale breasts and her little silver knickers. He removed them too, and then led her to a bedroom chair, where she sat, naked apart from her heels.

He removed his tie, and then his cufflinks. She was watch-ing his every move intently. She reminded him of a little hawk, just learning to track.

* * *

She noted everything.

Every button and every glimpse of his chest made her own chest tighten.

He removed his shirt and Violet watched as his gorgeous chest was revealed. She felt her bottom lift a little from the chair.

He kicked off his shoes and then he came closer. He placed one foot on her thigh and wordlessly, wondrously, she rolled down the black sock, exposing one long, elegant foot even as his hand pulled all the pins from her hair. She stroked the coffee-coloured skin of the foot on her thigh and then he removed it.

She crossed her legs, as if it might somehow calm the now swollen flesh between her legs.

Sahir presented his second socked foot, and as she slipped the other sock off his hand was loosening her hair. Then the sole of his foot slid between her legs, prising her thighs apart as if he knew the turmoil she felt between them.

He was looking between her legs as he unbelted his trousers, then slipped down his zipper. She felt her legs pressing back together of their own volition—not to hide, just in unfamiliar tension—as he removed the last of his clothing and she saw him erect, saw the gorgeous dark silky hair. The excitement of his arousal made her weak...

'Stay there,' he said.

And she continued to sit as he knelt down and pulled her bottom to the edge of the chair. He stroked her whilst easing her legs further apart. She touched his broad shoulders a little tentatively, as if he might suddenly disappear.

'Why aren't I shy?' she asked.

'It's just us...you don't need to be.'

He kissed her breasts, and she felt nicely lazy as he ministered to each one, his tongue perfection in its light suction, the small nips of his teeth. And then his head trailed down, and she looked at her breasts, wet from his mouth and unfamiliar with their budded nipples.

Her stomach was kissed deeply, and she leant back in the hard chair and closed her eyes. Then she moaned as his fingers parted her and his tongue explored her and it was the nicest, most unhurried moment. She looked down and saw his black hair, felt the tension in his shoulders, while her legs were so limp that he easily lifted them over him.

'I should do something…'

It was the vaguest ever offer to help—like offering to do the almost done dishes. Because she never wanted to move again. He ignored her anyway, just caressed her with his mouth, with his lips and his tongue.

'Sahir…' she said, sensation rippling through her.

His mouth was taking all the tension of the day, until it faded away with a sigh.

'Oh…'

She smiled down at him, then closed her eyes, wishing there was a switch that might flip the chair so she could lie back, breathless and pleasure-filled…

But then he removed her legs from his shoulders and kissed her, his lips made shiny from her delectably gentle first orgasm. And then he held her chin and met her eyes.

'You're sure?'

'More than sure…'

That said, she gulped when she looked at him. For she had thought him erect before, but he was even bigger now. Considerably. He held the tip to where she was still tender, stroking her, wetting her a little, and she watched, her thighs aching, her throat tight with anticipation.

'We'll go to bed,' he said.

At first it seemed a helpful suggestion, and she nodded. 'This chair's not very—'

Only her words caught—for suddenly she didn't want him to stop, and she forgot about hard chair backs and protruding arms and everything. She was entranced, just watching him nudge a little inside her.

'Can we please stay here?'

He pulled her bottom a little closer to the edge, and she

thought there was something heady about watching someone so strong and determined attempt and fail. Because as he hit resistance she tensed, and he careered a little to one side...

She reached down and felt the velvet of his skin, explored the veins. And then she just held him and stroked him.

'Bed,' he said.

But she liked them being here.

'No,' she insisted.

He closed a hand over her own, and as he nudged in again she couldn't help but voice the pain.

When he pulled out there was a little blood on his thick tip.

'Bed!'

Finally Violet agreed.

He scooped her up, and she had barely been lain down when he was over her. Violet's eager arms reached for him, holding his face as they kissed.

Sahir kissed her harder, making her mouth hot and swollen. He made her tongue dance with his and she felt him hard against her stomach and her pubic bone, moving lower. She felt the crush of his body as he kissed her neck. And then for the first time in her life Violet felt adored.

Utterly looked-after.

The most looked-after she'd ever felt.

'I am so glad it's you,' she said, putting her arms around his neck.

He answered in Arabic, and then his full lips hovered over her mouth. 'I am honoured that it is me.'

And now he took her, smothering her cries with his mouth, but she was ready. And he pushed through the last resistance... found her stretched, ready and, oh, so willing flesh.

The grip of her had his breath shuddering as his body fought for restraint. He held himself still within her as he kissed her slowly, hearing her low, throaty entreaties.

He was beyond logic now, and he drove in, closing his eyes in brief cognisance that he was bedding a virgin.

And he *was* bedding her.

* * *

'Sahir...'

She felt his hand slide to the small of her back, felt his stomach on hers, as if cradling the pressure within, as if absorbing it, giving her a moment to acclimatise, and when his mouth pulled back she watched his closed eyes open, knew they were both lost in themselves and yet so linked together.

He moved out a little and she pressed her lips tight, as if braced for the next push. She hummed as he slid in deeper, then nodded as he did the same again, only more precisely this time. Her thighs were shaking. Without intention she tried to wrap her legs around him—and promptly failed.

'I'm so unfit,' she admitted.

He laughed. She hadn't heard him laugh in that way, and it was as low and as sexy as the man himself. He took her leg and pushed it back further, and she did the same with the other leg. He took her with hard thrusts that made her weak, this glimpse of unbridled need both exciting and thrilling her.

'I want you wrapped around me,' he told her, and her less than agile legs attempted to do it again.

Nothing could prise her off him now, because he thrust, and then thrust again, and there was another glimpse of him, a surge of rawness that had her wanting more, and they were locked together...

He felt her breasts against his chest, her legs tight around his hips and her hands in his hair. It wasn't the smooth sex he was used to—it wasn't anything he was used to...

Sahir pulled the pillow out from beneath her head, and Violet felt as if there might be no mattress—because she was in freefall.

She felt the wave of her second orgasm, not at all comparable to the little butterflies she'd felt whilst on the chair. It was all-consuming. Her legs slipped away, joined by the delicious sensation of him rigid for a second before he achieved his own release.

'That was heavenly,' Violet told him, and it would seem he agreed. Because he came down by her side and pulled her into him and they just caught their breath.

'Are you okay?' he asked.

'About what?'

'You're not going to have major regrets?'

'Gosh, no.'

She felt as if the world had been put right. As if her every last hang-up had been taken care of. Every fear about men, sex, life…all were vanquished, at least for now.

'Though Grace must never, ever know.'

Violet let out a laugh that made him smile.

'We'll nod politely if we meet…'

Then she fell quiet.

Sahir was silent too.

Everything would be different when they next met, he knew.

Soon Grace would tell her of his royal status, or she'd find out for herself. Perhaps it was better that she heard that at least from him.

'I have appointments tomorrow.'

'I know…' Violet sighed. 'What time am I being kicked out?'

'Not yet.'

'Will we do it again?'

Sahir half laughed and pulled her closer, so her head was on his chest, and she lay there, feeling as contented as she ever had.

'Tomorrow night I fly to Janana,' he told her.

'You said.'

She played with the gorgeous hair on his stomach. She loved lying relaxed and naked in his arms, half asleep and simply talking—it was another new adventure for Violet, and she loved the lulling of his low voice.

'Carter does some work there?' she checked.

'Yes.'

'Rebuilding some ancient palace.' She stroked the lovely black hair. 'Are you working on it with him?'

'I am. I studied historical architecture.'

Her voice was sleepy, yet she didn't want to give in, wanted every minute of their night. 'Is that the same as what Carter does?'

'No, he's an architect.'

He thought of the years it had taken to get to this point with the project.

'It's a very ancient structure,' he told her.

'Mmm…'

'One wing was destroyed in an earthquake more than a century ago. There are a lot of people opposed to disturbing the ruins.'

If she hushed him, he'd say no more, Sahir decided.

'How come?'

'Many were killed—including the then Queen.'

He felt her stir of interest, the way her thigh moved across him, how her head moved a little, as if her ears had pricked up in curiosity.

'The King fell into deep grief…he killed himself a couple of weeks later.'

'Goodness.'

'There was a lot of turmoil in the country. A new king had to be appointed, with a whole new lineage. Rules were put in place so it could never happen again.'

'You can't prevent an earthquake.'

'I mean rules to ensure that a king could never again jeopardise his country's future because of his personal emotions.'

'You can't stop—'

'There is no love allowed in a royal marriage.' He stared at the ceiling. 'It must be a purely business arrangement.'

'Wow…' She seemed to ponder that for a moment. 'Are there bodies still buried in the ruins?'

'No.' He found that he'd smiled at her question, squeezed her arm in affectionate rebuke. 'Your thoughts are very dark.'

'Oh, yes.'

He felt her relax back into him.

'So, what happens now?' she asked.

'We are waiting for the council to approve the plans.'

'Well, if it's anything like our local council…'

'No!' He gave a half-laugh. He knew she was teasing, yet she made the serious subject a little lighter, made him want to explain their curious ways.

Her breathing was slowing and her eyes were closing, he was sure, but then she jolted herself awake, and he wanted to make love to her all over again.

But first…

If he didn't want her to hear it from Grace…

Sahir made himself say it.

'The new wing of the palace is where I shall reside…'

He felt her jolt again, saw the raising of her head from his chest, and then he heard her question.

'When?'

'When I am King.'

CHAPTER SIX

'KING?' VIOLET STARTED to laugh.

Sahir didn't.

Her eyes were wide open now and she actually sat up. 'So, you're a prince?'

'The Crown Prince.'

'Crikey.'

'A few hours from now I have a function to attend, then I fly back to Janana later that night.'

'Oh.' She stared at him. 'I honestly don't know what to say.'

'I am just trying to explain that I have to leave and why I—'

She put a hand to his mouth. 'You don't have to explain the next part.'

'What next part?'

'That I'm a very unsuitable date for a future king.'

'You'd be a wonderful date, but...'

Unsuitable in ways she could not begin to comprehend.

He had told her more than he'd ever told any other woman, and he already felt close to her in ways the laws strictly dictated he avoid, but... 'I'm needed back home.'

'I get it. Well...' She frowned. 'Of course, I don't...'

Violet turned on the light.

'What are you doing?'

'I knew there was something.'

She didn't sound daunted or overwhelmed. Truly just thrilled to have spent the night with him.

'Something?' Sahir checked.

'You're so formal...' She pinched his nipple. 'When you're not being sexy.'

He caught her wrist and held it there, and looked up at those blue eyes smiling down at him.

And nothing—not a thing—had changed.

'Come here,' he told her, taking her head and pulling it down to his.

There would be no sleeping tonight...

None.

At dawn he ran them a bath, and Violet rather gingerly climbed in so that she faced him.

'Ouch, ouch, ouch...' she said, lowering herself down, and then sinking into the relief of the warm water. 'You have chased this horrible week away,' she told him as she soaped his chest. 'Honestly, when I look back I am going to smile now, and remind myself there's always a silver lining...'

'Good.'

It was his turn with the soap now. He washed first her arms, her hands, her fingers, and then he washed her breasts.

He moved her onto his lap...

But even as they kissed the world was waking up—his phone was bleeping from the bedroom.

'Ignore it...' she told him.

Sahir was tempted to bolt all entrances.

'Violet...'

She looked up, wrapped in a towel and gathering up her clothes.

'Stay for breakfast.'

'There are people arriving...'

'I know. Look, I can't miss today.'

'I get that.'

And Violet absolutely did. He was the person who was leaving, the man who could never be, and right now that thought didn't scare her. She had never dared so much as to hope for even one such wonderful, magical night and Sahir had given her that.

'I know you're busy.'

'Yes. However, would you like to spend the day here?'

'Why?'

'I don't want you to feel I'm rushing off. I can delay the

flight…we can have a late dinner tonight—only this time without so much company.'

She knew what he meant. As wonderful as the whole night
had been, for Violet, the best moments had been those spent
alone with him.

'Just us,' he added.

'I'd love that.'

Violet needed little persuading. She had thought goodbye
was imminent, and she accepted the reprieve with delight.

'I have to get dressed,' he told her.

'It's a bit late to be shy,' Violet said, and smiled, but then he
explained he had someone coming in to assist him.

'Formal attire,' he said.

'Oh!'

While she wasn't in the least embarrassed with Sahir, she
was not going to sit around with someone else here.

Before he let someone called Faisal in, she pulled on her gorgeous silk gown, then opened the French windows and stepped
onto the balcony, feeling the gorgeous breeze… A helicopter
was hovering in the blue, blue sky and she stretched her arms
up and arched her neck, then gazed out at the new and beautiful morning.

How long she stood there, Violet wasn't sure. She was just
daydreaming, and reliving the night they'd shared.

'Hey…'

She turned and caught her breath. Sahir wore a white robe
and his *kafir* was tied with gold braid. He looked magnificent.

'Look at you…'

'I was just enjoying looking at *you*,' he responded. 'Your
breakfast is here.'

It was the most beautiful Sunday she had ever known, Violet decided as she swapped her hired gown for a robe and
climbed into bed.

Sahir placed a tray across her lap.

'I might watch a movie,' she said, buttering a muffin with
jam. But then, glancing around, she saw there was no television. 'Or sleep…'

He picked up a little remote, and a huge screen popped up as if from the end of the bed.

'Anything you need, just use the phone.'

'Does it work for Florentines?' she teased.

'It works for anything.'

'Do I get a kiss?'

'No.' He looked at her strawberry-jam-covered fingers and lips. 'But I'll make up for that tonight.'

'Good luck, then,' she said, and gave him a smile. 'Hurry back!'

Sahir left her in a cloud of white linen, working her way through a pot of tea.

He swept downstairs and spoke with Faisal about dinner—and arranged for a treat to be delivered to her.

As he went to leave, Sahir paused. Last night had been in-credible. Not just the sex, but the before and after. He simply could not imagine sitting down to dinner with Violet tonight and boarding his jet straight afterwards. Certainly she deserved more than that—and, most rarely for Sahir, he wanted more of a lover's company...

For the last two years he had worked non-stop—in contrast with his younger brother, Ibrahim, who did very little, and his sister, Jasmine, who did... Well, nothing much at all.

While Sahir had certainly lived a decadent life at times, duty had always outweighed everything else. Perhaps it was time for his siblings to step up when required.

Because right now, Sahir felt more time with Violet was required.

Life was going to be hectic once he returned, and while he knew Violet should be spending this week looking for work, he did want to indulge her and mark the preciousness of last night.

In the dining room, his escorts were waiting, and as Faisal made the final adjustments to his *kafir* he spoke with Pria.

'I am going to be staying in London for another week. Can you make the necessary arrangements?'

'Sir...?' Aadil glanced over. 'We are scheduled to depart tonight.'

'The schedule has changed,' Sahir responded.

Certainly he didn't need to explain his reasons, simply order it to be arranged.

Still, as he got into the waiting vehicle, Sahir knew that the sudden delay to his return would already be causing a stir—both amongst his staff here in London and at the palace in Janana.

That was quickly confirmed when, moments later, a call came through from the King.

'Another week in London?' he snapped.

'Correct,' Sahir told his father. 'Thanks to the delays with the council over the palace refurbishment, I have a clear schedule.'

'King Abdul has asked for a meeting. I was relying on you to take it.'

'You have three heirs. Ibrahim or Jasmine can step up.'

'Jasmine gets too worked up.'

'I'm aware.'

'And your brother is on vacation.'

Again? Sahir was tempted to say, but instead he offered a more personal response. 'So am I.'

Yes, he was taking a vacation—his first week off in more than one hundred—and God it felt good.

'I have to go now,' Sahir informed his father.

As the car moved forward to enter the formal procession Sahir ended the conversation with the courtliness expected of him.

'Your Majesty.'

Violet completely *loved* not being a virgin!

Especially so when sitting propped up on cushions in Sahir's sumptuous bed, eating the Florentines that had been served on a pretty plate!

'Where on earth…?' Violet had blinked when they'd arrived, then been told His Highness had arranged a delivery.

The only thing she had to worry about was deciding which movie to watch.

She flicked happily past all the news channels—misery had no place in this day. But then something, or rather *someone*, caught Violet's attention and she quickly flicked back.

'It's me!' she gasped.

It really was!

Florentines forgotten, Violet stared at herself on screen. Her head was thrown back and both arms stretched out, as if in salutation to the glorious morning. Her gorgeous gown billowed in the morning breeze.

Oh, she wished she could record the image—because it captured precisely how happy she felt, how perfect.

'A glorious London morning,' the plummy newsreader was saying. 'And for our viewers just joining us, let's take a quick look back—these are the first arrivals, making their way down The Mall.'

'Oh, who cares?' Violet muttered. 'Get back to me.'

But then, realising that Sahir might be in one of the cars on screen, she found that she did care after all, and started trying to work out who was who.

However, she was vain enough to smile in delight when the camera cut back to her.

'Somebody is clearly enjoying the view...' the newsreader said.

They were talking about her, Violet realised as the camera zoomed in on the balcony. But her brief revelling in celebrity vanished, vanity forgotten, and her breath caught as on the screen the most beautiful man in the world stepped through the French windows. It was Sahir, *kafir* on, wearing his formal robes, and looking as delectable as ever.

Then they were back to the cars.

Was it vanity or lust that had her scouring the internet trying to find more images of them?

Violet wanted that moment captured, wanted it saved on her phone, but it was nowhere to be found.

She hit rewind on the news channel, tried to go back fifteen minutes...ten...thirty. But there was nothing...

'Where am I?' she muttered.

She tried for ages, but found nothing, so she lay back in bed, sulking but happy, watching all the dignitaries arrive. Her eyes were growing heavy at the presenter's drone, yet she fought to keep them open in the hope of catching a glimpse of Sahir.

But there was no sign of him, and after such a brilliant night of dancing, talking and being so gloriously 'bedded'—as Sahir would say—her lack of sleep was finally catching up.

She lay curled up in the bed, excited at the prospect of Sahir coming back this evening. She'd honestly thought she'd be back in her little flat by now...

Her bravado wavered a fraction as she slid towards slumber. She'd known all they had was one night... But the thought of stepping into her empty flat and peeling off her dress... Even the prospect of a week off work didn't help—she'd rather be there, be busy...

Instead, she'd be returning her dress. Looking for a job.

She thought of what Sahir had said last night.

'We all have our own mountain to climb.'

Violet half wondered about his. Certainly, she'd faced many mountains in her time—starting over with a new family, saying goodbye to her own. New people...new faces... Endless goodbyes and people walking away.

With Sahir it felt different.

Her heavy eyelids fluttered open in a brief attempt to face this new mountain she was about to climb, yet she was daunted by the prospect of saying goodbye to Sahir.

The little mountain seemed to have turned into the Alps— only they weren't inviting. They were icy and cold, with dark clouds hiding their peaks. And, really, she didn't want to know what was up there.

She glimpsed missing Sahir, getting over their wonderful night, facing a whole world without him...

Violet had a very good trick for when panic hit.

She hid.

Pulling the crisp linen over her head, she closed her eyes and gave in to the bliss of sleep.

Sahir rarely missed a beat at these events.

Yet today he struggled to focus on his conversations, and Pria had to subtly prompt him to offer his condolences to the Sultan.

Certainly, the Sultan didn't get the extended, effusive words of sympathy that Aadil had suggested...

For the first time Sahir just wanted this over and to head home.

Not *home*, home...

But back to his bolthole in London, where Violet was waiting.

'Your Highness...' As he mingled in the grounds, Pria discreetly pulled him aside. 'There might be a slight issue.'

He frowned.

'Some footage of your balcony was briefly aired on television. Aadil was straight on it and it's been taken down.'

'I see.' Sahir immediately understood the concern. 'Was it just my guest the cameras captured?' he enquired.

Sahir wouldn't be so crass as to look at his phone in the current surrounds.

'Layla has the footage. She thinks you might have been glimpsed, although there's no sign of you on anything else we've seen...' She glanced to her own assistant, Kumu, who shook her head in agreement. 'As I said, sir,' Pria continued, 'it's all been taken down, and Aadil is going to speak to your guest and ensure that she doesn't go back out onto the balcony.'

'I would prefer for you to be the person to speak with her,' Sahir said. He knew Aadil would be by far too abrupt, and that Pria would be tactful and kind. 'Kumu can take over here.'

'Sir...' Pria said, and she swallowed.

Sahir was aware that Kumu was new and it was her first foreign trip.

'We'll be fine.' Sahir nodded. 'Let me know if there are any updates.'

There were none.

The reception was magnificent, the company interesting at times, but even so, for Sahir, the day seemed to move at a ridiculously slow pace.

It had nothing to do with the lack of sleep—it was his mind all too often drifting to the night ahead, to last night...

It was most unlike Sahir, but he even found his gaze wandering, looking for Pria. Or even Aadil.

He just wanted to know that Violet was okay.

Finally the formalities were over, and he was more than relieved to climb into his private vehicle, with both Kumu and Layla joining him.

'Where's Pria?' He frowned.

'I'm not sure,' Layla admitted.

'I sent her to the house a while ago. What about Aadil...?'

'I haven't seen him. I had a message to say that all the footage has been taken down, though there's the occasional photo popping up...'

Of course she had them stored, and Sahir glanced at the photo on Layla's phone and had to force himself not to take it from her just to get a better look. Actually, he had to force himself not to smile—for there was Violet, just as he recalled seeing her this morning, only this was an aerial shot.

'Hardly incriminating,' he said.

He'd been over and over that moment in his head, and aside from that, Sahir always took great care.

'What about the footage?' he asked, and Layla handed him the phone and he played the short video.

Violet stood there, her face turned to the skies, her arms waving as if she was standing on the bow in the *Titanic* movie, looking so wonderful and free.

And for the rest of the week he would be too.

'Oh,' Kumu said. 'The King is asking you to call him.' Her eyes were wide with alarm, and she was clearly struggling with Pria's tablet. 'The request came through an hour ago.'

'It's fine,' Sahir said, quietly certain that his father wanted to discuss the futility of sending an unversed Ibrahim or a nervous Jasmine to meet with King Abdul.

God, it had been a long day...

He glanced out of the window and realised the car had barely moved. Pressing a button, he opened the screen between himself and the driver.

'What's the delay?'

'We're just about to exit, sir.'

There were many other dignitaries leaving, and as they left the official event and blended into the traffic the crowds slowly started to disperse, with pedestrians ignoring traffic signals and crossing roads en masse.

'We're still well ahead of schedule,' Layla added, perhaps noticing that the usually measured Crown Prince was impatiently drumming the fingers of his free hand on the armrest.

Sahir halted the small gesture, for he rarely allowed his body to betray his thoughts or emotions.

Anyway, Layla was wrong. Sahir wasn't worrying about the schedule—he was feeling restless in the slow-moving vehicle. Or rather, he felt a sense of impatience building. He had a previously unknown desire to get home and tell Violet he'd taken the week off, work out what they might do with this precious slice of time he had engineered.

Sahir closed his eyes for a moment and arched his neck to one side as Kumu read through the messages that had piled up in his brief absence. He thought of Violet's smile when he told her tonight over dinner that they would be spending the week together. And then his mind drifted to how he'd left her, sitting in his bed, her lips and fingers sticky with jam, and it was not his taste buds that needed satisfying...

The kiss he'd been forced to deny her this morning would be delivered. More, if the house he was returning to was empty. He wanted to be messaging Violet now, warning her of his desirous approach. And he knew she would be there to greet him. Were it just the two of them, he doubted they'd make it up the stairs...

'Your Highness?' Kumu said. 'The council is being convened.'

Yes, Sahir thought. Now he'd taken a week off, suddenly they wanted to discuss his project.

They were pulling up at his residence. Maaz's unmarked car was blocking the entrance to the basement garage, but Sahir barely noticed it as he stepped onto the street.

'Your Highness,' Faisal greeted him. 'Is it possible...?'

'Later,' Sahir said.

He didn't want to discuss menus or such things now.

'Your Highness, forgive me...' Faisal persisted.

But Sahir was already opening the door to the principal bedroom.

'Violet?'

He frowned at the wall of silence that met him as he stepped in. The bed was made, her shoes and gown were gone, and he walked into the bathroom and saw it had been serviced.

'Where's my guest?' he asked, his voice bewildered as Faisal came to the door.

Layla was just behind him, her face pale. 'I just heard...' she said to Faisal, then addressed Sahir. 'Unfortunately, those images were seen.'

'I don't care about that now.' He turned to Faisal. 'Was my guest asked to leave? I specifically told Pria to be tactful.'

It was Faisal who spoke then. 'Aadil spoke with Miss Lewis before Pria arrived. It would seem the King had discussed matters with the elders and together with Aadil they all agreed...'

'Agreed to what?'

'That any further conversation should take place back in Janana.'

'And in due time it shall. Right now, I would like to speak with my guest...'

His patience was fast running out. The thought of Violet being bundled out of his home by Aadil incensed him. Violet deserved better than that.

'I need her address...'

He frowned at the intrusion as Maaz came bounding up the stairs. He nodded to Layla, as if confirming something, then cleared his throat.

'Sir, I have some information.'

'And?'

'The King felt that the situation was too volatile to leave your guest here...'

'I can see that.'

The room was empty, not even a trace of her perfume was in the air, and though he appeared outwardly unmoved he was cursing himself for not getting her number, or even her address.

'You have her details...' He looked to Layla. 'She would have been vetted.'

'Sir.' It was poor Faisal who told him at last. 'Your guest has been taken to Janana...'

'Taken?' Sahir checked, unsure he'd heard right, for his pulse was pounding in his ears.

'The royal jet took off an hour ago,' Faisal confirmed.

It was beyond comprehension that his father, the King, would sanction this.

'Where's Pria?' he asked.

'She went with her, sir. I believe she thought it for the best...'

Violet must be terrified. He thought he had left her safe, instead—

'I need...' Sahir halted.

He must not reveal his frantic thoughts, nor his overwhelming need to see her.

'Arrange a flight,' he told Kumu. His voice was not his own, for it sounded measured rather than raw, his orders imperious, even as he reminded himself how to breathe. 'Tell the palace I shall be arriving tonight, and that I trust my guest is being made most welcome and has been allocated the Inanna wing.'

The Inanna wing—or Venus wing—was reserved for the most esteemed female guests, and in allocating it to Violet he was letting the palace know the high regard in which he held her and that she was to receive only the best.

The dreadful news didn't end there, though.

'Your Highness, Miss Lewis isn't at the palace.'

Faisal's voice seemed to be coming from a long way off, for Sahir's mind really was in too many places.

'I beg your pardon?'

'Miss Lewis isn't at the palace, sir,' Faisal said again, doing his best to hold his head high as he attempted to meet Sahir's eyes. 'Your guest has been taken to the desert abode.'

Sahir felt as if a cricket bat had struck the back of his head.

Violet really had been taken.

CHAPTER SEVEN

VIOLET WAS VERY good at giving herself pep talks.

You've been through worse.

All through this terrifying, bewildering day she had said those words to herself over and over, and now, deep in the night and even deeper in the desert, she told herself the same thing...

You've been through worse.

And she had been.

As a child, she'd been taken from her bed at night by social workers, arriving in a new foster home as an emergency placement.

She'd become used to it, really. Had come to accept the constant upheavals.

Today's events hurt at a different level.

She'd learned that Crown Prince Sahir of Janana was soon to be married!

Aadil and Pria had left, and now Violet sat on a jade velvet cushion, the two maids she had been left with staring at her...

Actually, they had been very sweet.

A little unsure what to do with their unexpected guest, they had held out robes, but Violet had turned her face away.

A little later they had led her to a beautiful bathing area, parting lavish drapes, and she saw they had drawn her a scented bath. But even though she ached to climb in and let the water absorb some of her tension, Violet had again shaken her head.

The older maid had moved to undo her zip. 'No!' Violet had said abruptly, and then shooed them out. Actually, seeing her crestfallen face, Violet had felt dreadful for doing that, but she'd really needed the loo. She'd also filled the pretty basin with water and washed her hands and face, then stared at her reflection.

Through it all she hadn't cried.

Not once.

Violet never cried.

Well, she had yesterday, and Sahir had wiped away her tears...

She'd trusted him then.

For the first time in her life she'd completely trusted someone.

Never again.

Never, ever...

When she'd returned to her cushion the maids had brought out endless refreshments, but again she had declined, shaking her head and drinking only water.

By now she'd worked out their names. Bedra was the older lady, and Amal seemed to be around Violet's age.

They both seemed concerned, and now they had unearthed a wooden trunk, holding up some English books.

'No, thank you,' she said.

Bedra, the older one, frowned.

'*Laa,*' Violet tried.

She knew a very few words of Arabic from her work in the library, but then she remembered one of her clients telling her that simply saying no—*laa*—could sound abrupt.

She reminded herself that it wasn't their fault she was here.

It was Sahir's.

'*Laa, shukran,*' Violet declined, more politely, and Bedra gave her a smile.

Then she gestured to Amal to help her carry the trunk into what were to be Violet's sleeping quarters.

Oh, yes.

Because when a nervous Pria had earlier shown her the Crown Prince's lavish sleeping area, Violet had loudly demanded an area of her own.

Pria had apologised, and started to cry, and Violet wasn't proud of causing her tears.

Gosh, she'd really been a rather demanding unexpected guest!

Now she sat bolt upright, her ears strained for any sound, her wary eyes taking in every detail of her luxurious surroundings. From the bells that tinkled softly as she entered an area or left one, to the lavish rugs that dulled her footsteps. The jewelled daggers and swords on display had been noted, as well as the heavy, thick rope that hung over the velvet-draped bed where presumably Sahir slept.

She heard a sound—a low hum, steadier than the erratic wind.

She saw Bedra sit up straight, then abruptly stand. Amal moved quickly too. As the sound drew closer she was lighting lamps and stoking the central fire, as Bedra lit incense and filled two silver goblets with wine.

Then she heard the jangle of bells, and Bedra speaking urgent words she didn't understand. But her gestures and meaning were clear.

His Highness is here. Stand. Hurry, you must stand.

Never.

Never, ever...

But then she saw the confusion and urgency in Bedra's eyes, and knew that to sit as he entered would embarrass her and cause great offence. So Violet pushed herself up from the cushion, watching the drapes part, expecting a stranger.

An arrogant, ruthless stranger who had hurt her right to her core.

But she held back a gasp when she saw the same man who had left her this morning, dressed in the same robes.

It was the same Sahir.

His robes were less pristine, his *kafir* was gone and his complexion had a grey tinge, and when he saw her she saw a spark of something in his eyes that looked like relief.

On the maids' quiet urging she briefly bowed her head, then returned her gaze to his.

Violet was standing.

Sahir had considered more than a thousand ways he might find her.

Sobbing on a bed, frantic with panic or even lunging at him in crazed anger.

Not once—not even for a second—had he expected to be met with such dignity.

Her blonde hair was tousled, her silk gown somewhat crushed, but she looked as elegant and beautiful as she had last night, as captivating as when she had climbed from that taxi. She looked angry, rather than scared, but pale, and her lips were white, her blue eyes glinting as if they were striking flint.

She *was* scared, though. Of that he was certain.

'Are you okay?'

It was possibly the most ridiculous question, because nothing about this was okay, but he wanted to deal with the practical first.

She didn't answer.

'Violet…' He inhaled deeply, dragging air into lungs that in recent hours had felt too taut to breathe. Seeing her again, he wanted so badly to reach for her, to take her in his arms, yet protocol did not allow for that and her stance warned him not to, for she stood ramrod-straight.

'I apologise.'

He saw her blink, and young Amal seemed to start a little. Perhaps he should have cleared the room first.

'I have just come from the palace. I spoke briefly with the King and his aide. It would seem there has been a misunderstanding.'

'Sahir…' She put up a hand and corrected herself. 'Your Highness.'

For the first time she used his title, though he knew that the courtesy was not for his benefit, but for the maids. Her voice was clear and determined, but it held the tiniest tremble, which she seemed to swallow down.

'May we speak alone?' she asked.

'Of course.'

But there were certain traditions, and Bedra approached with a goblet for him. He nodded and took it.

He watched as Amal handed Violet a goblet too.

'*Shukran,*' she said, and he was surprised to hear her thank Amal in Arabic.

'She has taken no refreshment,' Bedra informed him quietly.

He nodded, and though he knew they should both drink now, then replace the goblets on the tray, he saw Violet made no attempt to do so. Downing his wine, he replaced his own goblet and asked the maids to leave.

They stood there, staring silently as they heard the bells, and then softer bells, as the women made their way to the far end of the abode and finally they were alone.

'What happened?' he asked.

'You know damn well.'

'No, I want to hear it from you. I want to know all that occurred.'

'I was kidnapped!' Violet shouted, tossing her wine into the fire and throwing down the goblet—possibly the first person ever to display raw emotion in a royal abode. 'That's what "occurred".'

'There was a misunderstanding—' he started, but again she put up her hand.

'Please don't,' Violet interrupted. 'I have three things I would like to say…'

A sound from outside the tent halted her, and as he listened to the sound of the helicopter taking off he knew her planned speech had been thwarted.

'We shan't be leaving tonight…' he began.

Once more she put up her hand to halt him.

'Then that leaves me with two things I have to say.' She took a breath, as if running through a speech in her head, then lifted her gaze to his. 'Do you remember me telling you that this dress is a rental—due back tomorrow?'

Sahir frowned deeply. She had been taken to another country, whisked off to the desert, and she was worried about a dress? She *really* was like no one he had ever met.

'Can we not worry about the dress?'

'I *am* worried—and not just about my deposit. I gave them my word that it would be back.'

She was, to his bewilderment, clearly distraught about the gown.

'It's for a wedding!'

'I'll sort out the damned dress!' he told her.

'Oh, you'd better. I won't have you ruining that woman's dream day the same way you ruined our night.'

She took a breath, and he knew the damage that had been done. He would rectify that, Sahir swore to himself, but right now he'd deal with her list.

'What else?'

'You're engaged.'

'Who told you that?'

'The same man who told me there had been a security breach and we had to leave your house immediately.'

Sahir wanted details, but she told him very little.

'Adal...?'

'Aadil.' His jaw hardened, but his anger would not help matters. 'Tell me more.'

'No. Ask the relevant staff. Because I don't report to you, Sahir.'

She stood so strong, refusing to give him anything—not even a glimpse of the woman who had cried before his eyes, who had laughed and danced in his arms.

'Especially when you haven't answered my question. Are you to marry soon?'

'Apparently so.'

Sahir was not being deliberately evasive, but the mist of panic that had hit him was lifting a little, and while he did not understand all that had occurred, he knew Aadil's unexpected arrival in London should have been a sign, as well as the fact that the council had been convened.

'It's a yes or no answer, Sahir.'

A smile almost ghosted his lips at her demand for a straightforward answer. It was not the time to explain the intricate laws and the mysterious ways of his land, but neither would he lie.

'Yes.'

'I abhor violence...' Violet stepped forward. 'And I've always said there's no excuse for it—whatever the circumstance. Even so, never say never!'

She slapped his cheek.

He could have stopped her—he had reflexes like lightning and was the most skilled warrior—yet he let the slap land before catching her wrist. He'd allow her to have that one...and not just because he deserved it, but because now he had contact.

He could feel her pulse hammering beneath his fingers. Knew that despite appearances she was not just furious but petrified. And, yes, again he inhaled her fear…

'Violet…'

His voice halted, but not because he was without words. Just with the simple act of her reclaiming her hand, all they had shared—all the laughter and affection and trust, everything so easily built—had dissolved and he fought for its return.

'You're safe,' he told her.

'How can you even say that?'

'I swear you are safe.'

'I shall never forgive you,' Violet promised.

For the first time since arriving he saw the shimmer of tears, and he could feel not just her terror but her devastation.

'You slept with me, and now I find out that you're getting married.'

He reached for her. 'It's not how it seems…'

'Don't!'

She took back her wrist, turned and walked away.

'Where are you going?' he demanded.

Not only was he not used to anyone walking away from him, he had thought there was much more to discuss. As well as that, she was walking towards the music area.

'To bed,' she told him.

'That is the musicians' area.'

'Not just for musicians…' She threw the words over her shoulder as she walked off. 'Pria gave me a tour. She called it your "entertainment area".' She was shouting again now. 'I believe she meant it's where members of your harem await their summons.'

'Yes, had I lived a century ago.'

'Bedra showed me the cord above your bed.'

And now, instead of storming off to bed, she abruptly changed direction, taking a dagger from one of the walls.

He watched as she crossed the tent.

He didn't follow, but knew full well what she was doing. The ancient bells in the musicians' area jangled as she went into his sleeping quarters and cut through the cord over his bed. That was followed by a whip-like noise from above as the velvet was severed.

'Sorted,' she said, walking out again. 'And for your information, I don't answer to bells.'

'I would never expect you to.'

She marched into the musicians' room—her sleeping area.

'Violet, we need to—'

'I don't want to.'

'You need to eat.'

'Don't tell me what I need,' she said from behind the partition. 'I'm going to get some sleep.'

'Let me at least have the dress so I can send it back...'

He almost instantly regretted his suggestion when, through the fabric partition, he saw that she was stripping off.

Violet was correct that this room had once been where the harem awaited its summons.

But now Sahir came here for deep reflection, and always alone.

It was also where the monarch came after his wedding, or when the teller had informed the council that the time was ripe for an heir.

It was subtly erotic by design.

He turned his back, but her near naked shadow danced on the far wall.

So he looked up at the ceiling.

More Violets. A kaleidoscope of Violets, all dancing naked across the walls of the tent.

He examined his thumbnails until she threw out the violet dress.

'That needs to be urgently sorted,' she told him. 'You had better not let *another* bride down.'

'I don't have a bride.' He took a breath. 'Here, a royal marriage is very different. I don't even know who she'll—'

'La-la-la!' she shouted.

Here, that meant, 'No, no, no.' He knew what she meant, though, for he could see her shadow covering its ears, and also that whatever she wore it was see-through...

'Violet...'

Should he tell her she was as good as naked?

She'd soon work it out.

'I am going to go to—'

'Hell!' she finished for him, and Sahir knew there was no chance of reasonable conversation tonight.

He should leave things for now; they could speak tomorrow.

Her anger he accepted.

What he could not accept was the certain knowledge that she was scared.

And from what Bedra had told him she was probably hungry too.

Finally, there was something he could do.

Although perhaps not very well...

Violet didn't know where he was—just that he had gone.

She poured some water from the jug by the bed and drank a glass down, and as her temper left her she shivered.

Away from the fire it was cold, and the flimsy muslin nightdress that had been left out for her offered no warmth.

The wind was shrieking outside, and suddenly she was shaky. It was as if she'd held on to her nerve since the moment she'd realised she was being taken, and only now was her terror surfacing.

Now that *he* was here.

Bedra had left a few of the books by the bedside, and Violet had just climbed into the bed with one when Sahir spoke to her from the other side of the flimsy wall.

'I've brought you a drink and something to eat,' he said.

'I don't want it.'

'I'll bring it in.'

'Please don't.'

He ignored her, and she lay staring up at him as he walked in with a tray.

'So, no privacy?'

'I won't enter here again unless asked,' he said, moving the jug and glass, replacing them with a small plate and a tall red glass with ornate silver handles. 'You can hate me if you want, but you need to eat. I made some—'

'*You* made?' she sneered.

He looked down at her where she lay. 'That face you just pulled doesn't suit you.' He curled the side of his top lip. 'You look like a camel!'

She gave a shocked gasp. 'How rude.'

'Just an observation. And as for your supper...? I did make it—well, I made the drink.'

She turned and looked at the silver plate.

'I cannot take credit for the *gaz*,' he told her. 'It is very sweet...like nougat.'

She turned her head and stared straight ahead.

'I am going to go to the stables now.'

Please don't go, she wanted to say. But she didn't want to admit to Sahir how nervous she was at the thought of being here alone.

'I shouldn't be long. But there's a satellite phone there, and if I am to sort out the dress...'

'And a helicopter?'

'The wind is too high now to fly safely tonight,' he responded. 'The pilot was hesitant to bring me out—that is why the helicopter returned so quickly.' He looked at her for a moment. 'We can discuss all that in the morning. For now, you need to eat and sleep. We will talk tomorrow.'

'I don't want to talk to you.'

She felt her mouth curl, and then thought of camels and closed it again, but she knew she was still pouting.

'That's better.'

He gave her a tired smile, and she didn't understand why. Goodness, he looked dreadful. Still beautiful, but compared to the man she'd seen this morning he looked utterly drained. Shattered...

He glanced at the books that had been placed by her bed. 'You've got something to read. That's good.'

'Yes, it's as if I've been given a toy box to entertain me...' Her words faded. Violet knew her acrimony was misplaced. But the gesture was a painful reminder of her past.

He peered into the trunk. 'It looks like my mother's old school books.'

She said nothing.

'I won't disturb you again,' he told her. 'You have your privacy, I promise. I won't come in.' He was very direct. 'I can assure you nothing will happen here.'

'Oh…' Her voice was dark with warning. 'It had better not.'

'Violet, I am appalled at what has occurred. Tomorrow, if you're willing, I want to hear about it, so I can deal appropriately with my staff,' he said. 'I am not putting you on a helicopter with anyone who has mistreated you.'

Violet swallowed. She hadn't really been mistreated; the only thing that had been wounded was her heart.

'If you need me—'

'I won't need you.'

'You might hear—'

'I'm not scared of things that go bump in the night.'

She looked at him then—really looked. At his liquorice eyes, at his gorgeous tall frame, at the man she should perhaps hate, but didn't. Certainly hating him would be the safer alternative.

'I don't need anyone, Sahir,' Violet said, and picked up one of the books. 'I worked that out a long time ago.'

'I shall make that call and then come back. If you have any questions—'

'I won't.'

The bells signalled his leaving.

She was too weary to think about the day's events, and yet too wired to sleep.

She was also bored with her hunger strike—especially when such treats had been placed by her side.

The *gaz* was lovely, and the hot chocolate delicious—especially because he'd made it. It was sweet, but with a bitter edge, and so creamy that even after she'd finished it, even after she'd turned off the lamp, she could taste the sweet remnants on her lips as she lay there waiting for sleep.

She should be exhausted, surely?

But there was that prickly feeling that came from being alone in a new place, and it was a feeling that was all too familiar.

She made a quick dash for the loo, and attempted an even

quicker dash back, because this tent was by far too big to be alone in, but on her way back she saw his softly lit room.

Poor Pria...

How Violet had shouted when she'd first seen it, and demanded a space of her own.

She stood at the entrance, feeling less terrified now he'd arrived.

Softly lit lamps illuminated the very masculine, sensual space. There the rugs weren't patterned, but thick and soft. Some looked like fur.

There was a lit fire with a huge dome above it—like a huge candle snuffer, should the heat get too much. And well it might, for she could feel the warmth even from where she stood.

Everything deserved to be explored, but her eyes were drawn to the vast bed. To call it a four-poster would be an injustice. There was an intricate patterned headboard that stretched right up to the dark wood ceiling—it really was like a room within a room. The heavy drapes were neatly tied back, and she wondered what it would be like to lie in that bed with them closed. They were of the same dark jade velvet of the cushion she'd sat on, and given how long she'd waited on it, Violet knew how soft they would feel.

Still, she walked over and ran her hand over one, then stroked the bedcover. The fabric was cool to the touch, while her body felt warm from the fire.

How could she still want him?

How could she want to climb in and close the drapes and wait for him to return?

Hide from the world with him?

No.

She went back to her own bed—in her far cooler, hastily made-up room—and lay looking at the ceiling, wishing it was last night, when she'd been in his arms with no idea of what was to come.

It had been the most peace she'd ever known...

The tent's roof really did move...and the one thing her first helicopter ride had taught her was that she really was in the middle of nowhere.

Oh, where was he?

Unable to sleep, she needed distraction, not to dwell on her plight, so she turned on the lamp and picked up a beautifully bound book.

Goodness, it belonged behind glass, Violet thought, or she should be wearing gloves. Because it was exquisite…

She opened the book slowly and looked at the carefully scripted name inside.

Anousheh.

Was that his mother's name?

It really was a gorgeous book, Violet thought. And it was beautifully illustrated.

She read a poem and didn't really get it. But then, while she might normally have skimmed over it, she saw a tiny scribbled note that helped.

Such need!

She looked at the words, which had been underlined, and read the poem again, with widening eyes.

Were Sahir here she might be tempted to tell him that she doubted this was one of his mother's old school books.

These poems were sensual…and so erotic.

Not all of them, but the Queen's underlining habit made it easy to find the good parts, and Violet lay reading about buds and clamshells and such…

So engrossed was she, she barely glanced up when she heard the bells that signalled his return. But as he turned off the lamps in the living area she knew she should turn out her own.

Then she heard running water, and wondered if he was going to have a bath or a shower. She did her very best not to picture him naked, and hoped he'd be ages, because she wanted to read just one more poem.

Oh, my goodness!

She glanced up as his lamp went on, and of course she could hear him. Surely that was by design, for there should be strings being plucked and beauties reclining upon the cushions. Well, there would have been a hundred or so years ago.

Unfortunately, her bedtime reading had moved on from

clamshells to 'tumescence', heavily underlined. It was like reading a diary, while at the same time not.

It was timeless pleasure that was being addressed here.

Placing the book face-down, she realised she could see the shadow of Sahir's member through the tent's wall. He was not erect, but he was certainly not flaccid, either, and she found that her hand had slipped from her shoulder and she was cupping her own breast.

She pulled it away, telling herself that he couldn't see her, and got back to the gorgeous poem.

And the next.

Had she been a little hasty in her warning to him that nothing could take place?

'Stop it...' she said aloud, trying to talk sense into herself, then closed the book and turned off her own lamp.

She heard a soft 'clank' and realised the dome must have been lowered over the fire in the next room as darkness fell.

Thankfully there were no more shadows to mire her mind...

CHAPTER EIGHT

DESPITE THE LATE NIGHT, still Sahir rose early.

Ah, but so too had Violet.

He returned from his morning horse ride to the sight of Violet seated on a low couch, wearing a pale silver robe with her blonde hair worn loose. She was sorting some books and folders into piles.

'You look...' His voice tapered off, her eyes flashing him a warning that his opinion was not required. 'I hope you slept well.'

Violet didn't respond; instead she concentrated on the books she'd retrieved from the trunk.

Sahir took a seat at the low table where Bedra had set up breakfast. Violet was blushing, furious with herself for noticing how stunning he looked in a black robe, unshaven, and thinking of the body beneath...how she had watched his shadow...

She was confused that she wanted him still.

'Come and eat,' he said.

'No, thank you.'

'Violet...'

That was all he said—but, yes, she was starving, and also she wanted to know what was happening, so she stood and made her way over.

'This bread is sweet.' He showed her the selection, clearly remembering her preferences. 'Do you want mint tea?'

'No.'

He raised two gorgeous black eyebrows at her lack of manners, but she refused to play nice. She glanced at his cheek. Of course she hadn't left so much as a mark.

Damn!

She peeled apart some of the bread and saw that there was

a gorgeous gooey mix inside—dates, and nuts, and perhaps honey too—and, yes, it tasted delicious.

'Are you sure you don't want some tea?' He lifted the silver pot.

Too proud, again she shook her head. 'I prefer English Breakfast…'

'I'll ask Bedra if we have black tea.'

'Please don't,' Violet said, uncomfortable with the women's presence and wanting to talk to him alone. 'My tastes are very specific.'

'They weren't the other morning,' Sahir pointed out, slightly tongue in cheek.

'I liked you then,' Violet responded easily. 'I could forgive you for not having my exact choice.' She picked at the bread, and then filled the silence. 'Usually, I take them with me. My own teabags.'

'Really?'

She nodded.

'Take them where?'

'Work.' She glanced up. 'Or if I go away for a weekend or to a friend's.'

'I see.' He seemed to ponder that for a moment. 'You actually bring your own tea to work?'

'Yes.'

'Is it very expensive?'

'No.' She told him the brand. 'It's strong.'

'Well, this is delicate,' he told her. 'Baby mint leaves from the palace garden…spearmint leaves too. And I believe some green tea. And a little honey, from the palace bees… Perhaps not to your standards.'

'Fine…' She pushed forward a delicate glass and watched as the pale brew was poured. And, yes, it looked fresh, and gorgeous, and utterly perfect.

'Shame it doesn't come in teabags,' she said.

It was her first smile. Fleeting, but he felt a heady relief that it had returned to her features.

'Faisal is sorting out the dress,' he told her.

'I bet he can't get it back—'

'Violet,' he broke in. 'Consider it sorted.'

'Did you arrange my transport?'

'There is transport already scheduled in a few days.' He put down his glass. 'To use the phone for that would be…' He didn't know quite how to capture the word. '*Darar*. A disservice…misuse.'

'Of transport?'

'Of the desert,' he said. 'The line to the palace is for the most serious emergency.'

'Yet you sorted the dress.'

'Because you told me that was urgent. Time here is considered valuable. Exceptionally so.' He saw two straight lines form above her pretty nose. He smiled. 'If I call for…say, your teabags, yes, there is a temporary solution, but at a cost.'

'What cost?'

'You don't taste the fresh mint. More importantly, you don't speak. Or, if I am here alone, I don't get the space and the time to reflect.'

'But I should never have been brought here.'

'I agree, and I want to know all that has occurred.'

Violet frowned.

'I came back to find you gone,' he told her. 'Faisal was perturbed.'

'The butler?'

'Major-domo,' he corrected, but only so he could better explain. 'Faisal is the head of my household in London. He is distressed—as is Pria.'

'You had no right…'

'Violet.' He closed his eyes, about to remind her that this was not his doing, but she was his responsibility, and it was his own team that had done this, so he accepted her words. 'Can I speak?'

'No.'

'Explain?'

'No.' Violet refused to hear him. 'I want to go home.'

'As you wish. I shall make the call and we will never have to discuss this again. You can hate me for the rest of your life.'

'I don't hate,' she retorted, because that was an active choice she had made long ago. 'And I don't hate you.'

'Then why not listen?'

She looked up, and though she knew she ought to demand again to leave, so much of her wanted to stay...to at least understand what had occurred. Deep down, she knew that this was her only chance to have time with him, that if she left now she would have to live with so many unanswered questions.

She sat for a second, wanting to talk, but refusing to give in. Wanting to leave, while preferring to stay.

'I'm going for a walk,' she said at last.

'I'll come with you.'

'I don't need an escort.'

'Violet, you do. You should know there is wind, and there could be a sand storm.'

Bedra helped her strap on desert footwear and Violet was ticklish. Both women laughed.

All smiles faded, though, as she stepped with him into the desert. It was dazzling, and bright, and she was glad not to be out here alone—not that she'd admit that.

'It's like being a prisoner, walking with an escort.'

'Violet, this is not a prison,' he told her again. 'If you want to leave—'

She interrupted him, because that hadn't been what she meant. And she truly didn't know if she wanted to leave without hearing all he had to say.

'My father was in and out of prison when I was growing up,' she said, and then she paused, knowing from experience the next question people asked, so just answered it. 'Fighting, assault, theft, public disorder...' There was quite a list. 'I always had to have someone with me when I visited him. Even if we went for a walk.'

'Where was your mother?'

'Who knows?' Violet shrugged.

As she walked, she could feel his eyes on her, but he made no shocked comment—his silence was his only enquiry.

'She tended to run wild when my father was inside,' she told him. 'I'd generally be placed in foster care till he got out.

Or if he partied too hard on his return.' She didn't quite know why she was telling him this, yet there was an odd sense of relief in telling him the truth. 'I'm sure the palace staff would be horrified at you sleeping with such riff-raff.'

'Violet, I did not say that and nor would I.' He asked a question. 'Where are they now?'

'I don't know,' she admitted.

'How long since you've seen them?'

'I got my own place at sixteen.' She shrugged. He could do the maths himself—it felt too awful to admit it had been nine years. 'There have been a couple of phone calls. Normally when they want money.' She shook her head. 'I don't want to talk about it. I was just saying that this reminds me of that—walking with a stranger.'

'I'm not a stranger.'

'You are to me.'

Even so, being out in the desert was far less daunting with Sahir by her side—though she didn't really want to admit that. Actually, everything—from weddings with angry mothers of the bride to highbrow receptions and, yes, even sex—was far less daunting with Sahir.

'The desert abode is set so it cannot easily be seen. Good for enemies...not so much for English roses walking alone.'

'I'm hardly an English rose...'

'A violet.'

'More like an overheated tulip,' she said, and the return of his low laugh caught her by surprise.

She was starting to understand that his laughter was rare.

What they had found had been rare.

Yet it was all sullied now.

She followed him into the stables, but stood back as he checked on the animals.

'This is Noghré.'

Violet stood back as he patted the stallion he'd ridden this morning.

'Now, you have to see his foal.'

Violet followed him further into the stables, and closed her eyes at the shaded cool.

A stable hand let out a tiny foal. She was white, prancing, and she bounded to Violet with enthusiasm.

Violet took a step back.

'You can stroke her...'

'No, thank you.' She declined the nudges from the foal. 'I don't want to get fond of her.'

Wow, she knew how to guard that heart, Sahir thought, and it hollowed him out, thinking of the trust she'd placed in him the other night and how badly she'd been let down since then.

As the stable hand took the foal back to her pen he glanced over at Violet, still refusing to look at it, and he walked over to another stall and gave a low whistle.

The sweetest head popped out.

'Hey, Josie,' he said. 'You've been cheating on your diet, I hear.'

'Don't be mean,' Violet said as she went over.

Then she giggled when she looked in—because, yes, Josie was rather the exception to the muscled horses she'd seen so far.

Nervously, she patted her lovely nose. 'I've never stroked a horse before,' she said, and smiled, feeling the hot air from the mare's nostrils.

'She's gentle...nice to ride, if you want?'

'No, I'm fine stroking her. I always wanted a pet.'

'You've never kept an animal?'

'No.'

'What pet did you want?'

It was Violet who shook her head now.

She wasn't going to be telling him her thoughts and her hopes.

There was something, though, that Violet knew she should tell him...

Bedra prepared her a bath before dinner. Violet tried to help her with the jugs of water, but she shooed her away, telling her to sit down.

Violet couldn't, so she rinsed out her knickers and bra instead and felt so guilty. Everyone had been lovely. Well, apart from Aadil. But, given he'd told her that Sahir was to be married, perhaps it was a case of shooting the messenger?

She hadn't been mistreated. Not in the scheme of things. And she didn't want to get anyone into trouble.

'*Shukran,*' she said to Bedra. 'Bye.'

Violet waved—because, honestly, she knew otherwise she'd sit on the stool and watch, or offer to wash her hair.

The bath was bliss, and she lay with her eyes closed, listening to the wind, wishing she'd stroked that little foal, that she'd dared to say yes to riding Josie. Because even if she should be snarling and angry, in truth...

She stopped right there and hauled herself out of the bath, dashing across the lounge, while Sahir was in his quarters as Amal set up for dinner.

She thought the robe selection must have been left over from harem days, or everyone in the harem had been slender, because they all clung ridiculously.

As well as that, she'd just washed her only set of underwear.

She settled for a nice, safe pinkish beige robe, that had long sleeves. They were a bit tight and...too long.

Far too long.

She found that out at dinner, as they sat in candlelight and she tried to roll up her sleeves in case they dragged in the gorgeous food.

'Here.' He picked up her hand and took the hem of one sleeve, hooked it over her middle finger.

'Oh.' She let him do the other one, looking at her fingers peeking out of the silky fabric. 'I hope I don't ruin it.'

She was close to ruining *him*, Sahir thought. He had sworn nothing would happen, and then she'd walked out. And in candlelight the dress was the shade of nude flesh, outlining her hips, her waist and breasts.

Violet was determined to remain cross, but as they ate in silence she looked at the candelabras, the food and the goblets, and then she looked at the man opposite her.

She put down a very fat date and said what she knew she had to.

'Your staff were all kind. Well, there was one who was abrupt. But he was never rough or...'

'How did he get you onto the plane?'

'I was told there had been a security breach and that we needed to leave. I thought you were hurt or...' She took a shaky breath. 'Pria arrived as we were getting in the car. She seemed shocked. She was trying to call you, Faisal was too, but Aadil said it was on the King's orders.'

Sahir gave one nod.

'I thought you were on the plane.'

Violet had run up the steps, sure he would be there, but she didn't tell him that part!

'It took off. I went a bit crazy. It was then that Aadil told me to calm down. That he was trying to avoid a scandal because you were soon to marry.'

He closed his eyes, then opened them as she spoke on.

'Pria was lovely. She told me not to be scared, that you would sort it out.'

'What about the helicopter?'

'It was waiting at the palace. Like I said, no one was dreadful. I just don't get it.'

'I don't fully...' His voice was both serious and thoughtful. 'Your marriage age is thirty?'

Violet frowned.

'You said you hoped to marry by thirty. I was aiming to get to forty. I think things were being moved along.' He looked at her. 'And then you were seen on the balcony.'

'I'm hardly the first woman you've brought back home.'

'No, but after I left you, I demanded to take some time off. My father told me about an important meeting and I said my younger brother could step up. I don't usually. I just wanted...'

He met her eyes, and she could see the candlelight flickering in them, a dance of flames with dark corridors of desire behind them.

'Time,' he said.

'How much time?'

'A week.'

She swallowed, for his eyes told her that the week was to have been reserved for her.

'I was going to discuss spending the week with you. That has never happened before.'

He was clearly being honest.

'Oh.'

'I don't even know if you'd have wanted to spend more time with me.'

Violet averted her gaze because she had to. His eyes took her to a place where she was being made love to by him, and she refused to succumb, to nod, to say, *Yes, Sahir, I'd have wanted to spend a week with you.*

'A final fling before your marriage?' She took up her own goblet and drank the herby, syrupy brew.

'I've told you I didn't know it was about to happen.'

She swallowed, and saw his eyes were on her throat as she did so.

'Look, I don't expect you to understand, but here a marriage is not about love. Intimacy and conversation are separate.'

'How?'

'The King and Queen work together. For more trivial matters they can take a lover, or confidant.'

'Trivial?' Violet checked.

'These are the laws—country first, everything else second.'

'And you agree?'

'I don't make the rules. I'm not saying they have to take a lover. Just that they can.'

'I don't get it,' Violet said again.

'Of course you don't. You're not going to be a king or a queen.'

'I meant…' She could feel her skin hot under her robe. 'I mean, presumably there would have to be heirs.'

'Of course.'

'So how?' She looked at him. 'How would they…?'

'It's sex, Violet, it doesn't have to be about love.'

'So, in this strictly business marriage, do they meet once a month, or…?'

'The teller states when the time is right for an heir and then they come here.'

'Oh.' She blinked. 'So, this "teller" decides the stars have aligned and off to the desert they go?'

'It sounds clinical, but…'

'No,' Violet refuted. 'It sounds rather lovely. Well, the stars aligning and the coming to the desert part does. It's the long, lonely stretches in between that would get to me. I doubt I'd be in the mood if my husband was off taking care of *"trivial"* matters with someone else.' She shrugged. 'But what would I know?'

Sahir breathed through his nostrils.

Violet knew how to press certain buttons, how to voice the questions he asked himself at times, and yet she did it with a smile, in a vaguely dizzy voice, when she was anything but.

'As I said, taking a lover is an option.'

He took a cleansing breath, watched as she helped herself to more dessert. Of course she could never understand. It felt important, though, to explain to her what had occurred.

'I didn't know anything until I returned to the house and you were gone,' he told her. 'I first thought you had been taken to the palace. Emotion is something we don't allow, but I spoke angrily with my father.'

'The King?'

Sahir nodded.

'Don't you get on?'

'We are not close, but we're not enemies. I have my own office, my team. I'm perplexed. I still cannot believe he sanctioned it. He seemed to think he was doing us a favour by giving us some discreet time.'

'What did you say when you spoke to him?'

'I told him to stay the hell out of my business.'

'And what did he say?'

'That the welfare of the country is my only business.'

* * *

Violet didn't ask to be excused. Just removed herself from the table and went over to the trunk she'd dragged into the lounge area.

As her thoughts whirred she went through it.

She could see things from Sahir's point of view a little more. Not just from what he'd said, but because she remembered the grey tinge to his complexion when he'd arrived last night. The relief in his eyes when he'd first seen her.

He came and lay on the sofa, staring at the roof of the tent as if still trying to work things out.

It was a nice silence. Not the tense one of before. Just a little pause as she sorted the books into piles and the wind sounded like music in the distance.

She rummaged in the trunk, looking at all the papers and treasures.

'Bedra didn't mean to offend you by bringing you that.' He glanced over. 'I think she was just trying to help.'

'I know. It just felt like…' She looked over to the one person she was really able to turn off her fake smile for and decided to tell him why it had upset her so. 'I was placed in a lot of foster homes…'

'So you had a lot of toy boxes?'

She nodded and ran her hand over the ancient gleaming wood. 'Sometimes there would be a jigsaw…'

'Missing parts?'

'No time to finish it. Or I'd find something I liked and then it would be time to go and I'd have to leave it behind. It wasn't always the case. Things calmed down somewhat as I got older. And I spent a lot of time with Grace and her mother.'

'It must have hurt when Mrs Andrews accused you.'

'I'm very used to it.' She made light of the painful topic, but then caught his serious, patient eyes. 'I was mortified,' she admitted, and felt her throat tighten even as she spoke. 'I die on the inside whenever things go missing.'

'Why?'

'I'm terrified people will think it's me.'

'Mrs Andrews was clearly confused.'

Violet nodded. She could hear the wind howling outside and she felt so removed from the world. And, despite her situation, she simply felt free not to lie.

'It was Grace questioning me that really hurt.' She had never said that—not even to Grace. 'I don't blame her. I get that it was easier for her to think I'd taken something rather than that her mother was so ill. She's always trying to talk about it now, or say sorry.'

'You're still too angry to hear it?'

'Oh, no.' She shook her head. 'I was never angry—just terrified I was going to lose her friendship.'

'Violet…'

'Don't.'

She put up her hand and then went back to the trunk, grateful for the distraction.

Her heart came to a stop when she saw a photo of the late Queen Elizabeth II with… 'Oh, goodness.' Her emotions changed like the wind. 'I thought this was you.'

'Show me?'

'Is this in London?'

'Yes.' Sahir propped himself onto one elbow to look. 'That's my father.'

'He looks about twelve.'

'He'd have been about eighteen…' He took a moment, as if to work out the year it had been taken. 'No, he'd have been nineteen.'

'Where's your mother?'

'This was before they were married. It was his first solo tour. What else is in there?' he asked.

'Menus,' Violet said delightedly. 'Maybe they'll give me some ideas. At work, we all bring in something to eat on a Friday… Oh, well, I guess I won't be needing these…'

'You're going to miss working a lot?'

'Yes,' Violet admitted, flicking through the cards. 'But maybe it's the change I need. I mean I always—and I mean always—wanted to be a librarian. I was also keen to study, but I didn't want to move away.'

'How come?' he probed. 'Why are you so reluctant to move away?'

She paused in flicking through the menu cards and met his gaze. She liked how he didn't react when she told him things, how his expression didn't change and he didn't judge. Sahir's calm made her feel able to admit something she never had before.

'I don't want to leave in case my parents ever decide to look me up.'

He nodded.

'They wouldn't be able to find me.'

He said nothing. Yes, she liked his calm...how he didn't react.

Inwardly Sahir did react.

I would find you, he wanted to say, but knew those words could only hurt.

She had put her career, her future, on hold, in the hope that one day her parents might look her up, or drop in.

He felt a real sadness. One he'd been taught not to feel, let alone reveal.

He felt everything now. Since Violet had appeared in his life he felt the world more intensely, and he breathed through the wave of anger that seemed to crush him for a moment as Violet got back to the menu cards.

'Ooh, what's Persian Love Cake?'

'Cake,' he responded gruffly. His voice betrayed him, so he corrected it and elaborated. 'With petals on. Tastes of rose water...'

'I'm going to make it,' Violet said. 'Once I've been freed.'

He took a deep breath.

'Kidding!' She looked over and gave him a small smile.

'Good.'

He stared at the tent roof as she went through all the menus and he realised he'd been right the first time—she did recover quickly.

The hurt was still there, though.

'You could get a job anywhere,' he said, in as even a tone as he could summon.

'Oh, please... I have no qualifications, no experience apart from at the library. And please don't offer to help,' she warned. 'I'd hate that.'

'Then I won't—and anyway, you don't need my help. You have a lot going for you.' He looked at her. 'You must be reliable, if you've worked there for so long. Loyal...'

She was many, many things, he thought.

'Maybe it's time to think about what you really want.'

'I'd like this.' Again, she changed the subject and held up another menu card. 'Christmas dinner at the Savoy. I'd love to go there.'

'I'm being serious.'

'So am I,' she said.

But she would not look up, and he knew she was hurting, and he loathed it that he did not know how to fix this, that she refused his help.

He sensed she did not want to discuss it further. 'What's on the menu?' he asked.

'Turkey,' she read. 'Sole.'

He smiled when she pulled a face at the thought of fish.

'Skip to the dessert, Violet,' he said. 'You know you want to.'

'Actually, no!'

She laughed, about to tell him she loathed fruit cake, but then she saw all the ticks beside a few of the dishes—neat little ticks that she recognised from the Queen's markings on the books.

'This is...' She was about to tell him, but then, turning the menu over, she abruptly stopped.

It was dated.

'What?' he asked.

Violet was silent, frantically doing the maths in her head.

'What?' he asked again, and she looked up, her face flushed.

'I was going to say it's less expensive than I thought it would be, but it's an old menu.'

It was from the Christmas before Sahir had been born.

Violet said nothing more, but went through the trunk with a keener interest now.

There were some gorgeous jewels contained in a little pouch. She poured them into her hand. 'Are these real?'

He barely glanced over.

'I would think so,' he said. 'We don't have any...'

'Costume jewellery?' She rolled her eyes. 'You are such a snob.'

She looked at the gorgeous sapphires, diamonds and rubies, all just exquisite, and then carefully replaced them in the pouch.

'Here's a report card...' she said. Then she read the name. 'It's your father's.'

'We went to the same school.' He rolled his eyes.

She read through it. 'It says that he's kind and thoughtful.'

'So long as he gets his own way. I think they probably only said such nice things because of his title.'

'Did they say nice things about you?'

'They did,' he agreed. 'Because I was an excellent student.'

'Arrogant?'

'"Confident", I believe they said...'

'Did you like boarding school?'

'I would have liked it a lot better without Aadil guarding me.'

'You really don't like him?'

'No. He was always snooping...reporting back to my father. He was the one who told me that my mother had died.'

'What did he tell you?' Violet asked.

'The truth.'

Violet frowned.

'He told me she was ill. That it was serious, and I was needed back home. I wanted to see her. He took a message after we boarded the jet and then started going through protocol.'

'Protocol?'

'For if the Queen dies, or the King, or whoever...'

Violet nodded, trying to imagine what that must be like— to be losing someone you love and having to think of protocol.

'I told him that I was aware of my role and that it was offensive of him to speak like that when she was fighting for her life...'

Violet nodded. 'I'd have felt the same.'

'Well, he barely glanced up from his papers, then he said, "The Queen has already died."'

Violet gasped. 'That's how he told you?'

'He then added "Your Highness", and offered his condolences, but, yes, that was how he told me.' He looked over. 'I think he was trying to provoke me.'

'Provoke?'

'He was hoping for a reaction. I think he thought it would be better for me to be upset at thirty thousand feet rather than on landing. I've told you—a royal cannot show emotion. It unsettles the people.'

'I think having a cold and unfeeling ruler would be more unsettling,' Violet said. 'At least that's how it would seem to me.'

'The people need to know their rulers won't fall apart in a crisis. I used to question it, but after my mother died...'

She stared at him, trying to demand with her eyes that he be honest—for she had been, after all.

'It was a turbulent time for our country,' Sahir said. 'My father had to work hard, make decisions that would impact the nation's future, and he did so unfailingly. I took a month out of school but I barely saw him. He was up at dawn, and would take morning briefings from Aadil in the gardens. I almost failed that year at school. Sometimes I would forget to eat...'

He was silent, remembering it.

'I managed all my royal duties, but only just. I knew if I got upset then Ibrahim and Jasmine would follow suit. I had to put aside my own guilt.'

He regretted his words immediately, because of course she pounced.

'Guilt?'

He stood up, ending the conversation. 'I believe most people feel that way when they lose someone.'

'But you're the Crown Prince,' Violet said. 'You don't get to feel.'

His back stiffened. 'No.' He turned around. 'And I don't get to share.' He nodded. 'Goodnight.'

'Stay.' She sat still, holding another book. 'Talk.'

'No.' He shook his head. 'Better not.'

He went to his rooms, shut off the fire, stripped and climbed into bed.

He watched the lounge darken.

Then saw Violet's shadow on the wall.

Politely he closed his eyes as she undressed, for she had clearly not worked out how erotic this space could be.

He opened them again and thankfully saw she was in bed. He could see her reading, her hair still up, and then he watched her turn her head to one side, picking up the howl of a lone Arabian wolf. She got back to reading.

Violet really was inquisitive rather than fearless.

And very sensible to have cut that silken cord.

How he ached to reach for it now...

The wind was soft, like a little whistle or a howl, and yet it was so still in here.

She paused in her reading and heard another wolf howling—or was it two, or three?

The poor Queen, Violet thought, stuck in her businesslike marriage. Because from all she'd read Anousheh hadn't just adored the sensual poets, but the romantic ones too.

She read a poem about ageing love and silver hair, and found there were tears in her eyes... Only she wasn't sure if they were for Queen Anousheh or for herself.

She wanted Sahir—more of Sahir—and yet she had warned him in no uncertain terms to stay back.

And she wanted to go riding, to play with the little foal and just explore this incredible place...

Then be sent away.

She got back to the sensual poems, reaching for a drink of water. But the glass was empty and she couldn't be bothered to fill it.

She saw her own shadow on the wall, and then looked up

and saw she was there on the ceiling too, her hand outstretched for the glass.

Her fingers were far longer than they were in real life...even the curls at the ends of her hair were magnified and somehow enhanced. Her eyes were heavy with sleep, and she thought she could even see her eyelashes flutter...

It was hypnotic...lying there, watching herself...

Her shadow self.

Or was it the real her?

Violet didn't know. And even though she got back to her book her shadow was still there, and apparently braver than she...more accepting of the low throb of desire in her stomach... The woman who danced across the walls as she lifted her leg and looked at her toes didn't mind where she was, or the circumstances that had brought her here.

Goodness, those poems made her bold—or was it something about the desert that lured her other side out? Was it simply that the man who had brought her here made her feel she could be whoever she really was?

Whoever she wanted to be?

Violet climbed out of the low bed and stood still. Oh, she was not *that* bold. She wasn't about to follow her shadow where it tempted her to go. No, she would not be slipping into Sahir's bed. Nor was she about to perform for him...

In the scheme of things, it could be considered tame. All she did was stand and lift the heavy jug by her bed, fill her goblet with water.

She did not glance up to check her shadow, nor did she intend to taunt.

Perhaps a little.

She took out the combs from her hair. Really, she only did what she might do at home...

It just felt very different here.

Sahir lay there.

He did not politely avert his gaze from her erect nipples...

He enjoyed the slow shake of her head as she loosened her hair and then climbed slowly into bed...

He knew that was for him.

Of course Violet would have worked it out.

And now she was taunting him for being the first to say goodnight.

When possibly she should be grateful that he wouldn't make her his lover tonight.

She could never be Queen.

A lover, a confidant—whatever the way it was described—that was all she could ever be for him.

Sahir knew one thing, and it kept him from turning on the lamp, beckoning her to his bed.

She deserved more.

CHAPTER NINE

VIOLET WOKE TO no shadows.

She lay there, staring and still a little more bold, more curious... And, no, she would not hide, or sulk, or even justify why she'd climbed out of bed last night as she heard him pass.

'Sahir...?'

He was just on his way out when she appeared, holding the curtain over her scant nightwear.

'Good morning, Violet.'

Her cheeks were red, and they stared at each other for a moment, both aware that last night he'd seen what lay behind the curtain.

'Can I come with you?' she asked.

'I'm going riding.'

'I know you are.' Violet nodded. 'I've decided I'd like to try.'

'You've never ridden?'

'I want to try new things, and you said Josie was a good horse to learn on.'

'I'll have the stable manager—'

'No,' Violet said. 'I don't want to go riding with someone I don't know.' Her eyes met his. 'When do we leave here?'

'Tomorrow night.'

'Then I might never get this chance again.'

'Very well. But a short lesson, or you'll be in agony.'

He stood outside the curtain as she pulled off her nightgown.

'What do I wear?' she asked.

'Just a robe. I shall sort out some chaps.'

'Chaps?' she asked from behind the screen, doing up the tiny buttons down the front of a lilac gown. 'What are they?'

'Leg coverings made of leather.'

'Sahir!' she chided in a voice she had never known she owned. 'We barely know each other!'

And he let her flirt, let her be free, and even if she didn't appreciate the way she'd arrived, oh, she knew she did not want to leave the desert.

Or him.

At the stables, he handed her the most awful-looking things. 'What on earth…?'

'You need to wear them,' he said, watching as she attempted to put the chaps on. 'The other way.'

'Can you at least help?' she asked, although she never usually did.

He glared but, ever polite, took the chaps and knelt.

And now he was being all gentlemanly, even as she lifted her robe, barely touching her as he buckled the straps.

As good as his word.

Aagh!

'Stay still…' he warned.

'I'm trying,' Violet said, feeling a touch deflated because he showed no reaction.

He seemed irritated, in fact.

'You're not a very nice teacher,' she said, when he snapped at her fourth attempt to mount a very placid Josie.

'Because I'm not a teacher,' he said. 'I offered the best horseman in Janana to give you a lesson. But, oh, no…'

'You're not very patient.'

'And you're not very good at listening.'

'I've never been so close to a dog, let alone a horse.'

He felt his heart crack as he thought of all the horses he had, the cats and the dogs, and the birds that tapped on the palace windows.

Then he thought of her not stroking the little foal, and how fiercely she guarded her heart. He could feel she was trusting him, knew she was flirting, and it felt like a gift.

He wanted that gift, and yet what did he offer in return?

'Can you move that stool?' she asked.

'It's called a mounting block,' he corrected. 'And it's where it should be.'

She stood up, trying it all over again.

'Balance your weight,' he told her.

'I am,' she said. 'It's the getting my leg…'

Josie really was rather large, and he saw Violet just couldn't stretch her leg far enough, so ended up lying prone over the saddle.

'Violet!' he snapped—but not in a terse way. It was more like the noise the velvet rope had made as it slithered over her head.

And then the tension gave, and he laughed. Not the mirthless shouts of laughter he occasionally gave, nor even the softer, shorter bursts. This was a low, deep laugh that he released as she lay there, face down. He even playfully slapped her bottom, and she almost cried with laughter as he prised her leg up and over and practically hauled her into position.

'I'm upright!'

Josie moved a couple of steps and she squeaked.

'Do I need a riding hat?'

'You do not.' He walked Josie around for a few moments. 'Look ahead,' he told her. 'You don't look down when you drive.'

'I can't drive,' she informed him. 'There's no need in London. Anyway, I have no sense of direction.' She smiled down at him. 'How am I doing?'

'Better,' he conceded.

'Can I trot?'

'Not yet.'

'Can I trot now?' she asked, all of six minutes later.

'Go on, then.' He nodded, confident in Josie, then frowned in bemusement as Violet made some clicking noises. 'Give her a few squeezes with your legs.'

She seemed reluctant to, and even Josie gave him a confused glance. He spoke in Arabic to the old girl.

'What are you saying to her?' asked Violet.

'That you are very confident for someone so clueless.'

He gave Josie a tap and Violet let out a shriek as the horse sped off, Violet jolting up and down as she fought to stay on.

'How do I make her stop?' she yelled.

'Pull on the reins.'

'It worked!' Josie slowed to a walk and Violet, breathless

and exhilarated, looked as if she felt she ruled the equestrian world. 'Can we go for a ride in the desert?'

'No.'

'I could do this at the local riding school at home.'

'You could—yet you never have,' he pointed out. 'You can't learn it all in one day. You're going to be sore.'

'I. Don't. Care,' Violet told him. 'I want a desert ride. It *is* my holiday, Sahir.'

'Holiday?'

'Well, it sort of is,' she said. 'And I don't want to waste it.' She gave him a smile. 'I've decided to embrace the time I have rather than endure it.'

And she was the most persuasive, guilt-inducing, incredible person he had ever met, because a short while later they were actually setting off, his beast chomping at the bit as Josie plodded along.

'How is it?' he asked as they left the tent far behind.

'So nice.' She closed her eyes. 'If I hadn't been kidnapped to get here, then this would be the best day of my life,' she teased.

He smiled, but it faded as his horse started to get stroppy. 'I'm going to stretch him—do you want to get off for a while?'

'No.'

'Violet…'

'I'll just keep walking.'

'But you won't…'

He felt it then—flashes of her deciding to trot, or gallop, or falling off…fears he did not allow himself to have.

And yet he'd been having them since the moment they'd met.

He kicked his horse, trying to outrun his thoughts, trying to rid his head of that moment when he hadn't cared what happened with King Abdul, or if he might be missed for a week.

And his head hadn't quite cleared even as he slowed and turned—for there she was, plodding along on Josie, her cheeks bright red and a smile on her face. He slowed his horse to a walk.

'We'll go back,' he told her.

'Not yet.' She looked at the endless dunes, and then she looked up to the sun. 'How do you find your way back?'

He told her about the observatory, how they were all taught about the stars…

'What if it's cloudy?'

'You'd know north.'

'No.'

'You'd know it.'

'I don't.' She shook her head. 'I must have missed that lesson. I'm not the brightest…'

'Violet.' He stopped her. 'You are one of the cleverest people I know.'

'I'm really not.'

'Oh, you are. We are all taught about the skies here, and the patterns of the land, the winds. It is just something I took for granted. The palace is built in the shape of a star…'

'I saw,' she said. 'Well, I noticed when the helicopter took off.'

'Were you terrified?'

'A bit.' She nodded as they rode on. 'But not adequately terrified.'

'What does that mean?'

'Just…given my situation, I wasn't that scared.'

As they rode he told her about the palace ruins his mother had loved.

'My father is adamant that they remain untouched. Or rather…' Sahir paused, for he did not discuss his thoughts with anyone, and yet he found that constantly challenged when he was with Violet.

He glanced over at her, saw the dreamy look in her eyes. She glanced back, as if expecting him to carry on speaking.

'The plans have to get passed by the council, and some of them are opposed.'

'But not all of them?'

'No.' He nodded. 'Unfortunately, it is the vocal few who are against change.'

'It always is.' She told him about the library committee. 'Honestly, it took for ever to get them to agree even to join social media.'

He smiled. 'We have the raw materials; the Bedouins have the skills.'

'They do for now.'

He frowned, unsure how Violet could speak so knowledgeably, but she turned and smiled.

'Use it or lose it.'

He laughed. 'I'll put that to the council.'

It was an incredible trip, and as they turned to head back, even though she'd been warned not to, Violet wasn't scared to persist with him.

'Can I ask a question?' Violet said. 'Just one.'

'One.'

'Why do you feel guilty about your mother?'

'Maybe because she was lonely, and unhappy.'

She knew when he was being evasive. And something told her that she was getting the standard Sahir reply.

'Don't bother answering if you're just going to fob me off,' she said.

'You really don't miss anything,' he said.

But then he paused, unsure whether or not to proceed. Yet she'd somehow trusted him, and now he felt the same way. It was something he had never shared before, though.

'She was breathless on our last walk,' he said. He had replayed that morning so many times. 'I should have noticed.'

'I'm out of breath now.'

'We've been out for two hours.' He gave her a slight smile, knowing she was trying to assuage his guilt, but it would never leave him.

They kept riding, the tent now in sight.

'She had a nosebleed. I caused it. I was scolding her...' He gave a pale smile at Violet's shocked expression. 'No, I did not hit my mother.'

'I know that, but...' She shook her head. 'What do you mean, you caused it?'

'My brother and sister had worked out that she had a confidant.'

He saw Violet holding in a gasp, trying to be as calm as he had been for her when she'd revealed her truth.

'I had always known. Aadil seemed to know too. He was my protection officer then, but his father was an elder on the council.' He glanced over, aware he probably wasn't making much sense, but Violet nodded.

'So, a bit of a stickler for the rules?'

'Correct.' He gave her a half-smile. 'As I've told you, there is a lot of leeway, but discretion is the absolute rule.'

'And she wasn't being discreet?'

'No. I was very concerned that she was going to get in trouble. And so I told her off. I told her to be more careful.'

'What did she say?'

'She started to laugh.'

They were almost back, and Sahir found he didn't want to be.

'Mother thought it was hilarious. She told me I was staid, and like my father, but then she was kind. She was always a bit wild, but she said she would be more careful, told me not to worry... And then her nose started bleeding.'

They were so close to the stables, to other people, and the horses seemed to intuit that, for they stopped.

'She had leukaemia.'

'You couldn't have known.'

He said nothing.

'Sahir?' She questioned his self-imposed silence with his name. 'Were there other signs?'

'I believe my father had noticed a bruise on her back, another on her thigh. She told him she had been exploring the ruins...'

'And did he rush her to the palace doctor?'

'No.' His voice was black. 'He did not. I was told she fainted at breakfast.'

He saw her look over at him.

'The doctor knew immediately that she was gravely ill. She was taken to the royal hospital. I was called out of school. It was that fast.'

'That's so sad... What was your father like afterwards?'

'Much the same as he'd always been. He said the country had lost a brilliant queen.'

'What else?'

'Truly? Not much. He went straight back to work—not that he had a choice. The country was on the edge of war.'

'Here?'

He nodded. 'My father was taking breakfast meetings with aides the morning after her funeral. I know he had to be, but he should have made time for Jasmine, at least.'

'What about Ibrahim?'

'He wanted to go back to school pretty much straight after.'

'And you?'

'I was back by October. There were some formalities for me to attend to. After that, life just carried on. He barely mentions her now. I sometimes wonder if he misses her at all.'

The conversation was over. She knew that both from his curt tone and also because the stable hand was approaching.

She wished they had longer.

Even their whole week. Because it felt all too soon for their time to be over.

'Slowly…'

He guided her down and she felt her feet hit the ground. As she headed for the tent she saw a look pass between Sahir and the stable hand as she rather gingerly walked away.

'I warned you,' said Sahir.

'You did,' Violet said. 'I'm just a bit stiff…'

So was Sahir.

Back to being formal.

Even as she sank into the bath Bedra had prepared, Violet was naïve about the agony to come. Even as she sat and ate dinner, and tried to get comfortable on the floor, she had no idea what awaited her.

CHAPTER TEN

THEIR LAST MORNING and she didn't want it to be. Even before her eyes had opened she was dreading this day.

And then all her sorrows were dimmed by a new agony.

From her neck to her toes, Violet ached.

More than ached.

Somehow, she made it to the loo—and there was fresh agony there. It felt as if she was burning…

'Okay?' asked Sahir as she hobbled out, and there was nothing worse than feeling dreadful and being met by the sight of Sahir's toned body, naked apart from a black towel tied around his hips, on his way to bathe.

'I can barely move…'

'I warned you,' he said. 'I'll prepare you a bath.'

'Where's Bedra?'

'Morning prayers, probably,' he said. 'Do you want a bath or not?'

She nodded, and just had to stand as he poured jug after jug of water into the beautiful stone bath, with far more speed than Bedra. Like some doctor, he peered at various bottles and added oils and gorgeous scents, then bent over and beat at the water with his hand.

'It's quite warm…'

'I'm sure it will be perfect.' She forced a smile. 'Thank you.'

'You want me to leave?'

'Of course.'

'So you're going to get over the bath edge with the same dexterity you showed on the horse yesterday?'

He managed to sound practical even as he dripped sarcasm—enough so that she was cross enough not to blush as he helped her off with her nightgown.

'I'm so sore…'

'I know that you are,' he said. 'Check the temperature.'

She dipped her hand in and the water felt divine.

There was just one problem. Violet was so sore that she honestly wondered if she *could* get her leg over the edge, even with his help.

Sahir did not even attempt to solve that mystery. He just scooped her up and lowered her, bottom first, into the bath, trying not to remember when they'd bathed together. He recalled her protestations of discomfort that time…when she'd been sore for very different reasons.

'It's not funny,' she said, as he sat on the edge and pondered for a while.

'I'm not saying a word.'

He was watching her, wondering how it was possible to be this close to another person and to care this much, and yet also be a bit cross with them too, and annoyed with himself.

'It was foolish,' he said.

'Very,' Violet agreed. 'And now I can't move.'

More than that, nor could he move his heart. And he could not close it.

Foolish, indeed.

After he'd let her luxuriate in the warm water for a while he picked her up and carried her to the entrance to her own chamber. He lowered her down.

'You'll feel better soon—just move around.'

He gave his best advice and left, but then heard her moans as she tried to put her knickers on.

'Violet?' He called out to warn her that he was there. 'Can I come in?'

'Yes.'

'Where does it hurt?' he asked.

She was about to say *everywhere*, but the bath had in fact helped.

'My back…my thighs…'

'Where else?'

'My bottom.' She wasn't going to tell him about the bits in between. 'I had no idea. We only walked the horses.'

'Do you want a massage?'

'I'm not going to fall for that,' she shot back.

'Violet, I am offering to help with your pain, not to bed you.'

'*Bed* me...' she huffed. 'I should have known you were from the Dark Ages when you said that.'

'Do you want me to sort out your pain?'

'Yes.'

'We'll go to my room.'

'What's wrong with here?'

'Have you ever had a sports massage?'

'No.'

'It's far from sensual—and, believe me, I would fall off that little bed.'

He was so tall and wide she believed him.

'Fine,' she said.

And then she was being carried into his bedchamber, although on less sensual terms than she'd hoped. Certainly the poems she'd read hadn't prepared her for this.

He lowered her onto his bed and it was like falling into a cloud and being caught by angels.

'Your bed...' She sighed, but then her eyes narrowed. 'Shouldn't I be on a firm surface?'

'If you prefer, we can go on the floor—though I have found my bed has always sufficed.'

She felt jealous, wondering how many beauties had massaged his aches away right here, and wondering even more so as he reached to the bedside table and poured some oil into a dish.

'Is that your sex oil?'

'It's just oil,' Sahir corrected, taking off her towel, and instructing her to roll onto her stomach.

She was relieved that she had managed to get her knickers on.

'I've told you. I come here only to reflect.'

Violet wanted to verify if that meant he'd never brought a lover here. If that meant she was the first woman in this bed. But she decided it wasn't the time to ask.

He was being very formal.

Very much the Sahir she had first met.

'It might hurt a bit,' he told her.

'Okay.'

He started low on her neck and shoulders and it was far from sensual. His hands were almost rough as they worked on the knots. Then deftly he worked on her torso, and either side of her spine. Then he focussed on her tailbone for what seemed like for ever.

'Ow!'

'I know...'

Sahir closed his eyes, took a breath and found he was very grateful for his teachings—because he knew when he opened his eyes his voice would be stern as he told her to turn, and he was confident his features would be impassive.

She was slippery and warm as he turned her, and then his oiled hands came to her calves and her inner thighs, and he tried not to look at her breasts.

He even lifted her leg, like a physiotherapist, bending it at the knee and then doing the same with the other.

'Your hips are tight,' he said.

'Yes.'

He again refused to look at her breasts, or at her soft stomach, or even to focus too much on her face. Her eyes were tightly closed, and she gave just the occasional grimace, but then he felt her hips loosen and saw her slight smile.

'Better?'

'Somewhat...'

At least she was moving her legs now, and her back looked less stiff, though he knew she would not be telling him that she'd just found out what 'saddle sore' really meant.

Sahir knew, of course. And knew she must be in agony. But he would not be offering to sort that out. It was just nice to see her more relaxed.

'Walk around,' Sahir suggested. 'Loosen up.'

'I feel loose,' she said.

Too loose and limp to move. Though she made a half-hearted

attempt to put her arm over her breasts, but then gave in and let it fall by her side.

'I don't want to move.'

'Then don't,' Sahir said. 'But I won't be offering to move you to the lounge.'

She gave a half-laugh at the very notion and he lay down beside her.

'You might get a couple of bruises; your shoulders were very tight.'

'I'll forgive you,' she said, feeling all floaty from his hands, and perhaps too relaxed to be subtle as her mind flitted like a lazy butterfly to the next topic. 'If your parents slept apart, how did your father notice your mother's bruises?'

'Perhaps they had the occasional…' He nudged her. 'Please don't make me think about that.'

She laughed a little, then they both fell quiet.

Soon it would be time for goodbye.

'What time do we leave?' she asked.

'Sunset.'

They lay listening to the wind, and she could feel her eyes getting heavy. She loved nothing more than the thought of dozing in his arms.

'We've never actually slept together,' she said, and smiled.

'We're sleep virgins,' Sahir said.

Then together they laughed at his little joke and it seemed to startle them both.

They turned their faces to each other.

'Sahir…' she grumbled, and he saw her pretty lips pouting.

That gesture had always annoyed him in the past. Seriously. Usually he did not like sulking or pouting. And yet with Violet it felt more like a code…a secret only he knew. Or was it the subtle shift in tone that alerted him to more than her pretty mouth?

'I'm so sore,' she said.

'I know.'

'I don't think you know where…'

'I said nothing would happen.'

'Please take it back.'

And it would have taken a will greater than any Sahir possessed not to lower his head and briefly kiss her.

The kiss was light, and yet she felt its soft weight. And although he did not linger, the contact lasted a second too long to be considered brief. There was just enough weight to his mouth that when he removed it she felt the little buzz of contact remain, and his kiss had allowed enough time to deliver its sensual intent.

His head hovered above hers and she stared into his eyes, trying to work out if they were a deep brown or a dark navy or were they both? Like a deep ocean that changed with each view.

His chest was above her own, not touching, but his hip was over hers and she wanted to arch, to feel the hair of his chest and the warmth of his skin. She longed for Sahir to kiss her again, but he just hovered, and waited, and looked down at her mouth.

She was not a petulant person—or she hoped she wasn't—and she never complained. But there was a new Violet that Sahir allowed to emerge when she was this close to him.

'I'm very sore,' she reiterated. 'In a place I'd rather not say.'

'Poor Violet,' he said, and gave her a sad smile.

She blinked, as if there were real tears in her eyes.

'Can I help in any way?' he asked.

'I don't know…' She sighed bravely, gallantly. 'I'm sure I'll be okay…'

His eyes swept down her pink chest and his hand lightly brushed one breast as it moved to her stomach. Then his gaze returned to her face and met hers completely as that hand moved down to stroke the blonde hairs peeking from the top of her knickers.

'Is it sore here?'

'Not quite,' she admitted. 'But you're close.'

'I see…'

He was very serious, moving her aching thighs apart just a little—though she might have helped with that—and then he cupped her through her knickers, his hand warm and gentle, but really quite firm. It really was rather lovely.

'How's that?' he asked, his voice gravelly.

'A bit better.'

'Why don't I take a proper look?'

He slipped off her knickers and oiled his hand, and she almost cried out as he touched her swollen and tender body.

'It will go.'

He stroked her inner thighs again, and then he cupped her—and, gosh, she hadn't known how nice it was to feel the soft oil and his touch.

'Distraction might help,' he said, and now he kissed her, softly still, but not briefly, and her hands moved into his raven hair.

And he really was the most excellent distraction, for she was pulling him closer, encouraging him to move over her. And now she felt the bliss of his chest, and then he knelt, and she felt so fluid.

He moved her down the silk sheet and carefully took her. 'Does it hurt?'

She did not know how to respond; she was sore, and swollen, but deep inside she was soaring.

'Oh, please...'

She stared at his face as he looked down, as he refused to give her what she needed—what their bodies demanded, but what she would certainly regret.

For Sahir, the restraint was more than erotic. Here in the desert he was taken by her pleasure. Captivated, he watched her, and there was almost a physical shift within her. He did not change his slow, deep rhythm. Something important was building... something impossible to contain.

'Violet...'

His voice summoned her from a dreamy delirium and she saw something new, something that told her the world as she knew it had changed...

She inhaled sharply, bit her bottom lip, and then she just stared back as he took her slowly, precisely…

She felt just the slightest feather touch of him against her sore vulva, over and over as he moved deep inside. Even the increasing speed of his thrusts, the deepening intensity that brought little pinches of tension to her thighs, that had her sex tightening, her back arching, were almost secondary to the feel of her heart opening to him.

The game had stopped, and she put her arm over her eyes because she knew now that she loved him.

'Help me,' she said.

Because she did not want it to be true, and she did not want it to end.

And then she really was helpless, just a writhe of knots and this orgasm that would almost hurt if he did not hold her steady—that would be agony if he did not spill into her with the same precision and slight distance with which he'd taken her.

'I can't—' she choked, feeling him pulse inside her, trying to tell herself she could not love this man when soon it would be time to say goodbye.

'I know.'

She pulled back her arm as he carefully pulled out. She wasn't sore—or possibly she was, but this deep revelation was certainly a distraction.

'Better?' he asked as he laid her down.

She summoned her most flirty smile and nodded. 'So much better.'

And then they were back to the game—but not quite. Because she lay in his arms and it was almost as before, his hands moving her hair from his face, then moving down to her arms and holding her, and yet she could hear the click of her thoughts in the silent air, and hoped he could not hear them too.

'That was bliss,' she said, trying to speak as she once had, to tone down the song in her heart.

She thought her world had changed when she'd met him. If she'd asked herself, she'd have named it as being then. But now, hearing the sound of his ragged breathing, seeing the look they were sharing, she felt as if they'd stumbled upon a new language. One only they knew or understood… And yet neither acknowledged it or denied it.

It hadn't been at the wedding.

Nor on boarding the plane.

Not even being alone in the desert.

For Violet they were all 'before'.

Now it was 'after'.

For the first time in her life she was completely in love.

And love made you brave.

'Can I stay?' She closed her eyes. 'I mean…'

Sahir felt her stiffen, as if braced for rejection, and from all she'd told him, from all he knew, he realised that Violet hadn't ever dared ask that question before.

'Just for a few more days?' she said.

He thought of her at the restaurant that first night, putting up her hand, not wanting a farewell speech. How she'd been prepared to leave that first morning.

She'd been forced to be independent. Had been let down over and over again. And he felt a great sense of responsibility as she now held out a piece of the heart that had been broken by so many.

'I can't leave you alone here,' he told her.

'I know.' She sat up. 'It was a silly idea. I was just…' She shrugged.

'Come to the palace.'

She swallowed.

'You would have to have your own wing, and it would be very different to here, but…' He refused to hide her—or, worse, send her away. 'I have to see King Abdul tomorrow. But we could meet for breakfast; you could have a day in the hammam…'

'Won't it cause problems?'

'You're a very nice problem to have.' He looked at her. 'Get dressed. I don't want the staff to find us in bed.'

As she climbed out, he couldn't help but smile at her oiled body and how she still hobbled a bit.

'Violet,' he said. 'You are my guest. Expect to be treated well.'

She gave a tentative nod, and as she went to her room to hurriedly dress he wanted to call her back. They needed to speak properly before they left for it would be impossible at the palace.

And it was impossible now, for he could hear their transport arriving.

Then it dawned on him.

He knew how they could speak.

His mother had taught him well...

Violet could hear terse conversation as she packed. She didn't need to be fluent in the language to know that Aadil was not best pleased.

Then all was silent, and she was terrified Sahir had changed his mind.

She picked up the poetry book, clutching it to her chest like a shield as she stepped out, but the tent was empty.

She went to replace the book in the trunk, but then knelt instead, picking up the Christmas menu she had found, turning it over, wondering if she should ask Sahir about it, or...

She felt too tumbled to think, so she just slipped it inside the book—then started when Aadil stepped into the living area.

'We depart shortly.'

'Fine.' Violet stood. 'I'm just going to say goodbye to Bedra.'

She went to walk off, but Aadil spoke again.

'It would be easier on him if you left.'

She said nothing.

'Just so you are aware.'

'I'm more than aware.' Violet turned around. 'You're the one who brought me here, Aadil.'

'At the King's command.'

Violet swallowed.

'Here in Janana we follow the rules.'

CHAPTER ELEVEN

VIOLET FOLLOWED THE RULES.

Desperate not to be like her parents, all her life she had followed the rules.

Yet something had changed, and now she refused to meekly surrender…to just nod and give up on love.

Not that she dared tell Sahir—after all, she knew how forbidden it was here, this love.

It was as the helicopter swept them across the desert that she accepted that.

The sun was a ball of orange fire as it lowered, and she looked over to Sahir, the first person she had ever truly given her heart to.

He sat opposite, staring out of the window, and she looked at his rough unshaven jaw and the mouth that could sink her to her knees. And then he turned and gave her a small smile—and, yes, she loved him.

Violet couldn't help but go misty-eyed at the sight of the palace from the sky. Last time she'd been too anxious to really take it all in, but now she truly didn't want to miss a thing.

Carved into the rocks—or from the rocks—it was incredible. Within the palace walls there was a beautiful central star, and from each point emerged a separate wing. From high up they looked like beams of light.

It was a fractured star, though, for as they hovered to descend she could see the rubble and the ruins Sahir was fighting to have rebuilt.

A plane was on the runway when they landed—not the royal plane that had brought her here, but the small dark one she had seen on the runway in London.

Sahir's private jet was all prepared and waiting…

Gosh, they really did want her gone.

She briefly met Aadil's gaze and then flicked her eyes away, feeling guilty at her own audacity in her refusal to leave.

She walked with Sahir, her stomach knotted as they passed through a beautiful arch and the mechanical world of jets and helicopters was left behind…

It was paradise—or it felt like it.

The sun was still low in the sky, and after the heat of the desert there was the cool shade of trees. Little birds perched on fountains, and huge butterflies hovered over flowers.

'It's beautiful,' she said.

'There are several gardens,' Sahir told her as they walked. 'This is the welcoming garden.'

'Really?' she asked with a slight edge, even as Aadil's eyes shot daggers into her back.

'You *are* welcome,' Sahir said. 'You are my guest and do not forget that.'

'Sahir. I'm sorry if this is—'

'Such a clear night,' he interrupted, glancing up at the sky.

She guessed they weren't allowed to discuss private matters.

'The view is magnificent from the Inanna wing,' he went on. 'That means Venus.'

'What's your wing called?'

Pria let out a small cough beside them and she realised her innocent question was not allowed either.

'I was just…' God, she always said the wrong thing. 'I can never remember the planets,' she said as they walked.

She stopped her nervous chatter; nobody was really listening anyway.

Two guards opened some doors and bowed to Sahir.

They entered, stepping onto a stone floor. Embedded within it was a golden star, where a bearded man paced. She thought it must be the teller.

Her eyes were drawn upwards to the huge arches and stairs, and to a central tower that stretched so high she had to put her head fully back to see the top.

'The observatory is above us,' Sahir said, still being formal. 'Beyond the ceiling are the tower windows.'

'It's incredible...'

'Violet?'

She pulled her chin down at the sound of her name and smiled at Pria.

'Bibi will take you to the Venus wing.'

She looked at Sahir, uncertain when she would see him again.

'Tomorrow we shall take breakfast in the East Garden before I leave, and then you can visit the hammam,' Sahir told her.

'Sounds wonderful.' She smiled. 'How do I get to the East Garden?'

It was Pria who responded. 'I shall come and collect you.' She turned to Sahir. 'The King is waiting to brief you on the agenda for tomorrow with King Abdul.'

'Of course.'

He nodded, and then there was a sudden stir—a slight flutter of panic from everyone except Sahir.

It was the arrival of the King.

'Sahir...' His father paused abruptly as he locked eyes with their unexpected guest.

Thankfully Violet copied Pria and bowed, grateful for her hurried advice.

'Respond only if he speaks...just light chit-chat.'

'Yes...' Violet breathed, as she came up to stand. At least she was good at that.

'Sahir, we have a meeting.' The King's eyes fell on Violet. 'Miss Lewis.'

'Your Majesty...'

'King Babek,' he invited. 'I trust you enjoyed your time in the desert?'

'Very much,' Violet said, and heard Aadil's low voice in her ear telling her to thank him.

Sahir watched as they all waited for Violet's suitable response. Never had he hated the stilted atmosphere of the palace more. He was tempted to open one of the arched windows and let her escape.

'The desert was wonderful,' Violet said. 'The flight there was a little hair-raising, but apart from that...'

Sahir suppressed a smile, certain that his father would simply stalk off. Yet he remained.

'You're from London?'

'I am.'

Sahir saw Violet's lips tremble as she smiled, but King Babek had already moved his attention to Sahir.

'How was Carter's wedding?'

'Excellent,' Sahir said, knowing damn well his father was reminding them both that it had been there that they'd met, and less than a week ago.

'I have fond memories of London,' King Babek said, and Sahir almost exhaled in relief. This was the polite, quiet conclusion to his brief greeting.

'Yes,' Violet said, clearly missing the signal that the King was about to leave. 'I saw a gorgeous photo of you there with the Queen.'

Nobody had been moving, but even so Violet felt everyone still. She knew she had spoken out of turn as she saw the King's eyes flare, and then she realised her mistake.

'The late Queen,' she hurriedly corrected, and then with slight horror realised her further mistake. 'I mean, *my* late queen. Queen Elizabeth...'

'Of course.' The King actually gave a small laugh, but then made it clear he was done. 'Goodnight, Miss Lewis.'

Damn! She screwed up her face as he walked off.

'Violet?' Sahir's calm voice allowed her to open her eyes. 'Well done.'

'I shouldn't have...'

'I have to go.' They looked right into each other's eyes, because here that was all they could do. 'I'll see you in the morning.'

'Yes.'

'You can stop smiling now,' he said gently, and Violet nodded, remembering the night they had met when he'd taken her into the garden.

* * *

She was brave, Sahir thought as she walked off into the unknown.

'The King is ready,' Aadil informed him.

'Thank you.'

He knew a measured approach was needed with his father,
and that emotion had no place inside these stone walls.

It had arrived, though, Sahir knew.

He'd just have to hide it for now—get through this meeting,
remain icily calm.

'Your Highness…'

Hakaam stepped out of the star and Sahir stood politely as
the teller, as always, briefed him on the skies before his meeting with the King.

'Neptune is in conjunction with Mercury. There may be
deception…'

'I see.'

'Irrational thinking. Emotions flaring.'

'Thank you.' Sahir gave him a polite smile.

There would be no emotions flaring. He'd face his father
with calm, and go through tomorrow's schedule.

Violet was referred to only once.

'Your guest is very talkative,' his father said.

'And very forgiving,' Sahir said. 'I could think of words
other than "hair-raising" to describe her journey to the desert.'

'I did what I could to give you a short holiday.'

Sahir looked up and met the challenge of his father's eyes,
which were as cold as black ice, in a face he'd barely seen smile.

This could have been him in twenty years' time, Sahir knew.
It might have been him had Violet not come into his life, warm
and effusive, volatile…

Perhaps Hakaam was correct.

His thoughts were somewhat irrational, he knew, for he
was glimpsing a future—and not the one he was destined for.

'It's time to get back to business, Sahir.'

'I understand.'

He saw Aadil's stance relax a little, and his father's nod—
only Sahir had not yet finished talking.

'Of course it would have been remiss to send a junior royal to meet with King Abdul. However, I *shall* resume my leave on my return.' He turned the page on his schedule. 'Let's move things along.'

Sahir wanted this meeting closed.

There was somewhere else he needed to be.

Oh, why did she always say the wrong thing?

Pria was very prim as she opened the door to the Venus wing. 'This way, Violet.'

It was bewildering to walk through a palace where love was forbidden. To walk into a suite and be braced for something cold and formal, yet find it was so beautiful her breath caught. The stone walls were a soft blue hue, and gorgeous lights hung like stars.

'A light supper?' Pria said.

A small table was dressed with silver and candlelit. It was inviting and opulent and Violet stood there, resisting the urge to say *wow*. To gape.

'Wow!' She couldn't help it. 'It's...' She looked at the sapphire and silver. 'So beautiful...'

'It is the alignments tonight.' Pria smiled. 'Prince Sahir thought you might want something to eat.'

'Thank you.'

'There are robes and perfumes for you to use, and I have arranged the hammam for you tomorrow, but first I shall take you to breakfast with the Prince. I have to go to the meeting now.' She gave Violet a lovely smile. 'You were fine.'

'I was dreadful.'

'Oh, no.' Pria shook her head. 'You should have heard Sahir when he found out what had happened. And I must say I told both Sahir and the King that I was not happy...'

'You were very kind to me that day,' Violet said, and was glad of the chance to thank her.

Pria left then, and Violet slipped off her shoes, thinking of what Sahir had said.

She could stop smiling now.

The supper was welcome, but best of all was the silver tray

of chocolates which she put by her bed. She showered and came out wrapped in a towel, wondering if she should have brought the nightdress from the desert.

She pulled open a few doors, but saw nothing to wear, then finally found a cupboard full of gowns—but clearly they were meant for daytime.

She ran her hand down one. It was sapphire-coloured, like the wax catcher on the candelabra, and it was far too stunning to sleep in. But she could hardly sleep in the nude.

A candle might get knocked over, Violet thought, imagining a fire in the night and another awkward encounter with the King.

She pulled it over her naked body.

Oh, it felt like velvet against her skin…

She stared into a long free-standing mirror and saw herself for the first time since the desert… There had only been hand mirrors there.

Her hair was lighter, just from that ride in the sun, but that wasn't the only change…

She looked at her breasts. She wore no bra, and the sapphire gown clung. Her nipples grew erect just at the memory of that afternoon.

No, she could never be Queen—and not just because of her lack of status.

More because of her love for Sahir and how she ached to see him.

She wondered how they'd be at breakfast…sitting apart, unable to touch.

The poetry book was by the bed, and rather than get under the sheets she lay on top, bringing a candle to the bedside.

'You'll ruin your eyes, Violet,' she warned herself, biting into a bitter chocolate.

She cringed all over again when she thought of what she'd said to the King.

Oh, it wasn't so much the hair-raising bit where she'd messed up, it was mentioning his late wife…

She thought of his flare of anger as she'd spoken out of turn.

No, not anger…

Violet shook her head, refusing to think about it and turned to a very dog-eared page in the book.

Pablo Neruda
Every Day You Play...

Boring, she decided. She didn't want to read about playing. But there were a lot of notes in the margin, so she gave it a go.

Oh, my...!

It was very sensual.

It was not a poem to read when you'd been thoroughly made love to and now had to spend the night alone.

Queen Anousheh's notes and underscores explained it better than any teacher, and the poem made the cold night air feel like a midday furnace.

Violet read of suffering and savage, solitary souls, and thought of Sahir—and then she thought that absolutely she was ordering this book when she got home...

Then she lay back, wondering if she'd let him down, but then she recalled his dark eyes as he told her she could relax, as he had that first night. She could stop smiling now.

'It's just us.'

It wasn't, though. They were an entire palace apart. She didn't even know which wing he was in...

It didn't matter, Violet suddenly realised, opening her eyes and slowly sitting up.

He'd been telling her about the observatory, the clear night, the view.

Sahir hadn't been being formal.

He'd been telling her where they could meet.

Hadn't he?

Opening her bedroom door, she peered down the long corridor. There was a maid sitting at the end.

'Goodnight,' Violet said, and slunk back inside.

Then she looked up at the ceiling, but there was no clue there. Then her gaze came down, and she looked at the many doors, one with a yellow gold and silver circle embedded in it...

Venus.

Inanna.

There seemed to be just a brick wall behind it, but then she saw that there was the same gold and silver circle embedded on the other side.

Violet picked up the candle and peered into the void. She saw that to one side there was a set of steep stairs.

It was creepy, and the candelabra was so heavy. And then it puffed out, so she left it on the first turn.

What if she was wrong?

She persisted on the slim chance that she was right.

She climbed up, ever up, and then she came to a door. Pushing it open, she came to a platform with four small arched windows and the whole of Janana stretched out below...

'Hey!'

He startled her. She was breathless from the climb.

'You...' she gasped, and then his arms were around her waist, as he held her from behind. 'I'm sorry if I said the wrong thing back there.'

'Stop,' he told her, lifting her hair, his hands on her breasts, naked beneath the sapphire gown. 'I've been thinking of you.'

His mouth was hot on her neck, his hands rough, pinching her nipples. And then his hot palms smoothed over her breasts, making her ache for the fabric to dissolve, so much... He was slipping a hand in the neckline. Only it was too high...

His growl was impatient as he dropped contact, and then took her wrist to guide her back to the stairwell.

'What if we get caught?' she asked.

'We won't if we're quiet.'

'But...'

His jaw gritted, and he looked at her, and she saw the glint in the eyes of a man who did not want to sneak like a thief in his home, even if it was a palace.

She watched him walk to the door she'd just come through, and he lifted the latch on the heavy bolt. She heard the scrape of it closing.

'It's just us,' he said.

She smiled.

The moon was behind her and she could see her own shadow on the stone wall. She stood, aroused, flushed and breathless, as he approached.

He gathered her into him, his body a wedge of muscle. His tongue prised open her mouth, and she kissed him back with all her might.

'I thought...'

She was panting, on the edge of crying at the final bliss of this day, at how she'd thought she'd be on her way home.

'We can't last,' she said, as his hands clasped her bottom. 'I know that.'

She was frantic. His hands had pulled up the velvet material and she could feel the cold night air on her bottom as she searched for the opening in his robe.

'Sahir...'

She did not know it could be this urgent—that she would choose a cold stone stairwell to be devoured in, rather than be made love to under a starry sky.

Their mouths were one...his hands were still on her bottom, pressing in and then stroking.

'Take me...' she said, and he lifted her. 'Ow,' she said, for the muscles of her inner thighs were too taut to stretch.

And yet they did so, because she ordered them to, wrapping her legs around him, sobbing as he smoothly entered her. Her back was to the wall and he was wild, tearing the front of the sapphire robe. His mouth was hot on her breast, and then he moved it back to her lips. That was foreplay, and all she required.

'I want to...' She held on to him. She wanted to stay. She did not want to be sent home. She was sobbing as he took her.

'Sahir...'

She was ready to beg him to keep her. His body was hard and his breathing ragged. The tension of him untamed was bringing her to the edge of honesty.

'Please let me stay. I'll be your lover...your concubine. I'll be—'

'Shh...'

His hand came over her mouth and she licked his palm. He

thrust into her hard, and then he stilled, and it was Sahir who let out a low shout that must startle the skies because it was primal.

Violet was climaxing so deeply that it almost hurt. Even her thighs contracted as he spilled inside her. It was everything she needed, all she desired, and she kissed his mouth.

She felt his firm hands lowering her down and she leant against him, his arms and body the only things that kept her standing.

Somehow she had to forget what she'd discovered today.

How much she loved Sahir.

CHAPTER TWELVE

THEY WENT UP to the observatory.

Her legs were shaky from the sex, and from the endless excitement he brought to her soul.

'You should first see the stars lying down,' Sahir told her as they reached the top. 'Close your eyes.'

She stood, eyes closed, and felt it was oddly silent. The echoes from the stairwell were gone, and the air was very cool. She could feel it on her exposed breasts. He took her hand and she walked on cold stone.

'When did you work it out?' he asked.

'I was reading on the bed...' She paused, frowning, as beneath her feet she suddenly felt a soft rug.

'Keep your eyes closed and lower yourself.'

She wanted to feel behind her, but she held his hands and lowered herself down—not to a cold, hard floor, but onto a soft cushion.

'How...?'

'No questions,' Sahir said. 'Lie back.'

It was disorientating. Her body was braced to be lying on stone, but instead she felt enveloped in silk.

Violet lay waiting as he joined her and took her in his arms. 'Can I look now?'

'When you are ready.'

She could never have been ready.

Violet opened her eyes, and nothing could have prepared her for the feast in the sky. There were more stars than she could even begin to count. Everywhere her eyes fell there were more, yet more, and everything she'd thought she knew or believed, or didn't know and did not believe, vanished—because she was staring at something so impossible, so divine, it was impossible not to lie there in awe. The sight was impossible to fathom... silvers, pinks, blues, gold. Endless beauty.

'I'll never forget this,' Violet said, gazing into the magnificence. 'How do you even begin to learn about them?'

'Hakaam is the last of his school. He was one of seven. They learned from ancient almanacs, or calendars, first written in clay. Even as he passes on his knowledge, they still discover more.'

He showed her the stars, some planets...

'Spica...' He guided her to the tiny light. 'That is actually two stars—maybe more—so close together, orbiting each other.'

'How close?'

'Eleven million miles apart.'

Unfathomable.

Like them.

'I know we can't last,' she said again, staring up to the sky. 'I know that, but I wouldn't change things.'

'You're a pessimist.'

'Yes.'

'What happened to sunny, happy Violet?'

'I don't have to be her when I'm with you.'

'You don't.'

'I'm scared you'll marry and bring your wife to visit Carter and Grace...'

'Violet.' He halted her. 'Can I ask you to trust me enough to know that I shall sort this out?'

'I don't see how.'

'Nor do I yet,' Sahir admitted. 'You're a very new puzzle.'

She turned to look at him, and he truly was as stunning as the sky. 'I'm scared I'll only be your lover.'

'Do you really think I'd want that?'

'Yes.' Violet nodded. 'If that's the only way.'

She sat up and tucked up her knees, looked at all the lovely cushions and rugs. There were even jugs and glasses and little sweet treats.

'Did the maids do this?'

'No, my mother taught me. I didn't realise it at the time, but she was teaching me all the secret places...'

'To take a lover?'

'She was romantic. I guess she wanted me to be too.'

'Well, she taught you well.'

'I'm furious with my father, Violet,' he admitted. 'We have never got on, but we have always worked together well. I don't see how we can now.'

'You have to.'

'I don't know... He should know better than to mess with my private life.'

'It's not just him, Sahir, it's the council, the elders... Of course they want you married to someone suitable to have heirs.'

'I told them maybe when I am forty.'

She inhaled sharply, understanding now what he'd been saying that first night, and she hated it that she cried. Because five years from now...

'Come here.' He pulled her down into his arms as she cried, and it felt nice. 'I'm going to fight for us,' he told her.

She gave a mirthless, tear-choked laugh and tried to pull away. 'I don't believe you, Sahir. Nobody's ever fought to keep me.'

It was, Sahir knew, going to take more than a few nights to wipe out a lifetime of hurt for her. And even though he didn't tell her, Sahir could not see how.

They slept, bathed by the stars, and in his arms she was perfection.

Sunrise woke him.

Sahir looked at Violet's soft, round cheeks. They were usually pink, sometimes blushing, occasionally pale with anger, even fear, like when she'd first bravely faced him here. This morning, though...

He could not quite say. Perhaps they were the palest pink, and yet she was glowing. The desert sun had added little freckles to her nose, and as he put up a hand and touched her cheek it felt like a soft petal...

'Morning...' she said.

'We have to go,' Sahir said. 'Pria will be arriving to escort you to breakfast soon.'

'That's right.'

They had to hide all the cushions in some cupboards and he locked them away.

'Did your mother teach you that too?'

'She did.' He rolled his eyes. 'She was a bit…wild.'

'She was wonderful,' Violet said. 'Well, her taste in poetry was impeccable. There was one I read last night…' Violet stopped.

'Please don't tell me any more about my mother's private life.'

'I won't.'

Only that hadn't been the reason she'd stopped talking. Her head was spinning as she thought about the words in that poem as Sahir led her down the stairs. So much so that she went to the wrong entrance and was about to press the handle.

'Violet!' He halted her, pointed to the gold sun etched into the door. 'That would take you to my father's wing.'

'Whoops!'

'Hurry! Have a quick wash and put on a fresh robe. Pria is always early.'

She was right about the meaning of that poem, Violet was certain. And even though she had to get ready for Pria, she was barely inside her room before she opened the poetry book and found the earmarked page.

This poem Anousheh had loved so, Violet had been so sure it was about the King…

Yet she frowned and read the lines again.

Or was it *from* the King?

'Sahir…' She dipped a piece of fruit in some honey as they shared a breakfast in the garden. 'Do you think your parents ever…?'

He looked over.

'Used the secret staircases?'

'Violet!' He laughed at the very notion.

'Only…' She stopped as more tea was poured and knew this really wasn't the place to have this conversation.

'What?'

'Nothing.' She smiled. 'When is your flight?'

'When I board,' he said, and then conceded. 'Now.' He stood as Pria approached. 'You'll be okay?'

'Of course.'

'Go to the hammam,' he suggested. 'If you still ache.'

'Oh, I do.'

He did not kiss her goodbye, but she didn't need it to feel the warmth in his parting, and she knew he would come to her tonight, in the observatory.

Violet took her time to finish her breakfast, then went to stand at a huge arch as Sahir and his entourage walked through the Welcome Gardens, lingering to watch the royal jet soar into the sky.

Nervous about the future, she still dared to feel happy. She even wore a smile on her face as she walked through the central star and glanced up, thinking of last night and more certain with each step that she was right about Queen Anousheh.

Pushing the door open to her wing, she walked down the long corridor, then turned into her suite.

'Bibi?'

She frowned, because the maid was crying. She met the unwelcome glare of Aadil.

'What's going on…?'

'I was just moving your glass,' Bibi sobbed.

Violet felt her heart plummet as she glanced down at the floor and saw the scattered stones—diamonds, emeralds and rubies—and the little square of silk Sahir had given to her the first day they'd met.

It was her worst nightmare…

'What's going on?'

She heard both Layla's voice and her footsteps.

'Oh…' Her face fell when she saw the jewels.

'They are Queen Anousheh's,' Aadil said. 'I believe they have been missing for some time.' As Layla went to scoop them up, he halted her. 'Don't touch them. We've called for the palace jeweller.'

Violet, when she should be protesting her innocence, was shivering.

'I found them in the trunk.' She felt as if she might vomit. 'I left them there.'

She wasn't crying or pleading, which astounded her, and she just let Layla take her by the shoulders and sit her down.

'It's a simple mistake.' Layla glared at Aadil. 'Please leave us.'

'Not till the palace jeweller is here.'

It was dreadful—the awful silence as the jeweller arrived and with white gloves collected the stones, each and every one. It took ages.

Aadil took the square of silk.

Oh, why didn't she say something? State her case?

Because it was hopeless.

She didn't want to see the doubt in Sahir's eyes, or the disappointment—or, on the impossible chance that he believed her, watch him having to defend her. To people who wanted her gone.

'It's a misunderstanding,' Layla said, when all had left.

'Why aren't you with Sahir?' asked Violet.

'I'm on my day off.' Layla smiled and took her cold hands. 'It's okay, you're shocked. I am going to contact Pria. She can tell Sahir—'

'No.' Violet shook her head. 'Please don't.'

'He has to know.'

'Not yet.' She shook her head again. 'Not until I've gone.'

'Violet? There's no need for that.'

'I'm not running away. If the police need to see me...'

'No police.'

'I just want to go home,' she said. 'As soon as possible. Can that be arranged, or should I do it myself?'

'It can be arranged.' Layla nodded sadly. 'Of course.'

'Thank you.'

She sat there for ages. Layla kept bringing tea, and even offered her some brandy.

'I don't like brandy.' Violet stood. 'I might go for a walk. Get some air before the flight.'

'The pilot will be here in an hour, but you can still change your mind.'

'I won't.'

No, she'd spent a lifetime under a cloud of suspicion, and she was not living like that again. Furthermore, even as they'd made love last night, she'd known it was too wonderful to last.

She picked up the book, wanting to bury her face in something rather than actually read, just to see the next hour out.

She wandered blindly around the fragrant gardens, barely noticing the gorgeous blooms, wishing she'd known this morning that it would be their final goodbye.

Then she looked ahead and saw a man sitting beneath the shade of a tree and her heart stopped. For a tiny second she'd thought it was Sahir, but it was the King, sitting alone...

'Your Majesty.'

'This is my private garden,' he snarled.

'I got lost...' She took a breath. 'I'm leaving shortly. I wanted to say thank you.'

He huffed and waved her away. Only she found he didn't scare her out here. Given where she'd visited her father, a pretty garden with one angry man really didn't daunt her.

'Leave me in peace,' he snapped.

'Of course,' Violet said, and turned to walk away.

But then she looked at him, so upright and so rigid, so hostile.

So lonely?

'I found something.'

'I heard.'

He gave a mirthless laugh, and Violet knew he was referring to the jewels.

'It's a menu. I thought it might have been misplaced. I didn't know if I should ask Sahir, or just ignore it, or...'

He looked over at her as she opened the poetry book and took out the folded card she'd slipped inside.

His hand was trembling a little as she handed the cream sheet of paper to him, and she swore that in those dark eyes there was the shimmer of tears. And then a smile had the years falling from his features, and the agony, and the grief...

'Where did you find this?'

'In the same trunk as those jewels—which were then planted

in my room to put Sahir off me.' The King glanced sideways. 'Anyway, I found it in there. It's a Christmas menu from the Savoy. There are little ticks...the Queen's writing.' Violet watched as he traced the handwriting. 'She kept a lot of things.'

'I didn't know.'

And suddenly Violet was brave—perhaps because she was leaving. 'That's the Christmas before Sahir was born.'

The King didn't move, didn't blink, but she felt the silence in the quiet garden and knew he did not need to read the date on the lavish card. He recalled it exactly.

'Have you told Sahir?'

'Of course not.'

'Not yet?' he said accusingly. 'If you are here to blackmail me, don't bother. The elders would crush you—and anyway, who would care now?'

'I don't blackmail people,' Violet told him, and knew that his threats were not really aimed at her, but born of fear. For if she had guessed correctly then this must be such a secret. 'And I certainly haven't told Sahir.'

'You will,' he accused.

'No.' Violet shook her head. 'It's not my secret to share.' She stood still, thinking of the huge secret she had stumbled upon. 'He ought to be told, though.'

'Never.'

'I thought as much. Would you like to...?'

'What?'

'Well, if you haven't been able to talk about it with anyone...' She knew that must hurt. 'I would never say anything,' Violet blurted out, and was rewarded with a disbelieving laugh.

She had been like that once—as a little girl she had smiled and laughed, but it had been an act. Inside she'd been pinched, refusing to trust a soul. Eventually, while she'd still guarded a lot of her heart, she had learnt to trust certain people—like Grace, Mrs Andrews before she'd got ill, an especially kind social worker, and lately Sahir.

Especially Sahir.

She had trusted her body to him...her heart. But, more, he had taught her to trust another person.

Herself.

That was Sahir's gift to her, Violet realised. Trust in her own judgement. And that made her brave enough to persist—not with 'the King', but with this man who sat alone on the bench.

'It must be hard not to talk about the times you two shared,' she suggested gently. 'I will have to go home and lie to my best friend...pretend I didn't spend my time here having the most wonderful time.'

'If she's your best friend, why can't you tell her?'

'Because I don't want to place her in the position of not telling her husband. And I don't want things to be awkward in the future.' Violet took a breath. 'I am guessing Carter and Sahir will remain friends, and that means we'll see each other on occasion.' She could feel tears trickling down the back of her throat, but she swallowed them down. 'Sahir and I agreed on the night we met to keep things just between us.'

The King remained silent, and Violet didn't blame him for not trusting her.

'Your Majesty...' She nodded her head and was just about to walk off when the King suddenly spoke.

'We met at a debating competition in London. Our universities were in the final.' He gave a hollow laugh. 'My father was surprised when I put my hand up to do that.'

Violet smiled.

'We managed one day alone. She wanted to try a British Christmas dinner.' He laughed. 'We thought mince pies would at least have meat in them, but instead they were filled with fruit.'

'I can't stand them,' Violet told him.

She imagined expecting a mince pie to be full of meat, instead of sweet fruit, and it made her laugh.

The King reluctantly laughed too. 'There was Christmas pudding...'

'Yuk.'

He smiled.

'Did you enjoy the meal?'

'I can't say the food was quite as I expected. But it was still

the best meal of my life,' he said fondly. 'There were consequences, though...'

She guessed that meant Sahir! 'A long lunch, then!'

He smiled at her cheeky response.

'A very long lunch,' he agreed.

He did not say they'd married because of Sahir, but it was
very clear...

'There was a lot of urgent discussion, the council met and
with help from a couple of very select people my bride was
"chosen". Believe me, with all the unrest between our countries
she would not normally have been considered. Except then...'
His voice grew husky. 'She was the most wonderful queen.
She brought passion and vigorous debate into every room, but
peace into the desert and the gardens.'

'Yet you hid your love? Even from your children?'

'We had to. The King's promise to the country is for a steady
ruler, free from emotional ties to any other.' He halted. 'Very
few people knew the truth, and they helped keep our secret at
great personal risk.'

'Can I ask something?' Violet said, because truly she didn't
understand. 'You loved your wife very much?'

'Yes.'

'Yet you don't want the same love for your own children?'

'Anousheh did. She had many projects, and changing the
laws regarding marriage was one of her priorities. She knew
it would be an uphill fight—we both knew.' He grew serious
then. 'I always thought it was just nonsense, having to hide
like a thief to be with my wife, having to treat her like a col-
league. Yet, after I lost my queen I was...'

He said some words in Arabic.

'It means distracted...wandering,' he told Violet. He looked
at her. 'There is a reason why love is not always wise. I was
lost for at least two years. At the time there was a lot of insta-
bility with some neighbouring countries. Had it not been for
the guidance of Aadil and his father I might have made some
less than wise choices.'

He shook his head.

'I never want that kind of danger for my people.' He glanced over at her. 'To lead a troubled country when grieving is an agony... I wouldn't wish that on an enemy, let alone my son. You can support him quietly, be there, but...'

'Not fully?'

'Correct.' He nodded. 'I'm offering you a compromise.'

'I'm tired of compromising.'

Violet stared at her hands, placed together in her lap, recalling Sahir's fingers closed around her own. She gripped her own fingers tighter, offering her own support to herself.

'Your son has taught me that I deserve better than to be second best.'

'Think about it.'

'I want a family of my own,' Violet said. 'It's all I've ever wanted. And, while Queen Anousheh sounds incredible, I'm no good at debate, nor playing on the other side.'

'Will you tell Sahir?'

'No. I gave you my word.'

Violet wanted to tell him that that he, too, had been entitled to love, but his secret was too big and so she shook her head. She thought of Sahir...how he hated the memory of that final conversation he'd had with his mother...how he loathed Aadil, when in truth, he was on their side.

'I do wish you'd tell him,' she said.

'No.'

'Please?'

'I said no.' The King was clearly regretting that this conversation had even taken place. 'What time is your flight?'

'Soon.'

Violet stood there, sad and defeated, because she did not know how to fight, how to be mean, how to persuade another person just to get what she wanted. But she would stand up for Sahir.

'He told his mother off,' she told the King. 'That was the last conversation he had with her. He was trying to protect her from being caught...' But, no, she could never play mean. 'You have my word, Your Majesty.'

CHAPTER THIRTEEN

SAHIR DID NOT walk from the royal jet.

He strode.

Not to his father's office, but to the Venus wing. Hakaam didn't halt him with his predictions or warnings. He just stood by the star, wringing his hands.

It was grief. Sahir knew that as he stepped into the bedroom suite...

There were the gowns she had worn still hanging, and he picked up the book by her bed, hurt for her because she hadn't taken it.

Opening it, he saw his mother's name—and closed it abruptly.

'You can be so staid at times.' He could almost hear her voice. *'Just like your father.'*

No.

He was not staid. Had not been staid from the second Violet had arrived in his life. He preferred himself now...missed her more than he knew how to miss another person.

And she was the priority.

It could be no other way.

The people would understand—or not.

Simply, it was right.

So he stood and walked away at pace.

Hakaam was still pacing around the star, and when he saw the direction Sahir was taking he pounced. 'Your Highness...'

'Not now,' Sahir barked. 'I have to speak with the King.'

'The planets in fire are misaligned. There is no harmony,' Hakaam urged. 'Please show restraint...'

'Too late.'

He parted the guards and walked past Aadil, and it was the King who hurriedly asked for the room to be cleared.

'You have no idea what you've done.' The doors had barely closed before he told his father the consequences of his actions. 'The jet is being refuelled. I leave for London as soon as the pilots are here.'

'You cannot leave now,' the King said. 'It's not possible.'

'It's what is happening. I am leaving tonight. I shall discuss my schedule later, but for now I shall be in London, sorting out the mess you have made. I might marry there—if she can forgive what has occurred.'

'Any marriage would be void here.'

'Then I shall be a bitter, lonely ruler like you—save for the times when I am overseas.'

'What about heirs?'

'That is a matter for you and the council.'

'They would never agree. They would demand your banishment.'

'I shall not go voluntarily—you would have to rescind my titles. Know this, though: you will get to explain why I am overseas. How dare Aadil plant those jewels?'

'She was caught red-handed,' the King sneered.

Sahir's curse told his father what he thought of that.

'Look…' the King said, and he opened a file, handed Sahir a sheaf of papers clipped to a photo of Violet on the balcony. 'Take a look…'

'I don't need to.'

'Of course you do!'

Sahir skimmed through the papers, his throat tightening as he realised how Violet had toned down the horrors of her childhood for him. He now learned that she had been taken from her parents at birth, rehomed over and over, then sent out alone into the world at sixteen.

'Hardly impressive reading,' his father said.

'On the contrary,' Sahir said. 'I find it very impressive that, despite all that, Violet is warm and strong.'

'She didn't even finish school.'

Sahir put down the file. 'I believe you yourself said never to mistake education for intelligence.'

'Her father has been repeatedly jailed. It's reprehensible!'

'Yes, both Violet and I have fathers whose behaviour has

been reprehensible.' Sahir came right up to his face. 'It's brought us closer.'

'You are infatuated,' the King said. 'You are in *love*.'

Sahir drew in a breath.

Hakaam might well be right, he thought. Restraint was required. Because to admit to love would be the death knell for both of them. It would mean that Violet could never be his wife.

'I'm going to London.'

'Sahir, please take another look at the photo.'

Angrily he swiped up the file and looked at the image—and then he understood why Hakaam had been pacing, for perhaps this really was a most perilous moment.

'Look at you, Sahir,' said the King.

His eyes moved to his own image. He was in the background, standing by the French windows, watching Violet. Her arms were raised…she was soaking in the morning. He barely recognised his own features, the look in his eyes, the soft smile he wore…

His father had known before he had.

'Love is a poor decision-maker,' his father said. 'An Achilles heel—a weakness that can be manipulated. Our people have suffered enough for that. Their king—'

'I'm aware of what happened, and why the laws are in place. How my mother suffered for them.'

'What did she say to you?' He watched his father's features darken. 'Your lover is both a thief and a liar.'

'She's neither,' Sahir said. 'I haven't spoken to Violet. I don't need to, to know.'

'Your mother did not suffer.'

'Oh, no? I'll tell you this. If you had—' He pulled back from the edge. From talking about the bruises his father had dismissed. His own guilt clashed within him as he fought not to lay blame. 'Don't lecture me about love.'

Sahir turned away.

'You can't leave now.'

'Watch me.'

Sahir walked to the huge doors, expecting his father to call him back—which he did. But he had never anticipated the words he would choose.

'I am to undergo surgery.'

The King let that sink in for just a moment, watching his eldest son, the most composed of men, recover from only the briefest falter and then turn around.

'It is delicate surgery…neurological…'

'You didn't think to tell me?'

'I had an…episode a couple of weeks ago.'

'And?'

'Aadil thought it should be checked out.'

'No.' Sahir shook his head. 'Aadil would never have left you and come to London if you were ill…'

'It didn't seem that serious then. I was just…'

'More worried than you let on to Aadil?' Sahir said. 'So it was time to push ahead on my marriage…' He frowned. 'What happened on Saturday?'

'I don't know what you are referring to.'

'Don't lie now.'

'A small seizure. Hakaam overreacted and hit the panic alarm.'

'I should have been informed.'

'I myself have only just found out the extent of the…growth.'

'Growth?' He stood, stunned, watching his father discuss a brain tumour and his possible demise in such a matter-of-fact fashion.

'I want to go into surgery knowing the future is taken care of. I want you married to a suitable bride—not giddy with love. I have fought hard to give you a peaceful land to rule over.'

'Are you dying?'

'We'll know more after the surgery. Or you'll know more and I'll be gone…'

'You cold bastard.' Sahir stood. 'How can you tell me like this?' Then he looked at this man who had once so coldly sanctioned his aide to tell a teenager his mother had died. 'Does it never enter your head that I might care?'

'Sahir, this is not a time to be weak. I am explaining why you cannot leave.'

'Do you know why I'm going to ask Violet to marry me?' Sahir's voice was like a knife. 'Because I want everything my mother never had. I want my children to laugh with their father. Not to stand and be told he is dying as if he is simply getting a new robe.'

'I am not scared of death.'

'Good for you.'

'Sahir!' His father called him back. 'Clearly you cannot leave now.'

'You don't get to play the emotions card when you have none,' Sahir said. 'The only way I stay is if I can marry the woman I love.'

'The elders would never accept her.'

'Then see that they do. If Violet is to return, I won't keep her hidden. One day, she *will* be Queen...'

'Sahir—'

He wasn't listening. He was walking out. But then he heard the crack in his father's voice.

'Do not walk out...please...'

Sahir heard that ever-steady voice tremble, and on a day he had not thought could get any worse it simply did.

'How can I fear dying when I will be with my beloved Anousheh once again?'

'Father...?'

And then he watched as his father beat himself with the same stick Sahir had beaten himself with for decades.

'She had bruises... I should have insisted she get checked out.'

'No,' Sahir said, a little awkwardly putting an arm around his father.

'I did love her—and she loved me.'

'What are you saying?'

'Ask Violet...' his father sobbed. 'She knows your mother was loved.'

'Are you having another episode?' Sahir asked, in all seriousness. 'How on earth can she know?'

'She's so easy to talk to...'

Oh, she was.

And never had Sahir missed her more.

CHAPTER FOURTEEN

YOU'VE BEEN THROUGH WORSE.

Violet repeated this to herself over and over.

The world wasn't scary without Sahir.

It wasn't impossible either.

She just didn't like it as much.

She refused to limp through the week. She smiled and chatted with the regulars at the library, and told everyone about Grace's incredible wedding—oh, and although she didn't share the location, or the company she'd kept, she told them about her horse-riding lessons and made her colleagues laugh,

She'd changed her mobile number at Heathrow and regretted it already, but it was done.

She checked online all the time. To see if there was any gossip from Janana…anything…

Nothing.

It was her final day of work and she pulled on a tight skirt, and a dark blouse, and somehow she felt strong.

But also sad.

Especially when she saw some drooping tulips in the window of the local florist.

They look like me…

There was a place inside her that could never quite be healed. This loss hurt more than anything else ever had, and she hoped she would never hurt more, but she was above all tough.

And she was loved.

Mrs Hunt was dabbing her eyes. She knew the decision to let Violet go had been impossible.

'Don't cry.' She hugged her wonderful boss. 'I'm going to be fine.'

Her heart was pummelled but her spirit was strong. She'd ended the lease on her flat, applied for new and exciting jobs, and made Persian Love Cake for her own party.

She even gave a little speech.

'I don't want to leave, but the truth is if I hadn't been pushed I'd never have gone,' Violet said. 'Which means I'd have ended up watching you all leave...'

It wasn't a very good speech, but today it was the best she could do.

'I love you all—and thank you.'

And that was that.

She dragged the ladder to the poetry section, determined to find something at least similar to the book Anousheh had had.

She couldn't find anything like it, though, and close to tears, halfway up the ladder, she felt herself sway slightly.

'Careful.'

She felt hands on her hips, and any other touch would have made her jump. But never his. Always his touch felt steadying, as if it were a part of her...as if it was helping her right herself.

'Slowly,' Sahir said, guiding her down the steps and turning her to face him. 'You are very pale.'

'I've been on a diet.'

'Diet?' He frowned. 'Why?'

'A health kick.'

'So healthy you faint up ladders?' he scolded.

He was all shaved and suited, and she had to force herself to look at him. 'I didn't take those jewels.'

'I know that.'

She blinked.

'Had you not dumped your phone, you'd know that.'

'I honestly didn't—'

'Violet, stop. I'm not here about that. I would like to invite you to dinner.'

'No, thank you.'

'You are refusing?'

'Yes,' Violet said. 'We've had a big lunch for my leaving...' But she refused to lie. 'I'm saying no because I don't want to spend the rest of my life wondering if you are in London, or if you might drop in... Anyway, it won't matter soon. I'm moving.'

'I shall always seek you out.'

'Kidnap *and* stalking…' Her eyes narrowed. 'Are you married yet?'

'No.'

'Engaged?'

'We don't have engagements.'

'Oh, that's right—no romance. So, is there a wedding planned?'

'Not yet.'

And she was weakening…wanting to know. 'Has your bride been chosen?'

'I am not discussing such issues here,' Sahir said. 'Let's have dinner later. There is a car outside that will take you home to prepare.'

'Hardly spontaneous…'

'I want to dine with the woman I first met.' He looked down at her drab skirt and blouse, and then to her pale cheeks and lips. 'Not her shadow.'

'Her shadow,' Violet said, 'is the sexy one.'

He smiled, and it was such a treat to see it, such a contrast to the severe man she'd met.

'Very well, I'll come to dinner—but not at your house. I won't be hidden.' She stared at him.

'Oh? So what happened to private and intimate?' He shrugged. 'Very well, we shall dine at the Savoy.'

She gasped. 'I didn't mean that fancy.'

'You've said you want to dine there, so now is your chance.'

'I don't want your car picking me up. I'll take a taxi.' She stared at him. 'There and back.'

With her time at the library for ever over and tearful goodbyes said, running eternally late, she dashed home to her little flat. There she hurriedly peeled off her skirt and blouse, then stood in the bath and used the overhead shower.

There was but one dress, and it was possibly too much even for such a luxury hotel—unless it was for a ball of course. But the restaurant…?

And yet she loved it.

And it was hers now.

The purple rental dress that she would keep for ever.

Maybe she'd end up doing the housework in it, but tonight it was calling to her.

'Come on,' she said, taking the gorgeous gown out of the wardrobe. 'We're going out. One last time.'

She dressed it down. Belted it and wore pretty flat sandals. Kept her hair loose.

She saw Sahir as she entered the restaurant, and he stood as she approached his table.

Her first instinct was to run to him—to somehow leap across the tables and rush to the man her heart desired.

Her second instinct was to run in the opposite direction. To flag down a taxi and race home. Because, yes, he made her feel strong—and yet somehow he weakened her too. She was terrified of capitulating...of agreeing to tonight, tomorrow, to a whole lifetime, even...

'Sahir.'

She took a seat and tried not to meet his eyes, yet she felt the seductive pull of him flood every pore. She saw a beautifully wrapped gift by her plate and recognised what it was. She tried to ignore it.

Even as his raised hand told the waiter to wait for a moment she recalled the heat of his palm on her skin, the touch of his fingers... And not just the intimate touches, but the way that hand had held her own.

She met his eyes. Today, so many things had ended. And while she might not have wanted them to...

'You haven't opened your gift.'

She would have liked to be strong enough to refuse it, but amongst all her regrets was one that she had no memento of their time together.

It was wrapped in silk and tied with gold cord, but she saw it was the book of poems and she held it to her face and inhaled it, shivering with delight.

'Thank you.' She put it on the table, but then changed her mind and put it in her bag, along with the silk and the cord. 'I don't want to spill anything on it.'

'Of course not.'

Violet put down the menu. 'Can I say something?'

She couldn't order and make it through a meal, just carry on eating, flirting, falling a little more under his spell.

She knew she was strong, but part of knowing your own strength was knowing your weakness—and Sahir would be hers for ever.

'I don't want to be your mistress.'

'Violet…'

'Please.' She put up her hand now, just as he had done as he told the waiter he did not want any interruptions. 'I knew you'd come. Maybe not today, but some day. But perhaps I'm being unjust. Maybe when you marry…'

She wanted him to be the man she wanted for herself.

The heat of the candle had her moving her hand, but he singed it with his fingers, and now she could touch him. She felt his lovely cheek and strong jaw.

'I don't steal.'

'Violet, please can we not—?'

'Please let me speak, Sahir.' She was finding it hard enough to articulate. 'I do have a compass, but not north and south… If I was your second wife, or whatever, it would be stealing. I believe a heart belongs to one person, and I couldn't do that to another woman. It would be taking something that wasn't mine, just because I want it, and it would hurt her. Anyway, I'm sick of being second best.'

He said nothing.

'I think I should go,' she said.

'Dine with me.'

'No.' Violet shook her head. 'Because then I'll forget all my own rules and we'll end up in bed. You know that. I know that…' She glanced over to where Layla and Maaz sat. 'They know that.'

'Okay,' he said. 'Can I speak now? Uninterrupted?'

'I won't stay.'

'You had your chance to speak,' he said.

She glanced over and waved to Maaz and Layla. 'Am I to be kidnapped again? Will they not let me leave?'

'You can leave any time. I just ask that you hear what I have to say. Although I would prefer us to have this conversation in private. I have a suite here…'

'I'm not falling for that. Like your massage.' She shook her head. She knew if she went to his suite they'd tumble into bed. And then she'd love him even more. And… 'No.'

'Why don't we just have dessert?'

She nodded, and stared at the menu, but then he spoke with the waiter and the gorgeous velvet folder was removed.

'I hadn't chosen.'

'Violet…' He sighed in exasperation. 'I'm trying to have a serious conversation.'

She'd hoped to sneak a copy of the menu, use it as a bookmark. But of course she couldn't tell him that, so she nodded, and stopped thinking about strawberry tarts and lemon meringues—oh, and chocolate and chestnut terrine.

'After that first night, when those images of us were briefly aired, my father saw them. He knew that his son was in love…'

She looked up.

'We barely knew each other then—' she attempted.

'Violet,' Sahir interrupted. 'We might not have realised it, but my father did. Aadil had alerted him to the threat, and then I called, requesting a week off.' He reached for her hand. 'I think by the end of that week perhaps we would have caught up with the same idea?'

She stared at his face, right into those eyes, and it was like watching a door open. It was as if she was being invited in—as if the noisy restaurant had disappeared and they were alone in the desert, or in a garden in London, or even her tiny flat.

It mattered not. They were in love…

'My father panicked…knew the danger. Because it is completely forbidden. A ruler can only…'

'I know the law.'

'My father…' He looked at her. 'He, more than most, knew the difficulties ahead if I broke that law.'

She wouldn't tell him what his father had shared with her, Sahir realised, and he was so proud of her for that.

* * *

Violet frowned as the waiter came over, carrying a silver tray. He removed the cloche and lit up the dessert so it danced with blue fire.

'I'll give it a miss,' she said, and gave him a smile.

'You don't want dessert?' asked Sahir.

'I don't like fruit cake, or pudding, or anything…' She went to grab her bag. 'I really must go.'

'Well, I asked the chef to prepare it especially. Apparently, it was my parents' favourite treat when they were in London…'

'Oh?' Violet said airily, as if she didn't already know.

'Now…' He took a jug and poured a very generous amount of cream over the dessert, and then scooped up some brandy butter with a silver spoon and held it out.

She reached forward, took the spoon in her mouth—because at least a mouthful of pudding would stop her from being indiscreet.

Oh, dear.

She loathed brandy, but this tasted of rum—and she hated that even more. It was so thick and rich, and he was watching her chewing it, forcing it down, and then taking a drink of water…

'Here,' he said, taking another scoop, still watching as she grimaced for a second time. 'Violet, I know you and my father spoke.'

Thank goodness her mouth was full. She kept chewing.

'I know.' He nodded. 'My father was stunned that you hadn't told me.' He took her hand. 'I wasn't. I was proud. Violet, he panicked because he's unwell…'

He stopped. And as his eyes lifted Violet saw agony. She knew then just how serious this conversation was, especially with Layla and Maaz so close.

'Perhaps we could speak in private,' she said.

'Thank you.'

She was shaking as he led her out, and yet still she did not want to break the King's confidence, unsure just how much Sahir knew.

'We're not staying in the same suite they did…' he told her.

Her eyes widened. 'I'm not staying at all,' she corrected. 'We're just talking.'

'Of course.'

He opened a door, and the second it closed behind them she turned frantic eyes to him.

'The King is okay,' he said. 'Although last week they thought he needed surgery.'

'Where?'

'On his brain.'

She started to cry.

'Violet, it's going to be treated with radiation, and the tumour is very slow-growing. We pray he's going to be okay, but I couldn't come to you straight away.'

'Of course not.'

'I had to sort things out.'

'I know.'

'Come on.'

She walked into his suite and never before had she felt as if she was coming home. Here, in a hotel she'd never been to, for the first time in her life she felt as if she were home.

There were pale pink tulips in vases... And on the television screen there she was—standing on his balcony, her dress shimmering in the morning sun... And there was a trolley with the entire dessert menu laid out on it... And then she gasped, because on the mantelpiece there was a photo of her, with Sahir standing behind her, watching her.

'I've never been on someone's mantelpiece.'

There were little pieces of her everywhere.

'My favourite tea,' she said, and smiled, opening the jar.

'In case you decide to stay a little while.'

'I'm too needy to be a mistress. And I'm not just being moral—honestly, I'll be the most dreadful, demanding...'

'I only want you,' Sahir told her. 'You come first.'

Those words stopped her from speaking, from breathing. It was as if a terror she hadn't even known had left her.

'Hold out your hand.'

'Stop it.'

She wasn't sure this was happening—especially when he told her to place her palm up.

'Here...' He reached into his jacket pocket and pulled out not a ring, but a vial. In her palm she felt a cold sensation. Opening her eyes, she stared at the small heap of orange sand from his land.

'You pour it back into my palm,' Sahir said. 'If you want this to continue.'

'If I want *what* to continue?' Violet frowned.

Oh, what the hell?

She poured it into his palm and ground it in. And then she threw it away and kissed him, because those lips were irresistible.

'Violet...'

He moved to peel her back, but their time apart meant that was impossible, and he kissed her back so hard, so deeply, that she was sinking. And then she was being carried to a bed and kissed again. And it still felt like home because soon she was being made love to, her violet gown ruched around her waist and pulled down at the top, being kissed all over...

Being made love to by Sahir was what made it feel like home.

'You made me wait a week...' She smiled over to him.

'I had to source this.'

He reached over and opened a drawer. She saw a gorgeous polished wood box with a beautiful clasp.

'Purple diamonds are very rare.'

'Violet,' she corrected.

'Violet diamonds are even rarer.'

The ring was absolutely exquisite, almost in the shape of a heart, and he slipped it on her finger. But she was crying, and a little cross.

'You put me through hell for a week to get this? You could have called the library, or...'

He kissed her nose.

'It's complicated when a prince chooses his bride. I had to

go to the desert for deep reflection—even though my decision was already made. Even though the council already approved.'

'The council approves?'

'They know I will not hide, and they know I will not take this lightly, so they agreed I could select the sand for our wedding.'

'I don't understand...'

'The sand you just threw...' He kissed her mouth. 'We have to find every grain.'

Her eyes widened.

'Will you marry me, Violet?' He put his hand up before she could answer. 'Before you say yes or no, know that if you accept then one day you will be Queen.'

'On one condition,' she said.

'It's a yes or no answer.'

'On one condition,' she said again, and stated her demand.

'That's never happened before.' He shook his head as she lay there silent. 'I can't see it working...'

'I can,' Violet said.

'Very well.' He nodded.

'Then I would love to be your wife.'

EPILOGUE

THE SERVICE WAS SIMPLE.

Marriage between a future king and his bride had always been a very low-key, matter-of-fact affair.

At least as far as the elders were concerned.

There were no bridesmaids, as such—well, not officially. But Grace helped Violet get into her gown.

'You look incredible…' Grace had tears in her eyes, watching love come alive.

'So do you,' Violet said, glancing at the tiny little bump that contained her niece or nephew, although not officially. 'I'm scared.'

'Of…?'

'Tripping over.'

'Not of marrying a prince and living overseas?'

'None of that,' Violet said. 'I just don't want to fall or…'

'You won't,' Grace said. 'And even if you do…'

Pria came to the door. It was time for Grace to take her place for the service.

She smiled at Violet. 'Whenever you are ready.'

'Thank you.'

It was very different from all the weddings she'd known before, because she could sit here alone for as long as she liked!

And actually Violet felt a little sick, with excited nerves—so, yes, she would make him wait, and make a little more dramatic entrance.

So she popped a mint, topped up her lip-gloss and let herself out of the Venus wing, having spent her last night there.

The palace was almost empty now, with most of the staff outside.

'Aadil.' She smiled at him.

'Violet,' he said, for the last time.

She'd be titled when they spoke next, and they were friends now. Each understood where the other was coming from.

'Your prince awaits,' he told her.

'Thank you,' she said as he opened the door to the King's private garden.

She made her way through the garden and there Sahir stood in a silver robe, beneath the tree where his parents had married, deeply in love, his mother pregnant with Sahir.

There were differences, though. For Sahir didn't hide his smile of delight when he saw his bride. In fact, they gazed at each other with that same look that had first got them into trouble.

Violet's heart felt as if it were full of sparklers, all fizzing as she walked towards him.

She wore a simple white dress with sliver slippers, and on her head she wore Queen Anousheh's favourite tiara, which the King had kindly offered for her to wear.

She wore her violet diamond engagement ring…and instead of flowers she carried a beautiful book that felt like a gift from above.

The King was smiling, and doing very well, seated with Ibrahim and Jasmine, who sat alongside Carter and Grace.

'You look beautiful,' Sahir told her. 'You always do.'

'Thank you.' She accepted his compliment. 'I did make quite an effort.' She looked at him, all trimmed and perfect, and she ached to kiss him, or pinch him—but of course did not. 'You did too.'

He nodded, and they turned to Hakaam.

Sahir poured some sand into her palm and Violet found out how she should have reacted the last time he'd done so.

Hakaam spoke. 'The sand always returns to the desert, but for now you share the wonders of the land.'

She carefully poured it back into Sahir's palm and it was carefully returned to two vials. Her palm was dusted, and so too was Sahir's, and both vials were sealed in golden wax by a very serious Hakaam as all the elders gathered round.

Violet closed her eyes when she thought of how she'd just brushed the sand to the floor and then kissed him.

Then Sahir gave her his promises.

'I accept,' Violet said.

She gave him her promises, and Sahir accepted them, adding that he would cherish them.

And, yes, there were more differences, and Hakaam had had to rework his charts. Because instead of being taken deep into the desert straight away, they were returning to the palace.

They stood outside the long doors and waited for them to be opened, and now Violet's one condition was to be met.

'This time, I *choose* to be photographed on the balcony,' she said.

They walked out to cheers, and photographers in helicopters, who captured the groom gazing at his wife, and the bride in a gown that was shot with silver catching the late-afternoon breeze.

And then it seemed Sahir could not resist, because he turned her around and she stared.

'You said no kissing.'

'Just a small one.'

It was scandalous, delicious and perfect, and she felt Sahir grip her hand.

Things would be different now.

And how the people cheered to see their grumpy king smiling. To see their crown prince with his gorgeous bride.

Love was no longer a secret, or something to fear in a ruler.

Today they all agreed that love made the world better.

At last they were flown into the desert, and the helicopter left them. But instead of heading to the tent, to attempt making the first of the many, many babies Violet wanted, Sahir stopped them.

'We have to check on the horses,' he said.

'On our wedding night?'

'No maids, no groomsmen—just us.'

'What's the point of being a princess?' she teased as they walked to the stables.

And there was Josie, squealing to be fed.

'If you want a pet, it comes with responsibility,' Sahir told her.

Then out she trotted, the gorgeous white foal, bounding towards her like an overgrown puppy, batting her lashes...
'She's *mine*?'
This time she embraced her without hesitation...absolutely.
Violet trusted in love.

* * * * *

Did you fall head over heels for
She Will Be Queen?

*Then you're sure to adore the first instalment
in the Wed into a Billionaire's World duet,*
Bride Under Contract

And don't miss these other Carol Marinelli stories!

The Greek's Cinderella Deal
Forbidden to the Powerful Greek
The Sicilian's Defiant Maid
Innocent Until His Forbidden Touch
Virgin's Stolen Nights with the Boss

Available now!

HIS HIGHNESS'S HIDDEN HEIR

DANI COLLINS

MILLS & BOON

To you, Dear Reader.

For loving romance, and reading mine,
and making this, my 60th Mills & Boon, possible.

Thank you!

CHAPTER ONE

THE ADAGE THAT SAID *If you want something done right, do it yourself* defined Lexi Alexander's twenty-five years of life.

Unfortunately, there were some things she simply couldn't do. For instance, she couldn't be famous and also be her own security detail.

Quietly cursing under her breath, she dismissed Nishan, the bodyguard her brother had hired, and left for the ballroom alone.

Poor Nishan hadn't meant to contract food poisoning. She knew that. Hadley was the real problem. Her brother had hired a man who hadn't been up to the task of protecting her even before he'd lost his lunch. Nishan hadn't known how to navigate her through the airports or the streets of Paris and there'd been a very un-reassuring alarm in his eyes as they'd run the gauntlet of paparazzi from the car to the hotel. He had allowed stylists to come and go from her room all afternoon without checking their bags. Now Lexi was without an escort as she joined the queue in the corridor, inching their way toward the ballroom.

She was perfectly safe, she reassured herself. The hotel was in a type of lockdown, given the guest list for this gala included muckety-mucks from across Europe. It wasn't as though she wore millions of dollars in jewels the way she used to when attending something like this. Her fall from grace two years ago meant she'd had to call in a favor to rent one of last year's gowns, and her jewelry was costume. Very good costume, but costume nonetheless.

The bloom was so far off her rose, she half expected to be refused entry.

Which would break her, financially and emotionally. She had dropped funds she couldn't afford on the flight, the hotel and the plate fee of a five-figure donation benefiting war-injured children. She was hoping her attendance would polish out some of the tarnish on her reputation, but was really here to "bump into" one of the other guests, a French woman Lexi desperately wanted to direct her in an adaptation she was trying to get off the ground.

All of this was high-stakes gambling, something Lexi objected to in principle, but she had so few choices. Being famous since childhood meant she was perceived as rich and powerful. That made her a favorite target for paparazzi and others who were even less savory. She would love to get a job as a barista and live a quiet life above a bookstore, but that option wasn't available to her. She had cut back as much as she could, but she still needed an income that would pay the mortgage on her high-security mansion and allow her to keep her staff.

"Ms. Alexander." A young woman in a little black dress greeted her with a smile of recognition when Lexi arrived at the front of the line. It was the delighted smile Lexi had seen most of her life. The one that seemed to exclaim, *You're that girl from that show!*

The young woman's expression faltered, the way they all did these days, as she recalled the more recent headlines: Unapproved Ingredients. Chemical Burns. Class Action Lawsuit.

The young woman touched her earpiece and flashed Lexi a more sober look. "May I ask you to step to the side with me, please?"

No. Lexi kept her star-powered smile frozen in place. "Is there a problem?"

"Not at all. Only…" As they moved to the left of the entryway, the young woman looked back the way Lexi had come.

Lexi followed her gaze and watched all the people in their tuxedos and evening gowns, designer shoes and sparkling jewels, step toward the wall. Some bowed their heads.

She heard someone murmur, "Your Highness," right before a man—an absolute *Viking*—appeared.

He was tall, six four at least. He led his entourage like an invading party, ignoring everyone as he marched toward the ballroom, head high with his right to cut the line.

Maybe Lexi was supposed to lower her gaze, too, but she was too dazzled.

He wore a gorgeous tuxedo with a white jacket that hugged his broad shoulders. A sash of midnight blue was tucked beneath it, running diagonally from his left shoulder to his right hip where the silk protruded. It was pinned with a silver emblem shaped like a starburst. A row of medals sat in a line above his pocket square and a crest of some kind was embroidered on the pocket.

His dark blond hair was combed back from his forehead, revealing the rugged bone structure of his brow and cheeks and jaw. His nose was hawkish, his mouth wide and accentuated by his closely trimmed bronze beard.

All of that was mesmerizing enough, but his *eyes*. They were such a vivid blue, they made her shiver as his gaze slammed into hers while he approached.

He turned his head as he passed her, holding her gaze an extra second, never missing a step in his long, ground-eating stride.

Then she was staring at the pewter wolf's head that secured his long hair at his nape.

He melted into the crowded ballroom, taking all his dynamic energy with him, leaving a wake of rippling voices.

"Whew!" Lexi heard beside her. She had completely forgotten the young woman who was now blushing and fanning her face. "They told me to let him go by without stopping him. You can go in now. Thank you for waiting."

Lexi dragged her mind back to where she was and what she was supposed to be doing, but her thoughts were scattered like stars across the sky.

"Who, um, who is he?" she asked under her breath.

"Prince Magnus of Isleif."

"Of course." She pretended that meant something to her, but she was an American born in Scottsdale, Arizona. She'd been raised on film sets and didn't know much about the royals of Europe. Isleif was an island somewhere between Denmark and Greenland, if she recalled her online geography classes correctly. Otherwise, she knew nothing about it.

With a nod of thanks, she entered the busy ballroom.

She hated to enter a crowd alone. *I'm safe*, she affirmed to herself. The hotel had its own security in place and that young woman at the door was only letting in the approved guest list. These were all sophisticated people who cared very little for American actors turned failed online influencers.

But there had been some *terrible* posts over the years, especially after that most recent lawsuit.

She ignored the anxiety that tried to churn her belly and scanned the crowd, looking for her target, Bernadette Garnier.

Lexi wasn't short. She was five eight and wore five-inch heels, but it was still difficult to spot the director. The room lights were dimmed. Balloons floated above highboy tables and streamers draped from the ceiling. Clusters of people were shifting and pressing around the silent auction tables. More were jockeying at the bar. Waitstaff circulated, offering champagne.

She waved that off, moving closer to where an ensemble played a lively tune that was barely audible over the din of voices.

"Paisley!" A man close to her age brightened with discovery as she tried to excuse herself past him.

This was why she preferred to have a bodyguard with her.

"Guilty." Lexi forced a friendly smile and offered her hand. "My real name is Lexi Alexander."

Yes. My mother named me Alexandra Alexander, she often had to add.

"No, you're Paisley Pockets," he insisted. "My sister made me watch your show when we were kids." He leaned in to add in a tone that bordered on creepy, "Then I made her watch *Bungalow Bingo*."

This was typical from a man. *He* hadn't enjoyed a show

about a girl who could travel in pockets, but he couldn't wait to brag about ogling her in her later work, when she'd worn short shorts and a bandeau.

"Can we get a photo?" He threw his arm around her and brought up his phone.

It was always more expedient to agree than protest that this was an invasion of her time and privacy, but damn Hadley for hiring such a green bodyguard. Who ate a shrimp-filled croissant from a street vendor's cart?

She smiled sunnily for the photo, experiencing a prickle of awareness as she did.

It took all her control to wait until the photo was taken before she glanced left, to where her inner radar was pulling her attention.

Prince Magnus was watching them. *Her.* He was tall enough he stood like a lighthouse amid the streaming crowd. As she held his stare, an itching sensation rose behind her breastbone, making the rest of her tingle.

The prince blinked once and glanced away, leaving her deflated at losing his attention.

"Darling." A woman arrived to grip her fan's arm, digging her nails into his sleeve.

"Look," he said with an excited wave at Lexi. "It's Paisley Pockets."

"Lexi Alexander. Hi." Lexi always offered her real name with her hand, even though she was resigned to having Paisley Pockets on her tombstone.

The woman offered a flat, dismissive smile. She ignored Lexi's hand and insisted to the man, "You need to meet my friend." She mumbled something in his ear.

The man shot Lexi a look and the tension in Lexi's belly twisted into a blistering knot.

That look was becoming familiar, too. *Don't speak to her. She's radioactive.*

"Excuse me," she said, even though they were already turning away.

This was why she was in Europe, taking long shots at finding work. No one in the American film industry would touch her.

You just have to stay in the game, her mother would say cheerfully, but Lexi was growing tired of the fight.

If she had other options she would take them, but this was all she had and the press loved to chum the waters with her old mistakes, making it impossible for her to outswim her past.

The next hour was a roller coaster of similar encounters. She wound her way around the auction items, bidding on the ones she knew she would lose since she couldn't afford any of them.

She didn't find Bernadette. Was she even here? People were still arriving, but she was very done with being here. This evening was starting to smell like a huge mistake.

The music paused for speeches. Lexi listened with half an ear, scanning the faces as best she could until she joined the polite applause. A gorgeous couple took to the dance floor in an elegant waltz.

"Shall we?" The deep, accented voice stirred the fine hairs near her ear while a wide, hot palm took possession of her hip.

She turned her head and her cheekbone grazed the silky whiskers of the Prince's chin. He essentially surrounded her, causing her heart to belatedly leap. She was snared. Caught. *Claimed.*

A dozen thoughts zipped through her mind—one of

them that he couldn't possibly know who she was—but he was trailing his hand across her lower back, thumb grazing where her gown dipped to reveal her spine, leaving a spark of electricity against her skin.

He removed his touch and caught her hand, tugging her toward the dance floor.

It was as though a barbed hook in her chest pulled her to follow him, instantly painful yet impossible to resist.

He gathered her a little too close. Close enough that her legs brushed his as they moved, causing the silk lining of her gown to caress her thighs.

She knew how to dance, but she'd never moved so fluidly with anyone. Not without weeks of rehearsal. She was instantly in sync with him, her body giving over to his dominant lead with instinctive trust.

Don't, a protective voice warned. She'd learned the hard way that trust needed to be earned. Even then, it was conditional. She'd been hurt too many times to take anyone at face value, even a prince. What did he want? Sex?

"What's your name?" he asked in his accented English.

"You don't know?" She was genuinely surprised.

"Should I?"

"I'm Lexi Alexander, an actor from America." She didn't mention the cosmetic thing. "I would have thought someone on your team had recognized me." And warned him not to talk to her, let alone dance with her. People were noticing.

She glanced toward his entourage and saw a silver-haired man wearing an expression of subtle horror.

It wasn't funny, but she had a dark enough sense of humor to be amused.

"You didn't know who I was when you saw me," the prince chided. "I could tell by the way you looked at me."

"How was that?" She lifted her lashes, curious, and was instantly snared by the banked heat behind his startlingly blue irises.

"As a man."

Oh. Her heart lurched. He did want sex.

But maybe she did, too? A sensual weight seemed to land in her belly, one that emanated intense warmth through her torso, arriving in pinpoints at the tips of her breasts and between her thighs.

It was disconcerting enough to make her cheeks sting. She lowered her gaze, embarrassed at having such a visceral, obvious reaction.

"You're very beautiful." His voice deepened with admiration. Intimacy. "I couldn't help noticing you, too."

She knew she was judged to be beautiful. Hollywood told her that all the time, not that she believed her beauty was anything more than symmetrical features and above-average height. She did have genuinely nice hair, but the honey-gold streaks were placed there by her mother. Rhonda Alexander had trained in hair and makeup before Lexi was born, then treated her daughter as her own personal dress-up doll, an asset to be polished and shown off.

Thus, Lexi knew how to emphasize her eyes so they seemed bigger and shape her mouth into more of a sensual pout. She wore push-up bras and kept her weight audition-ready. Her nails were always manicured, her fashion choices edgy, but flattering.

"Beauty is in the eye of the beholder," she dismissed lightly.

"Aren't I the lucky one to be holding it." His mouth twitched. "You're here alone?"

"I am, but—" She gave a barely perceptible shake of her head, regretting that she had to rebuff him. It made her throat feel raw, but it was necessary. She was used often enough that she wouldn't do that to a stranger for a bit of positive press, no matter how badly she needed it.

The way his expression hardened told her he wasn't used to being refused what he wanted. And he wanted her. Not the way other men did, either. This was different. She understood that at a cellular level, as his hands subtly tightened on her. He wasn't intent on possessing a pretty object. No, this was elemental sexual desire—the kind she had never really experienced. She only recognized it in him because it was coming alive in her blood and nerve endings, sharpening her senses and filling her with craving.

Her heart tipped unsteadily in her chest. The pull toward him was so profound, the need to be near him so acute, it was terrifying. She wanted to fall into him and damn the consequences, which conversely made her want to run the other way out of self-protection.

"You need to t-talk to your people." She stopped dancing and pressed for him to release her.

He turned to stone, holding her in place without effort for three crashing heartbeats.

The strength in his arms was an iron cage, but he held her more with the pierce of his gaze. Then he dropped his touch and gave her a disinterested nod.

She had to do some of her best acting as he walked away, hiding how bereft she was as she moving in the opposite direction.

He left the gala moments later. She felt the energy in the room change. Maybe it was the awareness inside her that dimmed. Either way, she was dejected and swimming in loss.

She told herself it was because she hadn't managed to find Bernadette. She went back to the entrance of the ballroom and asked the greeter if the director had turned up.

The young woman checked her tablet. "It doesn't seem so."

Damn. Everything about this trip had become a complete waste of resources.

Lexi threw in the towel, unwilling to go back into the ballroom and face the growing stares. They were even more rude and speculative now that she'd danced with the prince.

He had probably wanted distance after being informed about her. She imagined he was furious that she'd compromised him.

For some reason that ate at her worse than the money she'd thrown away by coming here. Why? He was a total stranger. He meant nothing to her.

Yet she couldn't stop thinking about him as she made her way down the corridor to the elevators, worrying over their brief interaction like an abscessed tooth, poking at all the most painful aspects.

She had to keep an unbothered look on her face as she went. Small groups of people were chatting in alcoves and she had to step aside for another entourage of royals.

Wait. Was that—? It was!

Lexi was rarely starstruck, but she paused to watch Queen Claudine and her husband, King Felipe, continue toward the ballroom. Claudine had been a beauty contestant from New York, competing in Nazarine when she'd fallen in love with its crown prince. He had since ascended to the throne. Their courtship was straight out of a romance novel, the kind Lexi would love to develop into a movie and star in, not that she could touch Queen Claudine's natural beauty—

"Lexi!" a male voice called.

She glanced to the end of the corridor where it ended at the mezzanine. A man stood on the far side of the circular rail that looked onto the hotel's entrance foyer below. He lifted his camera to point it at her.

The paparazzi was roped off outside, but that wasn't just any photographer. Her heart nearly came out her throat as she recognized her stalker.

Instinctively, she pushed through the nearest door.

She had an impression of half a dozen men, including Prince Magnus, before someone grabbed her. Shock rendered her meager self-defense training useless. Her right arm was twisted into the middle of her back and her scream was still trapped in her throat when her face smacked into the wall.

CHAPTER TWO

MAGNUS THOROLF HAD already been in a foul mood when he arrived at this hotel. It was a version of the foul mood he'd been stewing in for the last fourteen years, ever since he'd been plucked from his training session on a ski hill in Norway and shuffled into a van by men in suits and sunglasses.

One blood test later, he was deemed the legitimate heir to the Isleif throne, something his mother could have told him at any time in the previous eighteen years of his life.

I was afraid they would take you away from me, she cried when the truth came out.

That was exactly what had happened.

His life, which at the time had been filled with endless possibility, had shrunk to duty and protocol and service to a crown he had no desire to wear.

Which suggested he didn't love Isleif, but that was the furthest thing from the truth. The best memories of his life were summers and Christmases at his mother's cottage in the windy island nation, chasing his brother and sister down a beach or across a snow-covered field. He couldn't think of that time without a knife of nostalgia turning in him.

Ignorance really was bliss.

It certainly had been an hour ago, when a woman had snared his attention and he'd thought he might have amenable company in his bed tonight.

He wasn't even sure how or why she'd caught his eye. Yes, she was beautiful. Her blond hair was swept to the side, exposing one of her high cheekbones. Her pillowy lips were painted an earthy red, her eyeshadow bronze to match her gown.

The gown itself had been both elegant and sexy as hell. The silk had wrapped her throat then left her shoulders bare as it parted to cradle her ample breasts. It was fitted to her waist and hips, then fell open across one thigh, making the most of her stunning figure.

So, yes, she was easy to look at, but beautiful women made themselves available to him all the time, not that Magnus took full advantage of that small perk of his title. He'd had lovers, obviously. They were always vetted to within an inch of their life and his private secretary, Ulmer, damned near applied the condoms to Magnus himself.

Given the absolute dearth of spontaneity and the growing pressure to find a "suitable" partner and produce an heir, Magnus mostly eschewed sex—which probably contributed to his terrible disposition.

He'd grown numb to all of it.

Tonight, however, he'd felt something besides the frustration of living in a cage. Sure, it had been lust, but it was overwhelming lust. The sight of that woman had shaken him awake, spurring him with fierce need. When they danced, her voice and scent and grace had piqued his appetite. Not just for sex, although in his mind her legs had already been around his waist. No, he'd wanted *her*. It wasn't rational or even civilized, but he didn't care.

From the moment their eyes had met, he'd made up his mind that she would come to his room.

Then she'd rejected him.

You should talk to your people.

He hated talking to his people. He hated what they said.

Not a good look, sir. Absolutely not.

Magnus had walked out of the gala, loathing these hellish appearances anyway.

He'd bumped into King Felipe of Nazarine on his way to the elevators. They had a friendly acquaintance, both facing a similar challenge of representing a small island nation on the greater world stage. They'd stepped into this breakout room long enough to agree to support each other's position at an upcoming climate conference, then Felipe had escorted his wife, Claudine, to the ballroom.

"I saw a photographer in the mezzanine," Ulmer said, barely looking up from his tablet. "We can avoid him by using the service elevator." He signaled one of the bodyguards to check the catering hall.

At that moment, the door thrust inward.

Magnus caught a glimpse of bronze and blonde, heard a cry of alarm, then his guard shoved the intruder against the wall with far too much force.

"Let her go!" Magnus was across the room before any of the security protocols that had been drilled into him could register. He clasped his bodyguard's shoulder in the bite of his hand and yanked him away from her, damned near throwing him across the room.

"Sir!" That was Ulmer, trying to prevent a scuffle as his bodyguard turned on Magnus in reflex before realizing his employer was the one attacking him.

"She could be armed, sir," the bodyguard said, tugging his jacket straight and keeping a watchful eye on Lexi.

She turned so her back was to the wall, but her shoulders were hunched and her arms were folded upward defensively. She had one hand pressed to her cheek.

"In that dress? Use your eyes!" Magnus took hold of her wrist, trying to draw her hand down so he could examine her cheek.

She shook him off and slid sideways, still darting frightened looks around the room.

"Let me see," Magnus ordered.

He placed himself between her and the rest of the men, trying to remember to be gentle as he crooked his finger under her chin, but he was beside himself with unnatural fury, especially when he saw how red her cheekbone was.

"If this bruises, I'll give you one to match it," he told his bodyguard in Isleifisch. It was a modern version of Old Norse that was more a dialect between Danish and Norwegian, given Isleif's close ties to both countries.

Lexi brushed his hand off her face, still trembling.

"You're safe," Magnus assured her, belatedly switching to English.

She made a choked noise that held such lack of belief, the hair on the back of his neck rose. Then something caught her attention beyond him.

"There's nothing in there but my phone and room card," she protested crossly. "And that clutch is on loan. Kindly don't destroy it."

Magnus swore and held out his hand to Ulmer, who had turned out the lining of her rhinestone-bedecked handbag.

Ulmer was about to tear the silk open, but replaced the contents and disdainfully handed it to Magnus.

"It's our job to protect you, sir," Ulmer said in English, no hint of apology in his tone. "She's already damaged your reputation. Now she's followed you in here? Why?" He directed that last imperious query to Lexi.

"I wanted privacy to use my phone." She snatched the clutch from Magnus. "You can all go to hell. I have my own threats to deal with." She slid along the wall again, distancing herself as she placed a call.

"All clear, sir." The bodyguard who'd been sent into the service hall came in the far door.

"Even more reason to use a discreet exit," Ulmer muttered and looked expectantly to Magnus.

Magnus ignored the hint to leave. His hackles were still up, his attention fixated on Lexi. He sensed aggression rising off her, but it wasn't directed at them despite how she'd been treated. It was the defensive kind that hunched her shoulders forward.

"Pick up the phone, you— Oh!" She halted as she arrived at the corner and kept her face to the wall. Her voice seethed through her clenched teeth. "How does Carmichael know where I am? Because he's *here*. In Paris. At my *hotel*. Did Janet post about this trip? Because I told her to wait until I was home. And that *child* you hired as a bodyguard ate a bad shrimp and can't leave the—"

She turned to pace the other way and froze as she saw they were all watching and listening. The flags of color across her cheekbones deepened to crimson. Her mouth tightened.

"Call me back." She ended the call and let her arm fall to her side. Her throat flexed as she swallowed, but she kept her chin up. "Which one of you is in charge?" she asked loftily.

"Ha!" Magnus barked. "Who the hell do you think?"

Her spine stiffened a fraction more. "If you needed a bodyguard right now, immediately, who would you call?"

"Money is no object?"

"It's definitely an object, but so long as I get my money's worth, I'll pay whatever is necessary." She was pretending to take all of this in stride, but he heard the quaver of real fear underpinning her words.

It was disturbing, further abrading his protective instincts.

Magnus touched his smartwatch, sliding his fingertip to place a call.

"Your Royal Highness," a pleasant female voice answered. "How may I assist you?"

"I need someone in Paris as soon as possible, Kiran."

"Can you wait one moment, please?" She put him on hold long enough for Ulmer to mutter a dismay-laden, "Sir."

Magnus understood his private secretary's concern. Magnus was involving the very security firm that trained his own men, but they *were* the best. And they hadn't become the best by allowing themselves to be compromised by actresses with soiled reputations. Involving them would allow Magnus to run a dossier on Lexi and learn very quickly if she posed any real threat to him.

"Sir?" Kiran's voice returned. "My brother, Vijay, is on his way to Paris as we speak. He said he will join you first thing in the morning. If your team forwards more information, he should have everything you require in place by then. Will that suffice?"

"Thank you, Kiran. Lexi Alexander has a stalker, last name Carmichael." He glanced at Lexi.

"Aaron," she provided. "There's ample coverage of it online. I have a restraining order against him."

"Did you get all that? He's here in our hotel," Magnus added.

"I'll make hotel security aware of that and have them forward tapes for any legal action that may arise. Shall I ask them to provide a guard for Ms. Alexander?"

"No," Magnus decided with a leap of dark satisfaction. "She'll be safe with me until Vijay arrives."

Magnus ended the call, then waved Lexi toward the door to the service hall, where one of his bodyguards was still stationed.

She hesitated, but when she thought of walking out to the mezzanine and around to the elevators, toward Carmichael, her blood congealed.

Forcing a swallow past her dry throat, she complied. She ought to protest that she only needed an escort to her own room, but the fact was, she really needed a moment of feeling safe so she could compose herself and think this through.

Not that her brain managed anything except sparking awareness, crammed into an elevator with the prince and three other men. She pressed into the back to make room. Magnus joined her there, facing her, while the rest of the men entered and faced front.

Disapproval was wafting like musky cologne from the white-haired man who'd gone through her handbag. He didn't like her *at all*.

Prince Magnus didn't seem to care. He touched beneath her chin again, angling her face slightly before he caressed her still-tender cheek with the pad of his thumb.

"It's fading."

She touched where the knock had happened, probing, but also using it as an excuse to brush away his touch because it was far too disturbing, sending trickles of sensual awareness into her throat and down to her chest.

"Why are you helping me?" she asked.

"You know why."

A learned cynicism had her wondering if he expected sex in exchange for his help, but she wasn't sure she minded if he did. Which was a troubling thought.

The elevator stopped and opened, allowing fresh oxygen to rush in.

They had arrived in a laundry room where a guard waited. He nodded a confirmation that seemed to reassure everyone.

Magnus took her hand, sending a zing of electricity up her arm and into her torso. He led her through a kitchen where two staff stopped to nod as they went by.

"Are you hungry?" he asked as they moved through a dining area into a luxurious lounge decorated in shades of gray and ivory with accents of sapphire blue. The drapes were closed and several table lamps glowed.

"No. Thank you." She wriggled her hand free of his, then closed it into a fist, holding on to the sensation of his fingers woven between her own.

His bodyguards dispersed in all directions, checking behind doors and stepping onto the terrace, then checking beyond the door to the hall.

"Are *you* in danger?" she was compelled to ask. "You seem to have a lot of protection."

"An abundance of caution. The previous king—my father —" his lip curled with irony "—was assassinated."

"I'm so sorry. That must have been horrible for you."

"It happened years ago. I never met him." He shrugged off his tuxedo jacket and removed his sash, handing them to that circumspect fellow who was still giving off vibes of hostility and suspicion. "Sit. I'll save you the trouble of looking me up."

Magnus hitched his tuxedo trousers and lowered into an armchair that faced the sofa, instantly turning the chair into a throne with the simple act of lounging his magnificent body upon it. He pulled his bow tie free and discarded it on the side table, then released the button at his throat, shoulders relaxing.

She lowered into the corner of the sofa, sparing a moment for how surreal this was, sitting to converse with a prince. The force of his undivided attention was like a spotlight, hot and blinding.

"Isleif was on the brink of financial collapse and King Einer was living high. I mean that literally as well as figuratively. He was a fan of party drugs and places where they're offered in abundance. He had built a network within the government that was helping him cut inside deals for offshore drilling. In exchange for greasing those wheels, he was given anything he wanted. I'm not telling you anything that isn't in the six-part documentary series."

"He sounds…" She cleared her throat. "Larger than life."

"*Corrupt* is the word most use. It's a wonder he only had the one illegitimate child."

"You?" She widened her eyes.

"Yes. And believe me, I've looked for more. So has Queen Katla, his legitimate heir. She took the throne when he died, but she has never been able to conceive. There had long been rumors in the palace that the king had fathered a child with a commoner, after he lost his son, Katla's older brother. She found me and I was brought to the palace as her successor."

"That sounds like a fairy tale."

"Written by the Brothers Grimm, perhaps."

The grumpy assistant returned. He carried an ice bucket and two wineglasses. He showed Magnus the label on the bottle and Magnus nodded.

"No wine for me, thank you. I don't drink alcohol," Lexi said.

"What would you prefer?" Magnus asked.

"Soda with lime?"

He held up two fingers and the other man disappeared with the wine.

"I don't mind if you drink," she said. "My teetotaling is for PR purposes."

His brows lifted in a command for her to elaborate.

Since she was rarely given a chance to tell her side of things, she did.

"When I was sixteen, one of my brother's friends put drugs in my bag. It was hard stuff that I never would have touched. My father managed to keep me from being charged, but I did a stint in rehab, then a year of community service."

In some ways, the counseling had been a blessing. She probably would be a drug addict by now without that perspective, given all she'd been through. At the time, however, her counselor had feared she was in denial, lying about not having a drug issue.

"I live sober now," she added. "It's simpler."

Her phone burbled in her clutch, but she ignored it.

"Probably my brother calling me back," she said when the Prince's gaze dropped to the noise. "Half brother," she clarified. "He runs the entertainment agency that manages me." The agency her career had built, if she wanted to be petty about it, which she definitely did. "Our father was an entertainment lawyer. Mom worked in hair and makeup before I was born. They had an affair, but he was already married. I was born on the wrong side of the blanket, too."

A choked noise came out of Ulmer as he set a soda with lime on the table beside her.

Magnus gave the man a laconic blink. "You have an opinion you wish to share?"

"You know my opinion, sir."

"I do. Pack it with your things from your room."

"You're not firing him!" Lexi blurted. "I get way worse from trolls online. And I know what the press says about me. I don't blame him for wanting to keep you out of that blast radius."

"If only I could fire him," Magnus said with pained tolerance. "Ulmer serves at the pleasure of the queen. Her goal is that I experience no pleasure at all. I'm actually doing him a favor, giving him the means to report truthfully that he made every effort to offer you a bed that wasn't mine, including providing his own."

"I—" Her throat tightened, cutting off her voice while heat suffused her chest. He was taking a lot for granted! Wasn't he?

Maybe not. She kept imagining how it would feel to straddle him in that wide chair while she finished unbuttoning his shirt.

He held her gaze in a way that suggested he knew exactly what she was thinking. And wanted that, too.

The heat under her skin sizzled into her cheeks and streaked downward into the pit of her belly.

"The hotel is full. Ulmer will need to stay in your room. Give him your key. Unless you have something to hide?" Prince Magnus was like a cat, she realized with a leap of her pulse. He appeared lazy and bored, then surprised with a lightning move that trapped his prey in his sharp claws.

"Only a racy historical romance on the night table. Don't lose my place in it," she said as she opened her clutch.

"Send back something for her to wear in the morning," Magnus instructed.

Lexi thought about insisting on going back to her room. She could ask hotel security to check it, but she knew from experience they were no more qualified than Nishan. She would lie awake all night, fretting they had missed something, terrified by every footfall outside her door, waiting for Carmichael or someone else to break in.

"Will you have one of the men look for cameras, please?" she asked as she offered her key. "That's what Carmichael did the last time he got into my hotel room." She shuddered remembering all the snippets of film that had been shown in court.

Ulmer plucked the card from her with a *tsk*.

"I don't want to need protection," she said shakily, using anger to cover the way she was inwardly cringing with shame. She knew exactly how badly she had already tarnished the prince's reputation. Judging from what he'd said of his father, he couldn't afford any smudges.

"I'll see that you have something comfortable to sleep in, too," Ulmer said stiffly.

"Are you suggesting my bed isn't comfortable?" Magnus taunted at the man's back.

Ulmer sniffed and walked away.

"Please don't make this worse for me," Lexi pleaded. "If you needle him, he's liable to plant something incriminating in my room as retaliation."

"He won't. That could blow back on me. Besides, he prefers to tattle so I can be called on the carpet for a lecture from my sister. It's very tiresome. Let's talk about something else."

"Such as?"

"Tell me why your reputation is so far in the gutter."

"Your people haven't told you?"

"They told me you were involved in a lawsuit. That you are a lightning rod for sensationalism. That you encourage it."

"That last part is not true." She sat back and exhaled, wishing there was somewhere far enough she could retreat to. A remote jungle in Indonesia, perhaps? "I've always tried very hard to be professional and a decent role model to the younger generation."

"You've been acting from a young age, Ulmer said."

"I was famous before I knew what acting was. I was a cute baby so Mom put me in commercials for diapers and whatnot. She didn't need the money. Dad paid her support. He paid her to stay in Scottsdale, let's be real. But I had a temperament for it."

"Acting?"

"Being on set and doing as I was told, yes. I'm patient.

A bit of a pleaser. I was then, anyway. I was cast in a soap opera and that led to Paisley Pockets."

His brows went up again.

"A girl who shrinks and travels in pockets. That went for six years and it was very wholesome. Then I did some coming-of-age movies and campy comedies and had just landed a part in a superhero movie when the drugs were found. That was my first scandal and a huge setback career-wise. I tried to drop acting, actually, and went back to college, but notoriety followed me. Frat houses would claim I was at their party and it would turn into a riot when fans showed up and I wasn't there. The dean asked me to leave. My father had just died and Hadley took over the agency. I needed to support myself so I let him talk me into doing a reality show that was bikini-based. The money was great, but it got me a fan base I *really* wish I could undo."

"Like the stalker?"

She nodded jerkily. "Carmichael got off on a technicality. I could have appealed, but I had already lost three years of my life to him. And the cost." She rolled her eyes. "There was no upside to staying in that fight. Half the time the press framed it as a stunt I had pulled because I was an attention whore." Tightness invaded her chest. If only people knew how badly she would love to disappear into obscurity. "From a producer's viewpoint, I was too expensive to hire because I need on-set protection. My image was blonde bimbo from the reality series so no one was considering me for serious roles. I couldn't get work, but I needed security."

"From Carmichael? Or are there others?"

"From everyone." She lifted helpless hands. "Most of

my fans are perfectly rational and nice, but the volume is challenging. I need walls and gates. Long story short, I became the face of a cosmetic brand that paid for all of that until they switched out some ingredients due to supply chain issues. It was something the FDA hadn't approved. It reacted with other products and people started getting chemical burns."

He swore under his breath.

"It was very bad," she agreed, nauseated every time she thought of it. "I did everything I could to make it right. I took responsibility for promoting it and paid a huge fine. I sold a bunch of my assets to pay the legal fees because people wanted to sue *me*, even though I had nothing to do with creating the actual product. Anyway, I'm not allowed to put my name behind anything anymore, not that anyone wants it. That's another drawback to hiring me. These days, every film has merchandising licenses attached to it. No one wants me to be the next action figure sold to children. I've made a million apologies and I've donated to every organization I can find, but the bottom-feeding gossip sites still frame me as a monster who doesn't care who she harms so long as she gets ahead."

"Tonight was another photo op? Is that why you danced with me?" His tone held a lash of cynicism.

"That's why I stopped dancing with you," she corrected frostily, but her insides shriveled. "I don't want to be performative about giving to charity. I know how icky that is." She hated that she was reduced to this. "But if my mistakes are going to be made into headlines, I might as well have some good press to balance it. Mostly I came here to meet a director who was supposed to attend. Bernadette Garnier." She rubbed her eyebrow. "I have a project I genuinely think she would find interesting. One that could help me stage a comeback or at least keep the lights on a little longer. She wasn't there, though."

He sat in a comfortable slouch as he regarded her, so casually sexy it was difficult to look at him without more fantasies exploding in her head.

He couldn't want her now, though. Not after she'd laid bare all her flaws and drawbacks. He ought to ask her to leave.

Ulmer stalked back into the room. He held a small valise and paused behind Magnus to send her a hard glare over the prince's shoulder.

She held her breath, awaiting banishment.

"I'll text if I need anything," Magnus said without so much as turning his head.

Ulmer's mouth tightened. Seconds later, the door closed firmly behind him.

"He's not wrong," she pointed out, still wobbly on the inside. "I'm accepting your help because I don't have many friends left. I had to come all the way to Europe for a *chance* at work. You don't want to be associated with me."

"True."

The single word was an arrow straight into her chest, stopping her heart and lungs before radiating a sharp pain through her entire being.

He rose in a graceful move that was so abrupt it took her heart on a fresh dip and roll, and offered his hand. "I'll show you to your room."

CHAPTER THREE

HER FINGERS HAD gone cold. She noticed because his hand was hot. His firm clasp seemed to envelop her entire being as he drew her to stand. She felt lifted off the floor, as though she floated behind him as he led her down the hall.

To *her* room.

He paused in the hall where an open door looked into an empty bedroom.

"Use it if you want to. I'll wake you in the morning when Vijay arrives."

She started to walk through, kind of in a daze, but halted belatedly as his words hit her ears. Her equilibrium teetered.

"If I want to?"

Oh, don't, she warned herself. This man was dangerous. Maybe not violent, but he possessed the sort of power that could destroy what was left of her free will and peace of mind.

"I want this night with you, Lexi. I want *you*." His voice was quiet, yet it reverberated enough to make her cells quiver. "You want me, too."

A painful sense of exposure made her feel naked and obvious. She tried to reassemble her inner defenses, but it was too late. She already knew he'd breached them. So did he.

"But this is not a quid pro quo." The sea of his eyes roiled with the same frustrated conflict she'd seen on the dance floor. He was exerting supreme control over himself, but it took effort for him to leash his most barbaric instincts—which he had in abundance.

Recognizing that atavistic side of him should have terrified her. On some distant plane of consciousness, it did. Another part responded to that wolfish power that wanted to run her to ground, mostly because she already knew he didn't want to kill her. He wanted to *mate*.

It was such a wild, instinctual knowledge, she felt drunk on it. Petrified, yet excited.

"If I go in here, you won't follow me?" She set her hands behind her against the doorjamb, telling herself to step inside and close the door.

Make the smart choice, Lexi.

"I will not. This is your decision."

He braced his hand above her head, as though grasping at the only thing that would keep him from tipping into the room. He stepped close enough she had to tilt her chin up to hold his gaze. Her heart was going a mile a minute.

"Sleep alone or come to my room where you won't get much sleep at all," he clarified thickly.

Raw electricity pulsed through her torso, out to her limbs.

He wasn't touching her, but she felt compressed by his wide presence. Squeezed into making a decision. Move into the bedroom or step into the hall. Reject him or abandon herself.

"Are you trying to force me to make the decision for both of us? So you can say I seduced you?"

"You seduced me the moment you looked at me."

Same. She swallowed.

"The whole world already saw us together. Things will be said regardless." His gaze traveled all over her face, as though memorizing its contours. "Go inside and close the door. It's the best thing for both of us. I'll only hate you a little for it," he added with a sardonic curl of his lip.

A tiny whimper throbbed in her throat. Being hated didn't bother her. Or, rather, she'd grown numb to it. And he was joking. He wasn't trying to manipulate her. She didn't feel a need to appease him and *make* him like her. No, this yearning went deeper than that. She kept thinking of him saying she'd seen the man in him.

She had the sense he saw the woman in her. He wasn't staring at her chest. He was looking into her eyes. He wasn't sneering at her sordid history. He had asked her to tell him about it and wanted her in spite of it. She wanted what he was really offering her: acceptance.

"I'll hate myself either way," she acknowledged. "What's one more night?"

A growling noise resounded from his chest. Disapproval? Agreement?

He leaned closer. His free hand cupped her throat above the collar of silk, so she became ultra-aware of her quickened pulse as it thumped against his palm. Her breath stuttered.

He nuzzled the corner of her mouth with restless lips, sharpening the yearning within her to a razor's edge. Her hands were trapped in the small of her back as he used his weight to press her into the doorjamb. The wool of his trousers abraded the silk of her gown, shifting the slit open so she felt the coarse fabric against her inner thigh.

She tried to catch her breath, but her breasts were crushed by his chest. A small, helpless sigh escaped her, parting her lips. Her mouth wanted to find his. He was toying with her, though. Touching soft, soft kisses to her chin and the indent of her upper lip and beneath the pout of her lower one.

Her lips stung with anticipation as he teased her. When she couldn't stand it any longer, she flicked out her tongue, striking against the smooth flesh of his bottom lip.

With a gruff noise, he angled his mouth across hers, smothering her small cry of surprise as he swept her into a stark, untamed place. Colors shot behind her closed eyelids.

In an instant, she was both trapped and utterly free. Soaring. There was a vague discomfort at the back of her head where it was pressed to uneven wood, but she was far more conscious of the hardness against her abdomen, his arousal unmistakable despite the layers of their clothes.

"This is what you want?" His mouth roamed across her cheek and his teeth lightly clamped near the stud in her ear. Every hair on her body stood up.

She shouldn't want this. Of the many things she wanted, above all she wanted to feel safe. This man was not safe. He wouldn't hurt her. She was as sure about that as she could be, but he wasn't promising more than a few hours of pleasure. Her instincts for self-preservation, honed to a fine point by a lifetime of dealing with users and sycophants, were utterly failing her where he was concerned. She could feel herself succumbing to him because she was unwilling to fight herself.

One night, she kept repeating to herself. One night of pleasure. Of forgetting. She was entitled, wasn't she?

It wouldn't be enough. She already knew that. She wanted to know him more than physically. She wanted to know him intimately—even though she had the sense he would remain an enigma his whole life, never allowing anyone to really know him.

Everything about their coming together was tragically ill-advised, but her desire to be in his orbit, to feel his touch and hold his attention and *be* his for even a very short while, was too tempting to resist.

With a small shudder, she let go of doubt and worry about repercussions and surrendered to the inevitable. "Yes."

He lifted his head and stepped back. "Go to my room, then."

Her stomach was full of butterflies that soared into her chest. She led him to the end of the hall on shaking legs, hyperaware of his heavy steps behind her.

His room was extravagantly beautiful. The ceiling gleamed with copper tiles that glowed like a sunset above the wide, turned-down bed. Frothy sheers over solid drapes covered the tall windows. A thickly loomed area rug cushioned her step, making the click of the door lock seem overly loud.

She was staring at the bed, mouth dry, when he came up behind her. He swept her hair to the front of her shoulder. The snug collar of her gown eased as he released its two buttons.

"I don't…do this," she said, voice unsteady.

He paused in unhooking the clasp above the zip near her tailbone. "Have one-night stands? Or have sex? You're not a virgin."

"I don't have casual sex." She rarely had sex. Her attempts at relationships always fizzled. Too many men were trophy hunters or manipulators, but that was why Magnus appealed to her so much. He didn't want anything from her but *her*.

"Neither do I." His fingertips trailed absently along her spine, down and up and down again. "But this doesn't feel casual."

He was right. It felt profound.

He released the hook and slid the short zipper.

"This gown is on loan. I need to be careful with it," she said as she caught the front.

He helped her step out of it, then gave it a light shake before draping it across the bench at the end of the bed. He turned to look at her as he popped his cuffs and opened the buttons on his shirt.

"It's not very sexy." She had stood before cameras often enough in minimal clothing that she shouldn't have been so self-conscious in her underwear. Heck, the black halter bra and high-cut, tummy-control panties were more modest than most bikinis she wore.

Nevertheless, as his attention wandered leisurely over her, she shifted on her heels.

"I'm not mad at it." He opened his fly and dragged his shirt out, baring most of his torso as he padded toward her. "These straps are kind of hot." He traced from where they met behind her neck down to the corset-like underband beneath her breasts. His fingers splayed against the cups, plumping her breasts into the deep cut of the cleavage.

She didn't know where to put her hands and let them settle nervously on his sleeves.

He was really…everything. Powerful. Broad and muscular and emanating a spicy masculine scent that she knew she would remember for the rest of her life.

She didn't want to look and think and wonder where to put her hands, though. She wanted the blind passion that made her *feel*. She stepped forward, gaze on his mouth, and tilted hers up in invitation.

His mouth came down in a passionate crush, sweeping her back into that place where she didn't think about how she looked or who she was or what the consequence of this might be. She gave herself over to him, not realizing he was moving her with the same fluid confidence he'd used on the dance floor until the cool wall met her shoulder blades.

"What…um…?" She tried to catch her breath, but couldn't. Not when she was looking into raw lust glowing deep within his eyes.

He began to roll her underwear down her hips. He crouched to set a small kiss on the skin he exposed above her navel, then below it. Her mind blanked as his tender assault continued. Another kiss branded the point of her hip. He sent a soft "Hah" against her bared folds, stirring the fine hairs, making her flesh throb with anticipation.

His lips nuzzled the crease at the top of her thigh as he helped her step out of her panties.

"Do you know what high ceilings are good for?" he asked as he blew gently against her folds again.

She could hardly make sense of his words. She shook her head, thinking, *I can't breathe.*

In a formidable move, he swept his arms under her thighs, rising at the same time.

A startled scream escaped her. She scrambled for purchase against the wall, knocking a painting askew and catching a fistful of his bound hair.

"You're safe, goddess." His breath was between her legs, her thighs braced on his shoulders. His wide hands splayed under her butt supported her. "I'm here to worship. I won't let you fall."

Her choke of disbelief turned to a fresh cry of surprise when he set his teeth in playful warning against the sensitive skin of her inner thigh.

Her legs quivered in reaction, trying to close, but it was too late. He buried his mouth against her nether lips and scored her with the wet lash of his tongue.

She was at his mercy, completely unable to get away. It was raw intimacy and exquisite sensations.

He wanted to annihilate her, she thought wildly. Nothing would be the same after this. Nothing.

But as hot spears of pleasure emanated upward and outward, filling her with joyous light, she didn't care. She wanted him to wreck her. She pushed the back of her head against the wall and worked her hands with sensual agitation into his hair, not bothering to stifle her moans of pleasure. The bodyguards in the hall outside the suite could probably hear her and she didn't care.

No one had ever done this to her. *For* her. She *felt* worshipped. She felt like a goddess. Pure. Powerful. Deserving.

She arched her back, angled her hips and guided his head, gasping, "There. Please."

He found the perfect rhythm with his tongue, lavishing her with intensely sweet, generous attention. It was so good, it was almost painful, yet she begged him, "More. Don't stop." Waves of heat built in her core. Her stomach knotted with tension. Her legs stiffened and her toes pointed. She bit her lip, trying to reach the pinnacle. "Please, Magnus. Please."

Climax arrived with the blinding force of a lightning strike. While she shuddered and jolted in paroxysms of pleasure, her moans of ecstasy bounced off the high ceiling and echoed around the room.

Magnus was shaking with exertion when Lexi's body slumped into weighty gratification.

He let her slide down until he could catch her in the cradle of his arms. He was so acutely aroused he wanted to throw her on the bed and fling himself on top of her, driving into her like an animal.

"I need a condom," he reminded himself, and went into the bathroom to get them from his case. He splashed cold water onto his face while he was there, trying to regain some semblance of control.

She was magnificent. His perfect match. The fact he only had one night with her infuriated him. A lengthy affair with her was one more thing he couldn't have and he wanted to bellow his rage at the world for it.

He dried his beard and walked back into the bedroom to find her waiting in his bed, sitting against the pillows with a sheet pulled up to cover her breasts. The black straps of her bra were gone. Her shoes were on the floor beside the monogrammed slippers he never used.

All the bitter acrimony within him hardened into a diamond that glittered and sent out shards of hunger and anticipation and lust. *One night.* He would make the most of it.

He removed a condom from the box and left the box on the night table, then clutched the packet in his teeth while he pulled the cord from his hair. The pewter wolf's head landed next to the box. He gave his hair a loose comb with his fingers, shaking it out.

She watched him, keeping the edge of her lip in her teeth as he stripped off the rest of his clothes. By the time he was naked, her eyes had widened with wariness.

"Still with me, goddess?" he asked gruffly. The beast in him snarled, unwilling to be denied.

"Nervous," she said in a small voice.

"Why?" He applied the condom and threw back the covers, exposing her very enticing form.

She let out a squeak of surprise and wriggled sideways, leaving ample room on the mattress for him to settle beside her.

He braced on his elbow, appreciating the endless expanse of pale skin that held a hint of gold. Her full, up-tilted breasts had beige nipples pebbled with arousal, making his mouth water. Then there was the shadowy valley between her shyly clamped thighs, calling to him.

"Did I not demonstrate that I'm an extremely considerate lover?" He traced a light caress from her ankle to her knee, then up her thigh to her hip.

Her breasts quivered as she took a shaken breath.

"I plan to give you so many orgasms, you won't have the strength to say, *Thank you, Magnus.*"

The noise she made was a catch between a sob and a laugh. "I want to call you arrogant, but I'm afraid you're only telling the truth."

"Let's find out, shall we?" He scooped his arm around her hips, dragging her close enough he could open his mouth on one of the very pretty nipples that were tempting him so irresistibly.

As he rolled the firm berry against his tongue, she moaned and ran her hands into his hair.

"I didn't know I had a kink for men with long hair," she confided in a husky voice. "But I like how it feels."

"Don't talk about other men." He was not so hypocritical he thought women shouldn't take lovers, but he didn't want to think about her with anyone but him.

He rose enough to press her onto her back and swept his mouth to her other nipple, taking his time as he laved and sucked, enjoying the way she slid her fingers through his hair as he did.

When he couldn't wait any longer, he rose to kiss her, needing the feel of her lips opening against his own. Needing the brush of her tongue when he invaded.

And she was welcoming here, too. He strayed his hand between her thighs and found her soft and plump and slick. He wanted to taste her again. He wanted to live his life with the right to explore her like this, easing his touch into silken heat, feeling her muscles clamp snugly around his exploring finger while her breath hitched.

Her eyes were hazed with carnal need. He looked from that exquisite sight to the roll of her hips as she lifted to meet the slow thrust of his hand.

"Show me how you like to be touched." He needed to learn *exactly* how to please her, right now, because he didn't have a lifetime to learn it.

He didn't have a lifetime to practice, either.

"Magnus, please." She swept her hands across his shoulders, then wriggled her hand between them, closing her hand around his girth. "I want to feel this. *You*."

He could have lost himself right there, from only her soft grip and erotic words. It killed him to give up touching her, but he shifted to settle between her thighs, pushing them wide with his knees to make room for his hips.

"I'm a strong man, Lexi." He was built tall and wide and burned off a lot of sexual frustration in the weight room. "I *really* want you." More than he'd ever wanted anyone. Ever. But he wasn't going to dwell on how disconcerting that was. Not when he was at heaven's gate. "Stop me if I get too rough."

"You won't."

She didn't know, though. She didn't know how badly he wanted to make her his.

Leaning his weight on one elbow, he guided himself to her entrance and probed. Everything in him wanted to thrust to his root, but her nails bit into his upper arm.

He froze and looked at where she was pinching his biceps.

"Sorry." She rubbed the spot. "I really want this to be good for you."

"Look where I am." He nibbled the edge of her jaw. "This is very good."

He flared his nostrils to take in oxygen, trying to keep a few brain cells working as her heat closed around his tip, threatening to burn him alive. He let his weight do the work, slowly settling his pelvis onto hers as he forged his way into a sensation that dimmed his vision.

As he arrived deep inside her, his back flexed with pleasure.

"Oh," she breathed shakily, as though discovering something new. Then she bent her leg to sweep one foot against the back of his calf.

The movement drew him a fraction deeper into paradise. Her hands stroked his ribs and caressed his back and found his buttocks. She tilted back her head and made a noise of luxury.

The outside world disintegrated. All that existed was her and this: the drag and thrust of lovemaking and the profound pleasure it gave them both.

Lexi woke cotton-headed. She was in a dark room. The tangled weight of Magnus's limbs pinned her to the mattress.

He was entitled to his arrogance, was her first lazy thought. He had delivered a string of orgasms that had nearly broken her in half.

"Stay," he grumbled when she tried to pull away.

"Nature calls." She dragged herself to the bathroom and used the toilet, then slipped on the hotel robe while she washed off her makeup.

Magnus came in, casually naked and burnished bronze by the muted night-light. He wordlessly handed her a toothbrush from a drawer, still in its packet. Then he closed himself into the toilet stall, emerging a moment later to brush his own teeth.

"Do you mind?" She picked up his hairbrush.

"Help yourself."

Her hair was nothing but knots, given the styling products she'd used earlier, then the sweaty lovemaking while he had tumbled her this way and that on the bed. He had seemed determined to wring every last sensation from every position he could dream up, all while making her his in the most indelible ways.

It had worked. She had thought she had a low libido, never discovering true passion no matter how many toads she kissed.

Tonight she'd kissed a prince, she thought with amusement.

She watched him cup his hand under the running faucet to rinse his mouth. He straightened and used a hand towel to dry his beard, stilling when he noticed her watching.

"What are we thinking, pretty bird?"

"That this feels like a dream."

His rumbled noise might have been agreement. He took the hairbrush from her and moved behind her, running it smoothly through the length since she'd already done most of the work.

People fussed with her hair all the time, but this felt different. His hand petted behind every stroke, as though he took as much pleasure in this act as she did. He was a prince, for heaven's sake. What was he doing, playing attentive lady's maid?

A scald of heat arrived behind her eyes that didn't make any sense. Or rather, she didn't want to pick apart why she felt so emotive. In this moment, she felt cared for, truly cared for, even though this was only sex. Once morning arrived, they would never see each other again.

"I don't want to wake up." She didn't realize she said it aloud until his gaze met hers in the mirror.

The hairbrush landed next to the sink and his arms came around her, drawing her backward into him. One hand dived behind her lapel to cup her breast. Her nipple tightened to a point against his palm. His other hand burrowed below the tied belt, finding the quivering jump of her stomach.

"I don't want to sleep," he said in a graveled voice. He nuzzled against her hair, seeking her ear. "Are you sore? Or—? Mmm…" A satisfied noise left him as he traced into her folds and found her slick enough to bloom against his touch.

She was very tender, but his touch was lazy and gentle. Even so, she was so sensitized, the friction was almost too intense to bear.

She covered his hand, stilling his touch, but felt his erection against her bottom, through the thick velour of the robe.

"I'll be so careful, Lexi," he whispered against her ear, tongue dabbling into the whorls, teeth teasing the rim. "Do you really want me to stop?"

"No," she admitted, closing her eyes against the watchful glitter of his gaze.

His heavy hand lifted beneath the weight of hers. His touch was barely there, but the knot of nerves at the top of her sex was so swollen, the barest roll of his fingertip had her turning her face into his shoulder. A groan of helpless desire escaped her throat.

"Tell me no one else gives you this," he commanded.

"No one," she gasped, arching her bruised nipple into

his palming hand. Climax danced as elusively as his caress between her thighs.

"You make me feel like a god." He pressed his wide, claiming hand over her mound.

Her hips instinctively pushed into that firm hold and she broke, awash in sensations that melted her bones, but that was okay. His strong arms kept her from falling.

He woke her once more in the night, rolling away long enough to put on a condom, then stayed spooned behind her while they spent a long time simply enjoying the sensation of being joined, caressing and kissing what skin they could reach, sighing with bliss into the dark.

When orgasm arrived, it came in long, rolling pulses that took Lexi out to sea like a tide. She drifted to sleep still rocked by the waves of pleasure.

Magnus must have fallen asleep, too. She had a vague memory of waking with a start when he drew a breath and hardened inside her.

His arms tightened around her and he said something in his language before he asked, "Are you asleep?"

She made a noise between dismay and reassurance, wincing slightly at the sensation as he withdrew, but she didn't want to leave this liminal state between dream and waking.

He rolled away, then came back to envelop her and kiss her shoulder. They both sighed and slid back into dreamland.

CHAPTER FOUR

IF IT WERE up to Magnus, he would have kept Lexi in his bed indefinitely, but it was never up to him.

Resentment was a wasted emotion, though. He had wallowed in buckets of it through those early years of learning who he was, but it hadn't retrieved any of what he'd lost. The man he had believed was his father was still firmly gone, turning his back in a way that still tightened Magnus's chest.

His siblings hadn't known whose side to take and Magnus had been needed here so there'd been a wedge there, too. His brother and sister were strangers to him now. There was nothing left of their childhood camaraderie. He'd even lost his mother, to some extent. While he had come to understand and accept her reasons for hiding his paternity, he'd lost a measure of trust in her that could never be regained.

But sacrifice to the crown was not just expected or desired. It was required. Becoming a king meant he couldn't indulge the man within him.

Or keep the woman who had given that man more pleasure than he could stand.

Steeling himself against the ire and bitterness over what felt like yet another theft from his life, he finished dressing and went back into the shadowy bedroom where he sat on the edge of the bed.

Lexi's neck was warm and soft. Her shift into wakefulness stirred his desire to crawl back into those sheets and lose himself again, but he made himself pull his hand away before she had finished fluttering her eyelids.

She tried to get her bearings by glancing at the clock and the place where daylight was coming through the cracks in the drapes.

"I let you sleep as long as I could. Ulmer is running a bath in the guest room. Your clothes are there. Vijay will be here shortly."

He leaned to snap on a lamp, flooding the room with more harsh reality that made her wince. He made himself stand and lift the robe off the foot of the bed, holding it ready for her, catching a flash of stunned hurt on her expression before she schooled it.

He didn't allow it to move him. This was his life. There was no changing it.

"Ulmer has your gown. He'll make arrangements for its return."

She said a small "Thank you" before she started to sit up. A strangled groan left her.

"That's why the bath," he said drily. He had felt as though he'd been hit by a truck when he rose. There was a certain euphoria in the ache of his sore muscles, though. He liked it.

With another muted whimper, she rose to thread her arms into the robe, hurrying to close it and fumbling with the belt, head ducked.

It was a bit late for shyness or embarrassment. It wasn't shame, was it? That thought bothered him, but she hurried out and he could hear Vijay arriving so he went to the lounge.

Vijay Sahir was second in command at TecSec, a world-renowned private security firm. Vijay always wore a calm demeanor along with an exceptionally nice suit. Not flashy, but reassuringly authoritative. His wife and her twin were fashion designers. They knew how to make an impression and Vijay always made a quiet yet powerful one.

After a brief handshake, he accepted a coffee and told Magnus he had forwarded a report on Lexi and the various threats against her. And, because he was very good at his job, the report summarized the threats Lexi posed to Magnus.

While sipping his own coffee, Magnus read through them.

Her reputation was top of the list, obviously. It was sullied enough that their dance would have a knock-on effect to his own, but associating with him gave her social cache she badly needed. Was that why she had invaded the breakout room last night and come up here with him?

Magnus didn't want to believe it, but the state of her finances was listed as a potential threat. She had alluded to financial strain and a need to find work. The report didn't outright accuse her of looking for a bailout or a sugar daddy, but the implication was there.

As for threats against her, Vijay had identified possible malfeasance by the agency that her brother ran, but he couldn't rule out their colluding on those things.

Damn. Given his position, Magnus could not afford to be anything less than suspicious of her. Last night began to seem more calculated on Lexi's part. She was an actress, after all.

Her had already resigned himself to having to distance from her, but now it became imperative.

Lexi didn't linger in the tub of lavender-scented water, even though she was completely disoriented by all that had happened and really needed time alone to put it all in perspective.

She was most especially disturbed by the remoteness that had come over Magnus after their intimate, passionate night. He couldn't have made it more clear that their night was over. She had known it wasn't the start of anything long-lasting, but she hadn't expected him to turn off like a light switch.

His businesslike demeanor had made her feel self-conscious about her nudity and a sense of being *too* naked had her rising abruptly from the water without washing her hair.

She dressed in the dark purple suit with an oyster-colored blouse that Ulmer had brought for her. His attention to detail meant she had everything: underwear, shoes, even a small toiletry bag with her hairbrush and makeup to hide the shadows beneath her eyes.

When she left the bedroom, she looked as professional as she would on a press junket, but she felt horribly exposed as she entered the lounge.

A man of South Asian descent rose from the sofa.

Magnus stayed seated. He set aside a tablet and lifted his incisive gaze to her, making her hyperaware of herself. She had to concentrate on not letting her ankles wobble or her smile falter.

"You must be Vijay." She offered her hand. "Good morning."

"Ms. Alexander. It's a pleasure to meet you. My children have discovered reruns of your show. The theme song is embedded in my ears."

"I didn't write it, but I always feel I owe parents an apology for it." She took a seat on the sofa opposite Vijay. "Do you live here in Paris? I hope I didn't tear you away from vacation."

"My wife's family is here and we have an office here. It's very normal that I have business when we visit. Shall we get to it? I have some concerns."

"Oh?"

Vijay didn't look at Magnus, but she felt the prince's gaze on her. She had the very strong sense she was about to learn something Magnus already knew.

"The X-Calibur Entertainment Agency. Your father started it?"

"Yes, but why is that relevant?" Why was her body suddenly buzzing with adrenaline?

"I like a big picture view. It allows me to see patterns. You have a silent stake in the company. Is that correct?"

"I'm a client, so I don't have anything to do with the day-to-day running. That could raise conflicts of interest." Accusations that she was given opportunities based on nepotism, as opposed to merit.

"But you receive a share of profits."

"I do." She was starting to feel like Swiss cheese, given all the holes that Magnus was drilling into her with his gaze.

"X-Calibur manages all aspects of your career? Contracts, PR, legal."

"All aspects of my life, really. Everything down to the

guy who delivers my groceries. My father always had a 'keep it in the family' attitude."

"Which means you trust the agency?"

"Completely." She said it with confidence, but had the strangest sensation that the floor tilted beneath her couch. "Why? Is there a reason I shouldn't?"

Vijay briefly cocked his head, and she felt totally thrown off-balance.

"X-Calibur has a hundred clients," she rushed to say, as though it proved something. "It exists because of me and my early career. They wouldn't do anything to jeopardize my ability to make them money." It was cold-blooded, but it was the way it had always been.

"I think it's how they make that money that deserves a second look," Vijay said in a neutral tone.

Her heart took a dip. "What do you mean?"

"You pay them to protect you, but I don't see an incentive for them to actually do that. Not when bad publicity and court cases generate so much revenue for them."

"The incentive is that I'm a creative asset. I make them money by *acting*."

"Do you?" Magnus asked.

His simple question was a harsh one-two slap, both of them awful. No, she wasn't getting acting jobs lately, and he didn't have to rub her nose in it, thanks. But as she met his iced-over gaze, she heard the darker side of his question. The suspicion. Was she acting *now*? Had she been acting last night?

"You're accusing me of staging all of this?" She waved at her presence in his suite. "I didn't even know who you were yesterday. *You* asked *me* to dance. You brought me up here. I wish I could get men to do what I want just by thinking about it," she added in a mutter. "I'd rule the damned world."

Magnus only stroked his hand over his beard while he continued to watch her.

Whatever delicate threads of connection had formed between them overnight snapped, leaving her feeling adrift in the cold vacuum of space, but she was used to that. It was happening on more than one level, in real time, as she absorbed that her family was not looking after her best interest, content to line their pockets at her expense.

"Are you suggesting it's no accident that my bodyguard was underqualified and my stalker knew where to find me?" she asked Vijay.

"If it's not deliberate sabotage, it's gross incompetence."

She rose to take a few agitated steps, mind exploding under this new perspective on her relationship with her brother and sister.

There had always been petty jealousies from that quarter. Lexi had been a hot property as a child. The more involved her father was in her life and career, the more rights he had had to the money she generated. His legitimate children had resented her taking his attention and gaining his approval even as her work paid for their vacations and electronics and other frills.

Lexi had always believed that those frills were enough to keep them on her side. They wouldn't shoot down the rocket that was taking them to the moon, would they?

An old suspicion tickled at her. She had always wondered if Hadley had set her up with those drugs. Her father had refused to hear it, but Hadley had been a little too happy that she'd lost that superhero role. Then, after their father died, he had talked her into that reality series, constantly pushing an image of her as a sexpot, spoiling her chances at roles with more substance.

She began to shake with a mix of fury and fear, incensed with herself for being blind to what seemed obvious, now that it was pointed out to her. She was also daunted by the fight ahead of her, but her gut told her she had to cut ties with X-Calibur and Hadley and Janet along with it.

"Firing them will be a nightmare." She was thinking aloud. "They have the machine in place to destroy me before I could pull myself free. I would need resources I don't have."

"Vijay also has a machine." Magnus broke into her thoughts, making her heart lurch. "One that caters to clients with more to lose than an acting career. I'll cover whatever expenses exceed your budget."

Ulmer cleared his throat, registering his disapproval.

It was demoralizing enough that Magnus was learning how badly her family treated her—and was offering to give her *money*. It was even worse that the judgmental Ulmer was witnessing all of it.

She gathered what little dignity she had left and said, "That's not necessary. I'll figure it out."

"I have a vested interested in keeping my name out of it," Magnus stated, turning the knife. To Vijay, he said, "Whatever it costs to tidy this up is fine."

You bastard, Lexi thought, fighting the heat that rose behind her eyes. Last night, he couldn't keep his hands off her. Today he would pay any amount to have his hands washed clean of her.

"Once I sell my share in the agency, I'll have ample funds to pay you back." She would sell her soul to ensure she cleared any debt she incurred with him. "Why don't we take this to my room so we can hammer out an action plan?" she said to Vijay.

Magnus rose as Vijay did.

Did Magnus think he was invited? Hell, no.

"Vijay can keep you updated," she said, channeling the most haughty of daytime soap divas. "To reassure you that none of this will splash back on you. Thank you for your assistance, Your Royal Highness. I feel I'm in better hands already."

Did her comment border on bitchy? Yes. But she was feeling stung and cheapened and *paid for.*

The glint of cynical amusement in Magnus's eye told her the remark landed, which gave her no satisfaction. She only felt obvious in her disgrace.

"Your things have already been returned to your room, Ms. Alexander." Ulmer moved to the door. "Any future communication may go through Mr. Sahir."

It was an ultra-polite *I hope we never hear from you again.*

As she walked out the door, she flickered him a dour look that said, *Same.*

CHAPTER FIVE

"LET'S GET THIS over with," Magnus said as he strode into the queen of Isleif's formal receiving room.

"Do not be so dismissive," Katla said coldly. "No, you may not sit. And you. Out." She waved Ulmer and the palace secretary, Yngvar, from the room.

Ansgar Palace was built behind the original castle, which stood on a bluff overlooking Isleif's main port. This room of relics and modern conveniences had a sunny view past the north tower in the mornings, but today the harbor wore a carpet of mist that obscured all but the highest rigging on the container ships unloading their wares.

"I am thirty-two years old, Your Majesty," Magnus said with pithy, exaggerated patience. "I do not appreciate being treated as though I'm *two*."

"Welcome to the royal family, Magnus. It comes with expectations that you behave like an adult in order to be treated like one. When you fail to do that, you will be scolded. What were you *thinking*?" Her voice was not overloud, but held enough dismay to ring in his ears.

"That I wanted to get laid—which is a very adult occupation." His aim was to offend, but he immediately regretted his crudeness. Vijay might have handed him a bouquet of red flags where Lexi was concerned, but she had been more than a piece of tail.

"Get yourself a wife if that's what you want," Katla said.

"What century is this? I won't marry for sex."

"You'll marry because you must."

"No." Despite the way they locked horns, he didn't hate his half sister. He hated the way he had found out about her. He hated the world she had dragged him into. He hated the power she had over him, not because of her title, but because he liked and respected her. He hated that she held him to a higher standard than he wished to adhere to. He hated that he hated to disappoint her. He hated that she was almost always *right*.

"I can't have children, Magnus. I have tried." Her voice was pitched between the weariness of having to repeat herself and the steely tone she used when her emotions were riled. "It falls to you."

"Why?" he demanded, also weary with this conversation. "You were considering adoption before you found me. Why is that not still an option? You *want* children."

"I'm too busy with the colicky infant I have, aren't I?" She rose in a rustle of her bespoke pantsuit, walking away to hide her expression. "I have continued to hope that I could somehow…" Her voice trailed off, then resounded with heavy fatalism. "They won't let me try another surrogate. My frozen eggs have been deemed unviable."

She was fifty-four and had spent the better part of three decades trying to produce an heir. A twinge of pity had him backing down. Katla wanted children, truly wanted them. Not for the crown, although that was expected, but for herself and her husband, Prince Sorr.

Magnus didn't really understand the impulse. Yes, he

had fond memories from his youth, but he mostly remembered a desire to hurry those years. He'd been impatient to grow up so he could pursue his own interests. His younger siblings, with their shorter legs and dependence on his greater maturity, had been an encumbrance who had held him back.

An old spear of guilt went through him at taking them for granted. He would go back to those days in a heartbeat if he could, but he still didn't understand the urge to take responsibility for another human life. Katla already held responsibility for all the lives in a kingdom. Who the hell would want to raise a child with the expectation that they must shoulder the same burden? Given all Magnus had learned about duty to a crown, bringing a child into this role struck him as an act of cruelty.

As though Katla knew what he was thinking, she said, "You of all people should not be advocating I snatch a child from the street and turn them into my heir. No, Magnus, that is your cross to bear."

He knew. He could fight it all he wanted, but it had been drilled into him from the time his DNA had proved he came from the Thorolf bloodline that he would continue that line.

"Could you have chosen anyone more unsuitable with which to dally?" she grumbled.

"Shall I try?"

"I have already made a career of apologizing for one man's behavior." Katla turned to him, tall and regal and firm. Her expression was dispassionate. "Do not make your inability to keep your libido in check *my* cross to bear."

"It was one night," he said through his teeth. "As far as the world is concerned, we danced *once*." Thanks to

Vijay and his concisely worded threats to hotel management, any proof that Magnus had done anything more
with the notorious Lexi Alexander was firmly erased,
suppressed and filed under "unfounded gossip."

"Ulmer tells me you're paying for her security detail?"

"Why do you employ a man who can't keep his mouth
shut?" He turned to face the window. "File it under chari-
table donations," he added in an ironic drawl.

"You can't support her, Magnus. You had an affair,
fine. It's done. But let it be done."

"Paying for her protection is the most expedient way
to ensure my own. As long as I'm footing the bill, I'm as
much Vijay's client as she is."

That's why Vijay had given him the report that had
raised all of Magnus's suspicions around her motives. In
his quest to detach himself from her, Magnus had expected every reaction from wheedling to defensive anger.
She'd only been insulted. Hurt. And pale with shock over
what she'd learned about her family.

"I haven't spent the last two decades restoring peace
and prosperity so you can set us back by chasing skirt."
Katla's demeanor turned regal. This was no longer a discussion. It was a decree. "People need to see stability and
continuity. You must marry, Magnus. Produce children.
Show them what the future looks like."

It was not a future he longed for. Why would it inspire
anyone else?

"I've asked Ulmer to prepare a list. Introductions will
begin in the next few weeks." She rang the bell to dismiss him.

It might as well have been the rattle of a guillotine
blade coming down.

* * *

Over the next eight weeks, Lexi leaned heavily on the small but mighty team that Vijay had put in place for her. They were astonishingly competent, giving her the fairly simple task of stalling Hadley and any other calls from the agency while they quietly set up a chain of events like dominoes.

Thank goodness they were good at their jobs, because she was a wreck. She blamed her forgetfulness and moments of emotional tearfulness on the upheaval of realizing her family had absolutely no regard for her, but the deeper ache was Magnus.

Which was stupid. She'd spent one night with him, whereas Hadley and Janet were fixtures in her life. There had always been animosity there, though. With Magnus, for at least a few hours, she'd thought there'd been accord. Synchronicity. Something powerful that was—

An illusion, she reminded herself harshly.

Sex. They had had sex. It was good sex, which was nothing to be ashamed of. The shame was in her pining for a man who had wondered after the fact if she had singled him out for her own gain.

She was the one who had been used. Did he really believe she would do that to someone else?

Apparently, he did.

I have a vested interested in keeping my name out of it.

She felt sick, literally nauseous, every time she thought of that horrible morning.

Don't think of it.

Today was a big day. Not only did she finally have a meeting scheduled with Bernadette Garnier, but Lexi's new lawyer would walk into Hadley's office this afternoon and present her brother with the one-two punch of informing him that she was leaving as a client and also wanted to sell her share in the agency. Hadley had the right of first refusal, but she knew for a fact that her leaving the roster would impact the agency's value, especially if bad press followed.

Hadley had a decision to make. Did he want to sign an NDA and settle things quietly? Or cause them both to suffer financially by making it public that she was leaving? She had a very unflattering statement prepared on how poorly he'd treated her. He would want to think twice about starting a PR war.

At this point, Lexi didn't care how much money she came away with, so long as she was free. She hated herself for trusting Hadley as long as she had. It undermined her confidence in herself and her own decisions.

She also hated that she had Magnus to thank for bringing Vijay's shrewd assessment into the picture. It meant that she couldn't paint Magnus as a heartless villain and absolve herself of responsibility for their night together.

No, she'd been a very willing participant and she was a weak-minded fool for wishing she could have had more time with him.

With a frustrated groan, she left her walk-in closet, startled to find her mother setting up at the dressing table.

"What's wrong?" Rhonda asked.

"Nothing. I didn't realize you were here already." Lexi threw a handful of blouse selections onto the bed.

"Are you nervous?" Her mother waved at the seat. "Is that why you called me to do your makeup instead of using Sharla? You're going to be great, doll. You always land these things."

Not true, but Rhonda had never let Lexi wallow in discouragement. She was a faithful cheerleader, but she had also pushed her daughter too hard from too early an age.

"I hadn't seen you lately," Lexi prevaricated. "This was a good excuse to catch up." And she no longer trusted Sharla, who was yet another technician booked through the agency.

Lexi hadn't told her mother she was leaving X-Calibur. Rhonda still had a lot of ill will against Lexi's father. Lexi had learned a long time ago not to bring up her father's family at all with her mother if she could help it.

"How are things with Wayne?" she asked instead, listening as Rhonda complained about the car her boyfriend had bought her. He was twenty years her senior and had a very nice house in Malibu that her mother had moved into. Her mother had always known how to take care of herself.

"Why are you so pale?" Rhonda asked as she blended the foundation across Lexi's forehead and cheeks.

"I can't even go onto the balcony for sun. There was a drone out there the other day."

"Hmm. Well, I don't want you to look like you're trying too hard. I'm using a light hand. Wear the pink top." She flickered her gaze to the bed. "That will put some color into your face. But if I didn't know better..." She turned Lexi's face in each direction, expression concerned.

"What?" Lexi demanded.

"Nothing." Her mother dug through her case for a different brush. "You said it was only a dance. I believe you. You haven't been seeing anyone else, have you?" She slid a sideways look at Lexi.

"Like a man? I'm not pregnant, Mom!" Lexi didn't

have to act shocked. It genuinely hadn't occurred to her. They had used condoms.

"Good. I did my time with a baby on set. I won't go back to it." Her mother worked on her eyes, sweeping contouring strokes and colors over her closed eyelids. "The baby would be a prince or something, wouldn't it? Think of the security you'd need! And custody? You know how ugly things became with your father."

"Mom." She caught her mother's hand. "Please. Trust me. I'm not pregnant." Absolutely not. It couldn't happen. No, no, no.

But even her wildly unpredictable cycle had never gone a full two months without showing up.

A cold sweat took hold in Lexi's lower back as she realized she hadn't had a period since before Paris.

She couldn't be pregnant, though. Magnus had used condoms.

And he really would hate her if that happened.

I have a vested interest…

It took all her control to pretend she wasn't dizzy and clammy while her mother finished her makeup and did her hair.

"Break a leg, baby." Her mother kissed the air near her cheek. "Text me later, tell me how it goes."

"I will." She smiled weakly.

After her mother left, Lexi rose, still feeling lightheaded. She called to make a doctor's appointment while she dressed, then walked to her waiting car.

Her mind couldn't seem to grasp a proper thought. The drive through the city happened without her awareness. Suddenly Ola, her favorite bodyguard, was standing on the curb outside the open back door of the SUV.

"All right, Lexi?"

"Pardon? Yes. Just thinking."

Snap out of it, she berated herself.

But what would this mean for her chances for landing *any* role if she was pregnant? At least her shares in the agency provided her a small but predictable income. If—

No. She would worry about a baby if there was one. In this moment, she wasn't pregnant. She absolutely could not be.

She walked through the lobby of Bernadette's hotel feeling as though she walked through gelatin and found the director waiting at a table on the terrace. She was a sophisticated sixtysomething with a smooth gray bob.

The meeting went well. Bernadette had already read the book that Lexi wanted to adapt and not only saw Lexi in the lead role, she had ideas for additional financing.

Lexi walked out on unsteady legs, optimistic about her career for the first time in years. As she arrived home, she received a text from her lawyer.

X-Calibur has been notified. I'll call later with details.

Also good news, but it didn't stop her from running to the toilet, where she threw up every bite of food she'd eaten.

Aside from confirming with her doctor, Lexi told no one, still in a state of denial because a baby would be such a huge life change. She couldn't understand how it had happened. Why now? *No.*

The morning sickness said yes, but for the rest of each

day she was able to pretend it wasn't real, which was helpful because she couldn't fathom bringing a baby into this messy life of hers. Hadley was making a quiet fuss, trying to woo her back, but at least he wasn't taking it to the public sphere.

That threat of a scandal and a spotlight would always be present in her life, though, which meant any children she had would also live under a microscope. Actors might bring babies onto sets these days, but she knew the downfall of growing up on one.

She also knew parenting was *hard*. Her mother had always had ample funds, thanks to support payments from Lexi's father, but she had struggled in other ways. And Lexi knew for a fact that the most serene, sentimental moments of a mother holding a baby on film were achieved after hours of waiting for that baby to stop screaming its lungs out.

Parenting was not as easy and romantic as it was portrayed. This was a terrible time for her to become one.

She was pro-choice all the way so she didn't feel she *had* to have the baby, but each time she considered not having it, she couldn't hold on to the thought.

When Bernadette invited her to stay with her at her home in Nice, and said, "One of my regular investors is in Monte Carlo. You can help me charm him," Lexi eagerly went.

Filming was at least two years away. Her pregnancy wouldn't be a factor, but Lexi wanted to look for a new home. France had stricter privacy laws than the US and there were some very discreet maternity clinics in Switzerland.

She might be telling herself she hadn't made a decision, but she was making decisions as though she had decided.

What would Magnus say about her having his baby, she wondered? She would hide her pregnancy as long as possible, but once paparazzi got wind of it, they would speculate the baby was his. She had to warn him before that.

She wasn't ready to face him, though. Their night haunted her, sparking every emotion from erotic thrill to wistful longing to the ache of rejection. The only thing she couldn't seem to feel was regret.

Did he regret their affair? He might, once he learned about the baby. Would he blame her? Accuse her of orchestrating this? They'd been *his* condoms that he had applied. It wasn't her fault they'd failed.

Oh, she *dreaded* telling him she was pregnant. That was the real reason she was pretending it wasn't actually happening.

She would tell him when she had all the pieces in place to raise this baby alone, because that's what she planned to do. Yes. She had decided.

Then she walked into a cocktail party in Monte Carlo and there he was.

As a teen, Magnus had aspired to become an Olympic athlete, but he'd always seen the tech industry as his eventual career. Thanks to Katla's strategic marriage, Isleif was a growing hub of innovation. Magnus was continuing what Prince Sorr had started by attending trade conferences and high-level summits around every aspect of tech, most lately the impacts of AI, but he was also tasked with encouraging multinational tech companies to set up shop in Isleif.

Many heads of such conglomerates had homes in Monte Carlo, the most expensive real estate in the world. Going to a party there provided casual introductions and it was also a suitable place for a first date with the woman at the top of Ulmer's list of suitable brides.

Lady Annalise was visiting her cousin in Monaco, a woman who had married into the royal family here. Annalise ticked all the boxes for a future queen: she was a blue-blooded philanthropist, cultured, and had no troublesome scandals in her history. She was stylish and had a quick wit and knew how high-society games were played. She was not averse to moving to a tiny country in the North Atlantic. In fact, their marriage had the potential to strengthen ties with the royal family here in Monaco as well as her highly placed relatives in Denmark.

Magnus really wanted to feel something for her, but she left him stone cold.

They were standing on the terrace of a villa, listening to someone drone on about winning a painting at an auction when Magnus felt the air change. *Charge.* It was as though a thunderstorm gathered, but the sky remained clear and the breeze stayed soft.

He swiveled his head to the party inside and took an invisible kick to his gut.

Lexi. She stood at the top of the three shallow steps that led from the foyer into the columned living room. She was looking to the right while leaned down to hear the chic, gray-haired woman beside her.

Someone moved and Magnus was able to see her gown was an ethereal blue that looked as though it had been designed by the ancient Greeks. Its one-shoulder style was held up by braided silver cord against her golden skin. A matching band underscored her generous breasts while the skirt fell in a graceful curtain that hid the navel he'd kissed. The hips he'd bracketed with his hands. The thighs he'd pushed apart, then felt grip his waist.

He never allowed himself to search her name, even though she was top of mind from the moment he woke and through his colorless days, then into his fitful, erotic dreams. The few times he had broken down for a glimpse of her, all he saw were trolls and clickbait nonsense. That made him furious on her behalf, which brought on a wave of guilt because, for a few minutes that morning in Paris, *he* had thought the worst of her.

Aside from early attempts by the press to link them, however, she had managed to quash speculation that they were romantically involved.

Being a card-carrying hypocrite, he was quietly furious about that, too. He wanted her to betray some hint that she was as obsessed as he was. Because he still wanted her. She was an itch within him he couldn't scratch, one that was driving him mad.

His blood caught fire as he stared at her through the crowd.

She nodded at her friend, then cast her gaze around the party—and froze. Her pink lips parted in shock before she abruptly looked down at the steps and melted into the crowd.

There was a ripple of laughter in the people around him so he pulled his attention back to the conversation even as Annalise excused them, saying she was cold and wanted to step inside.

"Did you already know the punchline of his story?" she asked as they reentered the din of the party.

"No." Magnus didn't even remember what the man had been talking about.

"Oh. I thought you were bored with them. You seemed to check out on us. That's why I said we should come in."

What could he say? His inner beast was off-leash, stalking the crowd for—

"Oh, look! It's Paisley Pockets!" Annalise clutched his arm with subdued excitement.

No. His adrenaline surged and he followed her gaze, locking on Lexi, but whatever came into his face made Annalise sober.

"You didn't like her show? It's all I watched growing up. I *loved* it." Her tone panged with nostalgia.

"Are you referring to Lexi Alexander?" He glanced again in Lexi's direction, trying to sound disinterested while swallowing her with his eyes.

She had her back to him. Her hair was loosely braided. The tail sat between shoulder blades that struck him as tense, even from across the room.

She's been in trouble with the law.

That's what he should have said, but he couldn't bring himself to denigrate her. To gossip like a busybody neighbor.

"Would you like to meet her?" He was being *polite*.

"You know her?" Annalise brightened with curiosity.

"We met briefly in Paris earlier this year." It had been brief. Too brief.

"Will you think me ridiculous if I say yes?"

She didn't know the meaning of the word. This was *ab-*

surd, but he took her across the room to where Lexi was speaking to the gray-haired woman and a heavyset man.

Lexi was an exceptional actress because, after the slightest stiffening of shock, she beamed with courtesy and welcome.

"Your Royal Highness." Her gaze flickered over his tuxedo in a way that made him wish it was her hands before she swept her attention back to his face. "How nice to see you again."

"Ms. Alexander." He held her gaze, quietly affronted by her use of his title. He was Magnus and she was Lexi. God and goddess. Or had she forgotten? "Lady Annalise wanted to say hello."

"I was such a fan growing up," Annalise gushed, clasping both her hands around the one that Lexi offered.

"You're very kind." Lexi smoothly accepted the praise before introducing her friend, a film director, and a man in town for the high-stakes poker tournament that began tomorrow.

A lively discussion of the gamble of filmmaking ensued. As everyone bantered, Magnus waited for Lexi's gaze to come back to his, but she stubbornly looked at anyone *but* him, all while wearing a bright, engaged smile.

"When does filming start on your project?" he asked her directly.

"Oh. It's, um, not confirmed yet, so a year or two at least." Her gaze barely lifted above his bow tie and her expression remained stiff before she quickly looked to her friend. "When we do get a green light, Bernadette has a lot of work ahead of her while I—" She pressed her lips together and tucked a nonexistent strand of hair behind her ear. "My agent— My *new* agent." Her gaze finally crashed into his but veered away just as quickly. "She suggested I write a memoir before someone decides to write an unauthorized biography, so I'm on the hunt for a quiet place here in Europe to, um, do that."

Was she self-conscious about writing about herself? For anyone else it would be a vanity project, but her story of working from the time she'd been a baby was unique enough to make for an interesting read.

Everyone chimed in with location suggestions, then the man excused himself to speak to someone else.

"We should be on our way, too. We're staying in Nice and it's getting late," Lexi said, glancing at Bernadette.

They had just gotten here and it was only nine o'clock. The drive to Nice took twenty minutes, thirty if you obeyed the speed limit, but okay. After polite goodbyes, the pair of women left.

"She seems so down-to-earth. I wanted to ask her for a photo," Annalise mused.

Good God, that really would have taken this farce to a new height.

"I didn't think it was a good idea, seeing as you're involved with her."

He bristled. "What makes you say that?" It was a real question because he had been concentrating on not betraying anything and Lexi had been doing an excellent job of the same.

Annalise tucked her chin, and her mouth pinched with admonishment. "It was like being between a pair of magnets that were turned the wrong way."

His chest hardened like concrete. At the same time, he had the darkly amusing thought that Ulmer was right.

Annalise would have made him a good wife. She was observant and unwilling to put up with his BS.

"I'm not involved with her," he assured her. "It was brief and it's over."

"Is it?" she asked mildly. "If you don't mind, I'd rather leave. I don't think this will work."

He took her home and he was still brooding on her skeptical, "Is it?" an hour later when he received a text from Vijay.

Ms. Alexander said she saw you tonight in Monaco. She wonders if you have time for a coffee while you're in town.

The animal in him lurched against the chain that was strangling him. He wanted to make time. He wanted to gather a fleet of a thousand ships and storm Nice, bringing Lexi Alexander back to his bed by any means necessary.

They *were* over, though. They were impossible. If he saw her to tell her that, he would turn it into something that was liable to destroy them both.

The struggle between what he wanted and what he had to do flashed him back to those painful early days of moving into the palace at Isleif. His siblings had been as confused as he was, asking with bewilderment, "Are you ever coming home?"

It had been agony to accept that everything had changed. The painful weight of the crown forced him to put Isleif first, tearing a rift between them that he had never been able to repair, one that continued to make him ache with loss to this day.

He knew what he had to do with Lexi. He knew it would feel as though he was amputating his own limb, but he did it anyway. He texted Vijay that same brutal word.

No.

He didn't hear from her again.

CHAPTER SIX

VIJAY TEXTED MAGNUS five months later.

We need to chat. In person would be better.

Aside from that one text in March that he had re-
layed from Lexi, Vijay's only texts since Paris had been
a monthly reassurance of "no concerns." Today should
have been the seventh of those.
  Not that Magnus was counting.
  He was definitely counting.
  Magnus prompted him.

About?

Possible vulnerability. Important. Not yet urgent.

I'm due in New York tomorrow.

I can meet you there Wednesday.

See you then.

  "Is that a meeting I can take, sir?" Ulmer asked when

he received the request from Vijay's assistant to firm things up. "I understood all training is up to date with the security team. Your schedule in New York is already very full. If he's merely pitching—"

"Find room. Tack it on to the end if necessary."

"We can't put off the departure time. You're due in Reykjavík Thursday."

Outwardly, Reykjavík was a diplomatic engagement. In reality, it was a covert second date between Magnus and yet another woman who did nothing for him.

"Am I correct to assume your meeting with Mr. Sahir relates to Ms. Alexander?" Ulmer pried. He'd been deeply annoyed that her presence at the party in Monaco had slipped through his otherwise Big Brother–level surveillance.

"I'll let you know once he tells me."

"Her Majesty will not be pleased."

"Then don't tell her."

Katla was tied up before he left so Magnus was able to skip any stern warnings against seeing Lexi. Ulmer was likely correct, though. Magnus had no doubt Lexi was the subject of their meeting.

Landing in New York, he pushed himself through the meetings he had scheduled, counting down the minutes until Vijay arrived at his hotel suite.

When he did, Magnus brought him onto the terrace where they could have a modicum of privacy.

"This is about Lexi?" Magnus voiced the concern that had been grating in him. "Are there new threats against her?"

"No. Her team remains vigilant, but things have settled

down now that she has cut ties with her brother. He faces a defamation suit if her name passes his lips."

After she had said "my new agent," Magnus had quietly looked into her settlement from X-Calibur. It was an eyebrow-raising amount, making him think, *Good for her.*

"And her stalker?" he asked.

"She didn't want to pursue charges for his presence at the Paris hotel, but he's now on a no-fly list. He also knows we're watching his every move. If he tries to sell Ms. Alexander's likeness, it will trigger another lawsuit. It's enough of a threat that he's moved on."

"Where is she? Europe?" God, he was weak, but he had the sense she'd done exactly as she'd suggested and dropped off-grid to write her book.

"She's in Switzerland. I'm going to see her on my way back to India. She wants to settle up on the services that you've covered, then restructure her arrangement with me."

"Meaning you'll reimburse me and everything between you and Lexi becomes confidential." His gut tightened as he realized his last tie to her was about to be severed. "You mentioned a vulnerability?"

"I did." Vijay squeezed the back of his neck, betraying uncharacteristic hesitation. "I've struggled with how much to tell you. I discussed it with Killian, actually," he said, referring to the owner of TecSec. "He said he had a similar situation once. In that case, his mandate was to protect the entire family so the ethics were clearcut. In this case, Ms. Alexander gave me permission to share pertinent details with you, but my problem is that

I can't be one hundred percent certain this detail is pertinent to *you*."

"I am a busy man, Vijay," Magnus reminded him with a roll of his wrist.

"She asked me to prepare a quote for additional security. For the baby, once it arrives."

"The—" Magnus had only experienced this complete blankness once before in his life, when Ulmer had said to him, *It's our belief that your father is not your biological father.*

A strange, searing pain arrived at the periphery of his awareness. A recognition of a truth that was too painful to accept, one that would blind him when it was allowed in so he mentally held it off, staying safely inside a bubble of disbelief. Denial. It wasn't real. He'd misheard.

A thousand years and less than a minute passed.

Slowly he became aware of being on the terrace in New York. The sun was on his shoulders. City sounds were far below. Vijay's expression hadn't changed, but an acidic burn of betrayal began to seep into his bloodstream.

"It's mine?" he asked in a rasp.

"She didn't say." Vijay pushed his hands into his pockets, expression turning circumspect. "I felt you should be informed regardless, since assumptions will be made that it is. She wants everything in place two weeks before her due date. The math from the end of October calculates back to conception in January, about the time we all met in Paris."

"Math." You couldn't argue with math, could you?

"Take your time. My first was unplanned. I know how it scrambles the jets."

"It can't be mine," Magnus blurted.

He had used condoms. He was supposed to marry someone appropriate. Katla would have him flayed alive in the town square. He might chafe at her lectures and Ulmer's interference, but he understood the stakes. He needed to continue Katla's efforts to repair the royal family's image, not prove he was his father's son by having an illegitimate baby—

This was why he used condoms!

But he had a memory of drifting in the twilight of post-orgasmic bliss, exhausted by lovemaking, then lurching awake to a strange sensation. The condom was slipping as his erection faded.

He'd hardened as he'd awakened still inside her. That damned woman seemed to keep him in a perpetual state of erection. He was twitching with arousal just thinking of her and their night of sensual debauchery.

The rush of erotic memory was countered by a cooler thought, though. Had the condom slipped enough to fail? Even if it had, that didn't automatically mean he was the father. She could have slept with a dozen men before and after him.

Even as he had that thought, he recalled how frightened she'd been that night in Paris, after seeing her stalker. How angry she'd been when she'd said, *You're accusing me of staging this?*

And he could still hear her admitting in the shadows of his bedroom, *I don't do this.*

He ran his hand down his face, giving his beard a tug hard enough to hurt, grounding himself into this new reality.

"She's keeping it." Obviously. She was seven months

along and making arrangements for the baby's protection. "This will be a PR nightmare. But that's the least of it, isn't it?"

"If the baby is yours, broader decisions become necessary, yes," Vijay said evenly. "I'm here to assist any way that I can."

If the baby was his? Magnus knew it was. That's why she had looked so damned uncomfortable when she had told him she was going into hiding to write her memoir. That's why his brain was exploding.

Secrets had been kept from him *again*.

Lexi covered where the baby was pressing a foot against the side wall of her round belly and smiled while trying not to yearn for the baby's father to experience it with her.

How could she want to see him when she was still so mad at him?

The prince is unavailable.

That was what Vijay had texted back the night after she'd seen Magnus in Monte Carlo five months ago.

Because he'd been on a date with Lady Annalise?

God, it had hurt to see him with someone else. It had taken her very best acting to pretend she was unbothered by the sight of them together, and to claim that she was "always happy to speak with a fan," and that Portugal did sound like a wonderful place to hole up and write a book.

He had been horrible to her that morning in Paris and he stood there pretending nothing had ever happened between them at all while she had thought her pregnancy must be obvious to everyone. How could it not be?

As much as she had dreaded telling him, her conscience had demanded she reach out.

The arrogant jerk refused to see her.

Devastated by his fresh rejection, she hadn't pressed it. Had that been cowardly? Sure. Mostly, she'd been embarrassed at having asked to see him at all. She had felt like one of those needy women who couldn't take a hint that a man wasn't interested. She had never, ever wanted to be the sort of woman who couldn't live without a man, yet she felt like one. Or rather, she felt sometimes as though she couldn't live without that particular man.

When he had rebuffed her again, she had made herself move on to prove that she could. She seized his refusal to see her as an excuse to delay telling him about the baby, sold her mansion in California and leased a flat in Zurich until she began to show. Then she moved into this private clinic where she wrote between swimming and yoga and birthing classes.

She didn't love regurgitating her past for financial gain, but the generous advance had been a nice boon while she'd been waiting on Hadley's settlement. He had paid a pretty penny for her shares in X-Calibur and included an additional settlement to avoid a forensic audit and an investigation into his PR practices.

Lexi would always be sad that things had ended on such a sour note with him and Janet. In her heart of hearts, she had always hoped she and her father's children would develop a closer bond, but there was something cathartic in letting go of that dream as she started her own family with her baby.

Now that was finalized, she could settle up with Vijay—and Magnus. Then, and only then, would she insist Magnus speak to her so she could tell him about the baby.

She wouldn't let his dating life get in her way, either. Yes, she looked him up often enough to know he was wining and dining every eligible heiress around the globe—amid rumors that he was in search of a wife. That stung, too. And if he'd seemed serious about any of them, she might have felt guiltier about keeping him in the dark, but as he was photographed in various places with various women, her pride had hardened her silence around their baby. *Her* baby.

After today, however, she would be out of Magnus's debt. She had put an offer in on a house in France where she and her baby would reside when not on set. Between the book she was writing, and the movie, and other investments, she had enough income to raise their child without Magnus's involvement.

It will be fine, she kept telling herself.

Her baby didn't need a close relationship with its father. She hadn't had one. Not at first. Her father hadn't wanted anything to do with her until her career had taken off and, frankly, she would have been better off if he'd stayed out of her life.

So she could almost convince herself there would be a bright side if Magnus preferred to hide the fact he'd fathered her child.

It would hurt, though. It would crush her on their baby's behalf.

But she and the baby would be fine. Somehow, someway. She would make sure of it.

She checked the time. Almost ten. She made her way to the foyer, where Vijay would have to wait for her since guests were discouraged within the residential part of the clinic, to protect the privacy of its wealthy, high-profile clientele.

The clinic was a beautiful chalet-style building situated above a quiet village in the Alps, one that could easily be mistaken for an upscale spa with its kidney-shaped pool and serenity garden and five-star chef. It had treatment rooms for massage, a gym and three very well-equipped exam rooms, plus two birthing suites and an emergency OR. Between the midwife, the nutritionist and her doctor, Lexi was being very well cared for.

The receptionist was on the phone, but she held up two fingers, then pointed down the hall, indicating Vijay was waiting in room two of the visitor parlors.

Lexi nodded and turned the corner, surprised to see Vijay outside the closed door.

"Ms. Alexander," he greeted politely as she approached. "How are you feeling?"

"Fine. You?"

"Fine, but mine was a real question. Is everything going well? No high blood pressure or other concerns that could affect our meeting?"

"My back hurts when I sit too long. And I'm getting to the stage where I need the powder room constantly," she added wryly.

He didn't crack a smile, only nodded gravely.

"I'll use it before we start. I believe there's one in there." She pointed at the door he had yet to open.

"I need to explain something before we go in. When we started our arrangement in Paris, you agreed—"

The door was abruptly pulled inward, creating a vacuum that nearly pulled her soul from her body and into the towering figure that blocked the opening.

Magnus. He was broader and more imposing than she remembered. Angrier.

Lexi had an impression of a dark suit and a green tie and a sensation of all the blood leaving her head. She watched his impossibly blue irises sweep down to her middle. An inward thump might have been a kick from their baby, but it might have been the impact of her heart landing on the floor.

His gaze came back to hers, rife with accusation.

Her vision disintegrated at the edges. Had she forgotten to breathe?

"Ms. Alexander." Vijay's hand closed tightly around her upper arm.

She tried to grasp on to him, but her limbs had turned to overcooked pasta. A ringing sound filled her ears—

The sight of Lexi's undeniably pregnant figure was still hitting him when Magnus realized her color had drained. Her eyelids fluttered and her eyeballs rolled back.

Vijay was already starting to catch her, but Magnus reacted in a flash, stepping out to gather her crumpling form. If she'd gained any weight since the last time he'd held her, he didn't feel it. So much adrenaline was firing through his veins, he could have lifted her over his head and carried her across the continent. She felt no heavier than a long winter coat draped limply over his arms.

"I told you to let me warn her," Vijay snapped, as Magnus carried her to the sofa. "I'll get someone."

"You were taking too long," Magnus muttered, but the door was already closing.

Patience was not in his wheelhouse. That's why Magnus had insisted on accompanying Vijay to this clinic. When he'd heard the murmur of her voice beyond the door, he had wanted the answers he'd come here for.

He hadn't meant to startle her so badly she fainted. He forgot sometimes that he was such a big man. She was tall and lean, but flexible and strong. He had remembered her as assertive and surprisingly adept at rolling with punches.

In his mind, he'd begun to believe she was using this pregnancy as a form of extortion. By the time they'd landed in Zurich, he'd worked himself into seeing her as a threat and arrived ready to fight.

She was pregnant, though. Delicate? As he lifted her head to adjust the cushion beneath it, he noted the soft curve of her cheek, the shadows beneath her eyes.

"Lexi?" He hitched his hip beside hers and set two fingers in her throat where her pulse was strong, if uneven. She was breathing, but her lips were colorless. Her hand was lax when he picked it up.

The door opened and a fresh surge of protectiveness had him standing to face the intruder.

It was a woman in a white lab coat with a stethoscope hung around her neck. Vijay came in behind her and closed the door.

"I'm Dr. Rivera. Can you tell me what happened?" She barely looked at Magnus as she brushed him aside and gave Lexi's sternum a rub. "Lexi?"

Lexi winced and twitched away from the light that the doctor shone into her eyes.

"It's Dr. Rivera, Lexi. Are you in pain?"

"No," she murmured, blinking her eyes open. "What

hap—Oh." She saw Magnus and turned her face to the back of the couch.

"Do you want me to ask these men to leave?" Dr. Rivera asked.

"How many are there?" Lexi looked around, then said sullenly to Vijay, "Are you planning to ambush me with anyone else? My brother? My dead father, perhaps?"

"Don't be angry with Vijay." Magnus stayed behind the doctor where he could see that color was returning to her lips. "I wanted to see you and didn't give him a choice."

"I'm not giving you a choice, either." Dr. Rivera straightened and looped her stethoscope behind her neck. "Stay here while I get a wheelchair. I want you in an exam room while we check a few things. Oxygen, glucose. We'll put the fetal heart monitor on you, to be sure everything is as it should be. No stress please, gentlemen."

"I apologize, Ms. Alexander," Vijay said as the doctor left. "This wasn't how I wanted to handle this. At all." He glowered at Magnus.

"Leave us," Magnus said.

No one ever defied him, but Vijay folded his arms and said, "Ms. Alexander?"

"It's fine. I was going to ask you today if you could contact him for me." Her voice was quiet and heavy.

As the door closed behind Vijay, Lexi started to sit up.

Magnus pressed her shoulder into the sofa cushion. "The doctor said don't move."

"I can sit up." She tried to brush his hand off her, but he only caught it, keeping the weight of his fingertips against the hollow of her shoulder.

He was still unsettled by her faint. Her cool hand twitched in his grip before she twisted it free. Her brow flexed and she bit her bottom lip, gaze skating toward the back of the sofa again.

Reluctantly, he straightened so they were no longer touching.

"Why did you want to speak to me?" he asked.

Lexi released a humorless choke and looked toward the basketball that was her waistline.

"Mine." It wasn't really a question. It was more something that washed through him like a visceral sensation.

Not that he'd had any real doubt. No, the greater surprise was the nature of this feeling that swept through him. It wasn't a cold chill, the way he'd felt when he'd been told his father was really King Einer. When that had happened, a bleak weight had fallen on him, one that had severed him from his old life and left him sick with loss.

This was the opposite. His life had flipped again, reordering everything he believed to be true. A similar crushing sense of responsibility crashed over him, but this time it expanded a force within him. Strength pulsed through him. Determination. *Fire.*

Why? Everything about this was wrong, especially the part where he was becoming a father. What the hell did he know about parenting? Neither of the two men he referred to as his father had given him a good example to follow. They'd each cut him adrift in their own way, leaving him floundering in strange waters, abandoned and questioning his self-worth.

Yet he was the father of Lexi's baby. He had a thousand pressing matters that he'd disregarded to come here and all he could wonder was *Where is that damned doctor?* He needed to know the baby was okay. That Lexi was.

"You're not happy," Lexi said heavily.

He hadn't been happy, truly happy, since he'd beat his own record on a giant slalom the day he'd turned eighteen. Things had gone downhill even faster than he had, once Ulmer had introduced himself, but at least that memory reminded him what needed to be done as the doctor returned with the wheelchair.

"Let's get you down the hall for your tests," Dr. Rivera said to Lexi.

"Add one more," Magnus said. "Paternity."

He didn't believe the baby was his.

She shouldn't be surprised. Or insulted. But she was both.

Lexi agreed to have blood drawn for the paternity test along with the rest. A nurse helped her change into a hospital gown and she answered all the questions about what she had eaten today, submitted to various pokes and prods, then tried to relax while the monitor recorded the baby's heart rate.

It wasn't easy. Every time she closed her eyes, she saw the thunderous expression on Magnus's face when he had pulled open that door.

"They said I could come in as long as I don't upset you." He walked in with the energy of a caged lion and closed the door behind him.

She suppressed her jump of surprise, but decided she would rather get this discussion over with than sit in pre-performance jitters, feeling as though she was waiting to go on a talk show for a six-minute mea culpa.

He had removed his suit jacket and wore a pin in his tie over a crisp white shirt. His hair was smoothly pulled back, his brows low with consternation. His shoulders were *so* broad. Everything about him screamed power, intimidating her, yet she reacted in a potently sexual way, too. She was accosted by memories of his lips pressing her skin, his wide hand between her thighs. His body surging over hers while lightning gathered in her belly.

She tried to swallow and looked to the pastoral painting on the wall, pretending that her cheeks weren't stinging with a bloom of sexual heat.

"You're the one who's upset," she said stiffly. "I hope you believe me when I say I didn't mean for this to happen."

"The responsibility is mine. I never should have touched you."

Oh, Gawd. His disdainful tone made her shrivel inside.

"Why am I the last to know?" he asked in that same aloof voice.

"No one knows you're the father. Only a handful of medical professionals know I'm pregnant and Vijay only knows where I am because I asked him to meet me here. I wanted to clear my debt with you before I told you so you'll believe me when I say I'm not asking for anything from you. By hiding my pregnancy, I can say the baby was born by surrogate and keep you out of it completely."

"Am I supposed to be comforted by that?" His tone was even, but she heard the roil of emotion beneath it.

"I knew this wouldn't be welcome news," she said shakily, touching where the baby was giving a reassuringly strong kick at the top of her belly. "I know the challenges I'll face if we acknowledge this baby is yours. We *both* have a vested interest in keeping your name out of it."

Her deliberate use of his words landed on target because he narrowed his eyes.

"You're deluding yourself," he said flatly. "On several fronts. That baby is going to come out at five kilos wearing a horned hat. There won't be any doubt that it's mine."

"I...don't know how much that is."

"Big."

She was afraid of that. Had literally been worrying about it.

Magnus muttered something under his breath and flexed his hands.

"This is me keeping my temper so I don't upset you as I explain why I'm very angry that you kept this from me," he said in a tone that was exaggerated in its evenness.

"My body, my choice, Magnus."

"Agreed," he cut in, still with that suppressed emotion suffusing his deep voice. "I appreciate that pregnancy is a huge decision. You needed time to consider whether you wanted to continue with it. Fine. Hiding the pregnancy from the rest of the world is also fine. Hiding it from me strikes a very raw, personal nerve."

"I tried to meet you in Monte Carlo," she reminded in a hiss.

"You didn't try very hard," he snapped back.

She couldn't argue that so she didn't bother.

"I told you I never met my father. My biological father," he clarified. "Everything about my relationship to him was kept from me until it was thrown in my face on my eighteenth birthday."

"By whom?"

"Ulmer. He found me at a ski hill, showed me some identification and asked to speak with me. My mother was born on Isleif. She still had family there. I thought he was going to tell me someone we knew had died. Instead, he told me Queen Katla was approaching forty and was childless. She feared she would be the end of the Thorolf line so she was forced to determine whether I was her bastard half brother."

"He didn't call you that." Ulmer knew how to make a person feel small, but he didn't resort to insults. Did he?

"It quickly became obvious that's what I was," Magnus stated with a sweep of his hand through the air. "My mother wasn't married when I was conceived, only engaged to the man I came to believe was my father, Sveyn. She genuinely didn't know who the father was, but she feared the palace would take me if I turned out to be the king's. She talked Sveyn into moving to Norway."

"Did she tell *him*?"

"No. King Einer was killed six years later. By then Katla was married and trying for an heir. My mother thought it would never come up again."

"Sveyn never questioned it? Did you? Do you look like him?"

"Enough. We're all tall with similar coloring. I thought Ulmer was delusional when he said what he did. I consented to the blood test because it seemed the quickest way to make him go away. Within a few hours I was confronting my mother, blindsiding Sveyn in the process."

A chill settled into Lexi's chest. She bunched a handful of the sheet that covered her legs, feeling the anger and betrayal coming off him as waves of icy gales and scorching heat, understanding that some of that was directed at her, for hiding this baby from him.

"That must have been a difficult moment for all of you," she murmured.

"It broke their marriage," he said starkly. "Sveyn left.

I haven't spoken to him since. For years after, my brother and sister barely spoke to me."

"They blamed you?" She flashed a look up at his grim expression.

"They didn't know what to think of me. Everything we had in common, everything we believed about our family, was a lie. I had to move to Isleif so I wasn't there to… Hell, I don't even know what my side of it was, only that no one cared to hear it."

Her heart felt squeezed in a giant fist. "Magnus—"

"It's water under the bridge," he said bluntly. "What I'm saying is, I would never do something like that to my own child. I wouldn't hide their parent from them. That's why this—" he waved a finger to take in the clinic and her pregnancy "—infuriates me."

"I understand." And she hurt for the young man he'd been. It explained so much about how remote he was, walking around as though infused with the force of a hurricane. "But I didn't know any of that. And if we're talking childhoods, let me explain where I'm coming from. When *my* mother got pregnant, my father shuffled her off to Arizona and resentfully paid her support, angry that she insisted on having me. I was six when I realized I was the reason we had nice things, and that other little girls didn't play house on film sets every day. It was only when my career began to take off that my father showed an interest in me. Once he got involved on the contract side, the pressure to work really hit. And when Paisley Pockets became a hit, Mom and Dad got into a huge custody battle that had everything to do with the value of my renewal contract and nothing to do with *me*."

She glanced at the monitor to ensure that her strident voice and climb in temperature wasn't affecting the baby.

"*I* want this baby. It had to be my decision and I had to know I could raise it alone. You think I don't know how it looks? Your first thought had to be that I plotted to have the baby of a rich man. Don't deny it." She waved an accusing finger at him. "But that's not what this is. I need you to believe that. I was waiting until I was in a position to *not* need you before I told you."

"I don't think that's true."

"I'm not lying to you!" She dropped her hand to her side.

"No, you're lying to yourself." He glanced with concern at the monitor. "You wanted to cement yourself into a life where you can raise this baby alone because you knew what would happen as soon as you told me."

Her heart lurched and she splayed both hands on her bump. "You're not taking this baby from me, Magnus."

"Of course not. I just explained why it's paramount to me that my child knows both their parents from their first breath. No. For such a smart, ambitious, levelheaded woman, you have been remarkably naive, Lexi. I can only assume it's fear. You're not wrong to be frightened. It's a hellish life you chose for both of you when you decided to have that baby. But you did."

"No, Magnus." She dug her heels into the mattress, pushing her back into the pillows because she sensed whatever he was going to say would be too big to withstand.

His flinty gaze flickered to the monitor and he seemed to choose his words carefully.

"I wish things were different, Lexi. I do. But that's

not just any baby. You knew that the moment you found out you were pregnant. That's why you've been hiding it. You didn't want to admit what that means."

"It doesn't have to mean anything. That's what I'm saying. You don't—" Hot-cold shivers of premonition were washing over her. "You don't have to be involved." She forced the words through her tight throat, but they came out high and desperate. Panicked. "This is *my* baby. My body. My *life*. *I* decide what happens to me. To us."

He said nothing, only looked at her with pity in his expression. *Pity.*

Goose bumps rose on her arms and prickled down her back. Her whole life had been fishtailing on ice since she had learned of her pregnancy. No, since she had first locked eyes with him. She had thought she had begun taking control over the last months, but now a cliff seemed to loom before her, offering nothing but a huge, foggy void that she was about to plummet into.

"No, Magnus," she whispered.

"I have a duty to produce the next ruler, Lexi. Preferably within the sanctity of marriage, but that part has been overlooked before." His lip curled with cynicism.

"I'm not marrying you."

He snorted.

"You don't want to marry me," she hurried to continue. "You didn't even want to talk to me five months ago. The morning after, even!"

"Lexi—"

"No. It would be a disaster. *You know that.*" Her throat grew hot and so did the backs of her eyes. "Your people won't accept me. Your queen won't. No to everything you're saying. *No.*"

"Do you think I didn't try saying that when it happened to me?" Maybe if he had sounded patronizing, she wouldn't have welled up, but he sounded *sorry* for her.

"I'm not unreasonable, Magnus." She was in a fight for her life. Her heart rate picked up and tension gripped her. "I will grant you some say over what happens to our baby, but you don't get to make decisions for *me*."

"I'm not making these decisions, Lexi." He didn't raise his voice, but it rang with power all the same.

She was trying to sink through the pillows behind her, through the exam table and into the floor. Anything to escape the invisible force that seemed to emanate out of him, pushing against her like the wall of a bubble that was going to break only enough to pull her inside it where she would be trapped forever.

She couldn't breathe, not enough to speak. Not enough to tell him to quit talking.

"History is making this decision for both of us. People think rulers rule, but we are ruled by precedent and necessity and duty. There are perks. The royal chest can buy you all the nice things you want. Every physical need you have will be amply met from now on. What is unaffordable to me, however, and to you, is choice. We are bound by duty to the crown."

"You might be." She reached for a tissue and blew her nose. "I'm not. Not to your ruler or your rules. I'm not…"

"Lexi. It's done. Unless that paternity test comes back with a negative, we started down this path in Paris. There is no fork in the road now."

"There *is*," she insisted, but her lips were quivering too much for her to say more.

"I'm upsetting you." He came close enough to cup her

cheek and set the pad of this thumb against her trembling mouth. "Believe me when I say I know exactly how you feel. You put up a good fight and I admire you for it. It reassures me that you'll weather what's coming. But save your strength for other fights because this one is over."

"It's not." The tears brimming her eyes overflowed, infuriating her because she wasn't a weak woman. "I have a p-plan."

"Cry if you need to." He reached for a tissue and dried each of her cheeks, expression dispassionate. "But accept it. I'm taking you to Isleif and we're going to marry. I have to tell the queen."

He walked out, leaving her with a scream of frustration caught in her throat.

CHAPTER SEVEN

MAGNUS RECOGNIZED THE irony in telling Lexi to accept their situation when he was still wavering between denial and anger himself, wondering if the paternity test would let him off the hook.

He didn't want it to. That was the truth. Beneath the rubble of this disaster was a pulse of anticipation. Lexi would be his, whether she was prepared to accept it or not. She wasn't wrong that her reputation was inconvenient, but the rest was tremendously convenient. Now he could have a wife who lit his sexual fire.

And yes, that fact was hellishly dangerous, considering that giving in to his lust for her had put him in this life-altering position in the first place, but he still reveled in it.

Outside her exam room, he found two of his own guards waiting for him. They must have come in with Ulmer. Magnus had asked Vijay to release Ulmer from the purgatory of waiting in the car. He and Vijay were now in the room where Magnus had been shown when they arrived. Ulmer was tapping his tablet, as usual. Both men stood as Magnus entered.

"Did you tell the queen?" Magnus asked Ulmer.

"Her Majesty is aware there has been a detour." He still sounded frosted by it, even though it had been a solid ten hours since Magnus had ordered it. "I told her that explanations are best coming from you."

"You know why we're here, though." Magnus looked to Vijay, who kept his lips sealed and shook his head, indicating he hadn't said a word.

"The service this clinic offers, and Mr. Sahir's presence, speak for themselves." Ulmer looked to his tablet. "Mr. Sahir and I have been running potential scenarios, projecting to a time when you might have a family to protect."

By the time they left this facility, for instance. Ulmer might be a stuffy pain in Magnus's behind, but he was very good at his job.

"Ulmer and the rest of our team can take it from here," Magnus told Vijay. "One of my men can drive you to the airport."

"I'll find my own way. But may I offer you my congratulations, sir?" Vijay extended his hand.

It was a very normal thing to say to someone expecting a child, but Magnus was thrown by it. Every one of his thoughts from the moment he'd learned that Lexi was pregnant had been around how to mitigate this disaster. Even Lexi had said, *I knew this wouldn't be welcome news.*

Now, without irony, Vijay shook his hand and wished him the best, as though Magnus's impending parenthood was something to be celebrated. Not in the darkest corners of his heart because it meant he could trap Lexi into marriage, but because a new life was on its way.

Magnus thanked him, still dumbfounded, and Vijay left.

"I trust Ms. Alexander is well?" Ulmer said.

"Well enough." He'd made her faint and cry. He had not said *Thank you*. Or *I'm sorry*.

Magnus steeled himself against self-hatred because mercy was also not a luxury he could afford to offer either of them. There was no escape from who he was. He knew that better than anyone, so he didn't flinch from doing the other thing that he already knew would hurt a woman who didn't deserve it.

"Stay," he said to Ulmer as he called the palace secretary. "The queen is expecting my call," he said when Yngvar answered.

Katla's voice came on, crisp and wary. "Yes?"

"An heir is on its way, as requested."

Her breath hissed in. "Not—"

"Yes," he stated. "Lexi is due in October."

"Paternity is confirmed?"

"Not yet. But it's mine."

There was a long pause, then, "Keep this confidential. Send me the results as soon as they're available." She kept her voice steady and impassive, but Magnus knew this was a blow. For her, decades of trying had resulted in nothing but heartbreak, whereas his casually strewn oats had sown in one stolen night.

An apology rose to his tongue, but he wasn't sorry. Not nearly as sorry as he ought to be.

"You're on your way home?" she asked.

"Once the doctor confirms she can travel, yes."

"I'll see you soon." She ended the call.

Lexi was pronounced healthy and released from the exam room only for Magnus to call her into the visitor room where Ulmer also waited.

"I've settled your bill and procured a nurse to travel with us," Ulmer told her, barely glancing up from his tablet. "The dining room will prepare an early lunch for you while I pack your things. What would you like to wear for travel?" He gave her sundress a squint, deciding, "I'll leave out something appropriate for you."

"Why on earth would you help me go to Isleif?" Lexi asked him with a catch of askance laughter. "You *hate* me."

"I apologize if I gave you that impression, Ms. Alexander." Ulmer was nothing but smooth equanimity as he lowered his tablet and gave her his full, polite attention. "Please tell me how I can make that up to you. Your health and comfort are of paramount importance to me."

Lexi choked, then sent Magnus a look of disbelief, unable to find words.

"You see?" Magnus said mildly. "Even Ulmer doesn't have a choice. He has to be nice to you, now that you're a member of the royal family."

"But I'm *not*. And I don't intend to become one."

"Let's talk about that while we eat." Magnus escorted her to the dining room where they were seated in a sunny corner in an otherwise empty room.

Exasperated, she looked over her shoulder, suspecting Ulmer was gaining access to her suite despite her lack of permission for him to do so.

"Look, I accept that the baby deserves to know their father." She was trying to sound reasonable but also in charge. "Your having a say in our child's life was always on the table."

"Good. I want my child born in Isleif. All of Isleif will want their future ruler to be born there."

"I—" She clacked her teeth shut, feeling outmaneuvered. With a jerky nod, she said, "I can see that. But it doesn't mean I need to go there now. It doesn't mean we have to marry."

"We'll go there now because you've been cleared to travel. That could change as things progress. I had plans, too, you know." He waited until they'd been served cucumber water and a wedge salad before he continued. "Before I learned who I was, I aspired to ski in the Olympics. The minute I arrived at the palace, Katla told me that racing was too risky for a future king. I had to give it up. Where are you at with this film of yours?"

"If you're about to suggest I give that up, you'll hear another hard no." She had worked too hard for this chance to revive her career.

The truth was, however, acting was something she did because she was good at it and it provided the income she needed. As an art form, it allowed her to temporarily reinvent herself into someone else so she could escape the messiness of her real life, but she had often wished there was another way she could make her living that didn't cost so much of her soul.

Not that she was willing to confess that to Magnus.

"The film is based on a book about a sex worker, isn't it?" he asked. "That's not an ideal topic for someone taking on the role of my wife."

"Oh, is your wife a *role*? Why didn't you say so? Is there a script I could read before I commit? What's my character like? What's my motivation?" She blinked with facetious interest.

"I understand your resentment, but you'll have to let it go." Magnus let his eyelids droop to a bored half-mast.

"It's not appropriate to take things out on staff. Ulmer and I play a game of tit for tat, but he won't be able to retaliate with you. I won't allow it. Take a swipe at the queen at your own peril. She'll find a way to punish you that won't allow me to take the fall. That leaves bickering with me and that's not a healthy way for us to behave as parents."

A sting of helplessness rose behind her breastbone. She had weathered difficult times before. She had always found a way to move forward. To retrench and rebuild.

This was different. This wasn't a case of checking her contract and threatening to quit if it wasn't followed to the letter. She had a baby to think of.

Magnus was thinking of their baby, too, in his way. He might not be acting like the most lovingly engaged father in the world, but he didn't want their child to be harmed the way he had been when he'd learned the truth about his own paternity. She had to respect his desire to be part of their baby's life. But marriage?

"Look, I will concede to going to Isleif to have the baby. Okay? But surely we can wait on marrying? See how we feel?" She used her most reasonable tone.

"Our marriage is for your protection, Lexi. If I have any tips on navigating what you're about to face, it's to grab any power that you're offered."

"That sounds horribly calculating. Is that really how it is for you?"

"Often enough that you should get used to it," he said drily. The pensive tension around his mouth told her he wasn't joking. Not really.

"I don't want to get married, Magnus. Not like this."

"Like what? For the sake of our baby? What would you

rather? Something romantic? A declaration of love?" He was looking bored again.

"No, actually. I don't care about that." She did, though. She blindly stared out to the glare on the pool, thinking she had always wanted someone to love her. Her. Not Paisley Pockets or the girl in the bikini or any of the other roles she had played.

Her baby would love her, but could Magnus? Ever?

She had her doubts and she refused to hitch her life to something so futile.

"I'm not a romantic. I haven't been allowed to be." She chased a cherry tomato with her fork. "I've always been a product. A vehicle for someone else to make money on. My own parents did it." She shrugged that off, even though it was one of her deepest agonies. "People seek me out because I can make an introduction, or I'm a stepping stone to raise a fan's profile online. The love I receive is always superficial, but the transactions around it give me something—income or free publicity or a favor I can call in later. Marrying you gets me nothing. In fact, I would lose my identity to a man who doesn't even want me."

"We're talking about Monte Carlo again?" He hadn't finished his salad, but he pushed it aside.

"You only spoke to me because your friend wanted to meet me." The creak in her voice was humiliating, but she pressed on. "You refused to see me when I asked, but the minute you learned about this—" she waved at her middle "—you want to marry me. Do you have any idea how debasing that is? How unimportant I feel?"

"Yes." He didn't move, didn't blink. "As someone who carries DNA that forces me to live a life I didn't want, yes. I completely understand your bitterness."

Oh, she wanted to hate him for his cool logic and supreme detachment. At the same time, she hurt for him. He must have wanted to crawl out of his own skin when he learned the truth.

"Then you understand why I don't want to be your wife."

"Princess," he corrected drily. "Queen, eventually."

"Now you're mocking me, which tells me I don't even have your respect." She pushed her own salad away.

"I'm speaking the truth. You might not think those titles have value, but they do."

She offered a distracted smile when their plates were removed, but on the inside she was a fractured mirror, everything offset and webbed with cracks.

"You said this pregnancy was your fault," she reminded him. "But I know you're suspicious of me. Do you realize that you need trust between players to make a role convincing?" Her eyes were hot, her heart heavy. "How could I pretend we're happily married when our marriage doesn't even have the most basic foundation? We have *nothing*, Magnus."

"Lexi." He set his hands on the tablecloth between them, palms up. Then he waited patiently for her to get the message that he expected her to give him her hands.

It was pure weakness on her part, but she couldn't resist touching him.

The moment she hesitantly settled her fingers into the heat of his palms, a sensual jolt traveled up her arms and into her chest where it rang like a bell.

He closed his grip before she could reflexively pull away.

"You know what we have." He squeezed again, as

though deliberately causing that jolt of power in her chest. Her breath grew tight and the spark in his gaze flew into her, setting her heart alight.

"Passion doesn't last forever," she whispered.

"Nothing does." His thumbs swept across the backs of her wrists. He might as well have caressed her from head to toe, given how her whole body felt brushed by velvet. "That's why we should enjoy it while we can."

Her pulse was skipping under the caress of his fingertips.

"I don't know—" she had to clear the rasp from her throat "—if I can do that."

The doctor had said there was no physical reason she couldn't have sex, but Lexi wasn't sure if she wanted to. She wasn't the svelte woman Magnus had lifted onto his shoulders and pinned to a wall. She felt unlike herself. Awkward and far too vulnerable to withstand that kind of intimacy, especially when she couldn't shake the feeling of being rejected. *Unwanted.*

At least, that's how she felt before he chided, "You think I didn't ask?" in a way that sent a sensual shiver down her spine. "There's no physical reason you can't." His expression sobered and he released one of her hands so he could tenderly sweep a tendril of hair behind her ear. "I'll let that be your choice, though. I'm ready when you are."

"You left it in my hands last time," she reminded him on a choke of humorless laughter, sitting back and settling her hands on her bump. "I think that's your way of absolving yourself of responsibility."

"No. I meant it when I said the fault was mine."

"I don't want anyone to be at fault." She scowled, disgruntled at his continued use of that word. "That makes it sound like this baby is a mistake and I won't call them that."

"Fair enough." He sat back, too. "I do respect you, by the way. Otherwise, I would have restarted our affair in Monte Carlo and forced you to hide it."

Her heart swerved. She searched his deepwater eyes, then shook her head with uncertainty.

"No. You had already decided in Paris that I wasn't someone you could trust." She swallowed the lump that rose into her throat as she recollected that.

"You know what I think is strange?" His brows came together in puzzlement. "You say deeply personal things about yourself so it seems like you're an open book, but your actions tell a different story. *You* don't trust *me*. That's why you don't want to marry me. You don't want to rely on me. You're terrified to trust me. Aren't you? Be honest," he warned in a hint of taunt. "So we can start building this trust we need."

"No, I don't trust you," she admitted, feeling as though the admission peeled the skin from her chest, leaving her heart exposed. "I don't trust anyone. Everyone I've ever known has let me down or betrayed me. An hour ago, the man I paid *seven figures* to protect me broke my confidence and told you I was pregnant."

"Because you didn't pay him," he said with an ironic curl of his lip. "I told him not to take your money. But I hear you." He nodded, pensive. "I'll work on it. You'll need to be in Isleif for me to do that. Are you hungry? Or should we be on our way?"

CHAPTER EIGHT

By the time they were seated in his jet, the paternity result had come in. Magnus glanced at the word *Positive* and handed the tablet back to Ulmer.

"Send it to the queen."

"I'm definitely the mother?" Lexi asked with a guileless blink.

She was seated in the recliner opposite his own. Aside from Ulmer, his staff traveled in the aft cabin, on the other side of the galley, where they were seated in rows like commercial flights. In here, Ulmer kept to his cubicle while Magnus had a sofa and a dining table, a bigscreen television, and windows that tinted at the touch of a button.

There was also a door to a stateroom with a bed. It was midafternoon, but he couldn't help noticing the tension in Lexi's expression and the washed-out tone in her skin. He was frustrated by her continued resistance to marriage, but he couldn't press her too hard, not when he kept remembering the way she'd been so limp in his arms, or how emotional she'd been while she'd been hooked up to all those wires.

"I know it's a lame joke," she muttered, shifting restlessly. "Everything has been so heavy and serious. Like a military operation. Is it always like this?"

"Often enough you should get used to it."

She grimaced.

"How are you feeling? Tired?"

"Why do you ask? Do you have to be nice to me, too?" she challenged lightly.

"No."

Her eyes widened in shock.

"I'm genuinely worried about you. As soon as we level off, I'll show you to the bed so you can sleep."

"It's two o'clock in the afternoon. How long is the flight?"

"Four hours. But you'll meet the queen when we arrive. You'll want to feel rested. Also, I didn't sleep on the overnight from New York, but I'm not about to leave you slumped in a chair while I stretch out on the bed."

"Is sharing a bed another thing I don't have any choice over?"

"It's just a nap, Lexi. Unless you choose to make it into more."

"I won't," she muttered, and turned her frown of consternation to the window.

A few minutes later, however, she accompanied him into the stateroom. She didn't remove any clothing except her jacket and lay down on top of the bed in her maternity top and trousers.

He did the same, only removing his shoes and jacket, then his tie and belt before he draped a light blanket over her and joined her under it.

Did he want to reach for her? God, yes, but he was also

content—disturbingly content—to simply close his eyes with the knowledge that she was beside him.

Where she belonged.

A discreet ping woke him. The recessed lighting in the floor came on, signaling they were coming into Isleif airspace and it was time to rise.

Lexi rolled to face him, eyelids heavy with sleep. "Do you want to feel the baby move?"

A strange zing went through him. Surprise and apprehension, but also excitement?

"Is it kicking?" He reached out.

She brushed her loose top up and slid the elastic panel of her trousers down, baring her belly, then she guided his hand on the tense ball of her abdomen. Within him, something restless eased as he finally had contact with her soft skin. Her warmth.

"I wasn't sure how you felt about it," she said in a small voice. "I know this isn't what you wanted. You haven't asked about the baby."

"I asked the doctor about both of you. I'm still processing this. Making a baby was something I knew I was supposed to do at some point, but it was an abstra—"

He swore as something nudged his palm, striking Magnus like a punch to the heart. A choke of wonder left him.

"Bizarre, isn't it?" He heard the smile in her voice, but he was enraptured with the swell of her belly.

"Does it hurt?" He lightly explored, searching out more proof of life.

"Not really. Surprises me sometimes."

"All I've been thinking about is the ways I have to adjust my life, not fully realizing… All we did was have sex, Lexi. Now you're growing a *person*."

"Did you still believe they were found in a cabbage patch? Oh, Muffin. I'm sorry to be the one to disillusion you."

"I don't know what I believed," he admitted, smirking at himself as he continued exploring the taut shape of her belly. "That babies were objects? A goal? Not…" The realization was creeping over him that he would have to shape this person the way he'd been shaped. There would be arguments and resistance and weariness. His own resentment at his responsibilities would be mirrored back to him and it would sting.

Even so, there was anticipation in him, too. He wanted to know what this new human would be like. Would they have Lexi's eyes and smile and guarded heart?

Her resistance to trusting him had been bothering him since she'd admitted to it. It told him exactly how much she'd been hurt in the past. And really, was it any wonder she didn't trust him to look after her? They were together one night and he had gotten her pregnant. Now he was crashing her life.

"I keep thinking I should apologize to you. Probably to the baby, too." He drew a slow circle with his palm, searching for another nudge.

"Oh, Gawd, I feel so selfish for making this baby have me as a mother." Her voice held laughter, but also distress. "Now there's this mountain of royal duties on top of it. Do you think they'll ever forgive us?"

"Maybe not. But I keep trying to regret that night and I can't." He hadn't been interested in anyone else since her. The search for a "suitable" wife had only fed his sullenness. Now, however, a different fire was flickering to life within him.

It was passion. Obviously. He wanted this woman in ways that were very base and sexual. But there was another aspect he hesitated to examine. The darkness within him had become less dark the minute he'd had an excuse to fly across an ocean and confront her. To *see* her.

Now she was here in his bed, in his life. They had made a tiny being who would bind her to him forever. That pushed the darkness even further out, but at what cost?

He didn't let himself think of it, only slid closer and gathered her in, allowing his hand to run up her back beneath her shirt so he could mold her new shape to his front.

She stiffened in surprise, then gave a small shudder and relaxed. When he dipped his head to kiss her, she tucked her mouth into his chest.

"I haven't brushed my teeth."

"I don't care. Kiss me," he demanded.

He was in this strange headspace of tenderness and possessiveness and wanting to consume her. It took great effort to gentle his kiss when she let her head tip back. He reminded himself that her trust was tentative, that she was wary.

When she ran her hand into his loose hair, however, and pressed the back of his head while opening her mouth wider beneath his in hungry receptiveness, he abandoned restraint.

He crushed her mouth the way he'd been wanting to since he had glanced across a party in Monte Carlo and saw these pillowy lips part in shock. He slid his knee between hers and grabbed a handful of her lush ass and plundered her mouth with his tongue, trying to slake a thirst that had been driving him mad for months.

She moaned and ran her foot against his calf and slid her hand to the back of his neck, tongue sweeping out to find his.

The ample swell of her breast filled his hand, the silk and lace of her bra an erotic texture. He wanted what was beneath it—soft skin and the pebbled nipple. He swept his mouth down to gently bite through the layers of fabric, liking the way she gasped in pleasure.

"I was afraid you wouldn't find me sexy like this." Her hands were running over his shoulders and back, shifting his shirt against his skin as though she wanted to tear it off his body.

"What does this say about how sexy I think you are?" He moved so she could feel his erection against her thigh, then lifted his hips and opened his trousers, inviting her to caress him.

"This is just you waking up, isn't it?" She slid her hand into his loosened trousers and cupped his erection through his boxer briefs, dimming his ability to think.

"What about you? Are you waking up?" He worked his hands beneath the panel that was bunched beneath the roundness of her belly, finding the lace of her underwear.

She drew in a sharp breath, but she didn't stop him, not even when he slid his hand around to her backside, pushing the trousers off her ass, down to her thighs so he could come back and trace the vee of silk that covered her mound.

"We, um…"

He liked how she'd lost her ability to speak. He slid a

finger inside her panties and traced folds that were slippery and hot. *So* inviting.

Her mouth opened, but no sound came out, only the hiss of her breath. Her nails curled against shoulders and her breasts quivered.

"You said—" She bit her lip. Her eyelids fluttered. "Our seats?"

"We can circle the airport…" He let his fingertip roll around and around the engorged knot at the apex of her folds. "As long as you need."

She gave a small cry and pushed her face into his shoulder, but her hand found the top of his briefs and slipped inside. Her fist tightened around his erection as she slid her knee against his leg, opening her thighs for more of his touch.

"Let me kiss you again," he insisted.

She did. Passionately. They caressed each other as they feasted on each other, writhing and perspiring beneath the light blanket, gasping and moaning until she set her teeth in his bottom lip and groaned with ecstasy into his mouth.

As her hips bucked in orgasm, he let his own excitement take him over the edge, mindful of the fact they couldn't really stay in the air while he spent hours making love to her, even though this was exactly where he wanted to stay.

Lexi was still feeling undone when she took her seat.

She hadn't planned to fool around with Magnus. Her desire to see how he truly felt about the baby had turned into sexual desire and one thing led to another.

Discovering they still had a powerful physical connection wasn't as comforting as she'd imagined it would be.

All she'd really learned was that she had even less will-power around him than she had believed.

The way he looked at her as she joined him, with lazy satisfaction and knowing possessiveness, only made her feel more at his mercy—of which he seemed to have very little.

Trying to avoid his gaze, she looked out the window where the sun cast golden beams across a collection of jagged islands, all wearing coats of emerald and ivory.

"Is that it?" She touched her forehead to the cool glass, studying the largest one. It was shaped like a bowl rimmed in granite teeth. A long, silvery-blue fjord stretched in a jagged wedge up the middle. The coast-line was a cliff that had been broken off by the axe of an ancient ice age. In the distance, a half dozen smaller islands stood like weathered pyramids. "I expected it to be covered in snow."

"It's summer. And we're not as far north as people think. Also, the islands were formed by volcanoes, so we have enough thermal activity that the snow only sticks in the highest elevations."

"It's really pretty." She squashed her nose trying to keep it all in sight as they made their approach, growing more enchanted by the second. "Is that the palace?" She pointed to a grouping of stone towers with spires and tile roofs. Stairs led from lawns to halls to terraced court-yards. A fat wall surrounded all of it.

"That's the original castle. One of Queen Katla's first acts was to name it a heritage site and return it along with its contents to Isleif. It's open to the public for guided tours. The palace is the long building behind it."

"Where you live."

"We. Yes."

We. He wasn't going to let up for a second, was he?

The palace wasn't as fairy-tale-looking, but she imagined it was modernized and far more comfortable than that magical-looking castle.

Seconds later, they touched down. Her nerves dissipated the way they always did when she was about to go on stage. It was a convenient Zen-like state that bordered on disassociation. It probably wasn't healthy, but it had gotten her through a lot of difficult times so she didn't fight it.

"Crowds have gathered," Ulmer informed as he brought Lexi a long coat. "Ignore them and move quickly into the car."

Lexi glanced at Magnus as she buttoned and belted the light coat that would disguise her pregnancy. "Do they know I'm here with you?"

"A video of us boarding is circulating online."

She had a quick look at her phone and saw herself climbing the stairs into the jet. Magnus's hand was splayed in her lower back, his wide shoulders shielding her as much as possible, but she'd been caught in a compromising profile.

Baby Bump or Booty Call? was trending, with comments ranging from *I knew it* and *#StanMagLexi* to *#golddigger* and worse. She clicked off her phone and dropped it into her pocket.

"Welcome to the cage, pretty bird," Magnus said flintily. He looped a scarf around her neck and set a woolen hat on her head.

"It's too big." She brushed the hat back before it slipped over her eyes. "I don't need this, do I?" He had just reminded her it was August.

"No, but I want you to wear them."

"Because they're Isleif colors?" She picked up the tail of the scarf, recognizing the stripes of blue and white and green.

"Because they're mine." He gave the edge of the hat a third roll against her forehead, smoothing her hair back from her cheeks as he did. "And so are you."

That should not have sent a frisson of pleasure through her, but it did.

"Sir?" Ulmer prompted as the door was opened and a fresh-scented gust of air came in, one that was sweet and cool and beckoning.

Outside, a cheer rose only to be abruptly cut off when the crowd realized it was only Ulmer. He was not the star they were waiting for.

Magnus took her hand and drew her out the door where he paused on the top step, holding her firmly in the loop of his arm as he casually waved.

"I thought—" Lexi noted that Ulmer was glaring at them from the bottom of the steps.

"Wave." Magnus leaned down to speak next to her ear. "They love shots like this, that look like I had something to say that was so urgent and personal it couldn't wait."

"Something that implies we have private jokes?" She cupped his bearded cheek so she could look into his eyes with her most captivated expression. "Something that says, *I've never been so enamored with anyone in my life*?"

"Damn." His pupils flared. "You're good at this."

"I know." She smiled her cheekiest smile and gave the crowd a wave that caused them to roar. Then she and Magnus descended the stairs without hurry and climbed into the waiting car.

The windows were tinted and they had a police escort to allow them to exceed speed limits, not stopping for lights, but the road was lined with spectators, many waving Isleif flags.

"I feel like they don't...hate me?" she suggested tentatively.

"We've worked very hard to ensure the prince maintains a high approval rating," Ulmer said stiffly, attention on his tablet. "Weddings and babies are always popular. We're hoping that news will counter any negative attention that arises from y—"

"Ulmer," Magnus cut in, quiet and lethal. "We're not going to play the blame game. We're especially not going to make Lexi pay for my decisions."

"No, sir. Of course not," Ulmer said promptly, nodding contritely at her.

Ulmer and I play a game of tit for tat, but he won't be able to retaliate with you. I won't allow it.

"Ulmer?" Lexi bit her lip. Magnus could say he wouldn't tolerate pettiness against her, but she knew exactly how cold wars and passive-aggressiveness worked. She didn't want to be subjected to it if she could avoid it. "If you tell me what you need, I will stay on script and hit my mark every single time."

"I appreciate that, Ms. Alexander. Thank you." Ulmer sounded sincere, then looked to his tablet and added under his breath. "I can't tell you how refreshing that would be."

Lexi was given an hour to freshen up before meeting the queen.

Nothing like this had been in her plans so she was provided a small wardrobe from which she chose a three-quarter-length stony-green wrap dress. It was demure yet flattering and made by a local designer. Her hair went up in a simple chignon and she applied her own makeup in natural colors.

Before she could decide on jewelry, Magnus returned from wherever he'd gone. He held a gold coin dangling from a thick gold chain.

"It's an old custom to offer a woman a coin as a promise, usually when a man was leaving for a raid, in case he didn't return, especially if she had someone to provide for."

"It's pretty." She caught the coin to study it. It wasn't big, but it was surprisingly heavy, telling her it was solid gold. "Are you going somewhere?"

"After pulling this stunt? The dungeon, I imagine." He twirled his finger.

She turned so he could affix the chain around her neck. While he was there, he kissed her nape, sending a shiver down her spine.

"Thank you for the plane." His warm breath wafted against her skin as he nuzzled behind her ear. "I didn't get a chance to say that."

"Don't—" She blushed so hard her cheeks stung.

"Now you won't be so nervous." There was an amused glint in his eyes. He knew exactly what he had done to her.

"You're a menace," she muttered as she took the arm he offered her.

Ansgar Palace was as modern as a two-hundred-year-old building could be. It was full of historic art and odd echoes and staff who moved like ghosts, glimpsed briefly before they disappeared, leaving her to wonder if she'd actually seen them.

Not that Lexi was taking much of it in. She was more preoccupied with wondering if she could enlist the queen in delaying her marriage to Magnus.

Just when Lexi was about to ask *Are we there yet?* they arrived at a door with a guard outside it. Magnus rang a doorbell and a butler—footman?—let them into a formal receiving room, offering a deferential bow as he did.

Lexi barely got her bearings with a quick scan of a desk, a fireplace and a grouping of elegant furniture before Queen Katla demanded her attention without saying a word.

The queen was a handsome woman in a forest green dress. Her hair was pulled back from her face with pearl-studded combs, revealing tasteful chandelier earrings. She remained seated, expression dispassionate.

Lexi tightened her fist into Magnus's sleeve as he performed the introduction.

Lexi curtsied, murmuring, "It's an honor to meet you, Your Majesty."

"Sorr requires you," Queen Katla said to Magnus. "He's in his study."

"I'll stop in when we get back to that end of the palace."

"It's important."

"I doubt it."

A silent battle of wills waged between their locked stare.

"You forced my hand when you came off the plane," the queen said with muted fury. "You know you did. *Go.*"

Magnus looked to Lexi. His cheek ticked.

Her heart began battering inside her rib cage. She had thought Magnus was defying *Ulmer* when they'd waved from the plane, but he'd been playing power games with his sister.

"I would never leave you anywhere that you would be unsafe," he said, making her heart swerve. "I'll be back in fifteen minutes."

As she was left alone with the queen, Lexi drew a subtle, shaken breath, hoping she could believe him, but she couldn't help wondering if there really was a dungeon here, and whether his sister had the desire to consign her to it.

"Sit," Katla ordered with a nod at a nearby chair. It didn't look nearly as comfortable or ornate as her own. "Has Magnus explained that I've endured enough scandal and heartache for a dozen lifetimes, Alexandra?"

"Please call me Lexi. If you want to," she added weakly, swallowing under Katla's glare at being interrupted.

"My mother died from an undiagnosed heart defect when I was ten. My brother died by suicide a few years later. It's too easy to say that losing our mother made him give up hope. Our father was the more likely reason. He was not an easy man even when she was alive. He grew more demanding and intractable as time went on. I kept as many of his scandals behind palace walls as I could, but there was enough in the public record for six hours of a salacious, unauthorized documentary. His assassination was not unexpected, considering how many people he had crossed in his lifetime. I've since dedicated my life to righting his wrongs."

Lexi didn't move, didn't say anything. She barely dared breathe.

"Every decision, every sacrifice I have made, has been justified by my love for Isleif. I married a man I barely knew because he had the intelligence to create opportunity and prosperity for our people. Sorr has the heart of a good father, too. I saw my marriage as a means to build a better country and thus a better world to leave to my children. I very arrogantly believed I would produce a better ruler, too."

Ah. Here was the point she was making.

"I've never been able to conceive."

"Magnus said. I'm very sorry." Lexi self-consciously slid her hands off her bump and into what should have been her lap.

"It's not your fault, but I'll admit to being sick with envy. One and done? It's so unfair it's beyond cruel. I've learned to ignore such things because I still have the power to leave a better ruler, Alexandra."

Magnus. Everything within Lexi stilled.

"I know I'm not an ideal partner for him," Lexi said haltingly, seeing her chance. "That's why I've asked him to wait on marriage."

Katla snorted. "But you can see how he boxed us in by waving from the plane. He drives me mad at times, finding ways to get around me, but I can't complain about how shrewd and combative he is about getting his way. He needs qualities like that to rule well."

"What he doesn't need is a woman who drags him into the trash with her," Lexi acknowledged.

"Exactly."

Ouch. Lexi couldn't go back and change all the decisions in her life, though. Far too many had been made for her, leading up to this checkered history that followed her. She couldn't look at the queen. Her eyes were too hot, her humility too bone-deep. She willed the door to open and for Magnus to come in and save her, even though she doubted she would ever escape this sense of being judged unworthy.

"Magnus has made it clear that you are the wife he wants," Katla said quietly. "I *have* to believe he knows what he is doing. That somehow, this union will benefit not just him, but Isleif."

And the world? Lexi strangled a hysterical laugh. *No pressure.*

"I hope you'll use this chance to reset your image. Keep both of you out of the trash."

It was a harsh thing to say, but it also awakened Lexi to the possibility that this *was* a chance to reinvent herself. Marrying Magnus could be more than playing the part of someone "better." She could do better. *Be* better.

"I want to be someone my child can be proud of." The admission came from the depths of her dented soul, where she secretly wondered if she *deserved* for people to use her for their own ends. "I would like to be someone that Magnus, and Isleif, could be proud of. I hope…" She had to clear a thickness from her throat. "I hope you'll provide guidance when necessary?"

"I'm not shy with my opinions. Lexi."

Was that— It was sarcasm, but the friendly kind. A tiny glow of optimism flickered to life inside her.

The door thrust inward, making Lexi jump in surprise.

Magnus strode in on his own momentum, throwing

the door closed behind him with another bang that made her stiffen and widen her eyes at him.

"Eleven minutes. Did you run?" Katla said with a sniff. "You didn't even give yourself time to choose properly."

"I knew which one I wanted as soon as I saw it." He showed the ring pinched between his finger and thumb. "The emerald matches her eyes."

"I've always liked that one." The queen nodded approval. "It belonged to our great-grandmother. A gift from a Russian czar."

Lexi was speechless as Magnus picked up her hand. She wanted to remind him that she hadn't yet agreed to marry him, but he slid the ring onto her finger so quickly, she was only able to admire it once it was there.

It was gorgeous, with a green stone flanked by three white diamonds on either side in a gold setting of old-world craftsmanship.

"It's beautiful." Heavy.

This is a chance, she kept hearing Katla said. *A chance.*

But was she really up to the task? Because this wasn't a role. It was a position, one she couldn't leave once she took it.

Their engagement would give her time to think about it, though, so she pushed the ring a little more firmly onto her finger.

"When is the baby due?" Katla asked. "I'd like you married before it arrives."

"I told Ulmer to arrange it for Thursday," Magnus said.

"What?" Lexi gasped, very afraid she was about to faint again.

CHAPTER NINE

"FINALLY," MAGNUS SAID when Lexi walked out of her bedroom in a robe and slippers the following morning.

After a long, stilted dinner with Katla and Sorr, she'd left Magnus with a few cross words about things moving too fast and locked herself in her room to call her mother. He'd peeked in on her a few hours later, finding her fast asleep, so he'd left her to sleep alone.

Twelve hours later, he was concerned enough that he'd canceled a morning meeting. He set aside the report he was reading and rose to press the backs of his fingers against her cheeks and forehead. She was warm, but not too warm. Pink, but not flushed or glassy-eyed.

"I was about to put a mirror under your nose. Are you ill?"

"Yesterday was a lot." She blinked foggily. "So is assembling a baby." She sent a startled look to the servants who bustled in to reset the breakfast table for her. "It's only nine thirty, isn't it?"

"Yes, but we have a lunch engagement."

"Thank you." She smiled as a young woman set a dish of yogurt and berries in front of her. "Should I skip ordering eggs? What time is lunch? Will it be here?"

"Late. At the cottage." He nodded for the eggs.

"What cottage?" Lexi asked.

"My mother's. The one where she grew up. When I called to ask her to come for the wedding, she wanted to meet you right away so I had them flown in this morning."

"Them?"

"My sister and her family live with her. The house in Bergen is very big." Magnus had provided it once he had access to palace funds, so his mother would have the privacy she deserved. "I usually visit her there, but she still has her parents' cottage here. She's staying until the wedding."

"Magnus—"

"You need to meet her regardless, Lexi."

Lexi paused with her spoonful of berries halfway to her mouth. "I guess this is her grandchild, isn't it? Her first? No, you just said your sister has children."

"Two, yes. She's still on maternity leave with the second."

"What about your brother? Will he be there?"

"I don't know."

Lexi delved for more, but he looked away, signaling for a coffee he didn't want, loath to explain that the last time he'd seen Freyr had been his brother's wedding, but it had been strained by the fact that Sveyn had been there. They hadn't had much contact since.

Magnus couldn't seem to talk *to* his siblings. How was he supposed to talk about them? He turned to a more pleasant topic.

"We should discuss our honeymoon, since security will have to prescreen the location. I can only clear one week. Do you have any thoughts on where you'd like to spend it?"

"Seriously?" she asked snippily. "I've told you I'm not ready to marry you and, frankly, the only place I'm eager to go is back to bed—" She winced and covered her eyes. "I mean…"

"Oh, no." He chuckled, enjoying this. "You can't back out now. You said it so that's where we'll spend it. I'll tell Ulmer to keep a chiropractor on standby."

"Stop it," she said firmly, still blushing. "I'm saying I'm not interested in more travel. And if we don't get married, we don't need a honeymoon." She poked her tongue out at him!

They were getting married. He drew the line at bullying her into it, but he'd find a way to convince her.

In the meanwhile, he quietly told Ulmer they would honeymoon at the health spa on one of the smaller islands. It was a pretty location with natural pools of different temperatures. At least two of them were touted as beneficial in pregnancy so he knew it would be safe for her.

Whatever lightness had come into his mood while contemplating his honeymoon had dissipated by the time they left for the cottage.

The palace was situated on the south side of the mouth of the fjord. The cottage was all the way on the north side, but they took the ferry, which cut forty minutes off the drive.

Forty minutes that Magnus could have used to brood.

Family visits shouldn't be this oppressive! In many ways they were no different from other appearances. Dress up, show up, shake hands, listen politely, pose for a photo if asked.

They weren't even strangers. Well. They were to some extent, he supposed. He had a standing appointment in his calendar to call his mother and made a point of seeing her a few times a year, typically around birthdays or holidays.

He had attended his siblings' weddings and texted appropriate felicitations on other life events when prompted by Ulmer, but he was no longer close with them.

Today, that felt more significant than usual. He wasn't sure why. He wasn't worried that his mother would say something to upset Lexi or the other way around. He wasn't embarrassed by his roots, either.

His visits with family were always prickly, though. Rather than address things, they swept them under the rug, but they were still there—his mother's pain, his father's abandonment, Magnus's abrupt departure to Isleif and his sense of being cut off from his brother and sister against his will.

Yes, he did feel blamed for it, even though it was merely the hand he'd been dealt.

He had a feeling Lexi would navigate all of it without any problem, though. She was a people-pleaser, barely in the palace twenty-four hours and the staff was already charmed by her.

Something about introducing her to his family grated on him, though. Some of it was possessiveness, he acknowledged. They were new and she was his. He wasn't ready to share her, but there was more to it.

A latent fear that she would take sides, perhaps? Take *their* side?

"Are we here?" Lexi had been watching out the window with great interest and now sat up taller as they turned into the long drive. "How does she keep sheep if she doesn't live here?"

"She sharecrops with a neighbor and lets the house for vacation rentals. Security has gone through here. Don't worry."

"I can honestly say I've never felt so safe as when I'm with you," she said wryly.

That remark should have pleased him. It did, before the SUV rolled to a stop outside the stone cottage and an unexpected threat emerged with the rest of the people pouring out the front door.

First was his mother, Truda, with her white-blond hair coming out of its knot and her smile faltering as she shaded her eyes. His four-year-old niece was next. She jumped up and down and waved madly.

His sister, Dalla, hurried out to set her hand on the little girl's shoulder, trying to keep her feet on the ground. Dalla's husband came out with a swaddled infant against his shoulder. Then Magnus's brother Freyr and his red-headed wife. She looked almost as pregnant as Lexi.

Last was a man who had a lot more gray in his beard than he'd had when Magnus had spotted him at Freyr's wedding two years ago.

"Why the *hell* wasn't I advised he was here?" Magnus barked. And why was he looping his arm around Truda?

"He was on the list, sir." The bodyguard in the passenger seat took out his phone. "I understood it had been forwarded to you—"

"Oh, for God's sake. It doesn't matter now, does it?"

"Who—?" Lexi asked warily.

"My father. Sveyn."

As far as Lexi was concerned, it was a pleasant afternoon. Everyone was polite and friendly if careful not to overstep. The women had a lot of questions about her pregnancy and how Lexi and Magnus had met. The men asked if she knew this or that action star. The food was excellent and the children were adorable.

In many ways, they were the kind of close-knit family Lexi had always longed for, with their cheeky asides and small digressions into each other's lives.

It would have been a perfect day if Magnus hadn't been such a looming presence through it all, speaking very little, creating a tension that was so thick, it could have been spooned into bowls like porridge.

At one point, while Lexi was in the washroom, she heard a few sharp words in Isleifisch. When she came back, the room went silent. Everyone wore stiff expressions. Sveyn had left the room.

"Would you like to walk with me to the beach?" Lexi asked Magnus's niece, even though the little girl didn't speak English. It was a windy day, but Magnus had warned Lexi that they might walk so she'd worn short boots, wool trousers and a cowl-necked sweater with a short coat.

Dalla came with them. Lexi could see her trying to engage Magnus, trying to repair whatever disagreement had happened in those few minutes Lexi had been absent.

Lexi deliberately lagged behind them to study a tide pool, pointing to interest the little girl, trying to give Dalla a minute alone with Magnus, but he only stopped and waited for her, expression stoic.

When they got back to the cottage, Truda tried to speak to Magnus alone, but he insisted they had commitments at the palace to get back to.

Looking teary, Truda hugged Lexi and said, "I know you're both very busy, but we'll be here all week. Come by anytime. Anytime."

"Thank you. It was so lovely to meet you all." Lexi

said a warm goodbye, aware of Magnus only offering stiff nods.

He said nothing on the way back to the palace and they were both tied up for a few hours once they returned. She didn't know what mysterious meetings he had, but she was met by a stylist and her team of seamstresses who were assembling a wardrobe of maternity fashions to give Lexi an appropriate selection through the rest of her pregnancy.

The woman had a handful of wedding gowns for Lexi to try on, too.

Mindful of the fact the woman was only doing her job, Lexi went along with choosing one, but after their visit with his family, she had more doubts than ever about rushing into marriage to Magnus. If things didn't work out between them, would she wind up sitting in a room full of undercurrents like today? She wasn't sure if he was holding a grudge or what, but it had been very uncomfortable.

She was exhausted when she finished with the stylist, but she went looking for Magnus, determined to take a stand on the wedding before this runaway train arrived at the altar.

Their apartment took up two corners in this wing of the palace and his bedroom was suitably grand with a massive fireplace, a sitting area, a desk and a bed the size of an ice rink. He was seated in a wingback chair, a glass of something amber in his hand.

"Do I have to dress for dinner tonight?" she asked after he invited her to enter.

"It's just us. It's in the schedule," he said stonily.

She knew. She'd used the question as an excuse to come in here. Now she pressed the door closed behind her.

"Can we talk?" she asked.

"Not about my family," he clarified into his glass.

"About the wedding."

He gulped, then hissed out a breath. "My mother asked if my father could come as her date. They've reconciled."

"Oh." She didn't know what surprised her more. That statement or the fact that he was sharing it on the heels of insisting he didn't want to talk about his family. She came forward to perch in the chair that sat at an angle to his. "Did you tell her you'd rather not?"

"I said I didn't care. They're adults. They can do what they want." He took another hefty gulp.

She studied him, trying to read more in his expression than he was saying aloud, but he was very good at hiding his thoughts and feelings.

"It must have been a shock for him to learn his wife had had an affair, even though it was before they were married."

"It wasn't an affair," he said darkly.

"A—" *A hookup like us?* That was what she almost said, but her heart twisted in her chest as understanding dawned. Magnus wasn't sulking or holding a grudge. He was hurting. "Oh, Magnus."

He only curled his lip and sipped.

"Did the queen know?"

"Yes. She helped my mother leave the palace the night she was assaulted, then paid her to keep quiet. Or, I should say, she offered a settlement that my mother agreed was fair," he said pithily, as though quoting something he'd been told but didn't buy. "Once my father—Sveyn—realized it hadn't been consensual, he wanted the truth to come out, but my mother wouldn't hear of it."

"It's her story." Lexi had had her own run-ins with

handsy men over the years. It had never been as grave as what his mother had suffered, but she preferred to put those experiences as far behind her as possible, not revisit them. She completely understood Truda's desire to forget.

"My father couldn't see past his anger at the palace. Once I agreed to live here, I became one of them. The enemy."

"That's horrible. But his reaction is not your fault, Magnus."

"Don't psychoanalyze me." He flashed an icy glance at her. "I knew what I was doing when I agreed to come. More or less. I mean, I didn't want any of this, but Katla is very persuasive. She suspected from the time I was born that I was her brother. She said she *gave* me that time with my family. And that if she'd had her own children, she wouldn't have prevailed on me, but I was being called. What kind of man was I, at my core? The kind who knows he's needed and walks away?"

"That was a lot to put on you when you were barely a man." The words hit her like a ton of bricks. She could only imagine how they had landed on him.

"I thought my father would eventually see my side of it, that I didn't really have a choice, but he wouldn't talk to me. He didn't talk to any of us for a good year, not until he divorced my mother. Then he insisted on shared custody of Dalla and Freyr, driving us further apart."

"He turned them against you?"

"Maybe it would have happened anyway. I couldn't see much of any of them. I was here and they were still in Norway, but I speak to my mother every month. She never mentioned that she'd been seeing him since Freyr's wedding *two years ago*. He's been living at the house I bought her for *four months*."

"And this is the first you're hearing of it?"

"Yes."

"And it feels like another secret that was kept from you."

"That's exactly what it is." He drained the last of his drink and clacked the empty glass onto the side table.

She left her chair and slid into his lap.

He stiffened. "I don't want pity."

"It's comfort." She draped her legs over the armrest, ignoring his scowl. "That was very insensitive of them."

"I don't expect them to be sensitive," he muttered as his arm curved behind her back in a way that seemed more reactive than conscious. His other hand found her hip so he could pull her more snugly into him. "I expect them to be honest."

"Then be honest with me. You weren't happy about our going to see them even before we saw Sveyn was there. Why?"

"I don't know." He sounded irritated. "I knew they would like you and they did."

"I liked them."

"I knew you would." He hesitated, then he continued in a very low voice. "I knew you would have a place with them, that they would welcome you like you're one of them. But I don't have a place with them anymore. I didn't want to watch you go where I couldn't."

Oh, Magnus.

She tucked the side of her face into the hollow of his shoulder and cupped the silky whiskers on his jaw.

He caught her hand and drew it down, but held on to it.

"I feel like a ghost when I'm with them. I watch them

get on with their lives without me. Now even my father is back in the picture."

And it hurt him so much, he could hardly speak of it.

"I think they love you and don't know how to reach you," she said, thinking of the way they'd looked to Lexi to be that conduit, asking her questions that Magnus never would have answered.

"Because I'm *here*. And what the hell am I supposed to do about that?" he asked.

She didn't know, but she felt for his family, unable to scale the real and invisible walls that surrounded him. She had a suspicion he'd just told her more about his feelings for his family than he'd consciously clarified to himself before. And, if he was anything like her, he was about to pull back inside his protective walls and shut her out, rather than stay in a state of exposure.

But she was *here*. And this was the kind of intimacy she longed for between them. The kind that gave her hope and the confidence to reach out to him in a way they both could accept. A way that would reinforce these delicate emotional bridges.

She curled into him, lifting so she could set her mouth into the crook of his neck while she slid her hand up his arm to his chest, where she touched one of the buttons on his shirt.

His hold on her changed. He looked down with eyes narrowed in suspicion. "Still comfort?"

"Opportunity," she said lightly. "Unless you'd rather wait until after dinner?" She pretended to try leaving his lap.

"No." He gathered her as he stood and carried her to the bed.

* * *

"Lexi." Magnus brushed the hair off her neck and buried his lips against the spot that made her shiver and gasp. "You have to get up and get dressed."

"No," she grumbled, scowling at the daylight pouring through the open curtains, then glanced over her shoulder to see him sprawled on the bed behind her, fully dressed. "Why are you up already?"

"Because your mother is landing soon."

"Magnus." She rolled onto her back to glare at him.

He lifted onto his elbow. "I told you I was having her flown in for the wedding. Are you going to tell me you wanted your brother and sister here after all?"

"No. They're out of my life. But *I* told *you* that I'm not prepared to marry you in some rush-to-the-altar, shotgun wedding."

His expression cooled. "Was there something in the prenup that you didn't like?"

He had forwarded the documents after dinner last night, when she'd still been floating in the afterglow of their lovemaking. Then he'd left for a conference call.

Annoyed, she had nearly deleted them unread, but she never considered a role without reading the fine print of the offer so she had begrudgingly pored through them.

Despite seeming very fair, they had put her to sleep. He had come to bed later, not disturbing her beyond a spoon and a kiss, so they hadn't talked about the wedding and now her mother was here, expecting to see her daughter married.

"The terms are fine." She sat up. "It's the unreasonable demands of the director that are putting me off. You can't just book a wedding and order me to show up for it, Magnus. That's not how it works."

"Have you been paying attention at all?" He swung his legs off the bed and sat there a moment with his back to her.

She saw his fist clench before he smoothed his hand open and rubbed it on his thigh. Then he drew a breath and stood to look down on her.

"I will be at our wedding the day after tomorrow. Whether you join me at the altar depends on what kind of woman you are, doesn't it? What are you afraid of? That this life might be hard? It will be. Life is hard. This life, here in the palace, can be very hard. It is lonely and it is bigger than either of us, but you are carrying the next person who will shoulder this burden, Lexi. What are you going to tell them? That you didn't marry their father because you didn't have the guts for it? Fine. If that's true then you're right. You're not fit to wear my ring or a crown. I have places to be."

He walked out, pulling the door closed firmly behind him.

Lexi refused to cry, but she was still upset when she collected her mother from her guest room and brought her to the suite she shared with Magnus.

"I *knew* you did more than dance with him," Rhonda said the second they were alone. She wasn't looking at her, though. She was taking in the decor of rare art and hand-loomed carpets and luxurious furnishings. "I thought our room was nice. Did he make you sign a prenup?"

"Mom."

"What? Don't be stupid, Lexi. I presume he's making you give up your career. You'd better protect yourself."

Rhonda wasn't a bad person, merely ambitious. If an opportunity presented, she wanted a piece of it. And having watched the spikes and dips in Lexi's career, she knew things could change in a blink.

Always keep something for a rainy day was her motto.

"Are you?" Rhonda asked. "Giving up acting?"

"I've spoken to Bernadette," Lexi admitted reluctantly. "I told her I should be able to keep my funding in place, but that I can't commit to the role." Lexi had plenty to invest now. Magnus was covering her expenses and the prenup left all her previous assets in her own hands. Plus, it made arrangements for her support moving forward. It was actually very generous, not that she told her mother any of that.

"You're not sleeping." Rhonda spied the shadows beneath Lexi's eyes despite the cover-up she'd applied. "Nerves? It's one day. One performance."

Is that all this wedding was? Why was she agonizing then?

The performance part of it didn't bother her, even though the "family only" guest list had bloated to over a hundred and fifty dignitaries from Isleif and neighboring countries. The ceremony was being broadcast internationally and a parade was planned so the people of Isleif could glimpse their future queen in the flesh.

But that was Rhonda. *It doesn't matter if you're running a fever. The show must go on.*

"This is a lot of power, though," her mother mused as she cast another concerned look at the mural on the ceiling and the hand-carved molding and the portrait of the queen on the wall. "What if you decide to leave? What if they decide they don't want you here?"

"Magnus wouldn't throw me out. He wouldn't do that to our baby." She felt confident in that, at least. He had made it clear that he wanted their baby to know both its parents and he had confided how cut off he felt from his own family. "If he wanted to get rid of me, he wouldn't be marrying me."

"Or he's cementing his position."

"*Mom.* Don't be so cynical."

"You know better than to be naive about something like this. What happens to the baby if you divorce him?"

"The baby grows up here. It's their heritage. I respect that." She did. And she understood that meant her baby would always be here so she should be here, too.

What would happen if she didn't marry Magnus? Would he marry someone else who would not only be his queen, but would have influence over their child's life? *No.* That didn't sit well with her at all.

She didn't get a chance to talk privately to Magnus again. She saw him at dinner, but it was a small but formal thing with her mother, the queen, and a handful of royalty who were visiting for the wedding. The day before the wedding, Lexi entertained those wives while Magnus was in talks with their husbands. Queen Claudia, the one Lexi had been so awestruck by in Paris, along with Queen Cassiopeia—"call me Sopi"—and Princess Amy of Vallia were all delightfully down-to-earth, which reassured her that maybe she could rise to the station Magnus was offering her.

If he was still offering it. He'd been very cold yesterday. *I will be at our wedding*, he had said. But would he?

After such a busy day, she couldn't keep her eyes open and fell asleep before Magnus got back to their suite. Suddenly, she was waking to a light breakfast and more fussing than any red carpet she'd ever walked.

Her mother did her makeup and praised the A-line gown as "perfection" with its lace sleeves and chiffon overlay on the skirt. Queen Katla had provided a tiara to hold the veil and Magnus had gifted her beautiful tear-drop diamonds for her ears.

When it came to the ceremony itself, Lexi hadn't weighed in much. She'd been letting Magnus make all the decisions while she had stubbornly sat on the fence. As a result, he'd chosen a traditional vein and she was told that most of it would be performed in Isleifisch.

At the last second, she sent him a note with a request.

She didn't receive a response. She was only told that he'd seen it.

They arrived at the chapel and Lexi was an unchar-acteristic mass of nerves. It was worse than any stage fright she'd ever experienced, but it had nothing to do with the crowds or the unfamiliar words or the huge step she was taking.

Would he do as she'd asked? It felt hugely important that he make this one small concession. Would he?

The music began and his niece led the procession of bridesmaids out the door. Prince Sorr was supposed to es-cort her down the aisle. She could have asked her mother, but Lexi had grown up as something that her mother lent out. She didn't want to be "given away" by anyone. She didn't want to become something that Magnus acquired.

So Prince Sorr was already at the front of the chapel next to the queen. Lexi was forced to take on faith that her future husband understood her at least a little and would be waiting to walk down the aisle *with* her.

She stepped out of the anteroom, breath held, and there he was, acutely handsome in a green military-style jacket with blue cuffs and collar. It had gold epaulets and he wore his sash with various medals and other regalia. The hilt of a long sword sat against his hip.

He wore his long hair smoothed into its customary gather. His beard was freshly shaped. He held out his gloved hands and she went toward him without hesitation.

"I knew you wouldn't disappoint me." His rasped words and the glow of pride in his gaze brought tears to her eyes. "You were made for this, goddess. You were made to be mine."

Was marrying him a huge mistake? In this moment, it felt like the best and only decision she could make. She took his arm and walked down the aisle with him, feeling as though they were giving themselves to each other. It felt *right*.

When she spoke her vows, she did so with care, clearly and firmly even as her chest was filled with butterflies. They exchanged rings and were pronounced married and he lifted her veil.

Everything fell away—the pomp and the crowd and even the baby swelling her middle. In that eternal space between heartbeats, they were simply a man and a woman, pledging their lives to each other. He pressed his mouth to hers and it was done.

CHAPTER TEN

THEY DID SPEND much of their honeymoon in bed. At least, Lexi did. Magnus had always been a high-energy person so he went a little stir-crazy.

He swam a lot of laps while Lexi snoozed in their room at the spa, but it turned out to be a good choice. It was exclusive enough that the privacy expectations were already high. They mingled among the other guests and everyone was very respectful, but Lexi could only go in the cooler pools and she was never in them long anyway.

They made love a lot, usually with her on top which drove Magnus crazy in the best possible way. He wanted her to be comfortable and he wanted to be gentle, which meant it was slow and lazy and so delicious he nearly passed out from erotic joy.

They returned to the news that she had developed a small blood sugar issue. It wasn't severe enough to alarm the doctors, but they were adjusting her diet and were agreeing with Magnus's prediction that the baby would be big.

What the hell was it with people who wanted to touch her belly, though? After their honeymoon, they attended their first official function at a summit in Brussels. They were at a dinner and, in the middle of introducing her to an ambassador, the man bracketed her belly with both his hands as if he had every right to touch her!

Magnus nearly caused an international incident.

Lexi confided afterward that it wasn't the first time. "The irony is, I thought being married and very pregnant would put a stop to the groping. Joke's on me."

Magnus instructed their bodyguards to step in if he wasn't there to do it himself, but she only attended two more events before she begged to stay home.

She was still three weeks from her due date, but Magnus had an important presentation to offer at a climate conference in Dubai. He would only be gone a few days, but he was reluctant to leave her.

Her physician assured him everything was fine: her blood pressure was good, her glucose levels were under control, and her iron was exactly where it should be.

"If her body is telling her to rest then she should listen to it," the doctor said. "She might be experiencing an urge to nest, which could account for her desire to stay home. That's very normal, too."

Nest? They had staff to scrub baseboards and set up the nursery, but if she wanted to refold all the towels, he supposed he should get out of her way.

He left the following morning, but he was immediately discontent. Dubai was hot and dry and going back to his suite after his first meeting annoyed him. The rooms weren't empty. They were never empty. He was never alone, but the place *felt* empty. He much preferred when he could walk into a room and find Lexi reading a book or doing her stretches. She would tell him why the book she was reading would make a good movie or ask his opinion on the list of names she was compiling.

He would rub her feet and that would turn into fooling around. And even though she was up constantly through the night, disturbing him every time, he preferred to sleep with her than have the bed to himself.

He missed her. There. He had admitted it.

Now what? he thought with disgust.

He was accepting his second cup of coffee the following morning, glancing over the notes for his presentation, when she called him.

He frowned. It was only 4:00 a.m. at home.

"It's early," he said in lieu of a greeting. "Are you all right?"

"I think I'm in labor."

"Also early." That's why he'd been persuaded to keep this commitment. The guideline was that she could deliver two weeks on either side of her due date, but that window didn't open for another week. "Have you spoken to the doctor?"

"No."

"Why not?"

"Because I wasn't sure if that's what it was. Besides, what can he do about it?"

"Help you prepare to deliver the baby?" Magnus suggested. He snapped his fingers at Ulmer. "Lexi thinks she's in labor. Get hold of the palace and—"

Ulmer was already nodding and walking away with his own phone pressed to his ear.

"The doctor will be there shortly," Magnus assured her. "How long have you been having contractions?"

"On and off all night. They kept going away so I kept trying to go back to sleep. My water hasn't broken and it's not that bad—" She drew a small breath.

"Is that a pain? Ulmer!" he shouted.

"The physician is on his way to her room," Ulmer said, peeking around the door. "I'm speaking to the pilot."

"I don't want to have the baby if you're not here," Lexi's small voice said in his ear.

"Is that why you didn't call the doctor? Lex, I don't want that, either, but I don't think that's up to us. If it happens, it happens."

"I know, but..." She took a shaken breath that almost sounded as though she was fighting tears. "It's fine. I'll figure it out."

He suddenly recalled her saying *Everyone I've ever known has let me down.*

"Lex, I'm leaving right now," Magnus told her, impatiently waving at Ulmer who was trying to direct staff to pack. He didn't need his damned toothbrush! "I'll be home before—" He couldn't lie to her, much as he wanted to. "Before dinner."

Would the baby arrive by then? Would she have to deliver alone?

"I'm sorry," she murmured.

"Don't be sorry. I shouldn't have left."

"But that presentation—"

"Will be given by someone else. I'll see you soon." He kept the phone to his ear while Ulmer helped him with his jacket.

There was a long space of dead air, the kind that another couple would have filled with words like *I love you.*

That infernal buzz, the one that warned him of an upheaval arriving in his life, started to coalesce, but it was cut off as she spoke.

"I think the doctor is here."

"Can you get up to let him in or—"

"He came in. Hi. I'm sorry to bother you," he heard her say before she added, "Bye, Magnus."

"I'll be there soon," he promised, but she had ended the call.

He received updates every hour. She was definitely in labor. A midwife was staying with her and keeping her comfortable. Katla checked on her, but things were progressing slowly. Lexi's water broke so she had a shower. She was taken to the hospital.

It was excruciating and he wasn't the one in labor!

Finally, the plane landed and they sped through the streets to get to the hospital. Magnus hurried to the maternity wing where the palace physician gave him a worried look.

"Her labor isn't progressing. She's been stuck at three centimeters since she arrived. We're monitoring the fetus for stress. The baby is fine, but I'm concerned about the princess. She's hasn't accepted any pain relief, only the TENS and she abandoned it because it wasn't helping. She hasn't slept or eaten since last night."

"Then feed her."

"But if surgery becomes necessary—"

"Why would she need that?" he asked with alarm.

"The baby is larger than average. She would have struggled regardless, but when it comes time to push, I'm not sure she'll have the strength, now that she's distressed and exhausted."

"Let me talk to her."

Magnus walked into a darkened room that was a little too warm for comfort. Lexi wore a cotton nightgown rucked up to her thighs. She sat on an oversize ball, leaning forward, keening softly. The midwife sat in a chair before her, offering her arms to stabilize her.

"Lex, I'm here," he said softly.

He waited until Lexi quieted and started to sit up. Then he jerked his head to dismiss the midwife and took the seat. He cupped Lexi's elbows and set his feet on either side of the ball to keep it steady.

"What time is it?" she asked distractedly.

"They said you're not taking anything for the pain? Why not?"

"Because I need to stay sober, so I know what's going on." She clamped her hands around his forearms and winced. "These things are constant. Why aren't they *working*?"

She keened softly again, for a solid minute.

He waited, breath backed up in his lungs until she relaxed and panted.

"We talked about pain relief in birthing class. Remember? Let them give you something."

"I just told you." She squeezed his arms so hard it pinched. "They'll make me sick or stupid. I won't be able to walk. Walking is supposed to— *Argh!*"

Her cry was as much frustration as pain and it cut through him like a knife.

"Lexi." He tried to smooth her hair from falling over her eye, but she knocked his hand away. "Listen to me," he insisted. "They're worried. They want you to agree to surgery."

"They said the baby is fine." She touched the belt on her bump and snapped a look to the monitor.

"*You* are not. You're exhausted. You didn't sleep last night. You can't keep on like this."

"You don't know what I can do!" she cried. "You sure as hell aren't going to do it, are you? I have to do this myself. Oh my God." She folded forward.

He caught her before her knees hit the floor and gathered her into his lap. Her fist pressed into his shoulder in resistance even as she muffled her moan of agony in his chest.

"I don't know what to do," she said piteously, shoulders shuddering. "What if the baby needs me? I'll be unconscious. What if... I can't give up, Magnus?"

Give up control, she meant. She couldn't trust that she would be taken care of. That their baby would be.

"Lexi...*søta*." The endearment was one his father had used for his mother all through his childhood. Sweetie. It bordered on innocuous, but it wasn't something he threw around. He'd never called anyone that.

He had to wait while another paroxysm gripped her. He didn't know how else to soothe her except to hold her and try to absorb her pain and whisper, "I'm worried about *you*, *søta*."

Finally, she relaxed and panted, trying to recover before the next wave arrived.

"I'll be there the whole time, Lex. The baby will be safe and so will you. I promise you. I *promise*."

It wasn't something he could promise. He wasn't a surgeon. Things went wrong with childbirth. They'd made that clear in the classes.

She knew it, too. She lifted her head enough to give him a look of weary disillusionment, then her expression crumpled and she caught fistfuls of his shirt and groaned.

The urge to just give the order and make it happen was so strong, he had to lock his throat against it. She would never forgive him if he took this choice from her. Never.

So he waited until the contraction eased and she panted once again. Then he petted her sweaty hair and said, "Please, *søta*. Trust me. I know that's hard, but I won't let anything bad happen to you or the baby. We'll both be here when you wake up. I swear on my life. Trust *me*."

When the next contraction hit, she didn't stiffen. She collapsed into weeping.

"Okay," she sobbed.

"I can order the surgery?" He made her look at him.

Her eyes were streaming, her mouth trembling. She nodded, then ducked her head in defeat.

"It will be okay, *søta*. I swear it." God, he hoped he was telling her the truth.

He called out and the midwife hurried in.

Moments later, they had her on the bed and began preparing her.

"I feel like I'm failing," she said miserably.

"Don't you dare." Magnus braced himself over her. This beautiful fighter had waited for him. He knew that, deep in his heart. It humbled him. He swooped to give her one kiss before he was asked to step back and suit up in scrubs. Then he held her hand, walking beside the gurney as they wheeled her into the theater.

She didn't want the spinal block. She chose full anesthetic, but he was allowed to stay with her because he had damned well promised her he would. They would have to tranquilize him to get him to let go of her hand.

When it went limp in his, his breaths turned shallow. The next forty-eight minutes were the longest of his life.

He didn't watch the procedure. He watched her still face, torn between relief that she was no longer in pain and anguish over what she was going through. Because of him.

Then a squawk sounded behind the drape.

"A boy, Your Highness. A big one," the doctor said with a chuckle of wonder. "Do you want to cut the cord?"

His hand shook. The angry face of his son squinted at him. Magnus's vision blurred.

"Put him here. She wanted skin contact," Magnus insisted in an unsteady voice. He unbuttoned the top of her nightgown enough that the infant could rest on her chest while the midwife covered the baby in a warmed towel and gently dried him.

Magnus only realized he had picked up Lexi's hand again when the midwife asked if he wanted to hold his son.

The baby complained when he was taken from Lexi and loosely swaddled. He didn't want to be separated from his mama, but as Magnus took him into the crook of his arm, the buzzing arrived in his ears again.

"Is Lexi okay?" Magnus asked, mind split in two directions.

"It's going very well, sir. We're finishing up."

Magnus could hardly hear him, the buzz in his ears was so deafening. It filled him with a vibration that made him afraid he would drop this creature who blinked and looked so earnestly into his eyes. For some reason, Magnus wanted to laugh. It was an urge the likes of which he hadn't experienced since childhood.

"If you let me weigh him, sir, he can go with you into recovery with the princess."

"I don't want to let him go," he admitted. But he let the midwife take the baby and he picked up Lexi's hand again, holding on to her while he watched over her and their son.

* * *

Lexi slowly became aware of Magnus's voice. He was talking to someone in Isleifisch. He sounded...

She turned her head, still foggy.

"Why are you talking to a towel?" she asked.

"You see?" He tilted the rolled towel. "I told you she would wake soon."

"Oh," she sighed. One clumsy hand went to the bandage on her abdomen, where she felt weak and sore and empty. The other lifted, trying to reach the ruddy face scowling from the swaddle.

"Look at this young man you made." Magnus settled the baby half on her chest, so she could secure him with her arm and see his face. "Ten pounds, ten ounces. I made them convert it so you would know how big he was."

"Hello, Rolf," she said, smiling and touching his round little cheek.

Magnus gave a small exhale of exasperation and set his hand on the top of her head. His thumb caressed her brow.

"Since I witnessed what you had to endure, I will allow you to call our son Rolf Thorolf. But his given name will be Eryk and that is the name we will tell the queen." He kissed her brow. "I'm hoping you're still goofy from the anesthetic and won't remember I said that."

Maybe she was goofy from the anesthetic because she said, "I was afraid someone would take him while I was asleep, and he wouldn't be here when I woke up."

Magnus flinched and covered the hand that cradled their son. "I know. But I promised you that we would both be here, Lex, and I meant it. You can trust me now. Hmm?"

She nodded, starting to believe it.

CHAPTER ELEVEN

WHAT LEXI REALIZED over the next weeks was that trusting her husband meant she began to trust him with her heart. She was falling in love with him.

At first, she thought it was a side effect of the love she felt for her son. She was utterly enraptured with Prince Eryk Rolf Alexander Thorolf. He cried loud, consumed gallons and slept hard. He had fine blond hair and piercing blue eyes and smiled when he dreamed. He had two doting and underworked nannies because Lexi liked to keep him where she could see him.

She especially loved seeing him with his father.

That's when she began to recognize what was happening to her. Magnus would show up in the middle of the day and say, "I only have a minute before my next meeting, but I wanted to see what sort of trouble you two were getting into."

It was never more dramatic than nursing or snuggling while she read a book, but Magnus would kiss her and steal Rolf from her arms and tell him state secrets in Isle-ifisch before he handed him back and kissed her again.

She would just *melt* through those hit-and-run moments of affection, then she would begin counting the minutes until he came back for the evening.

Almost from the first night they had brought him home, after Rolf was bathed and fed, Magnus would take him to see the queen.

Lexi half suspected Magnus did it so she would get used to trusting that it was safe to let her baby out of her sight for a half hour. It caused her the normal amount of new-mother anxiety, but she also knew that her son needed to bond with his aunt, since Katla would provide him guidance on the role he would one day assume.

One evening, Magnus hadn't turned up by the time Rolf usually went up so Lexi took him. She was still recovering from her surgery, so she was moving slowly.

"You carried him up the stairs yourself?" Katla scolded. "Why didn't you take the pram and the elevator?"

Because that was an even longer walk, but Lexi didn't say so.

"Do not set back your recovery, Lexi. You need to attend that summit in New York with Magnus next month. Otherwise, your countrymen will think we're holding you hostage." She held Rolf aloft. "You're such a big, strong boy, aren't you?"

Lexi took her at her word. A few nights later, Magnus swept into their suite muttering impatiently, "These people who don't know how to end a meeting without telling you what they've already said." He looked around. "Where is he?"

"I sent him up." She set aside the book she was reading.

"Is he walking already? They really do grow up fast." He picked up her feet and sat, then set her feet in his lap, exactly as he had done so often while she'd been pregnant.

"Ulmer said that since we'll be in New York over

American Thanksgiving, he thinks I should host a charity dinner." She wrinkled her nose. "At first, I thought he meant serving meals at a soup kitchen, which I'm happy to do, but he means putting on a whole…thing."

"Why are you reluctant?"

"I was hoping I could stay here in the palace. Maybe never go outside again?"

"Ah. Well, I thought I could finally have someone prettier than Ulmer standing beside me while I make all my appearances."

"It's a tight race," she said with a grimace. "I'm not feeling very pretty."

"Why the hell not? Because I'm not crawling all over you, telling you how irresistible you are?" In a swift move, he was between her legs, wide hands easily dragging her hips down the sofa so he could loom over her and plant a long, lazy kiss on her mouth.

She caught her breath in surprise, then relaxed into the kiss, letting her leg curl around his waist. Her arms twined around his shoulders and she burrowed her fingers beneath the binding on his hair, looking for the heat of his neck.

"This sex ban is torture." He nipped lightly at her chin. "How are you not aware that I'm ogling your breasts at every opportunity? You are very, very beautiful, goddess. Let me show you off."

"People will judge," she said in a plaintive whisper, stroking his beard. "I didn't care before. Well, I did." It had hurt like hell. "But it was only me they were judging so I could stand it. Now they'll judge you for marrying me. It doesn't matter if I make a mistake or not, they'll find one and everything I do will reflect on you and Rolf."

"It will," he agreed in his no-nonsense way that always seemed to pull the rug on her. "But you are such a fierce warrior behind this angelic face of yours." He swept his fingertip along her brow and down her cheek. "I know that you'll slay them in your sly, ruthless way."

"What is that supposed to mean?" She pushed at his shoulder.

"Oh, please. You win people over with laser-focused charm. Even Ulmer has started to hyperventilate if he risks disappointing you. 'The princess will be waiting, sir,'" he mocked. "I caught the cook having a little cry because you gave her some things to send to her niece for her birthday. How did you even know it was her niece's birthday?"

"We were chatting. She's a fan of Paisley Pocket. I was being nice, not manipulative."

"I know. I'm not insulting you. It's a *strength*. That's why I want you by my side, Lexi. I'm proud of you. I like being out with you."

His words went into her like the sweetest blade, pushing tears into her eyes. Did he really say he was *proud* of her?

Magnus didn't say anything he didn't mean. She'd learned that much about him.

They kissed again and she clung to his shoulders, thinking, *I'm falling. This is what it means to fall in love.*

It was a visceral sensation that was both beautiful and terrifying. In another world, falling in love with her husband would be ideal, but as she regained her physical strength, she was losing the battle to keep her heart.

Did she need to guard it, though? Magnus was incredibly protective of her. As they began making appearances across Isleif, the slightest overstep by anyone was glared into apologies by her ferocious husband.

That was the real reason people fell over themselves to please her, she suspected wryly. But his defense of her built her confidence in their marriage and herself.

By the time they landed in New York, she had almost convinced herself she was not that old person the trolls loved to vilify.

They arrived to a crowd rabid with excitement and a friendly press conference that was mostly photos. Lexi did one softball interview with a morning show where she talked about being a new mother. Rolf made a brief appearance, sending the studio audience into coos of adoration. Being his father's son, Rolf scowled once at the lights and cameras, then ignored them in favor of rooting for her breast.

Lexi then attended a handful of meet-and-greets with Magnus, shaking hands with the president. She spent a couple of hours helping serve lunch at a shelter and visited children in a hospital.

High on her success, she came into their hotel bedroom to find Magnus undressing for his shower. She was in her robe, having just showered herself, since they were expected at a mixer this evening.

"I just did something scary."

"What's that?" He pulled off his belt and threw it on the chair.

"I told the nanny that we'll be out for several hours tomorrow, so I think we should have a small rehearsal. I pumped two bottles and told her to see if Rolf will take one when he wakes. Then I said I was going to rest for an hour and not to disturb me."

Magnus slid his gaze to the bed, then the clock on the table beside it.

"You're invited," she clarified. "In case you didn't know what day it is."

"I can count," he assured her as he padded toward her.

When his hand came out, she thought he was going to scoop her around the waist and drag her into him, but he turned the lock on the door behind her.

Then he used both hands to wrench open the robe, throwing it to the floor and leaving her naked and cutting off her scream of shock. She slapped her hand over her mouth, laughing, certain the staff would hear her, but he was already picking her up so her legs had to wind around his waist while he walked her to the bed and came down on top of her.

"I will make every single one of the next sixty minutes count," he promised as he dragged his mouth to her throat and left a wet kiss there.

"The doctor said it might be uncomfortable. I might need lube. There's some in my makeup bag." She looked toward the bathroom.

"I'll fetch it if we need it." He looked up from circling his tongue on her distended nipple, then reached between them to tear her underwear away, leaving a small friction burn near her hip. "But we never have before, have we?"

And down his mouth went, pausing to skim lightly over the numb line of her scar before he parted her folds and anointed her, preparing her. Driving her to the brink of orgasm within moments, then leaving her panting and whimpering in loss as he stood to tear off his own clothes.

When he came back down on her, she opened arms and legs to welcome him. She groaned with delight at the feel of his splayed hand possessing her ass, holding her steady as he carefully forged into her. She bit her lip, experiencing a virgin-like sting, but reveling in it because his nostrils were flaring and his eyes were blazing and he shook with the effort to hold on to his control.

She loved him, she acknowledged as a brilliant glow filled her. She loved this man who claimed her, groaning in helpless need, and folded himself across her.

This was the man she had met in Paris, the one who consumed her, but it was also the man who had come to know that she liked a caress in her lower back while they made love. One who knew he could rise on his knees and arch her over his arm and tell her to make herself come so he could feel it. One who held back so he could arouse her again and again, tipping her over the edge and picking her up until she was glassy-eyed with sexual excess, utterly his.

Then he unleashed himself, letting his shout of gratification fill the room.

And, because they still had eleven minutes, he dragged her into the shower where he gently soaped her and set tender kisses on her heavy eyelids and told her she was too sexy for words and that she would be his downfall.

She laughed, drunk on eroticism, but that word—downfall—came back to her later, haunting her.

CHAPTER TWELVE

As far as Magnus was concerned, he and his small family had conquered America. Their Thanksgiving-themed fundraiser had raised several million dollars for meals for underprivileged families. Lexi had been the belle of the ball in a sequin-covered creation of reds and golds like autumn leaves. Her profile lifted Isleif's and this time when they danced, they received applause.

They had earned a pseudo-honeymoon as they headed into a quieter December. Lexi was feeling more confident in her role as his wife and was finding a routine of sorts with their son. She was also bouncing back physically so she was very receptive to lovemaking.

A few mornings after their return, Magnus told her to stay in bed after she fed Rolf. He took the boy to their small dining room, burping him while he ate his own breakfast.

Rolf continued to put on weight and was growing stronger every day, holding up his head and pushing his arms and legs with determination, even though he didn't seem to have a destination in mind except to scale Magnus's shoulder. It was an amusing wrestling match, trying to keep a secure hold on him while trying to spread jam on his toast.

"Your Royal Highness." Ulmer paused to give Magnus a polite nod of greeting as he was shown in. "Good morning."

"Why are you here? My morning is free of engagements." Magnus had planned it that way. Once Rolf went down for his nap, he intended to rejoin his wife in their bed.

"Publicity concerns have cropped up." Ulmer swept his finger across his tablet. "I wanted to let you know we're aware of them and addressing them before…" Ulmer glanced toward the open door to the corridor that led to their bedroom. He smiled politely, but his lips were tight. "Good morning, Your Highness."

"Good morning, Ulmer." Lexi had secured a robe over her silk pajamas. It was hardly the first time Ulmer had seen her before she'd dressed, but she faltered. "I thought we had a free morning."

"I thought you were sleeping in?" Magnus countered.

"I'm hungry. Oh, yes, good morning to you, too. As if we haven't already said that." Her voice dropped to a gurgle of indulgence as she smoothed her hand over their son's fine hair. "You can't possibly be hungry, too? You *just* ate, you little glutton."

Hungry or not, Rolf wiggled harder, always aware when his mama was near and eager to be in her arms.

She took him and sat in the chair Ulmer held for her. Magnus moved his toast to where she could reach it and held up two fingers for the poached eggs she usually ate. Their server poured her decaf coffee and left.

"You were saying something about publicity concerns?" Lexi prompted Ulmer. "About me? I'm guessing it's not good."

"We're well aware that controversy sells clicks, ma'am. We're doing what we can to quash it, but they are being persistent."

"What are they saying?" Her voice was even, but Magnus heard the dread.

Ulmer looked as though he'd allow himself to be drawn and quartered before he repeated any of it.

"It doesn't matter," Magnus stated. "The staff are dealing with it so you don't have to. Carry on," he said, dismissing the man.

But later, after they'd made love and were sharing a lazy bath, he heard her "Tsk." He picked up his head off the back of the tub and found her reading headlines on a phone he didn't recognize.

"What are you doing? Where did you get this?" He took it from her, noting it was in a waterproof case.

"It's the one I keep in here for reading while I'm in the tub."

"Then read a book, not that garbage." He tossed it to the mat on the floor.

"They're saying I should have lost the baby weight by now."

"It's all in your chest. I think it's delightful." He slid his hand under the water so he could weigh the swell that overflowed his palm.

She didn't relax into him the way he'd hoped. "They think I'm lazy because I had a C-section instead of delivering naturally."

"'They' don't exist. One troll in the armpit of the internet is trying to profit off you. Are you really going to let them ruin our morning?"

"No," she said petulantly.

But it did cast a shadow, one that grew longer and darker as the month wore on.

Magnus didn't tell her that her post-pregnancy photos were being compared to ones that her stalker had posted a few years ago, but he had a suspicion she knew. She grew subdued while he grew frustrated. He had sworn she could rely on him to look after her, hadn't he? Why couldn't he protect her from something that caused her so much pain?

On Christmas day, he had his own history to face and thank God Lexi and Rolf were there to buffer him through it. Every few years, he had Christmas lunch at the cottage with his mother. This year, everyone was there, including Sveyn.

Snow was falling heavily. The sun had barely come up before it began to set, casting the day in a muted light. The babies were being passed around like plates of hors d'oeuvres and the women were caught up in lively conversation about sleep schedules and baby yoga.

When Freyr tilted his head at Magnus and said, "Sauna?" Magnus hesitated, not wanting to leave Lexi alone, but sitting in the sauna was something they had done throughout his childhood, boys and girls taking turns in the hut built for that purpose. He was here to take Rolf if Lexi and the women wanted to steam together later.

It was a setup, of course. He was no sooner seated on the top bench, sweating onto his towel, when Freyr invented a need to stoke the fire and took their brother-in-law with him, leaving Magnus with Sveyn.

Biting back a curse, Magnus demanded, "What is it?"

There was a weighty, indrawn breath, then, "I want to ask your mother to marry me."

"You don't need my permission."

"But I want your blessing."

Magnus stared balefully at his father through the billows of steam. Sveyn had aged. That was the thought that recurred each time he'd seen him lately. He worked in insurance, but his hobbies had always been outdoor pastimes. He was still fit and lean, but now his shoulders were bony, his face deeply lined, his red beard heavily salted with white.

"I want your forgiveness," Sveyn admitted with emotion in his voice. "That is what I really want to ask you. It took me a long time, Magnus. Too long to realize this wasn't about me or what I thought our life should have been. Nothing was stolen from me that I didn't let go of through spite. I wish I could go back and fight for more time with you, but I can't. I'm sorry for that. Truly."

Magnus believed him and, really, what was the point in holding a grudge now?

"I was an adult. I made the decision to come here. I'm glad you're no longer punishing Mom for my actions."

"You didn't make a decision," Sveyn said with ire. "You made a sacrifice. So did she. It took me far too long to understand that. To accept that it was her right to decide—I couldn't fathom how she could carry any man's baby but mine, especially—" He gave an agitated rub of his beard. "Especially when she knew it didn't matter how much she loved you, she might have to give you up. It felt as though she made all of those decisions without me. Even though they affected me. I wanted to keep everything as it was. I wanted to keep my *son*. For myself. But I know now that was selfish of me. Incredibly selfish."

A skewer invaded Magnus's chest, making his breath burn. He told himself it was the scald of the hot, humid air, but it was the score of that word: *selfish*.

She knew it didn't matter how much she loved you, she might have to give you up.

"Can you forgive me?" His father's voice came from far away.

"Yes." He cleared his throat. "Of course." Because *he* was not a selfish man. Was he?

"Thank you, son." His father's hand came out and Magnus leaned forward to shake it, thinking this should have felt more healing, but those words—*sacrifice* and *selfish*—glinted like two sides of a coin tumbling through the clouds of steam.

For Christmas, Dalla had given Lexi tickets to a play in London starring her former Paisley Pockets costar, Josh, who had played her onscreen brother. Dalla had checked with Magnus beforehand and he had suggested booking the New Year's Eve performance, so they could watch the fireworks afterward.

"I haven't seen you in such a good mood in weeks," Magnus said as Lexi pulled on black palazzo pants shot with gold threads that glinted as she moved.

"I haven't seen Josh in years. We used to text, but... life." She shrugged on the matching jacket over a gold push-up bra. "Thank you for bringing me." She looped her arms around his back.

"It was Dalla's idea."

"I know, but you agreed, even though the paps will be a nightmare about it." Those awful nudes of hers that Carmichael had peddled had been churned up along with comments that she was "poisoning" the royal line and turning Prince Magnus into his father. No matter what she did, she couldn't seem to burn away that old reputation and rise above it, which left her feeling guilty and ashamed for exposing her husband and child to the same ridicule.

"How many times do I have to tell you I don't care what the press says about you?" He set her back and slid his gaze down her front. "Anyone with eyes will say you look stunning."

"Thank you." She appreciated the compliment, but he didn't kiss her or try to distract her. He'd been growing more and more withdrawn lately and it was starting to distress her.

"We should go. The play will start whether we arrive on time or not. I'm guessing you don't want to miss any of it."

She didn't, but she also didn't like this feeling that he might *say* he didn't care about her reputation, but she couldn't fully believe him because her reputation had been an issue from the very beginning. A lifetime in an industry of broken promises and last-minute rejections had trained her to be skeptical and to expect to be cut adrift at any moment.

She wanted to believe her husband when he told her it didn't matter. In many ways, she was living her best life with him. She loved Magnus, loved their son. She wanted to tell Magnus that and celebrate this wonderful life they were making together, but each time he pulled away that little bit, she lost her nerve, feeling insecure and uncertain.

She trusted him with her life, but she didn't have enough trust in his feelings toward her to risk her own.

Her brooding thoughts were set aside for ninety minutes while they watched the play, a mystery that was suspenseful enough to silence the audience for long minutes at a time. When it concluded, Lexi was the first to leap to her feet, clapping wildly for Josh and the rest of the talented cast.

She had sent a note backstage when they arrived, telling Josh to break a leg, as if their presence in the audience wouldn't have been noted otherwise. They had been a distraction on and off throughout, but they were escorted backstage where they were greeted with great excitement.

After a small gauntlet of handshaking, they entered Josh's dressing room and Lexi flew into the arms of her old friend.

"You jerk," Josh grumbled as he squeezed her. "You made me so nervous, knowing you were in the audience." He had his hair dyed red for his role and wore traces of his stage makeup, but he gave her a second hug, picking her up and crushing her like a long-lost relative.

"You were amazing," she assured him. "But put me down so I can introduce you to Magnus."

"Excellent performance," Magnus said politely as he shook Josh's hand.

"A far cry from pretending to pick you out of garbage disposals, isn't it?" Josh joked to Lexi. "Ooh, let's start rumors of a reboot." He pulled his phone from his robe pocket.

"Wait. Let me do it on mine." Lexi wrinkled her nose. "Magnus has to be in it or the trolls will claim I'm having an affair."

"Please. I'm out and proud these days, Lex. If anything, they'll think I'm after your husband. Oh! Come to our party tonight! Meet my partner, David. You'll know so many people. I'm *dying* to hear why you left X-Calibur. And you have a *baby*?"

"We do have a son and we have to get back to him," she said smoothly. "But here. Magnus will take the photo and I'll send it to you. Post it whenever you want, but *please* say something boring. You have no idea what I'm going through."

"Babe, I was outed by a podcast host so they could boost their ratings. I have some idea." Josh slid his arm around her waist and tilted his head against hers, smiling wide as Magnus used his long arm to snap the photo of the three of them. "Did you really drop out of the project with Bernadette Garnier? It's *Bernadette Garnier*, Lex. And that role would be perfect for you."

"I know, but..." Lexi shrugged that off as she glanced at the photo, then asked for Josh's number so she could send it to him. "Even funding it is an issue. I believe in the story, but the trolls are finding the topic too darned salacious. Guard my number with your life, please. Otherwise, I'll have to change it and we'll lose touch again."

"I will. *I miss you.*" He hugged her again.

She kissed his cheek and they said their goodbyes.

When they were in the car, Magnus asked, "Text him for the address if you want to go to the party. I don't mind."

"It's not worth it. The trolls will turn it into me abandoning our son and accuse me of falling back into drugs or something."

"Lexi. You can't keep living around what strangers are

saying about you, especially when it's said in bad faith. If you want to see your friend, do it. If you want to keep a foot in acting, let's talk about how to make that happen."

"I don't." She looked to him with puzzlement. "That part of my life is over."

"What part? The happy part?"

"I'm happy," she defended.

"Don't lie to me," he snapped.

They didn't speak again until they were back in their suite at the hotel on the Thames. Rolf was down for the night so Lexi took the baby monitor and dismissed the nanny.

"Why do you think I'm not happy?" she asked as they changed from their evening wear.

"Because you looked happy tonight in a way I haven't seen in weeks. Or were you *acting* happy? Because it was either him or being around actors that made you light up like that. If it's acting, and you want to go back to it, then we should talk about it."

And add bad reviews to her already full plate of negative feedback?

"Josh and I grew up together. He's like a brother to me. But he's always been gay, Magnus. If you think there's something between us—"

"I'm not jealous," he said pithily.

Ouch.

"Good," she claimed. "Because you don't have any reason to be."

"But I can't be your whole life," he added.

"You're not. Rolf is." She was stooping to being mean, but he was standing right on her heart.

They glared at each other, but she looked away first.

"Do you *want* me to go back to acting?" she asked with trepidation. Was this his way of pushing her out of his life now that she'd produced the heir he needed?

"I don't want the guilt of keeping you from something you love."

"You're not. I'm making a choice."

"You're making a sacrifice."

"For my *son*."

"Exactly."

"I don't even know what we're fighting about," she muttered, leaving her couture clothes on the floor and yanking to tie the belt on her robe.

"We're fighting about the fact that I stole your life from you."

"What life?" she cried. "I chose to have him, Magnus. Not because I wanted to be the mother of a king, but because I wanted to be a *mother*. This is not the way I imagined my life would turn out, that's true, but it's a very good life. I—" Oh, she would have to say it. "I'm in this life because I love you."

"Don't say that." He winced and looked away.

He might as well have knocked her off the top of the building into the Thames. She sucked in a breath, unable to find words.

"Lex—"

"No," she choked, holding up a hand. "*Now* you've given me a reason to look for fulfillment elsewhere."

"Let me explain what I meant," he said tightly.

"Do you love me?" she demanded.

He hesitated and his expression became that stony horrible one that gave away nothing, which finished crushing her heart.

On the monitor, Rolf began to fuss. She snatched it up and headed for the door, thankful that she wouldn't complete her humiliation by crying in front of Magnus.

He could have called out to her, though. He could have told her to ask the nanny to get their son and stay here to work this out.

He could have fought for her.

But he didn't.

He let her walk out.

And she was devastated.

He shouldn't have let her walk out. He should have said, *Yes. I love you. I love you in ways I didn't know I could love.*

Because he did. And it made him feel as though he was being boiled alive.

From the time Sveyn had talked to him about sacrifice and selfishness, Magnus could only see himself as selfish where Lexi was concerned. He had wanted her from the moment he spotted her. He had balked at being told he couldn't have her and had found a way to stay in the periphery of her life even when he shouldn't have. The very second that he'd had an excuse to drag her into his world, he'd acted ruthlessly to do so.

And he'd been watching her suffer for it the whole time. She might have chosen to carry the pregnancy and become a mother, but she hadn't wanted the strictures of royal life. She had known their marriage would make her that much more of a target of attention, especially the negative kind.

Magnus had countered all of those downsides with his own rationalizations. He protected her. He supported her and the child they'd made. He gave her as much physical pleasure as they could bear. He had given her a family, such as his was, to replace the one he'd cost her by exposing their treachery.

Then, tonight, Magnus had seen for the first time that she did have a family she loved. A life where she was welcomed and celebrated. Her childhood friend had put carefree laughter into her eyes, if only for a few moments.

A ferocious tightening had sat in his chest while Magnus had watched them. Their connection had been similar to the way Freyr still hugged Dalla sometimes. It had struck Magnus as too similar. Had he broken her away from a place where she felt loved and accepted? Why? So she could live inside the boundaries of his life and still suffer the anguish of what strangers said about her?

When she asked if he loved her, he couldn't see how telling her would help. It wouldn't change anything. It would only make her feel obligated to accept this life he'd forced her to take on.

That's why he'd told her not to say it. If she loved him, it meant she would keep making sacrifices for him. He didn't want that from her. He wanted her to thrive. He wanted her to be the delightful force he knew her to be, with her strong personality and her cheeky remarks and her way of leading with her heart no matter how many times she'd been disappointed by those around her.

How could she even say she loved him? That was the real reason he'd told her not to say it. How could she love him after the things he'd done to cage her into this life with him? He'd done it out of selfishness, because he was so damned tired of being alone. How could she love *that*?

She didn't come to their bed, staying in Rolf's room

overnight. She didn't talk much the next morning either, keeping the baby and nannies and Ulmer between them as a buffer.

When they arrived back on Isleif, she said she had a headache so Magnus let her retreat to her room while he brooded on how he would pull them from this tailspin.

Before he saw Lexi the following morning, he was summoned to speak to Katla.

Irritated by what felt like a prime example of what had caused their fight—the fact that his obligation to the crown would always come before her—he strode into the formal receiving room with his usual flouting of protocol.

"Is this about Asia? I've already had discussions with Sorr. It's under control."

"No. That trip will be canceled. We have a personal matter to discuss."

"You are not going to attack me about Lexi. She's all but living under a veil. No, Katla. We have to learn to live with the bad press."

"Magnus," she said with quiet urgency. "I've been waiting until the diagnosis was confirmed. I have the same heart defect as my mother. I must abdicate."

CHAPTER THIRTEEN

THE WORLD FLIPPED on its axis.

No, he thought.

"Yes, Magnus," she said, making him realize he'd spoken his reaction aloud.

"It's really that serious?" The severity of this news—of her condition—drove him to his knee before her.

"Have you known me to be overly dramatic?" There were lines of distress around her eyes. Her lips were pale. "It's not as severe as hers, but I've been struggling to breathe lately. I can't continue with my duties, but with careful management, I should have a few years before I require a transplant."

"A transplant." That punched the air out of him.

"I'm being brutally honest with you, which I know is one of the things you hate most about me, but it's necessary."

"I don't hate you. I find your desire to do the right thing extremely annoying." He let himself fall onto his ass, turning as he did so his back landed against the chair that was angled toward hers. He braced his wrist on his upraised knee, trying to take it in.

"I don't want you to be ill." It was an understatement, but it was the most emotion he could allow himself to express without giving in to the shaken sensation in his chest. He and Katla clashed because they were knitted from the same chain-link armor, but she was as much his sibling as Dalla or Freyr. It would break his heart to lose her.

"I don't wish to be ill either, but it is a fact so we'll deal with it," she said with her own steely refusal to give in to emotion.

They would deal with it, but he had time to process what her illness meant to both of them. To help her find the care she needed to prolong her life, but the other part. King? He'd been preparing nearly fifteen years, but it still seemed like a bizarre fantasy so he brushed that aside to be parsed through in the coming hours and days.

No, in this moment, his most immediate concern was, "What do I do about Lexi?"

"What do you mean?"

"Come on, Katla. Look what I've done to her, forcing her into royal life the way you did to me. At least I had the DNA. What you did was necessary, but I essentially kidnapped her." There'd even been a level of emotional extortion when she had tried to delay their marriage and he'd challenged her on what kind of woman she was. He pinched the bridge of his nose, remembering their most recent argument. "When we were in London, I told her she should go back to acting if she wants to. Now I have to go walk that back? Tell her she has to stay here and become queen? I'd best have one of the bodyguards in the room with me. She's liable to kill me."

"Why on earth would you tell her to go back to acting?" Katla cried. "She's a perfect partner for you. She makes you *better*, Magnus."

"She makes me selfish," he argued, thrusting to his feet. "You know that. I could have made arrangements for her, let her raise Rolf away from all of this."

His chest felt ripped open at the thought. His son had become a part of him, but he shook off the sensation. At the time, his son hadn't been real to him. It had all been about Lexi. About his desire to drag her into his life.

"I wanted her and went around you to get her. But the weight of this is affecting her. I don't want to crush her and lose her. I love her too much to watch that happen."

"I know you do," Katla said with a choke of humorless laughter. "That's been obvious to me since I heard the defiance in your voice when you told me she was pregnant. You were so glad. So proud. It was—" She looked away and blinked.

"Katla." The unfairness of her infertility hit him anew.

"I do strive to do what's right." She folded her hands in her lap, gaze pensively fixed on the ring she wore. "I think often that if I'd been able to have children, I would not have had to force you to take this on. It was deeply unfair to you and your mother and your whole family. Sometimes there is no clear path that is wholly right, Magnus."

"I know, but…" He ran his hand over his face. "But what you have demonstrated to me again and again, what I know to be true, is that this is a life where my wants and needs are second to the greater good. How can I be good enough to take the crown if I don't have the strength of character to give her up, if that's what is right for *her*?"

He had to look away, to hide the fact that his eyes were growing damp. His chest was tight and there was a deep ache behind his sternum, one so acute it felt like a fracture.

"Oh, Magnus, I hope you know I'm not a saint. Look at this choice I'm making right now. Is it not selfish of me that I would rather step back from my duties in hopes of living longer?"

"*I* want that." He pointed to his chest. "I would rather you were here to provide advice than leave me to face this without you. Another self-serving act," he muttered with a derisive wave at himself.

"And I want to live so I may see you rule," she said quietly. In a rare moment of humanity, she let her mask slip and he saw affection and chagrin and humility. "I know you will rise to it, Magnus. You will make a wonderful king. I am so proud of you. I can't bear not to witness it."

Ah, hell. She was going to make him cry.

"When?" His voice thickened with emotion, because this wasn't a choice. It was his destiny.

"A month?"

He nodded, accepting it, but all he could think was, *What about Lexi?*

Lexi was very used to rejection. For every role she'd landed, she'd been turned down for dozens more. For every comment or post that called her a fashion icon or a "Mom Worth Modeling" there were a hundred others that tore her down.

She knew that you couldn't win if you didn't try, and that trying meant risking failure, but that was what was smothering her right now: a sense of failure.

She had risked her heart and the man she loved didn't love her back. She was married to him. They had a son— one who would one day be king of this country she had grown to love. She wanted to make Rolf proud. She wanted to make *Magnus* proud.

And she was failing.

She did the only thing she could do. She dismissed the nanny and cuddled her baby, soaking up Rolf's chubby warmth and the feel of his fingers curling into her shirt, his kicking legs and his wet mouth bapping her cheek.

"Lex?" Magnus came into their lounge, voice and expression grave enough to tighten her stomach. "We need to talk."

"Magnus, it's fine," she insisted while drowning in defensiveness and a desire to quickly move back to what they'd had while also wondering if that was even possible. "I knew love was not something you were offering when we married. I didn't mean to make you feel obligated."

"It's not fine. But I'd rather we weren't distracted." He rang for the nanny.

She closed her arms more firmly around Rolf. "You know he can't speak English any better than Isleifisch, right?"

Not one hint of amusement. Magnus was somber as he told the nanny they had some important matters to discuss and didn't want to be disturbed.

Lexi's heart lurched and she was reluctant to give Rolf up. Her arms felt empty as she followed Magnus into his office. Her chest ached with a chill of apprehension.

"Magnus—" She didn't even know what to say, she only knew that whatever he was planning to say would hurt.

"I need to tell you first that we're not going to Asia. Katla is ill. She's planning to abdicate within the next few weeks."

Lexi's shock was so great her mind blanked for several seconds.

"I know," he said, guiding her toward a chair. "Sit. It's a lot to take in."

"But... *How* ill? Magnus..." She searched his expression as she sank onto the cushion. Her stomach twisted into knots when she saw the shadows of worry behind his eyes.

"It's a heart condition similar to her mother's. If she reduces stress and makes resting a priority, she should be with us for a good while." It wasn't even lunch, but he poured himself a drink, then left it on a side table as he sat down to face her.

"She seems so young," Lexi said, voice coming out hushed because there was no wind in her. "Obviously, I knew you would become king eventually, but that felt like something that would happen years from now. I don't know what to say."

"Say you'll stay."

"What?" She lifted her head, only then realizing she had buried her face in her hands. "Of course I'll stay. I told you, I don't want to go back to acting. I want to—" She swallowed. "I want to be Rolf's mother."

"And my wife? My queen?" His expression flexed with some unnamed emotion. "Say you love me again."

Her mouth clamped reflexively into a hard line.

"Let me respond properly this time." He hitched forward in his seat and extended his hand.

"I don't want you to say something you don't mean." She bit her lips, trying to steady them. "I meant it when I said it's fine. I'll stay. You'll have more responsibilities and won't have as much flexibility for Rolf. It wouldn't be a good look for me to choose now to pursue my own interests. If you can stand my reputation, I'll take on the role of queen."

"You won't say it?" he asked grittily. "I killed those feelings in you? You are not that fickle." He rose and pointed at her, staring down his nose at her. "Fine. Don't say it. I told you not to say it because I didn't feel I deserved to hear it. I still don't." He turned his back on her.

"Oh, do you have some horrible nude photos that the internet keeps regurgitating?" she asked scathingly.

"That." He gave his beard a scrub as he turned to face her, pointing again. "That is one of the reasons I don't deserve your love. I can't make all that poison go away no matter how hard I try. I make it worse. Being my wife makes all of that worse for you." He exhaled, sounding exhausted, and dropped his hands to his sides. "When I talked to my father on Christmas Day, he told me he held on to his anger for so long because he hadn't had any choice in what had happened. That he felt my mother had made all his choices for him. When he said that, I realized that I hadn't given you a choice. At first, I was able to believe I was justified, but you haven't been happy, Lexi."

"Because I could tell *you* weren't happy. I thought it was because of all the bad press."

"I'm going to say this one last time." He closed his eyes and tilted his head to the ceiling. "Then we will never talk about it again. *Screw the press.* They can all go to hell. I know who you are, Lexi. And I love you. Exactly as you are."

Love was an arrow. It went into her chest with the sweetest burn, sitting there vibrating and stinging, putting tears into her eyes.

She hugged herself, voice a thin rattle. "Do you really?"

"Yes, damn you." His expression turned so tender, it broke her all over again. "I think it started in Paris, when you asked who was in charge. You knew damned well it was me. And you will never know how hard it was for me to say no to you in Monte Carlo."

"It was hard for me to ask," she muttered with a pang of remembered hurt.

"I know. And I will always be angry with myself for giving up that time I could have had with you, but I didn't know then how much you meant to me. I didn't really understand it until Rolf's birth. Everything about that day scared me, Lexi, especially when I realized I could lose you. I didn't want to face what that meant, though. I didn't accept how much I loved you until you accused me of being jealous of a gay man whom you think of as a brother and I was."

"You said you weren't!"

"I lied. I won't do it again," he promised, running his hand down his face and tugging at his beard. "But he made you smile in a way I hadn't seen in weeks. I couldn't stand that he could give you that and I didn't."

"It was nostalgia, Magnus. I didn't have a care in the world back then. We were children. You give me other things that are more important than candy bars stolen from craft services."

"Orgasms?" he scoffed.

"Our son. An identity that has substance. The power to affect lives."

"The weight of responsibility," he countered. "Duty. Expectations that are difficult to live up to."

"All true, but were you serious?" She rose and moved toward him, feeling as though she inched onto a plank over an abyss. "Do you love me? Have you given me your heart?"

"Yes," he said promptly. "It's all yours, Lexi. If you're not with me, then I don't have one." He cupped her face, looking into her eyes with such swirls of emotion in his that she felt lifted off the floor and plunged into a whirlpool at the same time. "Will you say it again?"

"I love you, Magnus. I love *you*. The man and the father and the king."

"You'll be my queen."

"I would be honored."

For a few seconds, his mask was completely gone and all she saw was love. So much love it should have frightened her. But the swell of her love for him was so great, it met and matched his, melding into something greater than both of them combined.

When he kissed her, it tasted as reverent and holy as renewing their vows. It was tender and loving and sweet. Eternal.

Then, because they were Magnus and Lexi, she tipped back her head, wrapped her arms around his neck and encouraged him to plunder.

He groaned and angled his head, then slid his hands down to her ass, picking her up so she wrapped her legs around his waist.

"How much time do we have?" he asked against her cheek.

"You told her not to disturb us. There's enough milk in the freezer to buy us a few hours."

"I should show more finesse," he said as he cleared

his desk with a sweep of his arm and pressed her back onto it. "But I hate fighting with you. I need to *feel* you, to know we're okay."

They barely undressed. Her slacks were thrown over a chair and her underwear was still dangling off her ankle when she hugged his ribs with her knees.

His entry stung. She wasn't completely ready for him, but he paused and kissed his apology onto the tip of her nose.

"I'm rushing you."

"It's makeup sex. I want to feel connected to you." She tugged his hair free of its band so it fell around her face.

He braced on his elbow, fingertips caressing her temple and cheekbone and the corner of her mouth while he seemed to memorize her features.

"I thought I was losing you," he admitted in a whisper. "I lost everyone I loved before and loving them wasn't enough. I need to know I'm giving you enough, Lexi."

"You do." She finished opening his shirt and ran her hands beneath it, mapping his bare shoulders. "I thought this was all we had, but we have so much more now. And it makes this even better."

"It does," he agreed. As he withdrew and returned, a wicked smile curved his lips. "I like watching your eyes haze like that."

"I like how safe you make me feel, even when you're burning down my world." She wrapped her thighs around his waist and arched, inviting the act. The energy of his powerful thrusts.

"I will spend the rest of my life making you sigh like that," he growled.

"Promise," she gasped.

"On my life."

They stopped talking, too caught up in the pleasure they were giving each other. And soon, the inferno engulfed them.

One month later...

Crowds had been pouring into Isleif for days. People of all ages lined the streets from the palace to the parliament building where Magnus would be declared king.

Security forces had been beefed up with help from allies, particularly the ones who were attending the coronation. It would not be a long ceremony, but every detail had been choreographed to the millisecond.

Their car arrived at the end of the red carpet that led into the building. A deafening roar rose around them as they left the car and walked the short distance into the building. Magnus had always been incredibly popular and, here in Isleif at least, Lexi grew more adored by the day.

Inside, cameras broadcast their short procession, flashing to Queen Katla seated with Sorr, holding Rolf who had the good manners to remain soundly asleep. They were flanked by Magnus's family, including his father, and Rhonda, who still wore an expression of astonishment that her daughter was becoming a queen.

After the formal declaration of Magnus as king, they would travel in a slow parade back to the palace for a full day of celebration. There would be a reception for various local dignitaries, a state dinner for the foreign ones and a midnight ball. The day had been declared a national holiday, so events were planned across the country. Every club, arena, pub and local diner would be packed.

"Magnus," Lexi whispered as the prime minister made his opening remarks. "You're shaking." He normally had nerves of steel.

His expression was the contained one that was difficult to read, but he flashed her a glance, allowing her to glimpse what was in his eyes. In his soul.

He leaned close to say in her ear, "I've always dreaded this day because I thought I would have to face it alone. But I have you." He picked up her hand and kissed the finger that held her wedding band. "Thank you for being here. Today and in my life. I love you."

He was going to make her cry and she'd taken such care with her makeup.

"I love you, too." The clip of her lips shaping those words would become a GIF shared millions of times around the world, but in those moments, they were spoken by a wife to her husband with the utmost sincerity.

Then the prime minister turned to Magnus and recognized them as, "King Magnus of Isfeild and Queen Alexandra."

EPILOGUE

"LEXI," MAGNUS SAID with exasperation as he strode into the royal chambers. "Ulmer just told me you booked us an hour-long meeting to discuss the decor in the royal apartment? We pay people to choose wallpaper. My choice is to not attend meetings that aren't necessary."

They had moved into the monarch suite as soon as Magnus was crowned, but eight months later, they still hadn't changed any of the furnishings. It was all period pieces and beautiful antiques, many of which he'd begun to complain lacked comfort.

But that wasn't exactly why Lexi had blocked out this time.

"It sounds like you're having a good day," she teased.

"I am dying a death of a thousand paper cuts, all caused by bureaucracy." He looked around. "Where's Rolf?"

"Auntie time." Queen Katla had kept her title, but was typically referred to as the Queen Matriarch. For Rolf, she was very much Auntie Katla. She had more time for him these days and absolutely doted on him.

"Oh?"

"Now his interest in wallpaper sharpens," she noted with amusement.

"Furnishings at least." He stalked toward her. "Pick

whatever you like, but make it sturdy." As he passed a writing desk, he gave it a wiggle, then swooped to wrap her in his arms, lifting her so she was eye to eye with him. "*Is* this meeting code for sex? Because I think I just developed a fascination with interior design. We might need a weekly appointment to explore color samples."

"I did want a private discussion without alerting staff." She gave his hair band a light tug, which was always a signal they were about to let their hair down.

"I'm listening."

He was not listening. He was burying his mouth in her neck, making it difficult for her to remember what she wanted to say.

"I, um, saw the doctor today."

He picked up his head, blue gaze darkening with concern. "About?"

"About whether it's too early to conceive again. I'd like the kids to be close in age, if possible. He said we could start trying. What do you think?"

"I think that I want my wife to have everything she wants, so we're going to squeeze lovemaking into my busy schedule every single day, if that's what's necessary to make it happen."

She chuckled. "You're willing to make that great sacrifice, are you?"

"My country can spare me." He walked her through to his bedroom, the one that was called his, but that they shared while hers was mostly a dressing room. "In fact, I would say it is my most solemn duty as king to make at least one more baby with you."

"I've been thinking I might want three. What do you think?"

"I think we'd better start applying ourselves," he said against her smiling lips.

They did. And because they were Magnus and Lexi, and they wanted to give each other everything and more, they welcomed twin girls within the year.

They had another boy two years after that, just for fun.

* * * * *

Did His Highness's Hidden Heir
leave you wanting more?
Then you're bound to love these other steamy
Dani Collins stories!

The Baby His Secretary Carries
The Secret of Their Billion-Dollar Baby
Her Billion-Dollar Bump
Marrying the Enemy
Husband for the Holidays

Available now!

MILLS & BOON®

Coming next month

GREEK'S ENEMY BRIDE
Caitlin Crews

The priest cleared his throat.

Jolie took one last look at Apostolis, soaking in this last moment of blessed widowhood before he became her husband.

He looked back, that gleaming gold thing in his gaze, but his expression unusually serious.

For a moment, it was as if she could read his mind.

For a long, electric moment, it was almost as if they were united in this bizarre enterprise after all, and her heart leaped inside her chest—

'Stepmother?' he said, with a soft ferocity. 'If you would be so kind?'

No, she told herself harshly. *There is no unity here. There is only and ever war. You will do well to remember that.*

And then, with remarkable swiftness and no interruption, Jolie relinquished her role as Apostolis's hated stepmother, and became his much-loathed wife instead.

Continue reading

GREEK'S ENEMY BRIDE
Caitlin Crews

Available next month
millsandboon.co.uk

COMING SOON!

We really hope you enjoyed reading this book.
If you're looking for more romance
be sure to head to the shops when
new books are available on

Thursday 19th December

To see which titles are coming soon, please visit

millsandboon.co.uk/nextmonth

MILLS & BOON

FOUR BRAND NEW BOOKS FROM
MILLS & BOON MODERN

The same great stories you love, a stylish new look!

OUT NOW

Eight Modern stories published every month, find them all at:

millsandboon.co.uk

LET'S TALK
Romance

For exclusive extracts, competitions and special offers, find us online:

- **f** MillsandBoon
- **X** @MillsandBoon
- **⊙** @MillsandBoonUK
- **♪** @MillsandBoonUK

Get in touch on 01413 063 232

afterglow BOOKS

Afterglow Books is a trend-led, trope-filled list of books with diverse, authentic and relatable characters, a wide array of voices and representations, plus real world trials and tribulations. Featuring all the tropes you could possibly want (think small-town settings, fake relationships, grumpy vs sunshine, enemies to lovers) and all with a generous dose of spice in every story.

♪ @millsandboonuk
⊙ @millsandboonuk
afterglowbooks.co.uk

#AfterglowBooks

For all the latest book news, exclusive content and giveaways scan the QR code below to sign up to the Afterglow newsletter:

SCAN ME

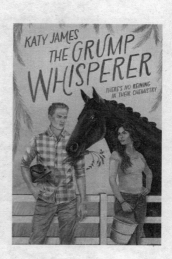
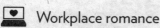
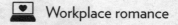
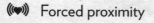
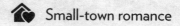

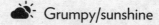

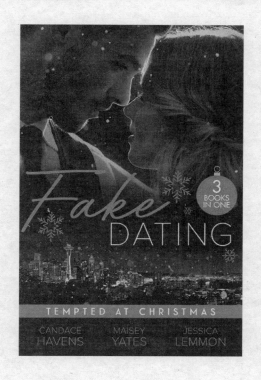